MURDER IN DRAGON CITY

MURDER IN DRAGON CITY

QIN MING

Translated by Alex Woodend

amazoncrossing

Text copyright © 2014 Qin Ming
Translation copyright © 2016 by Alex Woodend

Previously published as 第十一根手指 (法医秦明系列) (The Eleventh Finger) by Qin Ming in China in 2014. Translated from Chinese by Alex Woodend. First published in English by AmazonCrossing in 2016.

Published by AmazonCrossing, Seattle

www.apub.com

ISBN-13: 9781503939592
ISBN-10: 1503939596

Cover design by David Drummond

Printed in the United States of America

1

■

A dozen blue-and-white police cars sat in front of an abandoned factory, their flashing sirens and bright headlights making the secluded lot look like a busy nighttime market.

Inside, about ten people had their heads on the fetid ground, and as many heavily armed cops stood nearby. Flies swarmed around, and sewage ran openly.

The police captain walked to a rusty iron drum and banged his baton against its side.

Peng-peng.

"What the hell is wrong with you?" Wrinkling his brow, the captain peered into the drum and retched twice at the smell. "You let people eat this? It isn't fit for pigs!"

"It's just been used a little by restaurants. It'd never find its way into your mouth if you didn't go out to dinner so often," a skinny man blurted out from his position on the floor.

"What's that?" The captain glared at him. "How would I know if the cafeteria at work uses gutter oil?"

Just the day before, the provincial capital, Dragon City, had launched a campaign with a punchy name: "Fight the Four Wrongs;

Right the Four Rights." The police had already uncovered this black market operation that was recycling used cooking oil into disgusting, poisonous slop. Now they were here to put a stop to this evil.

The captain picked up a ladle and scooped up the swill, lifted it away from the barrel, then poured it slowly back in. "Look at this! Edible? The only word for this is 'horrific.'"

A yellow film clung to the bottom of the spoon. The captain examined it with growing dread. Then he turned around and asked the environmental protection officer next to him, "Have you ever seen a chicken toe this big?"

I was already a well-regarded forensic scientist when, in order to improve my investigation skills, I was sent for a year of training with the North Central District Squadron. Police life was interesting sometimes, but it could also get tedious—especially because it meant I barely got to see my new wife, Ling Dang. The squadron spent most of the year mediating civil disputes, arresting car-battery thieves, and chasing purse snatchers.

We couldn't decide whether to laugh or cry at some of the stuff we ran into. Like one time, a woman and her husband were fighting, and he hit her. In a rage, she came to report it, but we told her it wasn't under our jurisdiction. She said, "If domestic violence isn't your jurisdiction, whose is it? My book club's?" Another time, a man said his wife had been abducted. After several days of hard work, we realized that the so-called wife had long been married to another man.

My real passion was using my talent for forensic science to help solve murders. The county usually had only a few such cases each year, and most were solved quickly. I was lucky enough that, as soon as I was done with the training assignment, North Central got a sensational murder case that shook up the whole Ministry of Public Security, the federal agency that oversees China's police forces, before it was eventually, and thankfully, solved.

The night that case broke, I'd only just returned to my old department, and I was feeling both happy and out of place. Happy because I could again focus on the forensics of difficult cases without getting caught up in trivialities. And out of place because I'd gotten used to the camaraderie and adrenaline rush of police work, to pulling all-nighters, and chasing criminals. My body wasn't used to normal life anymore.

As I tossed and turned in bed, the phone rang. Ling Dang, sat up, startled, and said, "Who could be calling at this hour? I'm not used to the phone ringing in the middle of the night anymore!"

I grabbed for the receiver, my heart racing with excitement. "Hello? . . . Yes, Boss. No, no problem at all. I was awake anyway. I'll be right there!"

"What's going on? What's the rush?" I asked as I climbed into the car.

Chen, head of the forensic department and my boss, looked me over and laughed. "I want to know why you're still up at this hour. You and your little lady still in the honeymoon phase?"

I stared at him for a second, then changed the subject. "How many dead?"

"Well," he said solemnly, "it seems the public security bureau found a chicken toe."

"A chicken toe?" I was confused.

"That's right," Chen said. "Deep-fried."

No matter how many questions I asked, Chen just smiled and kept quiet. The car bounced along, and we soon arrived at the factory, way out on the edge of the city.

"Quite a display," I said.

On TV, they always show a whole fleet of police cars roaring to the scene, sirens wailing. But that's really just the director's imagination. If the police announced their arrival with that much commotion, the criminals would always flee the scene and no one would ever be arrested. Our general rule was to not cause a disturbance, so we'd always sneak in and out. Large-scale arrests like this were pretty rare.

We grabbed our kits and jumped out. Suddenly, a guy with little glasses popped up, TV station microphone in hand. "Are you with forensics? Cracking down on gutter oil needs a whole forensic team now?"

I backed up, startled by the questions and the microphone shoved in my face.

Chen cut him off. "Hey, buddy, what are you trying to do? Stuff that thing down his throat?"

The reporter faltered in embarrassment, and we took advantage of the opportunity to slip under the caution tape.

Inside the factory, the special police team was already preparing the suspects to be driven to the station for booking. Two civil officers seemed to be in charge. They squatted with their heads together over a bowl on the ground, talking intently. Their uniforms indicated that one was a first-class superintendent, the other a second-class inspector.

"Could be a fingerprint, huh?" the superintendent said.

"Yeah." The inspector nodded. "This really white part may be a mark left by a fingernail coming off."

"So maybe it's just a chicken toe?" the superintendent said.

"Probably from a *lou mei* restaurant," the inspector said. "But, then again, it just seems a little too wide."

Suddenly, the two men spotted Chen and me standing right behind them, and they nearly fell over. "Jesus Christ, are you guys part cat or something? What the hell do you want?"

The boss gave a slight smile and looked them straight in the eye.

The two policemen scrambled to their feet and saluted. "Hello, Director Chen. Heard so much about you. An honor to finally meet you, sir."

"This is Medical Examiner Qin," Chen said, gesturing to me. "And the man headed over is Lin Tao from trace detection."

We all shook hands.

"Okay, so bring us up to speed," the boss said.

"Oh, our unit just broke up a gutter-oil gang." The first-class superintendent pointed to the second-class inspector next to him and said, "But then our captain spotted something strange in the slop bucket."

Chen pulled his pant legs up a little and crouched next to the bowl with an oily yellow thing in it. "This little guy here?"

"Yessir. We're trying to figure out if it's a human finger or a chicken toe," the first-class superintendent said with a shy smile.

"Well, maybe the professionals should take a look, huh?" I muttered.

"Damn right," the boss said. "If just anyone could figure it out, why even have forensic scientists?"

I crouched down and squinted at the thing in the bowl.

It was a yellow cylinder, and I stuck out my finger for comparison. The thing was somewhat smaller. Even though it showed clear signs of being fried, I could still make out a faint grain. And there were two distinct bends that did look like joints.

"Huh, hard to say. It seems too thin and short to be a finger, but too thick to be a chicken toe."

Chen said, "If someone were to fry a woman's body, her finger could very well contract to this size."

I felt my scalp tighten. "Fry . . . fry a body?"

Boss took no notice of my frightened expression. "So tell me, Qin, how can we determine whether this is a human finger?"

I froze for a moment. Only when Chen turned and stared at me did I recover. "Huh? Oh, a DNA test, right?"

"Oh!" the two policemen exclaimed.

"Oh what?" Chen said, glaring at them a second. He turned back to me and said, "DNA? Is that really the best you can manage?"

My cheeks flushed with embarrassment. In school, I'd focused on forensic pathology—and neglected less exciting areas like forensic anthropology.

I quickly ran through my limited knowledge of species determination but didn't come up with anything. I shyly shook my head.

The boss grunted with disappointment. "Read up a little more in your spare time. Maybe you think that fundamentals aren't important, but when the critical moment comes, you need all your tools."

Chen put on gloves, opened his kit, and took out two pairs of hemostatic forceps. He gave me one, then took out a surgical knife handle and fitted on the blade.

He deftly sliced into the object, revealing muscle and ligaments. Separating the soft tissue required a lot of finesse, patience, and skill with the knife, and it took him, with all his experience, a full half hour to extract the bone.

"Whew . . ." The boss took a deep breath, wiping sweat from his brow. "Well, your 'Fight the Four Wrongs; Right the Four Rights' campaign seems to have uncovered a brutal murder!"

"You mean . . . ," the police captain said, trying not to gag. "It's a finger?"

Chen nodded. "The phalanges are some of the more distinctly shaped human bones. When humans were evolving, their shafts grew shorter, but the articular surface stayed relatively large so the hand could be more flexible. This is definitely a standard human finger."

I used forceps to clasp the soft tissue he'd removed—it was very hard.

"I see now," I said. "The soft-tissue water loss was extreme, which caused severe contracture, making it much smaller than a normal finger."

The boss and I exchanged a somber look. Frying a corpse was a rare, extraordinarily inhumane form of mutilation. The horrifying case would surely make headlines in all the papers and cause a public uproar. We had to solve it as fast as possible.

Ten minutes later, all the suspects had been escorted out, but dozens more police were arriving on-site.

Several forensic personnel wearing colored goggles searched for trace evidence. Uniformed officers rummaged through boxes in a corner. The boss stood in the middle of the room, looking around in all directions, hands on hips. "We've got our work cut out for us, men."

His sonorous voice reverberated through the building. Everyone stopped what they were doing.

Chen swallowed hard and said, "It's not going to be easy. Now we have to take these dozen slop barrels and filter out all the dregs."

The officers looked pained. Working in this space that stank to high heaven was hard enough without having to sift all the revolting scum from the stinking swill buckets. It would probably be the most disgusting thing they'd ever done.

Just then, Big Bao, my forensic intern, bolted in, a huge bundle in his arms.

"Boss, I got the stuff you wanted," Big Bao said to Chen, panting. "It took me quite a while kicking the door to wake up that medical supply store owner."

The boss unwrapped the bundle. Inside were several dozen white coats. He picked one up and took the lead by putting it on. He laughed and said, "A little present so your wives don't make you sleep outside when you get home."

2
■

And so the repulsive work began. We assigned each barrel a number, then divided ourselves into teams of three. The first person scooped out the slop, the second held a sieve, and the third scanned for possible human remains. The boss moved among the various groups, offering forensic guidance as needed.

With the slop stirred up, the stench became even more intense. It passed through the lab coats and adhered firmly to our clothes. Some of the men couldn't take it, and vomited again and again. But they pressed on.

Before we knew it, three hours had passed and all the sludge had been sifted. Only three teams had found tissue samples. There were twenty-one chunks, together making a pile roughly the size of a cell phone. Some had bones and were clearly identifiable as human. Others were just fat and muscle deformed by frying. Only DNA testing could confirm them as human.

I took off my white coat and sniffed my body. My sense of smell was deadened by then, but I was pretty sure the stink went right through me.

One detective moaned, "Oh man, we're going to have to burn these clothes. Even then, our families aren't going to let us into the house!"

"No one is headed home just yet, I'm afraid," the boss said. "All the tissue of interest was found in barrels one and thirteen, which means the body parts must have been discarded together. Forensics' next task is to create DNA profiles, and the detectives' task is to get the suspects to tell them where those two barrels came from."

The detective looked pained. "Tracking the origin of a particular barrel of rancid oil? That sounds impossible."

The boss smiled a little and said, "Depends how good a detective you are."

I just shook my head in horror. "Frying a corpse, how evil do you have to be?"

Chen thought a moment. "Maybe not that evil. Mutilation is most common in crimes committed by acquaintances—enemies. But lots of mutilation cases aren't necessarily that simple."

"Not that simple? It's simple to meet someone on the street, dismember them, and then methodically fry the body? What kind of mind-set is that?"

Chen waved me off, saying, "An abnormal one, sure. But let's not speculate too much at this point. We have to focus on using the remains to identify the victims. Only then can we hope to take a step toward breaking this case."

I nodded.

The boss turned to the exhausted team. "The hard work isn't done, brothers. When this case hits the papers in a few hours, it'll cause an uproar. So let's push through now to get a better grasp of the facts before reporters start getting in the way. We need all hands on deck."

We were carrying twenty-one evidence bags into the station when the DNA lab director, Ms. Zheng Hongzheng, walked in.

"What's so urgent?" she asked.

"We caught a real doozy of a case, Zheng," Chen said, feigning calm. "All the evidence is deep-fried. Can you sequence it?"

Zheng froze for a moment. "Deep-fried?"

The boss nodded.

Zheng lit up, suddenly wide-awake despite the early hour. "I remember reading something about a case like that—I'll find it. Leave it to me. I'll have the results for you by tomorrow morning. But what's that god-awful smell?" She waved her hand in front of her nose.

"Boss, can we go home to shower and sleep while we wait for the results?" I sniffed my pungent sleeve again.

"You wish!" Chen shouted before turning to Zheng again. "These samples are precious babies, so I can't hand them over just yet. I'll give you an hour to scan the literature, research some methods, do some prep. Then I'll give them to you."

"Precious babies?" Zheng asked, both of us looking at him in confusion.

"Don't worry about it—just do as I say."

Chen grabbed me, and we walked to the forensic pathology lab. He threw a sterile drop cloth over the lab bench, then lined up the tissue pieces on top of it and passed me a scalpel.

"Okay, Qin. First, we're going to strip fried tissue off the surface and try to separate it from the unaffected epidermal or dermal tissue. My hunch is that there are still some distinguishing features in there. Second, do you know what else these babies can still show us?"

I looked up, realized the boss was staring at me, and shook my head dumbly.

Chen gestured to a book on the shelf behind him and said, "Time to educate yourself, man. In every part of the human body, the muscle fibers' thickness and direction are different. We have to figure out which body parts this tissue belongs to."

I had a sudden realization but wasn't confident, so I started skimming through the book.

Earlier, my sense of smell had been paralyzed by the sheer heinousness of the factory. Now it came back, keen as ever, as the stench of the twenty-one "babies" filled the small lab. The visual and olfactory stimuli were enough to make even this not-so-rookie forensic scientist's stomach turn.

"Coarse muscle fiber, directed obliquely, each layer drawn tight." I looked back and forth between the tissue samples and the book. "These parts without bones all come from the buttocks."

"Not bad. You figured it out fast," the boss said, pleased. "And the ones with bones are either fingers or toes." He paused and sighed. "Unfortunately, I didn't find any distinguishing features."

At six o'clock that morning, a call came in. The boss told me he'd been summoned to a national coordination meeting about a series of robberies and murders. He'd be gone for a while, so he was entrusting me with the case.

"Not even a case this awful can keep you here?" I said.

He chuckled. "The case they called me in on is even worse."

"Are you sure I can handle all this on my own?" I asked.

"Go to the airport right now," he said. "Someone is coming to help you, and you need to pick them up."

"The airport?"

"I gotta go. Remember the flight number CZ9876. When you get there, you'll know."

How strange, I thought. Why keep me in suspense? I called Lin Tao. We hurried to put on our uniforms, then headed out to pick up our mystery helper.

It was still early, so there weren't many people waiting at the airport. Lin Tao and I stood around, feeling foolish in our starched uniforms as we expectantly watched everyone who came out. We got a lot of looks ourselves—well, mostly Lin Tao. I've long since gotten used to standing next to a better-looking guy.

"So, who do you think it could be?" I asked.

Lin Tao suddenly stiffened.

"Hey, I'm talking to you." I poked him with my elbow. Lin Tao still didn't answer, so I followed his gaze.

In the distance was a beautiful woman, waist-length hair, gold sunglasses, black silk shirt, graceful figure, pushing a wheelchair in which sat a white-haired elderly man. They were coming right toward us.

"You getting soft in your old age? I don't remember you paying attention to pretty girls before," I teased. "So there *are* girls who can get your attention."

"She's so hot." Lin Tao sighed.

"Ha, finally found your type? Want me to help you get her number?"

A short but very muscular, flat-headed man suddenly pushed Lin Tao. "What do you think you're looking at?"

Lin Tao's eyes widened in anger. "Get your hands off me!"

A tall, skinny guy helped me push the two men apart before things could escalate. I got a good look at the flat-headed guy's face and was suddenly overjoyed. "It's you!"

His rage dissipated, and I gave him a hug.

His name was Hua Long, and the tall guy with him was Bao Zhan. The beautiful woman was Su Mei, and that was Professor Liang in the wheelchair. The four were federal Ministry of Public Security special investigators, famous for cracking brutal, high-profile murder cases. I'd had the honor of working with them once during my year with North Central.

"Qin, a pleasure. Your boss is afraid this case might be a bit much for you to manage alone," Professor Liang said, smiling. "It sounds pretty vile."

"I'm so happy to see you all again." I shook their hands exuberantly.

"Yeah, man, you too," Hua Long said, then pointed at Lin Tao. "Just make sure this guy doesn't try anything with Su Mei."

I laughed, shepherded everyone to the van, and drove us back to the station for a task force meeting.

"All twenty-one tissue samples were human, female, and from the same person," Lab Director Zheng reported.

I took a deep breath.

"Little Qin," Professor Liang said, "remember in North Central when I had you arrange all those parts into a body?"

"I remember. But it won't work here. These pieces are too deformed to be spliced together."

Liang said, "That's okay. I just need to know which parts of the person they came from."

Great minds really do think alike.

"The boss and I worked on that yesterday," I exclaimed. "They're all from the buttocks, fingers, and toes."

"Good. And next I need to know where the frying oil came from," Liang said, rubbing the stubble on his chin.

The special team had clearly done its homework on the plane.

Our investigators were a little nervous when they first saw the famous foursome. The detective in charge cleared his throat and said, "Hello, gentlemen and, uh, lady. According to our colleagues at the sheriff's department, all the oil in those barrels came from twenty-eight restaurants on Northeastern Street in the Tiancang neighborhood. I have men checking out each one as we speak."

Liang shook his head and picked up some photos from the table. They were detailed shots I'd taken of the specimens.

"Little Qin," he said, "can you tell me what this black substance adhering to these specimens is?"

I frowned and looked. "Oh, I noticed that too and checked it out with a microscope. It's silt."

"And how do you imagine the tissue would get stained with mud?" Liang quizzed me.

The detective cut in. "Dirty kitchens, right?"

Liang shook his head. "If dirt got in there through negligence, its appearance would be random. But it's on seven or eight of the samples. It wasn't by chance but by default."

The detective looked puzzled.

I closed my eyes tightly for a moment, then said, "I know what you're getting at."

Liang looked at me with interest. "Oh yeah? Out with it, then."

"Gutter oil, apart from coming from restaurants . . . Well, some particularly unscrupulous criminals might also skim grease off the upper layer of residential sewage and mix it with the rest of the slop."

Liang nodded slightly. "Not bad, Qin. These body parts came from the sewer."

"The sewer? How disgusting," the detective said with a frown. "These gutter-oil people should hang."

"We all know what we have to do next, right?" Liang said. "Get the suspects to tell us which part of the sewer they skimmed the oil from. That's where we'll find more body parts."

"Right," I said. "So far we haven't found any distinguishing characteristics. No clues as to where the corpse came from."

"But," the detective interjected, "how are our officers going to find such tiny body parts in the sewers?"

Liang smiled and said, "That's why I asked Little Qin which parts of the body these came from. I think we'll find some useful clues rather quickly."

3

In a flash, I understood. "Right, this tissue was all cut off the buttocks."

The detective looked confused. "So?"

Bao Zhan jumped in. "In our last case, not a single part of the pelvis was damaged."

I nodded in agreement. "The pelvis consists of the sacrum and both parts of the ilium—really dense bones. Breaking it up is virtually impossible."

Professor Liang went on. "And the pelvis is one of the most important anatomical structures for forensics. Right, Little Qin?"

I nodded. "As soon as we hear back from the interrogators, we can start searching the sewers."

The police are always searching sewers on TV, but I'd never done it myself. The claustrophobic space and echoing voices seemed like they'd be pretty exciting.

But the interrogations were a letdown. None of the suspects was able to tell us exactly where they got the sewer oil.

With all of us feeling helpless, Su Mei said, "Someone get me a map of all the underground pipelines in the vicinity of the factory where these crooks operated. I can put together a computer simulation of all the currents to find the most likely location of the body."

Lin Tao jumped up and said, "I'm on it."

Half an hour later, Su Mei had a strange diagram on her computer screen with a red dot the size of a soybean flashing in the center.

"Right here," she said. "Give it a shot."

Once again, Lin Tao was the first to jump up. "I'll go get the equipment."

At the mouth of an apartment complex's sewer line, I suddenly wasn't feeling so adventurous. I shone my flashlight down into the hole. "It's too dark. Maybe we should come back in the morning?"

"It's just as dark down there during the day," Liang said, seeing right through me. "I'll give you men two hours."

Hua Long patted my shoulder, changed into tall rubber boots, and took the lead down the ladder. I glanced at the site survey team. "Let's get started, then."

As it turned out, the sewers weren't as terrifying as I'd feared. Under the light of several officers' headlamps, it was practically like daytime. The worst part was that the ceilings were so low that we had to squat down and half crawl along. A suffocating stench blew in our faces.

"Good Lord," I said. "I'm a forensic scientist, and even I can't stand the smell down here. Must be even worse for you guys, huh?"

The survey staff nodded, stone-faced.

Bao Zhan sniffed in several directions and pointed behind us. "That way."

I beamed. "Everyone says your nose is better than a police dog's! Can you really pick out the smell of a rotting body in this place?"

Bao Zhan just pushed me and said, "Screw you. *You're* the police dog."

We struggled forward for half an hour, and my legs got so stiff, they felt like lead.

Finally, Bao Zhan stopped and said, "Should be right around here. Time to dig."

The staff pulled small shovels from their packs and set to work, their pouring sweat adding to the sewer's stench.

After another half hour, Lin Tao shouted, "Never doubt Brother Bao's nose! We hit something."

Lin Tao handed me his find, and I used a glove to wipe the sludge from the surface. It was a femur. I held it to the side of my pants for comparison. "This woman . . . has some seriously long legs."

Bao Zhan turned and kept excavating. "We have to find more bones, especially the pelvis."

Another hour of work and we did find a female pelvis, plus over a dozen more bones.

"Okay, I'm calling it," Bao Zhan declared. "If we keep digging, this hole is going to be our grave too. Time to head back and regroup."

The incomplete skeleton lay on the dissection bed.

I folded my arms across my medical jumpsuit and squinted at the assembled bones. "This is the only way they can be put together, so why do I keep feeling something isn't quite right?"

"Each body is different, of course," Professor Liang replied. "Can you explain what seems wrong to you?"

I frowned and said, "Besides the two leg bones' being too long and too thick, some of the ribs don't quite line up."

The phone rang, and Lin Tao took the call.

"Investigators checked the local resident records for someone matching the age and height that you determined from the bones," he reported. "And there just aren't any twenty-five-year-old women around here who are five foot nine."

"Could she be a migrant worker?" Professor Liang said.

"Hang on—there is a twenty-five-year-old housewife in the neighborhood named Lian Qianqian," Lin Tao continued. "She usually sits outside with the old ladies, eating sunflower seeds, but no one has seen her for a couple weeks."

"Is she tall?" I asked.

"Under five three," Lin Tao said.

"That's kind of a big discrepancy," I said, frowning.

"A housewife?" Liang asked. "What's her husband do?"

"He's a restaurant manager."

"Restaurant?" Liang's eyes lit up. "Fried corpse, restaurant boss . . ."

"And there's more," Lin Tao continued. "The husband resigned two weeks ago, and he's missing too."

"What are we waiting for?" Liang said, excited. "Get a search warrant. Go check the house!"

I said, "But what about the height problem?"

Liang called Su Mei, asking her to come push his wheelchair, and said to me, "Well, we don't have complete bones, right? Maybe what we've got is misleading somehow."

Baffled, I stared at the bones, pulled out the tape measure, and checked one more time. "They may be incomplete, but there's no way this person was five foot three."

After the skeleton was transferred to the DNA testing room, Lin Tao and I tagged along to Lian Qianqian's doorstep with Hua Long and a group of detectives.

Bao Zhan sniffed. "Nice work, guys. I'm picking up some blood already."

"Really?" Just as I leaned up against the iron door to see if I could smell anything, Hua Long kicked it open with a loud bang.

"What are you waiting for?" he said, stepping into the residence, gun drawn.

Seeing the shock on my face, Lin Tao said quietly, "This guy's a piece of work."

With all the curtains drawn, the three-bedroom apartment was as dark as the underworld, and the smell of blood was unmistakable, even to me. What had been a new, tastefully decorated home now looked like a horrible crime scene. The front hall and main room were covered with drop-shaped bloodstains.

After searching, Hua Long holstered his gun. "Nobody."

Lin Tao began photographing the scene. I walked around, studying the blood patterns. After a few minutes, I said, "The drops seem to have fallen after the blood was diluted. They came from the bathroom, then went through the living room, through the corridor, and on to the kitchen."

"Diluted blood?" Hua Long asked, squatting next to me.

I nodded and said, "It didn't come directly from the veins. It mixed with water on the skin; then, as the body moved, it dripped off."

"What's that mean?"

I led Hua Long to the bathroom. "Look—the walls of the bathtub have these streamlike bloodstains. My hypothesis is that the murderer dismembered the body in the tub, then carried the parts to the kitchen."

"To fry them?" Hua Long's brow wrinkled for a second.

I nodded and went into the cramped kitchen. The wok on the stove was half-filled with a liquid the color of soy sauce, a white crust starting to form on the surface. The smell was ghastly.

I picked up a spoon and stirred the wok a little. The liquid felt very viscous and became clearer closer to the bottom where there was some solid matter—probably muscle fibers.

I raised my elbow and used my sleeve to rub my stinging nose. "This is where the corpse was fried."

"So some of the body parts got fried, others didn't, but then they all got thrown into the sewer," Big Bao said.

I nodded and asked Lin Tao, "Find any fingerprints?"

Lin Tao shook his head. "I looked in some key places, but there are only clear markings like from gloves."

"What's that mean?" Hua Long asked.

Lin Tao glared at Hua Long for a second and said sharply, "It means the murderer was wearing gloves for the duration of the homicide, dismemberment, and frying."

"So what?" Hua Long said. "Typical wife-killing and dismemberment case! Let's get an arrest warrant for this guy."

"Maybe," I said, frowning, "but if you're killing your own wife in your own house, do you wear gloves?"

Lin Tao nodded in agreement.

"Oh," Hua Long replied, "I see what you mean."

Big Bao, Lin Tao, and I carefully extracted every possible sample from the oil and prepared them to be taken for DNA testing, hoping for a surprise discovery.

There was a knock on the door. It was the director of the local police station. At our request, he wore a hat, gloves, and shoe covers into the scene. The stench nearly made him retch. Steadying himself, he said, "Gentlemen, the preliminary investigation into Lian Qianqian is taking shape."

We all stopped what we were doing and gathered around to listen.

Lian Qianqian, he told us, had moved to the city from a far-off village to work as a pedicurist. Xia Hong, the restaurant manager, took an interest in the pretty young woman. They'd dated for two years and gotten married six months ago—much like my wife and me, I reflected.

Xia Hong had grown up an orphan, but he'd used his smarts, charm, and people skills to become a middle manager in the competitive hospitality industry in less than three years. But Xia Hong's boss thought him timid, so he had trouble advancing.

The couple didn't have any family or close friends in the city. The cops had questioned the neighbors, but they all said there were no unusual signs before the pair's disappearance.

"Nothing unusual?" I said. "How about Xia quitting two weeks ago? Based on the blood degradation, I'd estimate the victim also died about two weeks ago. Maybe this Xia Hong is our man."

"Didn't you just say if you're killing someone in your own house, there's no need to wear gloves?" Hua Long asked.

I ignored him and gestured for the station director to finish his story.

"Apparently, another hotel conglomerate was trying to poach Xia Hong. He'd just accepted the offer and given his old company three weeks' notice. He finished up there two weeks ago and was preparing for the new position."

I nodded. "So a number of factors suggest Xia Hong might not be the murderer, but what kind of murderer would calmly fry a corpse in Xia's house, and where the hell did Xia go?"

The station director shook his head. I didn't press further. Now that we had our tissue samples safely bagged, Lin Tao and I started a closer search of the home.

"Look," Lin Tao said, pointing at the floor. "There are blood traces going from the bathroom to the master bedroom too."

We lay on our stomachs, and I turned on my flashlight to see the pale, directional blood spatter. A tetramethylbenzidine test confirmed it was blood.

"Huh. The killer took the body to the bedroom too," I said. "But this time, relatively little blood adhered to the floor and walls."

"The blood seems to lead here," called Bao Zhan from inside the room, pointing to a large wardrobe.

I put my hand on the handle, swallowed hard, and, closing my eyes, opened it.

Lin Tao and Bao Zhan screamed and stumbled backward.

4

The two were no strangers to ruthless murder scenes, so the shock on their faces now made my heart race as I summoned the courage to look.

Inside the closet hung a row of beautiful clothes, along with the bodies of two people that appeared to have been flattened and draped over hangers. One had long black hair covering the shoulders and chest, while the other just hung limp like a shabby coat.

"Wha-what is that?" I didn't dare get closer.

Bao Zhan gasped. "Skin!"

Two sheets of human skin.

Hua Long rushed into the bedroom. "The DNA lab called."

I stared at the wardrobe and nodded. "Don't tell me, Xia Hong is dead too."

"Yup. The skeleton wasn't fitting together right because it was actually two skeletons. The pelvis was a woman's, but the legs were a man's."

Hua Long observed me staring slack-jawed at the wardrobe, unsurprised by his news. Puzzled, he looked inside and shouted, "Holy shit, they were skinned?"

We took the two human skins off their hangers and laid them out on the floor. At the bottom of the wardrobe was a messy pile of clothes soaked with blood that had dripped down—probably what the victims had been wearing when they were killed. We found a man's dress shirt, jacket, underwear, and pants, but for the woman, just a dressing gown.

The bodies had been sliced open from the neck straight down to the pubic bone. The skin was then peeled off sideways from that incision, and the limbs were peeled starting along the superficial fascia. In some places, muscle tissue was still attached, which meant the tool used had been extremely sharp. Stuck together with masking tape, the stripped skin made a full bodysuit.

Hua Long lifted up the woman's skin, saying, "This guy's knife skills are even better than a forensic scientist's, huh?"

"Don't move!" I shouted, taking out my magnifying glass to get a closer look.

Both her breasts were still attached to the surrounding skin. I said to Lin Tao, "Look, right there—isn't that a dermal ridge?"

Lin Tao's face filled with surprise. "It is! I bet we can get a print!"

"Didn't you say the murderer was wearing gloves for the whole thing?" Hua Long asked.

"If he wanted to feel the breasts, he very well may have taken off his gloves."

Professor Liang addressed the task force. "Right now, the situation is pretty clear. The young couple, Xia Hong and Lian Qianqian, were murdered in their house, then skinned, cut into pieces, and fried. The nature of the crime is heinous. We have to catch whoever did this as soon as possible. Who's got ideas?"

"Simple!" Hua Long said. "We just have to figure out who had reason to hate these people enough to do something so horrible."

"But according to our preliminary investigation," Liang replied, "the couple was kind and well-liked. It's hard to imagine the two of them having enemies like that."

The room was silent for a moment.

I said, "We should use Su Mei's simulation to organize additional searches in the sewers. There may well be more body parts. Also, let's not forget that the house doors and windows were intact. The murderer probably didn't break in—he was invited."

"Are you saying the crime was committed by an acquaintance?" Liang asked.

"I wouldn't jump to that conclusion just yet."

"What about surveillance video?" Bao Zhan asked the station director.

"There's surveillance only at the entrance. And right now we have no idea when the murders took place, so reviewing several weeks of the tape isn't viable."

"Bao Zhan, you lead a team back to the sewers," Liang ordered. "Qin Ming, Lin Tao, and Su Mei, I want you to go back to the site and see if you can turn up any more clues."

I dragged myself from the meeting, worn down by several consecutive days of physical and mental overexertion. Lin Tao, on the other hand, was thrilled at the opportunity to spend some time with Su Mei.

Back at the house, apart from the drops of blood on the floors and the streaks in the bathtub, we didn't find anything unusual. We confirmed that the killer could not have come in through the windows because they all had security bars.

"Maybe it really was an acquaintance," Lin Tao said.

I shook my head. "When acquaintances commit crimes, the conflicts are almost always well established. If there had been anything, the local cops would have found out about it already."

"Do you guys notice anything strange about these drops of blood?" Su Mei asked.

"Nah," Lin Tao said, smiling at her.

"You see, these multidrip stains," I explained, "mean the killer carried body parts from the bathroom to the kitchen many times."

"But some of the stains are a different color."

Lin Tao and I didn't speak, just stared at the bloodstains. It seemed Su Mei was right.

"You're so good," Lin Tao said, trying to ingratiate himself. "I guess it's true that women are more sensitive to colors! Amazing how none of us saw it."

Su Mei gave him a tight smile, then took out her computer and a light, and got down to work. "A comparison under the same light source shows there is indeed a difference in the color."

I squatted on the ground and thought for a moment, then said, "The color reflects how long the blood has been exposed to air. The longer the exposure, the darker the color. At some crime scenes, during the first survey, the blood is red. Then two weeks later, during the resurvey, it's black. If these stains are so different, can we speculate that the killer returned to the scene of the crime multiple times over many days?"

"Right, that's exactly what I'm suggesting," Su Mei said.

Lin Tao got up, made a phone call, and then came to report back. "Okay, I confirmed that the house key was still in the deceased man's pocket."

"Then the killer had his own copy," I said.

"Who would have a key?" Lin Tao said. "Do you think one of them was having an affair?"

"No way to know yet. Let's see if we can find any documents. Sometimes the victims leave behind information that can tell us who the murderer is."

The couple hadn't been married long, so they hadn't accumulated too much, but we did turn up some diaries the man had kept and what appeared to be two ledger books.

◆ ◆ ◆

Returning to the task force, we found Bao Zhan's team had also made another find: the rest of the victims' bones. The soft tissue on the bones was nearly all gone; so badly decayed, it couldn't be distinguished from the mud.

"The way the sewers work in this neighborhood, they couldn't have carried the body parts far from where they were discarded. And since we found bones near a number of different openings, the killer must have moved all around the area to dispose of the evidence."

"What I take from that," Professor Liang said, "is that our killer can't be far."

"We did manage to get a fingerprint," Lin Tao said, "but this neighborhood has more than twenty large apartment buildings, each with dozens and dozens of households, and each household has two to five people in it. Getting prints from them all is not feasible."

"Plus, the area has a lot of rentals, a large transient population, so pinning anyone down would be hard," I said.

"We do have another lead," said Wang, the city bureau medical examiner. "The skulls of both deceased individuals were found. The flesh had been stripped, but judging from the bone damage, they died of severe brain injuries."

"Their heads got bashed in, you mean?" Hua Long said. "With what?"

"The instrument has relatively unique characteristics." Wang started a slide show.

The victims' heads had been stripped of all their skin and scalps. The facial muscles had decayed to the color of soy sauce. Around the eyes, the muscle texture was still clearly visible. The slide of the two heads on the dissection table was an eerie sight.

The female victim's skull had a huge cavity, which meant she suffered a blunt blow that caused a perforating fracture. The male victim had a round, depressed fracture. The two were killed by the same instrument, but the male's skull was thicker, so the damage was less severe.

As the picture was enlarged, the pattern on the edge of the victim's skull fracture grew gradually clearer. "Large round hammer," I concluded.

"Over four inches in diameter," Wang said.

"A big hammer like that, most people wouldn't have at home," Professor Liang said. "More often, they're for knocking down walls."

"Construction workers!" Lin Tao said. "That would explain why the killer had the victims' house key. And gloves!"

Su Mei, who'd had her head down, lifted it now and said, "But after their home was renovated, the victims changed the locks."

Su Mei had been busy looking through the documents we'd found. There was a diary that turned out to be a poetry collection in which he expressed his love for Lian Qianqian. It gave Su Mei goose bumps, and she quickly moved on to one of the ledger books. It detailed all the costs of their home-renovation project from six months earlier.

Professor Liang took the book and put on his reading glasses.

"There was doubtless another home renovation under way in the neighborhood two weeks ago, was there not?" Professor Liang said as he turned the pages.

"Sure, all the time," the station director replied.

"Would it be hard to track down workers from two weeks ago who could knock down walls and dredge sewers?" Professor Liang asked.

"Easy to find one that knocks down walls, but whether they know sewers too is hard to check," the detective said.

"Found one already!" Lin Tao said. "This is a photo I took when testing the camera in the elevator before we headed out to survey the crime scene."

The photo showed an elevator car with a corkboard covered in small ads. One of them said, "For wall demolition, spackling, drill work, and sewer cleaning, call: 139XXXXXXXX."

"But if the victims changed their locks, then why worry about construction workers?" Hua Long asked, confused.

Liang smiled and said, "Because Su Mei flagged something else in the records. About a month after they changed their locks, there's an entry for sewer cleaning."

"So? Just because someone was cleaning the sewer, why does that mean they did it?"

"Because the other recorded expenses are ordinary, but this one requires a stranger to come into the house," Liang said. "And Lin Tao's discovery is invaluable, because sewer cleaning is the type of service you only find advertised on random walls."

Su Mei smiled and looked at Lin Tao, who blushed.

"Okay, fine, they brought in a sewer guy, but why look for someone who was demolishing walls two weeks ago?" Hua Long asked.

"Because, according to Qin Ming's findings, the killer went back to the house multiple times. He must live in the neighborhood, or that would attract attention. And doing demolition work nearby would be a perfect cover for carrying the murder weapon."

Everyone was nodding.

"Now we just have to make an arrest," Liang said.

Hua Long sprang to his feet. "My favorite words!"

5

The phone number on the ad was registered to a man named Big Dog Li, and he'd been working in the neighborhood exactly two weeks prior. His home was immediately put under surveillance.

A few of us sat in a car across the street, quietly awaiting Hua Long's orders. Suddenly, Big Dog Li appeared at the front door.

"Where's this joker going in the middle of the night?" Big Bao said.

I shushed him.

"Okay, forensics," said Hua Long, his voice booming through my earpiece. "Once he's out of sight, use your tools to unlock the door. As soon as your team turns up any evidence, we'll move in and make the arrest."

A few minutes later, Lin Tao, Bao Zhan, and I were inside.

"Oh man," Lin Tao said. "This guy's got to be the killer." He gestured toward the bedroom wall.

The wall was full of contorted, ugly pencil drawings. Their primary subject was male and female genitals.

"Yeah, these do seem like the work of a psychopath," I said.

"Look at all this!" Hua Long picked up a snakeskin bag from the corner of the bed and poured out dozens of pairs of women's underwear.

I picked up a pillow—under it was lingerie. Most of it was red, but with darker red splotches. "Blood. Could very well be Lian Qianqian's."

"Oh, they totally are," Bao Zhan said. "There were only nightgowns and dressing gowns in the house, no women's underwear. We missed that before."

I activated my headset and said into the microphone, "Okay, I'm convinced. Your guys can move in now."

Hua Long's voice came right back. "Are ya? Good thing. I'm already standing on this dirtbag's head."

Crime scene evidence has three main roles. The first is to identify suspects. The second is to eliminate suspects. The third is to prove the suspects' guilt in court.

The fingerprint we found on the victim's breast would surely convince any judge.

Under the weight of hard evidence and Hua Long's show of force, Big Dog Li confessed to his crimes.

He'd done the sewer cleaning about a month after the renovations. Probably because of waste from the renovation, the drains got blocked, and the resulting regurgitation of sewage stank to high heaven. Lian Qianqian couldn't be home all the time to make it easier for the handyman to come and go, so, feeling he was an honest man, she gave him a key.

Big Dog Li had a keen interest in women's underwear, especially that of beautiful women. After a long day of work, he'd relax by smelling a few of his favorite pairs. He copied Lian Qianqian's key so he could steal some of hers.

Two weeks prior, he'd been at a nearby house tearing down walls and spackling. When his coworkers took their afternoon break, he pretended to be sick and snuck off to Lian Qianqian's home.

The house seemed dark and empty, so he figured no one was home.

But opening the door with his copied key, Big Dog Li ran straight into Lian Qianqian. Wrapped in a dressing gown, she was heating oil to fry dumplings for dinner. Without thinking, he raised his sledgehammer and brought it down on the horrified young woman's head.

While trying to decide whether to hide the body or simply flee, Big Dog Li caught a glimpse of white legs under the dressing gown. Hot blood surged into his evil brain, and he carried Lian Qianqian's lifeless body into the bathroom.

Just as Big Dog Li was contentedly pulling up his pants, he heard the front door opening. Xia Hong was back from signing his new contract. When the sledgehammer dented his skull, Xia Hong still wore the smile of someone excited to share good news with a loved one.

Big Dog Li locked the front door and admired the two bodies like works of art. On a whim, he took out his spackling blade, cut off Lian Qianqian's fingers, and threw them into the pot of bubbling oil. Watching the white fingers bob in the oil and turn crispy and yellow aroused him all over again.

Curious to see what other fun he could have, Big Dog Li meticulously peeled the skin off both bodies, dismembered them, and masturbated while he threw chunks of their buttocks into the pot. This gave him incredible pleasure.

Over the following days, every time he got off work, he'd go back to the house and pleasure himself at the sight and smell of frying corpse. Then one night, his job coming to a close, he took the body parts and threw them down various sewer grates. With the bodies gone, there'd be no trace of his crime. Or so he thought.

"Some new underwear tonight sure would be nice," Big Dog Li said to Hua Long. "You kicked me so hard, my back hurts!"

There was no sign of fear or guilt on that strange face, and I knew then that he was not really human. He was a demon.

"This Lian Qianqian chick was so naïve," Lin Tao said later. "Can't believe she gave someone the key to her home so easily."

"I guess she thought that since he'd worked on her house before, and since she got the key back, it wasn't a big risk," I said.

Professor Liang sighed. "No matter what, one must stay vigilant."

"Professor, after working so hard these past few days, we should all get a drink together. It's been a long time since we've gone out!"

Liang shook his head. "We're catching the first flight to Beijing in the morning—heard there's a new case."

Lin Tao looked at Su Mei and opened his mouth, but no words came out.

"That's a real shame," I said. "We'll have to wait till you come back, then."

"Unfortunately," Liang said with a laugh, "we never come under good circumstances."

At the airport the next morning, Thursday, June 6, Lin Tao and I stood outside the security barricade, watching Professor Liang and the other three disappear. Lin Tao's sense of loss was palpable.

"You really like Su Mei, huh?" I asked.

He didn't answer.

Big Bao suddenly ran up from behind, panting. "They're gone?"

"Yeah, they just left." I looked at Big Bao in confusion.

Big Bao swallowed hard. "Damn. If I'd been a second earlier, maybe I could've gotten them to stay—we could still use their help."

"What's happened?" I asked.

"Another murder," Big Bao said. "The car's outside. Hurry up."

6

"You think we can't handle some little murder without the big guns? Have a little faith, man."

"Well, the boss isn't here either, right?" Big Bao said. "The case they called him in on now is a pretty big deal. I don't think he'll be back to help us any time soon."

"Are murder cases necessarily so tough?" I pretended to be calm. "Don't worry, we'll solve it."

It had been great to have the special task force helping us, but I was determined not to call them again. If Chen was going to be away for a long time, I needed to step up and fill my mentor's shoes without their help. I was known for my forensic skills throughout the province. This was my big chance to show everyone my leadership skills as well.

Big Bao and I took a few steps before we realized Lin Tao was still standing at the security fence in a daze. I went back and gave him a light shove. "You want to go chase down the airplane and propose?"

◆ ◆ ◆

The new crime scene was at a garbage can outside a residential complex downtown.

"Did you discover the body parts?" a cop with a notebook was asking a bystander.

An old man in a street cleaner's uniform shut his eyes and shook his head hard. "No, no. I just saw some bloody goo and called the police."

There was a white plastic sheet on the ground, on which Han, the city public security forensic scientist, was placing body parts he'd pulled from the trash.

Big Bao and I pitched in with the sorting. Lin Tao took out a special light and checked for blood traces.

The white sheet already held quite a few body parts.

"You guys work fast."

"Yup," the city forensic scientist said. "We got guys checking other trash cans in the area. I think we already have everything besides the head and internal organs."

I kept looking at the two largest parts in the pile. One was the pelvis and upper thighs. The top was neatly cut off at a lumbar disc. The lower end was chopped off at the middle of each femur. The other large part was an armless upper torso. On both of them, it seemed the killer had used a knife to make a slit about an inch deep. A rope about the thickness of a thumb was wrapped twice around the wounds and tied in a knot, the cuts serving as grooves for the rope.

"Hey, Han, these weird grooves—do you think they're to make the bodies easier to carry?" I asked.

Han nodded. "Yeah, you're right. Without them, the rope would slip off easily."

"And none of this was wrapped up? He just hauled it right up to a residential complex?"

"Which makes me think he had some kind of vehicle," Han told me. "Walking down the street with unwrapped body parts would call too much attention."

"If that's true, why'd he bother with the grooves?" Big Bao asked.

I thought for a moment. "Maybe to be more efficient. Think about it—all tied up with a rope, he could get rid of most of the body in one go."

Han stopped what he was doing and used his forearm to wipe sweat from his brow. "There's something I don't understand. Even if there was no wrapping on the big pieces, all these smaller body parts must have been in something, but there's no packaging in here. Why would he take something that incriminating with him?"

"Well," Big Bao said, "I guess he wanted us to find them."

I broke into a cold sweat.

"Found the head!"

Another forensic scientist named Wang came running, a black evidence bag in his hand.

"Is it wrapped in anything?" Han and I asked at the same time.

Wang shook his head and said, "No, it was just thrown in a trash can by the residential complex's rear entrance. Also, we've confirmed that the organs weren't discarded in this area."

"The head was thrown away around back," Han said, "and the rest was thrown in the front. Why?"

"Toss far, bury close," Big Bao said. "That's the rule."

This was conventional wisdom among investigators. If a murderer made a real effort to hide the corpse, by burying it, for example, he was probably still relatively close. If the perpetrator didn't make much effort, he probably came from somewhere else.

I nodded and said, "But even if the killer is far away, that doesn't explain why the different parts were dumped in trash cans at the front and back."

"I bet it's just the route the murderer traveled," Han said. "That fits with the vehicle theory."

"We almost have the whole body, but no organs. Why wouldn't the killer get rid of those here too?" I asked.

"Well," Lin Tao jumped in, "what if he was after the organs?" Everyone turned pale.

On the autopsy table, a complete male body was gradually being pieced together.

The body's sternum had been broken open, and the internal organs carefully taken out. Looking at the precise cuts on the chest and abdomen, we thought of Lin Tao's conjecture, and chills ran down our spines.

"There're always rumors online about people getting murdered for their organs," Big Bao said, "but getting transplant organs that way would be stupid. They didn't go through blood-type matching, they were probably cut too crudely to survive, and murder conditions are hardly sterile."

"Can't be that anyway," I said. "The killer took almost all the organs, not just ones people want for transplants."

"It couldn't be . . ." Lin Tao trailed off, his face full of disgust, and then finished, "cannibalism?"

Everyone shot him a look of annoyance.

"What? Then why'd the killer scoop out the organs?" Lin Tao said.

"Come on," I said. "If the killer wanted the organs, why dismember the bodies? He could just disembowel them, right?"

Han tightened his lips, then said softly, "Looking at the cuts, the killer had some knowledge of anatomy, but not too much. He knew to cut at the intervertebral disc, but not the other joints. Dismembering the body definitely made it easier to dispose of."

"The killer must be pretty strong," Big Bao said. "This piece weighs a ton."

"Here's what strikes me," I said. "If the killer was trying to hide the corpse, it suggests he probably knew the victim. But then again, dismembering the body to get to the internal organs suggests he didn't."

"So you're thinking they were casual acquaintances?" Big Bao asked. Everyone nodded.

"Organs aside, we found the whole body, right?" I asked.

"Almost," Bao said. "We're missing a piece of tissue from the abdomen and an ear."

"Don't count on finding them." Lin Tao laughed. "By tomorrow, those tasty bits will have popped out a feral cat or dog's rear end."

"Such a nice-looking guy. Too bad about the potty mouth," I teased.

Lin Tao raised his thick eyebrows and said, "What do you mean? I'm classy as hell."

"The body shows no signs of asphyxia or injury," Big Bao said. "Right now there's no way to determine the cause of death."

"And there isn't even blood left to test for poisoning," Han lamented.

"When one door closes, try another!" Big Bao used his forearm to push up his glasses. "The bladder's still here, and there's urine! We could test that."

"Murder by poison is really rare, and it's usually committed by women," Han said.

"Can't imagine a woman did this," Big Bao said. "How could she even lift such heavy body parts?"

"If the car was driven right up to the trash can?" Han suggested.

"Not even then," Big Bao said. "And what woman could be so ruthless as to hack open a body, then disembowel and dismember it? Women don't have the psychological resilience."

"You never know," Han said. "See where the long bones of the limbs were cut? The bone chips indicate that it took over a dozen cuts to get through the thick parts. A large man could have done it in three to five."

"Oh, come on. Have you ever seen a case where a woman dismembered a body all by herself?" Big Bao said.

"Sure," Han replied with a smile. "It's the twenty-first century, man. Women can do anything these days."

As I listened, I squatted down by the pressure cooker we'd put the pubic symphysis in so we could get past the muscle, cartilage, and periosteum to examine the bone surface. Big Bao and Han both had good points.

"This'll be done boiling in a second," I said, interrupting their discussion. "Once we find the cause of death, it'll be a lot easier to plan our next steps."

The pressure cooker rattled and squeaked. Steam puffed from the holes in the lid, filling the room with a gag-inducing meaty smell.

"I will never drink bone broth again," Big Bao said, grimacing.

"Aw, come on, Bao." I lowered the heat and slowly opened the lid of the pressure cooker. "Work with the nervous system, eat with the digestive system. No reason to let one interfere with the other."

"Almost sounds like you're the one who's been disemboweled here, Qin," said Han.

I fished the pubic bone out of the milky pot of bone soup and set about peeling off the soft tissue with a hemostat. The surface morphology soon revealed itself.

"Our victim was probably about thirty years old," I said. "I'll take it back to get a more specific age. Also, we'd better get started on that toxicology test if we ever want to figure out how he died."

"Uh, you guys," Big Bao suddenly said, "why are there eleven fingers here?"

We hurried to the autopsy table. A victim with six fingers on one hand would make identification much easier.

"I don't understand," the intern said. "We already pieced the palm together. The victim didn't have six fingers."

It took me a moment to react. "What . . . What do you mean?"

It was Han who answered. "Means these body parts include a finger that doesn't belong to the victim."

"Oh," I said. "Damn. Looks like we've got two victims. How didn't we notice that when we were piecing the body together?"

"No, it's not like that," the intern said. "There weren't any incongruities besides this extra finger."

The autopsy room fell silent.

Disembowelment, rope grooves, no wrapping, a rogue finger. It was all pretty eerie.

"Hey, guys." Big Bao broke the silence. "Finger or no finger, we already know that the victim, the one all the rest of the parts belong to, is male, five foot nine, average weight, about thirty years old. Once the DNA results come back, I think we can get an ID."

"Right," Han chimed in. "And the cause of death might be poisoning. Time of death was around three days ago, around June third. We actually know a lot!"

They're trying to reassure themselves, I thought, not at all pleased. Is there a ghost among us? What is his finger doing here?

"Medical Examiner Qin." Xiao Hu from administration suddenly ran into the autopsy room. "I called your desk, but you didn't answer. Director Chen just called. He wants you to turn this homicide over to the city bureau, then take your team and hurry to Qingxiang City."

"What? What happened?" I asked.

"Seems a deputy mayor was killed."

"This case is complicated—I can't just turn it over!" I paused, then added, "I do forensic work to serve the people, not just the elite."

"Listen, Qin," Xiao Hu said. "The local forensic team doesn't want word getting out, so they need you. Besides, this is an order from Director Chen. You can keep your political opinions to yourself."

I opened my mouth, but couldn't find any words. I nodded to my team, and we reluctantly took off our lab coats.

7
■

By the time we arrived in Qingxiang City, night had fallen. With no time to rest, we followed a howling squad car to an upscale, secluded residential district.

There were a dozen or so police cars but few onlookers. The north side of the neighborhood had seven or eight six-story apartment buildings, while the south side had ten duplexes. Our crime scene was in one of the duplexes. Each duplex building was divided into east and west.

"Huh . . . fancy. Guess this is like a town house?" Big Bao asked.

"Okay, men, let's get to it." I noticed several city bureau inspectors packing up equipment, probably wrapping up the preliminary site survey.

A police inspector hopped out of the squad car we'd followed, walked over to me, and said quietly, "The eastern unit is the principal crime scene, but we've requisitioned the unoccupied western unit as a temporary operational headquarters. We'll go there first so you can meet with the party secretary."

"It's just a homicide," I said with a frown. "Why all the fuss?"

Lin Tao tugged on my sleeve and whispered, "Easy, Mr. Man of the People. Let's not make everyone think we province-level guys don't know politics."

We followed the officer inside.

"Gentlemen, this is our city's party secretary, Bao Chenbin," he said obsequiously.

The woman, dressed in a fitted black suit, was in her early thirties. She had long hair, a beautiful face, and arrogant brows. If it weren't for all the kowtowing, no one would have guessed such a young woman occupied such a high position.

Secretary Bao didn't deign to look up. She just glanced at her watch and said, "The city government attaches great important to this case. I hope you can solve it within a week. You can go now. Please try to be as fast and efficient as possible."

Who did this woman think she was? I dropped my notebook on the desk, pulled out a chair, and sat down unceremoniously. "First, tell me what work's already been done."

Secretary Bao stared at me solemnly. "That's confidential."

"Then I apologize," I said. "As an expert, I have the right to refuse to handle a case if I'm not provided with sufficient information."

I picked up my notebook and turned to leave.

The police inspector hurried over, gave Bao a fearful look, and pulled me out into an adjacent room.

"Take it easy, big guy. I'm Wang Jie, newly appointed commissioner of public security. Here's what we know: This afternoon, Deputy Mayor Ding's help reported that he had been killed."

"Help?"

"His maid, to be precise," Commissioner Wang said. "This maid usually comes every other day to clean Deputy Mayor Ding's house. But her mother passed away, so she's been off the past week. She got back to the deputy mayor's house around noon today and called the police."

The east and west units were separated by only a narrow hallway. As we talked, Wang led my team and me over to the crime scene.

"How is the smell so strong?" I covered my nose.

"Yeah," Wang said. "The body is already very decomposed. That's why the maid called the police as soon as she walked in."

I glanced at the thermometer by the entrance. It was eighty-eight degrees. "So it's been at least several days. And no one wondered why he didn't show up at work?"

"According to our preliminary investigation, the last person to see Deputy Mayor Ding was his driver," Wang said. "On the night of June first, he took him home. Deputy Mayor Ding said he would be working on a research article all week, so the driver shouldn't worry about coming by."

"A politician who wrote his own articles?" Lin Tao marveled. "And how did he manage his meals?"

"Ding really was a good deputy mayor," Wang said gloomily. "He was sent down from the Provincial Party Propaganda Department. His wife died young, and he raised his son alone and sent him to college. He was very down-to-earth, went out, cooked his own meals. This isn't even his house—the city provides it."

My initial resistance to the case evaporated.

"June first was Saturday. Today is Thursday, the sixth . . ." Big Bao cracked his knuckles.

We walked to the second-floor bedroom, the stench intensifying with each step. In the dim light, I glimpsed a dark outline on the bed.

"Listen, our forensic director is related to the suspect," Wang said. "Which meant our forensic guys couldn't work the case."

I was surprised. "There's already a suspect?"

Wang's gaze faltered. "Uh, yeah, but the city party committee requested confidentiality."

I didn't pursue it further and instead peered at the laptop on the desk. "Has this been inspected for traces?"

Wang looked to the deputy chief of the criminal police division, Chen Junyi, who'd joined us in the room. Chen nodded and said, "There are fingerprints, but all of them appear to be Ding's."

I saw the laptop was in standby mode, so I put on gloves and tapped a key.

The display lit up and a document appeared: "Feasibility Report on the City's Cultivation of Literary Works." There were only three lines written. I opened the document properties and found it had been last modified on June 1 at 22:05.

"The victim was probably attacked at this time," I said, pointing at the display.

"Uh . . . agreed," Big Bao said. "He must've been attacked right after he got started."

I walked around the bed. Besides the body, everything appeared undisturbed.

"Nothing else unusual has been found?" I asked.

"No," Chen said. "The house is extremely clean. There are a few dusty footprints, but they're messy, overlapping, and deteriorated—of little value."

"My God!" Big Bao suddenly shouted. "Why doesn't he have a face?"

When the police had arrived on the scene, the body was covered from head to toe in towels. Because there were no forensic scientists on-site, no one had removed the towels until now.

Big Bao's roar made my heart beat like a drum. I forced myself to calm down, went to the bedside, and looked at the corpse's head: a uniform green surface. You could vaguely make out a nose, but no other facial features.

In the dim light, it looked like a robber with a stocking over the face, or something out of a horror movie. I crouched down to get a closer look.

"How is that possible?" Deputy Chief Chen asked.

"Any chance it might not be the deputy mayor?" added Wang hopefully.

"Even if it's not Ding, it still shouldn't be faceless." I pressed my fingers against the green surface, and it wrinkled up immediately.

"Oh! The corpse's face is covered with several layers of paper. As the body decayed and leaked, the paper turned the same color as the victim's skin. In this bad light, it just seemed like it didn't have a face."

Even though it had only been five days, it was so hot and humid in there that the body was very far gone. The once-white sheets were stained by the dark green liquid.

The rotten corpse lay supine with its hands behind its back, probably tied there by someone. The feet were bound with wide yellow tape that was also wrapped around the bed. I lifted the body and saw its wrinkled hands were also bound with tape.

As I moved the body, the stench rushed out and made me feel faint. The movement also caused the paper mask to crack slightly, and the jawbone fell open. It was as if the rotting, faceless corpse suddenly unhinged its blood-bowl of a mouth and let ichor pour out.

Big Bao, who'd been looking under the bed, glanced up at the corpse and yelped. "Shit, go easy. You're gonna scare me to death."

Without the help of a local forensic team, and since funeral homes wouldn't transport a decayed body, Big Bao and I were going to have to move it ourselves.

I held the corpse's feet while Big Bao took the elbows. Gas had gotten under the skin, which, along with tissue liquefaction, caused the smooth surface to become greasy. Big Bao's hand slipped, and the corpse hit the bed with a bang, causing fluids to splash up. Bao gazed at the green patches of skin stuck to his gloves, then at the wet spots on his shirt—his face a mix of nausea and distress.

Liquid bubbled out of the broken skin on the corpse's dropped elbow, exposing the dense green pores of decayed subcutaneous tissue.

"Whoa! Nice work, clumsy," I said. "His elbow is injured. I couldn't see it until you ripped off the skin. Let's be sure to examine his joints for trauma."

◆　◆　◆

Bao and I worked well into the night in the morgue's blinding autopsy room.

The corpse was wearing boxers and an undershirt. Being an important official, he'd dress so sloppily only if he was certain he was home alone.

"We should be able to confirm the time of death soon," I said. "Based on the stomach contents, the victim likely died about five hours after his last meal. And we know that he ate dinner with his driver at six thirty p.m. on June first. Combined with the info from the documents on the computer, I'd say he probably died around eleven thirty that night."

"Attacked at ten, dead at eleven thirty, makes sense."

"Nail bed cyanosis, visceral bleeding." I cut into the heart and said, "No visible blood clot, just fluid decay. Blood there's noncondensable. Looks like he choked to death."

We opened each elbow, wrist, ankle, and knee joint one by one. If the murderer constrained these joints during the crime, there should be blood under the skin.

Sure enough, each showed signs of subcutaneous hemorrhage.

"What's this tell us?" I quizzed Bao, my voice muffled by my mask.

"It tells us the victim died after someone tied him up." Big Bao sounded a bit muffled too.

I shook my head. "One killer probably wouldn't have been able to control all of the joints."

Big Bao thought for a moment, then nodded hard. "So there were at least two. But there aren't any serious injuries on the body. And there's no bleeding around the mouth, nose, or neck, so how could he have suffocated?"

"What about these?" I pointed to several small parallel flaps of skin on the neck, half-hidden in the bloated folds.

"These are practically scratches," Big Bao said. "Scratches can't serve as the basis for mechanical asphyxia."

"I didn't say they were caused by choking," I said. "They're probably an intimidation wound."

"Oh! So we've got constraints, we've got intimidation—you think the murderer was interrogating him?"

"I'm thinking about how the hell I'm going to get the victim's fingerprints," said Lin Tao, who'd come to check on our progress. "As soon as I touch this skin, it comes off."

The buildup of liquid and gasses had separated the victim's upper and lower skin layers. I used a scalpel to make an incision around the wrist, then peeled the skin off the hand like a glove. I carefully fitted the "human leather" over my hand and said to Lin Tao, "Okay, then, let me at that fingerprint pad."

Lin Tao stared at me wide-eyed with shock. "Y-y-you, I—I—I . . ."

"You, me, what?" I laughed. "Come on already."

Lin Tao held up the fingerprint plate and mumbled, "You're so gross, I can't handle it . . ."

Big Bao was studying the body's face. "Qin, I got it. The stuff on his face is toilet paper, lots of it."

8

■

"What's the killer trying to say?" Big Bao asked. "What's the point of killing someone, then covering the face with a bunch of toilet paper? Why not just use a pillowcase? And he used towels to cover the rest of the body, so why toilet paper on the face? I really don't get it."

I was confused too. I held the stack of toilet paper sheets Big Bao had taken off and turned them back and forth. The side of the paper near the mouth was damaged, but not all the way through; on the other side, you could make out some kind of corrugation.

A lightbulb snapped on. "Weren't we trying to figure out how the victim suffocated? From this, of course."

"What?" Big Bao and Lin Tao asked in unison.

"Fortune Paste!" I said.

"Fortune Paste" is an ancient torture and interrogation method. Interrogators would wet mulberry paper and paste layer after layer of it on a prisoner's face until they either talked or died of suffocation. When the paper dried, it would have indentations from the prisoner's face like the mask worn onstage during a traditional "Fortune Dance."

"The victim shows no signs of mechanical asphyxia," I continued, "but there's this wad of toilet paper on his face. And it's damaged on the face side, I think because it was wet and the victim used his lips and tongue to try to break through and breathe. But the killer or killers pasted on ten or twenty sheets, and the victim suffocated."

Big Bao and Lin Tao both nodded in startled agreement.

I called Deputy Chief Chen down to the autopsy room and explained our findings. "Do you think the murderers wanted to get some kind of information from the deputy mayor?"

"Ding was in charge of culture and education," said Chen. "He wouldn't have had political secrets of interest to others."

"Could it have been robbery?" Lin Tao asked.

"No," Chen said. "All the doors and windows were intact—no signs of a break-in. Plus, there wasn't anything out of place in the house. Nothing points to a robbery."

"So it was probably an acquaintance?" I asked. "The deputy mayor wouldn't let strangers in late at night."

Chen looked reluctant. "I'm afraid I don't know any more than you. The city party secretary is insisting on confidentiality, and it's created a lot of mystery."

"Isn't she just a secretary?" Big Bao said. "Does she think she's a special agent or something?"

"Let's call it a night." I was exhausted. "We already got the cause and time of death. And we're pretty sure it was an acquaintance crime with two or more killers who restrained and threatened the victim—maybe to get information. That's enough for now. Tomorrow, Lin Tao will take a look at the tape from the victim's hands and feet and see if he can find anything."

Lin Tao shook his head, face full of disappointment. "No point, the murderers were wearing gloves."

◆　◆　◆

Back at the hotel, I couldn't help but call the provincial bureau chief. The strange case with the eleventh finger was still on my mind, and I had to admit it was distracting me from the deputy mayor.

"Chief Hu, how are you?" I asked. "Any new developments?"

"The toxicology test confirmed our hypothesis," Chief Hu said, sounding almost as tired as I was. "Tetramine in the victim's urine—the victim died of poisoning."

"I'm still thinking about that eleventh finger," I said. "Was it from another person?"

"Mm-hmm," Chief Hu said. "All the other body parts were verified as belonging to the same person. Just that one finger doesn't. It's another male's."

I opened my laptop and scanned through the photos of the dismemberment case.

"The finger was definitely dead before it was cut off," I said. "Means the killer couldn't have injured his own finger. There must be another body!"

Chief Hu said, "We sent out a group of officers and search dogs, but they came up with nothing."

I went silent for a moment, then asked, "What about IDing the body?"

"We've gone through missing persons files and compiled a list of individuals who meet the victim's description; we're hoping to find the family and ID the victim soon. We've got another group combing the tetramine black market to see if we can find the source. Tetramine is an illegal substance. If the murderer got hold of it, we want to know how."

Hanging up the phone, I collapsed into bed and, staring at the ceiling, my thoughts a mess, somehow fell asleep.

Early the next morning, Secretary Bao asked us to come to the temporary headquarters. The secretary seemed to have put away her contemptuous air for the moment.

"Please sit, gentlemen." She bowed slightly.

Her courtesy made me uneasy. Was the case at an impasse? Had my standing up to her yesterday weakened her pride?

"On behalf of the city party committee, I would like to tell you gentlemen about the preliminary case findings," Secretary Bao said with a stiff smile. "We had a suspect, another deputy mayor, Chen Feng. Chen and Ding were rivals—clashed politically. At meetings, they fought to the point where open conflict almost broke out on more than one occasion. Recently, when the provincial government was looking into promoting Chen, we received an anonymous tip that he'd accepted bribes. So not only did Chen's promotion go out the window; he was placed under disciplinary review. In short, we suspected Deputy Mayor Chen hired someone to kill Deputy Mayor Ding in revenge for exposing him."

I tilted my head and thought it over. "Could be. Based on what we've found, the killers subdued the victim, then threatened and coerced him, like they were trying to get some kind of information. They may have wanted Ding to confess to reporting Chen."

"That's the reason I asked you back here," Secretary Bao said, a little embarrassed. "After last night, we can exclude Deputy Mayor Chen and his family as suspects. We have determined that he didn't commit the murder, nor is it likely that he hired others to do it."

No wonder Secretary Bao had changed her tune. The case really was at an impasse: there was no lead, no evidence, no suspects. Now the arrogant lady realized our importance and her mistake.

"I see, of course. Well, you're in charge, Boss! Just call and we'll come running," I said with a sneer.

Lin Tao elbowed me and shot me a look that said, Shut up.

Secretary Bao gave Lin Tao a grateful nod. Indeed, if I kept talking, Secretary Bao would be humiliated in front of her subordinates.

"We'll get to work, give you our preliminary results tonight," I told her.

Back at the crime scene, we began a second survey of the room. It was daytime now and, with the window open, the sun shone in, revealing something I'd missed the night before.

"Lin Tao, come look and tell me what the color variation in this stain is from," I said, pointing at the massive green splotch on the bedsheets.

"It looks like residue left by a colorless liquid after evaporation," Lin Tao said, "but it's definitely not water."

Big Bao lifted the stained portion of the sheet, smelled it, and said, "It . . . I think it's alcohol."

"Alcohol?" Skeptical, I sniffed it as well but only got a noseful of rotten flesh. "I know you like to drink—you didn't by any chance go out alone last night, did you?"

"I don't remember swapping our Big Bao for that bloodhound Bao Zhan from the special task force—how 'bout you, Qin?" Lin Tao apparently didn't smell alcohol either. "Well, I'll take these sheets back for tests, and we'll see if he's right."

"This too." I picked up a soaked towel and stuffed it into Lin Tao's evidence bag.

It was getting close to noon, and we hadn't found anything else new. The elegantly decorated home was calm and still. With the body gone, it was as if nothing had happened. Birds sang cheerfully outside, and the sun was shining.

"Why would they have suspected Deputy Mayor Chen of hiring a hit man?" I was suddenly doubtful. "Think about it. If it were hit men, why would the victim have let them in?"

"Didn't they say they already ruled out the possibility that Chen hired someone?" Lin Tao asked.

"Another problem," I said. "Tell me what kind of person hears a knock at the door, answers it in his underwear, then invites the guest to his bedroom."

"You're right!" Big Bao said. "They would have stayed downstairs. And maybe other people don't have the decency to put on pants, but he was a deputy mayor!"

"So, we overlooked some really obvious clues," Lin Tao said. "Looks like you two are as distracted by the Eleventh Finger case as I am."

I went back to update Secretary Bao. "No matter how familiar the killers were, Mayor Ding wouldn't have brought anyone into his bedroom in the middle of the night if he was wearing only underwear and an undershirt. And Ding isn't even from around here."

Secretary Bao, whose job didn't normally involve criminal investigations, thought over my argument for a long time before responding. "So, what then? Weren't the doors and windows intact? How did the criminals get in?"

"Keys," Lin Tao and I said in unison.

"But only Mayor Ding had keys to that apartment." Secretary Bao thought a second, then corrected herself. "No, that's not true. The maid must've had a set too."

I smiled generously and said, "Your guys will want to interrogate her, huh?"

Lin Tao, Big Bao, and I went to Qingxiang City's physical and chemical laboratory to test the sheets and towel. This was the first nationally accredited lab in our province—talented people, sophisticated equipment. As for the maid, I had faith that the local detectives would have results within a few hours.

The graph on the chemical testing device jumped all over the place. Lin Tao didn't take his eyes off it. "Big Bao really does have a good nose—it's ethanol."

Big Bao scratched his head bashfully. "Heh . . . wild guess."

"Ethanol?" I wrinkled my brow. "How could it be ethanol? Which section did you test?"

"Several sections showed the same profile," Lin Tao said. "I'm confident that the color variation on the sheets was caused by evaporating ethanol. Furthermore, the towels from the body show traces of ethanol too."

"But we didn't smell any in the room."

"The body stank so much, it covered the alcohol," Big Bao pointed out.

"So only a drunk like you could smell it, huh?" I said with a laugh. "But there was no alcohol container on-site, so the killers must have taken it away with them."

"Why would there be so much alcohol on everything?" Lin Tao wondered aloud.

"The killers knew the victim, and they came to drink with him," Big Bao said hopefully. "They drank and drank, then started to fight, then the murderers killed him."

We ignored our enthusiastic intern.

"We've already established that the killers and victim probably didn't know one another," I said. "I suspect that the killers were hiding in the house ahead of time, waiting for an opportunity to strike."

"Still, where'd the ethanol come from?" Lin Tao asked.

"Examiner Qin," a detective said, running into the lab. "The maid has been questioned, and we have her in custody."

9

The maid's name was Fang Xiangyu. She was twenty-one, a high school graduate from the countryside, and quite plain. It hadn't taken much to get the young woman, still dazed from her mother's death and the discovery of Ding's body, to talk.

Fang Xiangyu knew Deputy Mayor Ding had spent most of his life as a bachelor. She confessed that, six months ago, he'd come home drunk after a business dinner and she'd taken the opportunity to seduce him.

After their tryst, Fang Xiangyu told Ding that if he didn't want to be reported, he had to double her salary. As a bonus, she'd let him make sexual demands of her anytime, at a rate of one thousand yuan per night.

According to Fang Xiangyu, Ding did not call on her services again. And while she admitted to blackmailing the deputy mayor, she firmly denied any involvement in his death.

"So we should release her?" the detective asked.

I nodded. "But the people around this Fang Xiangyu need to be investigated further, because apart from the victim, she was the only one with a key to the house. Oh right, one more thing. Did the local surveillance cameras catch anything?"

"We've looked closely at the footage from after ten p.m. on the night of June first," the detective said. "No suspicious vehicles came through, and only a few small groups of people left the neighborhood."

"What about the trash? How often is it picked up?"

"Usually once a day," the detective said.

"Shit. If it weren't way too late, we could check the trash cans for a bottle containing ethanol. We found traces of it all over the victim's room."

"There's a garbage center nearby," a district police officer chimed in. "If the container is relatively distinct, we might still be able to find it."

"Is it necessarily straight ethanol?" the detective said. "Could it be baijiu?"

"I thought it was baijiu too," Big Bao exclaimed at the mention of the potent liquor. "Ethanol just isn't that fragrant."

I felt like a rat rescued from a maze, suddenly refreshed and sober. "Let's get back to the site!"

Aside from the bedroom, there were two more upstairs rooms in Ding's house, but they were so neat and clean that we hadn't paid them much attention before. One was an unused guest room without so much as a blanket on the bed. The other was a study full of all kinds of books, as well as a shelf displaying a wide selection of baijiu bottles in decorative boxes. Fang Xiangyu must not have been a very thorough maid, because the shelf was covered in dust.

"Look down here." I pointed my flashlight at the shelf. One box had been moved recently, exposing a dustless area underneath.

Lin Tao put on gloves and carefully picked up the box. He turned to me and said, "Good eye, my friend. It's empty."

We checked the other boxes, all of which still had bottles of booze inside.

"Now we just need to confirm that the bottle of baijiu from this box was the one poured on the body. A chemical test could do that, right?" I asked.

"I can tell you right now!" Lin Tao said.

"Yeah?"

"Look at these markings. Whoever picked up the box was wearing gloves like the ones I found fibers from on the tape used to bind the victim's hands and feet."

"What?" I said. "Why would anyone wear gloves to get alcohol?"

We ran to the master bedroom and lay down on the floor.

"Oh!"

Back at temporary project headquarters, Secretary Bao sat at a dining table in the center of the room. We sat across from her, and several police officers and government officials arranged themselves on a sofa off to the side.

Having a task force meeting in an apartment felt pretty silly.

"If I'm not mistaken," I said, "Fang Xiangyu was cleaning other people's houses too?"

"Of course." Secretary Bao seemed a bit disappointed at my opening remark. Maybe she'd expected me to tell her who the killers were right away. "She worked only part-time for Deputy Mayor Ding. Commissioner Wang, give us a report on her whole working situation."

Wang flipped the pages of his notebook with gusto. "According to our investigation, Fang Xiangyu usually went to each family's house every other day for half the day. She worked for four families in total. That is to say, her schedule was relatively full. The four families, respectively, were Deputy Mayor Ding; Qian Yiran, who lives in one of the six-story buildings nearby; a family in another complex about a mile away called Scenic View—"

"Okay," I said, cutting him off. "What do we know about Qian Yiran?"

"But I'm not finished." Wang pointed to his notebook and looked at Secretary Bao. He was so used to reporting to this woman that he was anxious about not completely fulfilling her request.

"Answer my question," I said.

"Oh, okay." Maybe Wang had gotten a look of approval from Bao. "Qian Yiran is thirty-seven years old, previously ran a coal mine, but now he manages a restaurant in Qingxiang."

"Personal life?" I prompted.

"Divorced one, two, three, four, five, six—divorced six times, no kids," Wang said.

"Is Fang Xiangyu still here?" I turned my head to ask the detective behind me.

"We're in the process of releasing her now."

"Invite her to stay a little longer." I leaned closer and whispered a few words to him.

The detective turned and left.

Secretary Bao frowned, impatient for me to get to the point.

I smiled and said, "Don't worry, beautiful. I'll explain it to you. First of all, we already hypothesized that the killers and Ding probably didn't know one another, right?" I said.

Secretary Bao said, "Right, you think they had Deputy Mayor Ding's keys, broke in ahead of time, and waited for an opportunity to attack."

I nodded. "Right. Next, after thorough investigation, we discovered that after the killers struck, they went to the study and got a bottle of baijiu and poured it over the body, then took the bottle away from the scene with them. Why do you think the killers would pour baijiu on the body?"

I caught a flash of childishness in Bao's eyes. "Dunno, a toast?"

I smiled slightly and shook my head. "Wouldn't use that much to memorialize. I think the killers wanted to burn the body."

"Okay. What's that tell us?"

"Well, why burn a body?"

"To destroy evidence!" Bao's eyes shone.

"Yes, the primary motive would be to keep us from finding incriminating evidence," I said. "But crime scenes with burned bodies are usually in rural areas where a fire wouldn't immediately be seen by neighbors. Have you heard of anyone burning a body in an apartment complex?"

Bao opened her mouth but didn't speak.

"Many killers will try to hide the body so they have time to flee," I continued. "That's especially important if the murder occurred in the victim's home."

"But like you said, in an apartment, someone would notice before the killer could get away."

"Right." I grinned, warming up to the twist. "Which tells us that the killers didn't need time to run. After further surveying today, we found traces of alcohol leading to the door, and at the end there are slight burn marks. The killers made a line of baijiu and lit it before leaving, so that when the fire started, they'd be safe."

I looked right at Bao and said, "So now do you get it?"

Bao avoided my gaze and recovered her arrogant expression. "Sure. At least one of the killers lives nearby, so they didn't need to buy much time."

"Right, but the fire didn't catch. Guess again."

Bao suppressed her anger. "If the killers had a car outside, couldn't they just flee that way?"

"Don't be silly. The surveillance video shows no suspicious vehicles and few people leaving the complex."

"Are you saying Qian Yiran is a suspect?" Commissioner Wang asked.

"Yup," I said. "He didn't have to leave the complex."

"But why would he want to kill Ding?" Secretary Bao asked.

"Fang Xiangyu."

"We've got a lead!" A detective burst through the door with a bang. "Should I make the arrest, Boss?"

"Excuse yourself!" Commissioner Wang's eyes widened in fury. His men were embarrassing him in front of important city officials. "Now, back up. What did you find out?"

The detective said, "Fang Xiangyu says Qian Yiran was pursuing her, but she refused."

"Refused?" I was a bit surprised. "Wouldn't that woman do anything for money?"

"Don't judge her," Secretary Bao said. "You don't know her life."

The detective shook his head and said, "Qian Yiran is impotent."

Qian Yiran was issued a summons, and we went to search his home. Big Bao was wildly excited.

"See, Boss? I was right, right?" Big Bao said. "That brand of alcohol is about three thousand bucks a bottle, limited edition. I bet a thousand is just for the bottle. It's super pretty, with a concave bottom and old sailboat inside. The color of the sail changes with the temperature—it's exquisite. Everyone loves it, so this guy probably kept it as a collector's item."

Alcohol always brought out the eloquent side of Big Bao.

Fang Xiangyu must have had her work cut out for her cleaning Qian Yiran's place. She'd been gone only for a week, and it already looked like an outdoor market at closing time. There were empty beer cans all over the coffee table. The floor was covered in takeout wrappers, and the table was cluttered with food scraps and unwashed dishes.

Big Bao caught sight of a vase of roses prominently displayed in a bay window. The vase had a concave bottom and a vivid sailboat inside.

"Like I said!" Big Bao jumped three feet in the air. "See? Just call me Sherlock."

"Easy, big guy." I squeezed Big Bao's shoulder. "How do you know it's the bottle from Deputy Mayor Ding's house?"

Big Bao smoothly pulled out the roses, dumped the water into a nearby plant, and pointed at the bottom of the bottle. "This is a limited-edition, high-quality luxury product. Each bottle has a serial number!"

"And?" Lin Tao prompted, laughing at Bao's exuberance.

"And?" Big Bao pushed the glasses up on his nose. "And what? . . . Oh yeah, it matches the number on the box you found. I wrote it down so I could go online and check its authenticity."

"You're really committed to your baijiu." I laughed. "Okay, boys. That's a wrap, case closed!"

10

Qian Yiran was a romantic, but he'd been cursed with an uncoopera-
tive body.

As the boss of a coal mine, he'd been an important man. He had a
luxury car and designer clothes. But he couldn't make it happen with
women.

Whenever he got into a new relationship, it was a whirlwind of
romance and promises. They'd get married fast, but then Qian Yiran's
impotence, and his anger about it, led swiftly to divorce. Ashamed,
Qian Yiran gave each of his ex-wives some of his property if they'd
agree to keep things out of court. Eventually, all he had left was one
small restaurant.

Fang Xiangyu had come to work for him a year before. She was
no great beauty, but her honest temperament moved him. He thought
he'd finally found true love, but, of course, he'd thought that with all
six of his marriages.

Fang Xiangyu was not a shy girl, and soon made it clear that she
shared his interest. Qian Yiran tried to sweep her off her feet, but
his body let him down yet again. In a flash, Fang Xiangyu's interest
evaporated.

Do women really care about sex that much? Qian Yiran wondered. Xiangyu can't be so vulgar! She's a pure girl—she looks so innocent. I bet it's just that her family wants her to have children. Rural people are so traditional. It must be that. I'm sure she still cares for me anyway.

He didn't give up, believing his passion would make up for his bodily defect.

But one day he noticed with alarm that Fang Xiangyu was wearing new clothes and carrying a new handbag. She was in a suspiciously good mood. He started to track her every move and riffled through her cell phone while she was cleaning.

He found a text message she'd written to someone called "Ding": *If you want to, I'll come tonight.*

Qian Yiran spun with jealousy. Doesn't she work for someone named Ding? He lives just over in one of those town houses. A dirty old man sullying the young girl I love! He must have seduced her with sweet talk, with lies. That's why she hasn't wanted to be with me!

When Qian Yiran confronted her, Fang Xiangyu snatched her phone away. "What I do with my time and my body is none of your business."

After that, Qian Yiran couldn't sleep, couldn't eat. He needed to know if another man was tarnishing his girl.

You can't run a coal mine without knowing some thugs. Qian Yiran called up three he knew were still loyal.

The thugs couldn't pick locks, so Qian Yiran secretly copied Fang Xiangyu's keys.

That night, his body trembled as he tested the keys one by one. But when the front door gave way, he suddenly wasn't nervous at all. He and the men hid in a closet, waiting for Ding to come home.

Qian Yiran had learned about Fortune Paste from TV shows, and he knew it'd be just the thing for his little interrogation. First, he'd find out if this Ding had defiled his goddess. Second, he'd teach the old bastard a lesson.

But he blew it.

He'd only just started plastering toilet paper on Ding's face when the man stopped moving. Qian Yiran shook him. What the hell? How'd he die so fast?

The thugs started to panic and looked to their former boss. That reverence calmed him, took him back to the heyday of the coal mine when he'd felt powerful, manly. "It is what it is, boys. Let's burn the body, hide out at home for a while, and everything'll be all right."

The roses were to be a surprise for Fang Xiangyu, a little gift to ease the pain of her mother's death. With his rival out of the way, Qian Yiran was sure the innocent girl would finally be won over by the lovely flowers in their strangely beautiful vase.

11

"How's it going, Chief Hu?" I was panting, having raced up to the forensic pathology lab on the fifth floor of Dragon City's municipal public security bureau. When I heard they'd ID'd the corpse in the Eleventh Finger case, I'd asked our driver, Han Liang, to floor it.

"That was fast. Didn't you guys just leave?" Chief Hu said with surprise.

I picked up Chief Hu's cup of tea and downed it. "I've been dying to know—any developments in the Eleventh Finger case?"

"Heh, not a bad project name," Chief Hu said. "Eleventh Finger."

Big Bao, Lin Tao, and I sat down at the chief's desk, staring expectantly.

"No rush, no rush, let me tell you the whole story. The victim is a male named Zuo Fangjiang, thirty years old. Five years ago, he committed telecom fraud and used the capital from that to start the Tongtong Internet Company in Nanjiang City."

I wasn't too interested in this scumbag's history. "What's someone from Nanjiang doing in Dragon City?"

"He traveled alone by train to Dragon City on June second for business," Chief Hu said. "That night, after eating with a business partner at his hotel bar, he went back to his room by himself. Zuo Fangjiang's wife said she called him at midnight, and he didn't answer. When he didn't come home the next day as scheduled, she called again, but the phone was turned off."

"The hotel he stayed at, has it been searched yet?" I asked.

"The hotel realized two days ago that he still hadn't checked out, so they sent someone in to look. Everything was neat and tidy, nothing suspicious. So they moved his luggage to the front desk and called us."

"Now that we've ID'd the victim, the case should be easy to solve, right?" I stroked my stubble.

"I think not."

"No?" I said. "Dismembering a body is usually done to hide it. And hiding a body is usually done by acquaintances. So once you ID the victim, you're halfway there. Don't you think so?"

Chief Hu said, "Yeah, in general, but every case is different, Qin. As far as we can tell, this is the first time Zuo Fangjiang has visited Dragon City, so how could he know anyone?"

"He could have an enemy in Dragon City," Lin Tao said, "or one that followed him here."

Chief Hu shook his head. "I think we can rule out both those possibilities. Besides his partner, he hasn't contacted anyone since arriving in Dragon City. And if an enemy followed him, why would he bother to dismember the body instead of just getting out of town?"

"Good point," I said. "Then there's only one possibility—the business partner killed him."

"That's what we thought at first too, but the Security Ministry conducted a secret investigation of the business partner and was able to determine that he is definitely not the killer."

"So . . . no suspects, no motive? What's with this case?" Big Bao whined.

Lin Tao thought a moment. "If the killer was just a casual business contact, he wouldn't be too bothered by disemboweling and dismembering Zuo Fangjiang."

"Right. Did we find the victim's organs?" I said.

Chief Hu nodded. "We enlisted local firefighters to drain a nearby pond and found the organs there."

"It'd take a forensic scientist to remove all the internal organs in one go, right?" Lin Tao said. "I mean, I sure couldn't do it."

"You're right," Chief Hu said. "Based on their appearance, the organs were removed using forensic techniques."

"So our killer studied forensics?" I asked.

"Well, that's complicated," Chief Hu said. "The disembowelment shows strong familiarity with anatomy, but the dismemberment doesn't. My personal hunch is that the killer is actually a professional forensic scientist who deliberately messed up the dismemberment just to throw us off."

"So why would the killer take out the organs if he was just going to dump them?" I asked.

"To attract attention," Chief Hu said emphatically.

"Attract attention?" Big Bao said, puzzled. "Maybe the killer's insane?"

Chief Hu shook his head. "The key characteristic of crimes committed by the insane is that they ignore consequences; they're sloppy. But the body was dismembered with care, disemboweled with skill, special grooves were made for the ropes—all of it shows purposeful action. And talent."

"Okay, so what's the point of trying to attract attention?" I asked Hu.

"To make sure we'd find it," Chief Hu said, lowering his eyes. "Provoke the police."

I nodded. "Oh God. Dismembering the body wasn't to hide it. It was to make it easier for us to find, and more ghastly. Our opponent is directly challenging us."

"And he has some real anatomical knowledge," Chief Hu said. "I'd hate to imagine it could be one of our own. Can you guys think of anyone in forensics who might be a suspect?"

"Chief Hu," Forensic Scientist Han interrupted, looking surprised to see us. "You guys are back already? Didn't you go to work on that murdered politician case?"

"Solved it," I said, still thinking about what Hu had said.

Han lifted the transparent evidence bag in his hand. "Chief, we examined this again like you asked. The separation point doesn't show obvious signs of bleeding, and there appear to be multiple incisions, so we're pretty sure it was cut after death."

Inside the bag was a finger, slightly bent. The part where it had separated was black and red with bone chips sticking out of the soft tissue.

"I'm really stuck on this eleventh finger situation," I said. "What do you all think?"

"Yeah, DNA confirmed it doesn't belong to the victim," Hu said.

"And we can rule out the possibility of it being the killer's because of the lack of vital response." I took the evidence bag from Han. "It's really strange, all these fingers lately. On that gutter-oil case, the first thing we found was a finger. Now one shows up in this case too."

"I wonder what relationship there is between the two victims," Chief Hu said. "I mean, we don't know for sure that the eleventh finger and the disemboweled body are actually connected."

"Two unrelated dismembered bodies discarded in the same place?" I replied. "That'd be one hell of a coincidence."

"We've got people investigating Zuo Fangjiang's contacts, and others hunting for the rest of the body that goes with that finger. Other than that, we're at a bit of a loss."

I was still staring at the evidence bag. "What about timing? Have we looked into it?"

Han came over. "Can't infer time of death based on just a finger."

I glanced at the survey kit at our feet, then motioned to Big Bao. "Get me a fresh blade." I opened the evidence bag, ready to take the finger out.

The scalpels forensic scientists and surgeons use are the same. Each has a surgical knife handle, and the blade is replaced after each use.

Chief Hu was shocked. "Wait, right here? Hold on, I'll lay out some newspaper. This is a new desk, damn it. We gotta maintain hygiene, maintain hygiene!"

I couldn't help but laugh. After Chief Hu covered the desk in newspaper, I placed the finger on it and pulled on a pair of gloves.

"A finger's main structures are skin, fascia, and bones," I said. "Because the fascia is hard and tough, it will decay much slower than other tissue. This finger's skin is obviously turning black, and the soft tissue shows signs of blackening too."

"It's only been four or five days since the last examination," Han said.

"Yeah, a few days of decay definitely couldn't cause a finger to reach this level."

I cut the tip of the finger to expose the yellow-and-white subcutaneous fascia. "Look, the fascia has already softened, which means we're looking at a prolonged period of decomposition."

"You're saying the eleventh finger's owner and the body we examined didn't die at the same time?" Big Bao said.

"Definitely not," I said firmly. "There's no hard-and-fast rule to determine the exact correlation between time of death and decay of a certain body part. However, the fascia takes at least half a month to soften like this when it's not particularly hot out, so we're talking about a death sometime around mid-May."

"In other words, the body parts of these two victims weren't thrown in the garbage at the same time?" Big Bao said. "If the cases aren't related, I don't know if that's good or bad."

"Of course it's bad," Han said. "If there's no relation, that means two cases to solve, and the finger won't help us find out more about the other body."

"I actually think it'd be a good thing," Chief Hu said. "If it's one case and the killer just left an extra finger, then he's really trying to mess with us. With a well-prepared, professional enemy, we're out in the open, and he's holding all the cards. That's no good for us."

I shook my head. "Who said the bodies couldn't be discarded together just because they weren't killed together? What if the killer disposed of the first corpse earlier but kept this finger, then put it with Zuo Fangjiang's corpse?"

"That would be scary—it'd definitely be a provocation," Hu said. "Hopefully your famous jinx powers won't work this time."

"I'm afraid they will," I said, "but it's not jinxing; it's just judgment. What's more, I think the softening of the fascia could be more from having been frozen than from regular decay."

All forensic scientists know that if a body is frozen and then put back into a room-temperature environment, it'll decay faster. Some corpses decay so much while thawing that the skin turns blackish yellow.

"But we didn't freeze the eleventh finger after that last autopsy," Han said.

"Which means the killer may have frozen it before he discarded it with Zuo Fangjiang's corpse," I said.

This case was shaping up to be a doozy.

"Either way, the only place to start is by IDing that finger," Lin Tao said, breaking the silence. "If we're right so far, investigating Zuo Fangjiang's problematic social relationships won't do us much good."

"Whether it helps or not, we have to check," Hu said. "Forensics has done all it can—the only thing now is to wait for the criminal investigation part of the task force to give us some good news."

"True," I said. "It all depends on them. I'd like to talk to the detectives. IDing this finger is urgent. Also, have we made any progress on the cause of death?"

"Tetramine, a potentially lethal amount, was detected in the victim's urine," Hu replied. "We believe the murderer poisoned the victim's food or drink, but the incisions show a slight vital reaction. What we don't know is if that means the killer didn't wait until the victim was really dead to begin the disembowelment or just started it moments after he died."

"So, since we don't know if the victim was completely dead when the cutting began, we can't determine whether the main cause of death was poison or blood loss."

"Like I keep saying, poison cases are usually committed by women," Han said.

"Get off it, Han," Big Bao retorted. "No way could a woman be this brutal."

12

"By the way, where's Director Chen?" Chief Hu asked.

"A big shooter case," I said. "Several provinces, several killed. The perp's some kind of lunatic—started unloading as soon as the bank door opened, took the money, and ran. And I hear he broke through a heavy police blockade and keeps slipping right through our fingertips. The Ministry of Public Security is taking it very seriously, so they called the boss in to help. I doubt he'll be back before they solve it. I'm doing my best to fill in while he's gone."

"Oh, I know about that case, lots of chatter online." Hu nodded.

My cell phone started buzzing like a hornet in my pocket. Maybe it has to do with my line of work, but I've developed the unfortunate habit of jumping every time my phone rings.

"Shit! I just got back—still haven't gotten a chance to go home and see my wife! There can't be another case, can there?" I fumbled in my pocket.

"Uh . . . your exam glove's still on," Big Bao said.

I ripped off the tight gloves. "If I have to go on another work trip, Ling Dang will divorce me."

"Yeah, right," Lin Tao said with a smile. "She's so good to you, and you helped her family with that impossible case—she should be loyal to you for life."

"Qin! I'm deep in it over here, and you can't even be bothered to answer your phone?" Director Chen's voice boomed in my ear.

"Huh? What's going on?" I said. "Boss, sorry, have you been calling me? I just got back from Qingxiang City. I'm in Dragon City working a murder."

"Skip town for a case in Qingxiang, leave the office empty, don't answer your phone . . . Are you trying to piss me off?" Chen snarled.

I glared at my phone—the piece of junk was always missing calls. Time to burn a month's salary on a new one. "So sorry, Boss. What's up?"

"Liqiao City's got a new case. I didn't catch the details," Chen said. "You guys hurry over, see if you can help."

"Got it. On our way, Boss."

As soon as I hung up, I felt exhausted. "Damn, looks like we're not even going home."

◆　◆　◆

And so we jumped in a car and spent half that day on the highway. By nightfall we'd reached Liqiao City's public security bureau.

The conference room was lit only by a projector. Clouds of cigarette smoke slowly drifted through the beam of light, turning the space into an acrid fairyland. Even for a smoker like me, the room was suffocating.

"Ahem, hello, Director Qiang." I shook hands with the director. "Director Chen told us to get here as soon as possible, but we haven't heard any details yet."

"It's a pretty strange case," Director Qiang said with a bitter laugh. "We just started watching this surveillance video. Join us."

"This alley is located on the east side of town. It was built during the early Republican Era and is a level-three cultural heritage site," a detective said by way of introduction. "Most of the old housing in East City has been demolished, but the alleys have been preserved."

The detective took a sip of water and continued. "The area consists of seventeen north-south and east-west alleys that form a kind of a maze, so locals call them the 'Lost Lanes.' The Lost Lanes have twenty-one family dwellings, each a traditional courtyard building. Of the twenty-one households, sixteen are renters and five are long-term residents."

The detective aimed a laser pointer at the screen. "Because of a prior rape case, the local police station installed several surveillance cameras. This image was captured by one of the cameras."

The detective tapped on the computer, and the screen began to move. A man dressed in dark clothing passed through the frame. Then there were four or five minutes of just a blinking light in the corner of the alley. I yawned, rubbed my tired eyes, and looked up just in time to see a shadow flash across the screen.

The shadow belonged to a short-haired woman in a dress. She looked right into the camera, then, leaning on the wall, slowly turned away from it.

The detective spoke again. "Based on her body shape and clothing, we believe this to be Tao Zi, a missing person. After she came upon this camera, she realized the alley had come to an end, and she escaped in the other direction. Unfortunately, there's no camera there, so we couldn't see that."

On the screen, Tao Zi was squatting against the wall and covering her face with her hands.

"Watch the opposite corner."

As he spoke, a dark shadow appeared there, looking like the silhouette of a long-haired woman. Tao Zi leapt up. She grabbed her hair, then turned her face to the wall and covered her eyes.

"Looks like extreme fright, right?" Director Qiang said.

Seemingly terrified, Tao Zi rushed toward the corner of the alley, but as she was about to disappear from view, she fell. Her legs were still in the frame, but her upper body was obscured.

"Here's where it gets really bizarre," the detective said.

On the screen, the shadow of the long-haired woman slowly grew bigger and bigger until it covered Tao Zi's legs. Then, a hazy white light appeared to slink around the corner and envelop the fallen figure. The detective stopped the video with a click.

"We asked our video-processing colleagues to clarify this image, and this is the result."

In the enlarged picture, we could see that the shadowy white light was half a person—the other half was blocked by the wall. The visible half showed a long head of hair covering the face, and below it, a whole white body, but the arms and legs were not visible.

The Ring, I thought, shivering. It was the scariest movie I had ever seen. But being a forensic scientist, how could I believe in ghost stories? To comfort myself, I turned to Lin Tao and joked, "You believe in ghosts, right? This time, it's the real thing."

Lin Tao blanched. "Let's share a hotel room tonight. Big Bao can stay by himself."

"When a female officer reviewing the tape saw this part, she got so scared, she cried," the detective sneered. "She's convinced her district is haunted. In my opinion, it's just someone in a white sheet pretending to be a ghost. Don't they say ghosts don't have shadows? This one sure does."

The detective tapped his keyboard, and the video continued.

The white shadow seemed to squat down and edge closer to Tao Zi's body. Soon, the "ghost" stood up and dragged Tao Zi away.

The detective opened another image, a diagram of Lost Lanes. "The red dots mark the locations of our cameras. We retrieved all the video, and only this camera recorded Tao Zi before she went missing. After the footage you've just seen, Tao Zi and the white shadow just disappear."

"Disappear?" Lin Tao squeaked.

"Right," the detective said. "If the white shadow was very familiar with Lost Lanes, there were two routes they could have taken to get out without being seen."

"Or White Shadow lives somewhere in Lost Lanes," I said.

"Or she's a ghost," Lin Tao whispered.

"So what all do we know?" I said over Lin Tao, afraid the local cops would laugh at my superstitious friend.

The conference room lights were abruptly switched on, making me squint.

"So," Director Qiang said, "this morning, Commissioner Tao of Liqiao City's inland revenue department called the police to report that his sixteen-year-old daughter, Tao Zi, had gone missing. It seems that, around eight last night, Tao Zi got a call from a friend inviting her for karaoke at Guosheng KTV. When a taxi arrived, Commissioner Tao looked down from his balcony and saw three of her classmates inside, so he didn't worry. But Tao Zi still wasn't home by midnight, so Tao called some of her friends. They all said Tao Zi had headed home by herself at ten."

"How far is Guosheng KTV from Lost Lanes?" I asked.

"Not far," the detective said. "Probably a couple hundred yards. But the karaoke bar is on a major road, so it's easy to catch a cab. If Tao Zi was going home, there was no need to walk through Lost Lanes."

"Have we searched each of the Lost Lanes households yet?" I asked.

"We're just finishing going through all the video this afternoon, and we're just beginning an inquiry into the twenty-one households. Meanwhile, we're making contact with some of Tao Zi's classmates."

"And Tao Zi herself? Where is she?"

Everyone shook their heads. Qiang said, "We haven't found her yet."

I immediately felt uncomfortable. "Wait, why'd you call us in if you don't have a body?"

Qiang touched his head in embarrassment and gestured at Lin Tao. "The thing is, we called Director Chen to ask him to send Trace Technician Lin to help us find Tao Zi and examine some trace evidence we found. But Director Chen was busy with that big case and didn't have time to let me explain, so he sent your whole team down."

"Ah," I said curtly. "I see. So Big Bao and I can go home?"

Lin Tao grabbed my sleeve. "Don't go! Just wait a day or two and go back with me. Tomorrow's the weekend anyway, so there's nothing to do. Besides, if you take the car, how am I gonna get back?"

I knew he was afraid of staying here alone. "Nothing to do? Maybe I want to spend the weekend with my wife! You ever heard of newlyweds?"

"The truth is that we may well end up needing you, Examiner Qin," Qiang said. "From the looks of it, Tao Zi is not in good shape. I've got men sweeping the area. We might have something for you very soon."

"You shouldn't talk like that," I objected. "You're making it sound like the poor kid is doomed."

"We'll see," the detective said. "For now, it's only seven thirty. Why doesn't Trace Technician Lin come with us to take another look at the scene?"

Lin Tao flashed me a desperate look.

I smiled. "Y'know, I think Big Bao and I will come too."

In the dim light of the streetlamps, it really did feel like we were entering a maze. With the detective's help, we found the spot from the surveillance footage.

"According to our analysis using the light angle and shadow length," he said, "that white-looking shadow belonged to someone about five eight."

Lin Tao nodded, lay down on his stomach, and peered at the ground. "Did you protect this surface?"

The detective shook his head. "We didn't see the footage until ten hours after the fact, so by then there was no point."

Lin Tao jumped up and brushed the dust off his pants. "No use. Can't see any traces; they've all been destroyed."

"Didn't you say there are two ways out of Lost Lanes that bypass the cameras?" I asked.

The detective nodded.

"Then take us along those routes. Let Lin Tao see the walls there."

It wasn't until we were tracing the second route that Lin Tao found something.

"This looks useful!" Lin Tao shouted. "A palm print and a wipe trace."

I leaned in closer. "Huh? What's that mean?"

Lin Tao pointed at the wall. "The palm print wasn't made by direct contact with the wall, but through a very fine fabric. And there's a wipe mark about four inches above the print."

"Why would you get a print through fabric? It's too warm for gloves."

"The shadow in the video looked like someone wrapped in a sheet, right? So, if even their palm was covered and it touched the wall, it would leave this kind of mark!"

I nodded.

"Not only that," Lin Tao crowed, "there's also this wipe mark here, probably from fabric rubbing against the wall. Judging by the height, it was left by something being carried on the person's shoulders."

"You're saying someone wrapped in a sheet and carrying Tao Zi on their shoulders leaned against the wall right here?" I asked.

Lin Tao nodded.

"Awesome, so we've got White Shadow's route. Maybe she lives in this direction," the detective said.

"Not only that," I added.

13

"Carrying someone who might be unconscious on your back," I prompted, "shows what?"

"Shows this person isn't weak," Big Bao rushed to say.

"Not bad, little man," I said with a laugh. "Always so eager. Okay, so, the analysis showed that White Shadow is about five eight, and we know the individual must be quite strong. I'd say this White Shadow probably isn't a long-haired woman, but a man."

"So what?" the detective asked.

"If it's a man, he probably doesn't have that beautiful, long black hair we saw in the video," I said. "Which means we have another clue."

"We can look into wig sales!" the detective said.

"Also, now we know the perp acted alone. If there were two people, they could have carried her without having to throw her over their shoulders. In the surveillance video, Tao Zi didn't look especially tiny."

"Yeah," the detective agreed. "Commissioner Tao says she's five six, one thirty."

"This mark was probably caused when the person carrying Tao Zi stopped to lean on the wall," Lin Tao said. "If there were two people, they wouldn't have needed to rest."

"All right." I raised my wrist to look at my watch. It was already ten thirty. "Let's go. We should head to the hotel and get some sleep. We'll be able to do more in the morning."

"Let's stay in the same room," Lin Tao begged again.

Maybe because of all the stray fingers that had been popping up recently, I dreamed that night of chopped pepper chicken feet. I was taking a bite when I realized it wasn't a chicken foot, but a human hand. I felt my stomach churn. Mercifully, the hotel phone yanked me out of the nightmare.

I sat up and glanced over at Lin Tao. The poor guy had his head buried under the covers. What a scaredy-cat, I thought.

The clock said five something. Who could be calling this early? If they'd solved the case, did that mean I'd get to spend Sunday at home?

I grabbed the phone. "Hello?"

"Examiner Qin." It was Liqiao City's Forensic Scientist Wu. "I'm sorry to bother you so early, but there's been a big development in the case."

Adrenaline rushed through my veins. "What happened?"

"The search team found Tao Zi's body in Liqiao River."

My heart sank.

"Okay, I'll be there as soon as I can."

Liqiao River flows east-west through the city. The local government had taken advantage of this unique natural resource and turned it into a beautiful scenic area. Willows and flowering bushes covered both banks. There were picturesque bridges and a charming pavilion over the water.

The scene wasn't so charming this morning, though. Dawn had just broken, and flashing police lights reflected off the river. A group of officers was gathered around a large suitcase.

Director Qiang approached us with a look of frustration. "I knew Tao Zi's prospects weren't good. Around five, an old man doing his morning calisthenics saw something under the pavilion and called the police."

I looked at the water surface; it was crystal clear.

"Emergency one-one-oh dispatched our search group to this location, where we found a large suitcase with Tao Zi's body inside."

"How far are we from Lost Lanes?" I asked.

"Not too close, several miles," an officer said.

I nodded, knelt down, and looked at the body.

Tao Zi was completely naked, curled up in the suitcase, her clothes beside her.

"It couldn't be a mugging/rape case, right?" Qiang asked. "That'd be awful."

A technician photographed the suitcase, put on gloves, and along with Forensic Scientist Wu, lifted the body out of the luggage. Photographing a body before we start our work is critical. The technician photographed the face, neck, front, back, hands, head, and soles of the feet to record the body's original state. Then, we forensic scientists began to inspect the corpse's skin for damage, marks, and other clues.

"Rigor mortis hasn't fully set in." I tried to stretch the body flat. "The corneas are getting cloudy; livor mortis is starting to fade. It's been about thirty hours since the surveillance footage, so the timing's about right."

"You mean Tao Zi died shortly after the camera caught her falling down?" Qiang asked.

I looked at several abrasions on the face, which were consistent with how she fell, and nodded.

We laid the corpse flat—height and weight confirmed it was Tao Zi, as did the clothing and effects in the suitcase.

There was a lot of blood on the body. I waved a technician over to take a photograph, then found a roll of gauze in my survey kit, cut a piece off, and slowly wiped blood from the chest and abdomen.

Wu wrestled apart the body's legs, took a look, and sighed with relief. "Director Qiang, fortunately, there was no rape. The perineum's clean and the hymen's intact."

I had wiped most of the blood off, revealing many vertical and horizontal wounds on both shoulders.

Lin Tao's voice was shaky. "Wh-wh-what kind of wound is this? So dense and messy. Are they bites?"

"C'mon, you're the trace guy," I said. "These are clearly not bite marks."

"Hey, I only know human bite marks," Lin Tao said uneasily. "I've never seen ghost bites."

A nearby policewoman sniggered.

I gave Lin Tao an embarrassed look, then probed one of the little wounds with a hemostat. "Animal bites can be messy like this, but they tear. These wounds have neat edges, so they were definitely made with a sharp instrument. And the bones underneath are damaged, probably from repeated slashes."

"Slashes? Why?" Big Bao asked.

"The skin around the wound is crimped," I explained, "and the broken soft tissue doesn't show a clear vital reaction. The damage was done postmortem. It looks like someone wanted to dismember Tao Zi but lacked the anatomical knowledge to do so. Then the killer gave up on that idea, put her in the suitcase, and threw it in the river."

"Lacking anatomical knowledge? Dismemberment?" Big Bao said with surprise. He picked up Tao Zi's hands and examined them carefully.

"You've got the Eleventh Finger case on the brain too, huh, Big Bao?"

"Hold on, hold on," Lin Tao said, curious as always about forensic work. "We know they're slash marks, but why did they necessarily happen postmortem? Why couldn't they have been inflicted when the victim was alive? Look at all the blood in the suitcase and on the body. Don't dead people's wounds keep bleeding?"

"Of course," I said. "Wounds bleed when you're alive because the heart continues to pump. After death, there's no pump pushing blood, so a broken vessel will bleed, just not as much. Do you know what signs a corpse will show if it bled to death?"

"Pale livor mortis," Big Bao said.

I nodded. "Right. Because of blood loss, there won't be enough red blood cells to pool in part of the body and cause livor mortis. The livor mortis in Tao Zi's body is very significant and even shows some purple, so she definitely didn't bleed to death. But we can determine she was put in the suitcase and left here within twelve hours of death."

"I know why!" Lin Tao exclaimed. "Within twelve hours, livor mortis doesn't infiltrate the soft tissue, so when the position of the body changes, it shifts like sand in an hourglass to new parts. And Tao Zi's livor mortis is all on her lower left side, which is in line with the suitcase's position."

"So how'd Tao Zi die, then?" Qiang asked impatiently.

I looked at the body's eyelids and lips. There were no signs of mechanical asphyxia. No sign of force on the lips or neck either. "I need to examine the body further."

Dragging the cold scalpel along the body exposed the yellow fat below the skin. We went through all our procedures, but the young body offered up no secrets.

"Why can't we figure out the cause of death?" Lin Tao said.

"Who says we can't?" Big Bao seized the opportunity to show me what he knew. "Death typically falls into one of four categories. The first is mechanical injury—the rupture of blood vessels or organs, massive blood loss or head injury, damage of vital centers. This category also includes lightning strikes and skin corrosion. The second category is mechanical asphyxia caused by smothering, strangling, and drowning. The third is poisoning, and the fourth is sudden death due to things like organ failure."

He took a deep breath and went on. "So far, we've ruled out injury and suffocation. From the look of the corpse, it wasn't poisoning either. But we haven't ruled out sudden death syndrome!"

A detective laughed. "That reminds me of that Guo Degang stand-up bit about the dismemberment-suicide case. Ha!"

His cavalier attitude offended me. "Have a little respect for the dead, man. That's a kid's body in front of you. Besides, suicide and murder are ways of dying, but dismemberment is something that happens to someone after death, got it?"

The detective hung his head.

"So," Big Bao deduced, "in this case, maybe there was a sudden death that the kidnapper didn't want to take responsibility for, so he tried to dispose of the corpse?"

I didn't say anything, just began taking out the internal organs and examining them one by one.

Forensic Scientist Wu said, "Sudden death is typically caused by cardiovascular disease or cerebrovascular disease, but Tao Zi's probably too young for that. Do you think it could be cardiac failure or status thymicolymphaticus?"

I shook my head. "Cardiac inhibition usually occurs as a result of outside pressure that leads to cardiac arrest and death, so the skin around the chest would show corresponding damage. And a status thymicolymphaticus victim would show an enlarged thymus and development problems."

"Then what could it be?" Big Bao asked.

I cut open the deceased's heart. "These ventricles are very thick, and the size of the heart is strangely large. In most people, the heart is the size of their fist, and hers is about one and a half times that size."

The detective jumped up. "I'll go look into Tao Zi's family's medical records to see if there's a history of congenital heart problems."

"Good thinking," I agreed. "Also, please transport the victim's organs to the lab. I'll call Forensic Scientist Fang Jun—he's a pathology expert. Treating organ samples so they can be put under a microscope takes a long time, so we need him to get started right away.

"As for us," I said with a stretch, "let's go take a nap."

14

A bleary-eyed Lin Tao shook me. "Wake up! It's already five o'clock. We need to check in on the investigation."

Just as I looked at the time on my phone, it rang. It was Fang Jun from the forensic pathology lab. "Examiner Qin, I looked at the organs you sent over today. Based on the deceased's organ structure, we can diagnose pulmonary valve stenosis."

"Pulmonary stenosis?" I said. "Are you sure?"

"I am," Fang Jun said. "I can double-check using another section, but that will take some time."

"Looks like I guessed right," I said to Lin Tao with a yawn. "The victim really did have a heart condition that could lead to sudden death. We should let the task force know."

"You go talk to them. I want to look around the scene again."

When I reached the station, I found the number of people on the task force had dropped by half. I figured it was because they'd already heard the victim might have died of disease, so they reduced manpower.

"The victim had a congenital heart disorder, pulmonary valve stenosis," I announced. "Judging by the autopsy results, this is likely the cause of death."

"We heard," Director Qiang said. "So this is no longer a murder case, I suppose?"

"I'm not of that opinion," I said. "Who says sudden death can't still be murder? Don't forget the White Shadow video. Judging by the time of death, I believe the victim got frightened by that 'ghost,' which caused her condition to kill her. If it was just a prank, then it was negligence, but if White Shadow knew Tao Zi had a weak heart and wouldn't be able to stand the shock, then it could be a tricky method of murder."

Director Qiang thought it over. "Using a method like that to kill someone is pretty risky, though, don't you think?"

"Not necessarily," I said. "We were able to see in that processed screen shot that White Shadow wore a wig to cover his face, which means if he failed at scaring the victim to death, she wouldn't have been able to identify him. I think it's rather clever."

"Oh come on, Qin," the lead detective scoffed. "Life isn't a detective novel. No way the situation is that complicated. According to our investigation, two of the guys Tao Zi was doing karaoke with left shortly after she did."

"Right," another detective said. "And according to testimony from some of her friends, one of the two was always pursuing Tao Zi, but she always rejected him. Our theory is that the two boys wanted to punish her with a bad scare. It's totally the kind of corny thing teenagers do."

"Hm," I replied. I had no reason to argue with them, but something wasn't right. We'd have to wait to see what came of questioning the two boys.

◆ ◆ ◆

I ran into Lin Tao on my way back to the hotel room.

"What's with the long face?" he asked.

"Nothing," I said weakly. "The task force's initial determination is that Tao Zi's death was the result of some high school mischief gone wrong. They're looking into two male students who left right after her that night."

I shook my head, perplexed.

Lin Tao opened his bag, took out a map of the area, and spread it out on the hotel room table. "Well, I have two pieces of evidence to refute that this was done by high school students."

"Let's hear it," I said, suddenly excited. "These local cops think the murder was childish and accidental, fitting for high school kids. I don't think so at all. Frightening someone to death! Impressive, really."

Lin Tao nodded. "First of all, remember the mark we saw before? I looked again and confirmed that was from one person carrying Tao Zi and leaning against the wall to rest. There definitely weren't two people involved in the incident, or else the second one would have helped carry the body."

I smacked myself on the forehead. "Of course, how'd I forget that?"

"Second," Lin Tao went on, "I was thinking about a problem during my nap, which is why I wanted to get back and look at the site. Look."

Lin Tao sketched a line on the map. "Here's the route the killer took. Here's where he rested. There aren't any residences over that way, so he doesn't live in Lost Lanes, and he could only have exited this way."

I nodded in agreement.

"But that's right next to the highway," Lin Tao said. "Even at midnight, how could someone dressed as a ghost and carrying a body go unnoticed?"

I wrinkled my brow. "You're saying he was confident he wouldn't be seen."

"And why would he be confident of that?" Lin Tao raised his eyebrow provocatively, a look always popular with women.

"I got it," I said. "No one lives by that exit, so that's not a problem, but the only way not to be seen by the highway traffic would be to have a car waiting."

"Right," Lin Tao said with a smile. "A sixteen-year-old kid carries Tao Zi through complex alleys and down a path that cameras can't see, then hops into a getaway car? Does that make any sense? Does it sound like something a high school student would do?"

"Nope," I exclaimed as I took out my phone. "Hello, Director Qiang? I need two detectives to go have a chat with Commissioner Tao right away and then come straight to my hotel."

"It's really a shame about Tao Zi," one of the detectives said when they arrived. "Poor kid was actually abandoned near Commissioner Tao's house as a baby. They couldn't have their own child, so they adopted her. But shortly afterward, they found she had a congenital heart defect, which may have been why her biological parents abandoned her."

"What I'm worried about now is how many people knew about her heart," I said.

The detective took a sip of water. "More than a few. Commissioner Tao's neighbors and coworkers, as well as some doctors at the hospital. The question is, which of them would use that knowledge to murder a teenager?"

"Right, right, right."

"When we started asking about all that, Commissioner Tao got squirrelly," the detective said. "He kept stressing that he did what he did so he could get Tao Zi the treatment she needed."

"Treatment?" My head was muddled. "Did what?"

The detective shook his head. "Something was off in his face, so I decided not to push it until we'd checked in with you."

"If he's avoiding our questions," I said, "then it's nothing good."

"He's the commissioner of inland revenue." Lin Tao laughed. "We've got to be talking about corruption, right?"

"That was our guess too," the detective agreed.

"I would venture to guess," I said, looking at the ceiling, "that someone bribed Commissioner Tao, but didn't get what they wanted, so they killed Tao Zi. Make sense?"

"Makes a lot of sense," Big Bao said.

"And," Lin Tao said, "this person would have to know Commissioner Tao well enough to know about his kid's heart."

"Right," I said. "Also, someone who would murder a child in such a cunning way must have one hell of a twisted mind."

"We have some other info," Lin Tao added. "Our murderer has a car, and he's five eight, slim, knows Lost Lanes and the surrounding area very well—I mean, he knew the locations of all the Lost Lane surveillance cameras!"

"And he bought a wig!" I said.

The detective laughed. "With this many clues, shame on us if we can't find the guy!"

Maybe because I'd slept too much in the afternoon, I couldn't fall asleep all night.

I remembered in college when my forensic science professor taught us how to use each of our fingers during an autopsy. Which fingers to hold a knife with, which to hold a hemostat with, which fingers to probe the chambers of the heart with, to tie a suture knot with.

The professor had said, "When we forensic scientists do an autopsy, the finger we use the most is the eleventh finger—the scalpel."

And now we were all mixed up over an eleventh finger case.

Did the killer leave that extra finger as some kind of clue? I would definitely catch him, no doubt about it.

I couldn't stop thinking about that disemboweled, dismembered corpse and that black, curved finger.

Somehow dawn crept up and I woke Lin Tao. "You sure can sleep, friend. Guess you're still young."

"Somewhere around one hundred forty-two people knew about Tao Zi's heart condition," the detective said, holding up a list. "We were up all night checking them out and found four that fit the criteria. Oh, but we couldn't verify the buying-a-wig part. Two of the four weren't in town, so that leaves us with two suspects."

He cleared his throat and continued. "Zheng Xiaofeng, forty years old, Commissioner Tao's classmate, a pediatrician at People's Hospital. He made the original referral to the cardiologist who confirmed Tao Zi's condition. Zheng Xiaofeng is five eight, one hundred thirty-seven pounds, and lives in a new development near Lost Lanes. The only thing is, there's no evidence for motive or the kind of warped personality we'd expect. Zheng Xiaofeng is a kind, cheerful pediatrician, likes to joke."

I gently shook my head.

"Then there's He Hong, forty-six years old, used to be Commissioner Tao's neighbor, and was very close with him. He's five nine, one hundred twenty-eight pounds, introverted, runs a hotel."

"Runs a hotel?" I said, interrupting. "That's key. Someone who could be affected by Commissioner Tao's political decisions is definitely suspicious. And his height is well within the margin of error."

Big Bao barged through the door, holding something.

"One thing doesn't fit," the detective objected. "He Hong lives on the west side of the city, far from Lost Lanes. He probably doesn't know the neighborhood well at all."

"So that'd rule him out," Director Qiang said. "The White Shadow knew Lost Lanes inside out."

Catching his breath, Big Bao held up a picture he'd printed. "Is this He Hong?"

Big Bao had been going over surveillance footage to look for someone out of place, someone who didn't live in Lost Lanes but who was scouting the location.

The man in the picture was definitely He Hong.

"This person appeared in the surveillance footage only once," Big Bao said, "but he was holding a box. A bald officer down the hall recognized it as being from a wig store."

"Shall we make the arrest?" I smiled at the look of shock on Qiang's face.

15

He Hong and Commissioner Tao had been friends since they were little, and lived next to each other for over thirty years. Around the same time that He Hong's hotel began to rely on tax evasion to stay in business, Tao was named commissioner of inland revenue.

He Hong was thrilled to take advantage of this relationship to turn things around. What he didn't expect was for his old friend to use the tax evasion evidence as blackmail and constantly demand more money. Tao had always been dependable. Why had he turned on his old friend as soon as he became commissioner? Tao swore he didn't have a choice and that the money was to take care of his child, but He Hong thought that was bullshit—Tao must be playing him for a fool.

But the truth was, Tao Zi's medical bills really did exceed Tao's annual salary. And because Tao's wife didn't have a job, the family had no way to scrape together enough money for the surgery that would fix her heart once and for all.

He Hong wouldn't dare get a gun and shoot someone, but he decided to try something more subtle. Scaring Tao Zi enough to land her in the hospital, he figured, would be pretty good revenge on her ever-protective father.

He followed the girl to the karaoke bar and waited downstairs, then ran into her as if by coincidence and offered his neighbor a ride home. Saying he had to relieve himself, he parked near Lost Lanes and slipped away to get his wig and sheet. When he appeared as a ghost at the car window, Tao Zi ran. Luckily, she wasn't familiar with Lost Lanes, so he was able to corner her. Watching a fresh young life fade away before his eyes terrified He Hong, and he was even more terrified of getting caught. The plan to scare her into unconsciousness and leave hadn't worked out. He carried the corpse away from Lost Lanes as fast as he could.

He considered cremation, dismemberment, acid, lots of things, but didn't know how to go about any of them, so he crammed Tao Zi's body into a suitcase and threw it over the bridge and into Liqiao River.

Survey staff found traces of Tao Zi's blood in He Hong's bathroom. He had no way of denying his crime.

A disciplinary commission stepped in and investigated Commissioner Tao's blackmail.

The two old neighbors were admitted to the detention center together.

16

"Qin"—Big Bao ran into the room, panting—"I completely forgot, today's the anniversary of my grandma's death. I have to go back home to Qingxiang for the funeral."

I was sitting at the computer, looking through autopsy photos from solved murder cases. I planned to pick out a few for a lecture I was giving at the police academy. But my mind kept drifting to the Eleventh Finger case. Over the last couple weeks, detectives had looked closely into the victim's social circle. They'd also checked the places Zuo Fangjiang stayed, ate, and worked while he was in Dragon City, but they hadn't turned up a single clue. Meanwhile, our database had been looking for matches on the DNA of the eleventh finger, but still nothing. We had neither the identity of the finger's owner nor the body.

Because Zuo Fangjiang had been killed on June 3, six three, some people were calling it the "six-three case," a common way of naming important dates in China. The special task force was still in operation, but a lot of the men had become discouraged and resigned. They seemed to be waiting for a breakthrough before applying themselves.

I was just a forensic scientist, so my work on the case was already done. The investigation division didn't need my advice, but I couldn't help wondering, shouldn't we have some clues by now? Were we missing something?

Big Bao, seeing the glazed look in my eyes, tapped on the table. "Examiner Qin, did you hear me? The anniversary of my grandma's death, I have to go back for the burial."

I woke up as if from a dream. "Huh? Oh! Sorry, go mourn."

"Nah, no mourning, been mourning for a year, and don't forensic scientists see beyond life and death?"

"A year?" I asked, shaking off my trance. "Your grandma died a year ago, and you're only burying her now?"

"Yeah, so?" Big Bao said, confused. "Our custom there is to wait a year after the cremation to go to the cemetery and bury the urn."

"Oh." I nodded. "Where I'm from, when an old person dies, we bury their ashes right after cremation. I'll run you over to the bus station. Then I can check in and see if the task force has any leads in the Eleventh Finger case."

"Uh . . . that's okay, really," Big Bao said. "They're so strict about using the cars now. I'll take a cab."

I smiled and held up my moped keys. "Private car, private use."

As soon as the two of us climbed on the motorbike, there was a banging sound as the tire burst. I got off and squatted next to the deflated tire, holding my stomach.

Big Bao stood next to me, cracking up. I glared at him. "Your grandma's being buried today and you're laughing? Bad grandson."

A police car suddenly pulled up next to us, and Lin Tao waved from the passenger seat. "Hey, guys, what are you doing out here? Something came up—we've gotta go right now."

"A new case?" I struggled to drag the moped to a covered bike rack. "Why the rush? Can't I even stop home and pack some clean underwear?"

"Qingxiang City, two girls dead, just discovered," Lin Tao said. "We received orders to hurry."

"Qingxiang?" Big Bao's eyes lit up. "Looks like I can keep my bus fare."

◆　◆　◆

"'Provincial Public Security Bureau Evidence Identification Management Office: The bodies of two female workers were found in a bathroom at a suburban coal mine this morning. Preliminary evidence suggests homicide. With two deaths and a destroyed crime scene, the case poses great challenges, and we ask for national experts to come offer guidance and help solve the case.'"

In the rattling car, Lin Tao read every word of the fax. "'Forensic pathology and trace laboratory staff, please hurry to the scene. Signed, Director Zhang Xiaoxi, June twenty-ninth.' That's why I came to find you guys. Lucky you hadn't gotten far."

"Bathroom? Female workers?" Big Bao said, squinting at the roof of the car. "Last I heard news like this, two girls were arguing about who had nicer boobs and got in a fight. Think it's something like that? Murder-suicide?"

I didn't bother dignifying Big Bao's conjecture, determined to use the time in the car to get some shut-eye. Every time there was a difficult case, it affected my sleep. That may have been why I'd aged more than ten years in just seven on the job.

In my dream, I felt the car getting off the highway and pried open my reluctant eyes. As we were waiting to pay our toll, Qingxiang's Captain Nie suddenly hopped into our car and patted me on the shoulder. Young, handsome, and charming, Nie was one of our province's brightest young captains.

It's no exaggeration to say that Qingxiang City was built on coal. Ninety percent of its revenue comes from coal, and its landmarks are "Mine 1," "Mine 2," and "Mine 3." We made our way through a downtown bustling with people who had been making their living from coal for generations.

"I didn't know until this case," Captain Nie said, his face full of mystery, "just how many industries are connected to coal here. The murders actually took place at a property management company."

This news seemed to disappoint Big Bao. "Uh . . . what does it have to do with coal, then? Aren't there property management companies everywhere?"

Captain Nie gave a knowing smile. "But coal property management companies are clever."

◆ ◆ ◆

We were shocked to learn that the coal mine's property management company was actually a front for a dog-meat-selling operation. Their official responsibility was to work between the time when one coal pile was taken away and another was made to remove the mud and waste mixture underneath. "Waste" needs quotation marks, though.

The "waste" in coal industry jargon is called "coal slurry." When this management company removed the coal slurry, they'd mix it with actual coal. Even though the fifty-fifty mixture was much less effective than pure coal, it was hard for a buyer to identify. That way, they increased the amount of coal by fifty percent and shared the profit with coal resale middlemen.

As you can imagine, the underground coal-slurry business grew quickly.

The property management's annual fee for clearing away "waste" funded the entire company, which freed up the director to start his illegal side business.

"Guess how much the company nets annually," Captain Nie said.

"A million?" I guessed.

"Five million?" Lin Tao ventured.

Captain Nie shook his head. "Twenty."

"T-t-twenty million?" Big Bao stammered. "That's a lot of dirty money!"

"The property management company usually stores the slurry in a remote location," Captain Nie said. "Local villagers know they can make money working for them, so they do whatever they can to get in with these guys. If the company needs manual labor, they get the strongest man; if they want an accountant, they get the best; if they need marketing, they use the most beautiful girls."

"God, how many rich people are crooks?" I groaned.

"There are rich people in China who aren't?" Lin Tao said.

"Hey, that's going too far."

"So . . . ," Big Bao said, pausing slightly, "no one's paying attention to these corrupt property companies?"

"They will after this case," Captain Nie said. "If all that weren't enough, they also use child labor. The victims are under sixteen."

"Under sixteen?" Lin Tao said. "Shouldn't they be in school?"

"What can a girl that young do with coal?" Big Bao asked. "Only big guys can do that kind of work."

"PR," Captain Nie said. "You know PR? That kind of PR."

The confused looks on Big Bao's and Lin Tao's faces made me sigh, wishing I could be that innocent again. I headed off Nie's awful explanation. "You still haven't given us the basics of the murders."

"Oh right," Nie said, giving himself a smack on the head. "Here's what happened."

From June 25 to 28, Green Property Management took a four-day break, and all the employees caught shuttle buses to their hometowns. Only Huang Rong and Xie Linmiao, the two young teens, stayed behind to use the company's free Internet. The security guard on-site saw that they could take care of themselves, so he decided to go home too.

At dawn on the first day after the break, the security guard, Liu Jie, was the first to arrive.

After parking his motorcycle, he was eating breakfast in the security office when he heard rushing water coming from the showers.

Aside from the relatively nice main office building, the dormitories, bathrooms, toilets, and warehouses were very run-down. The women's bathroom was located in a corner of the compound in a redbrick bungalow with frosted glass windows. A group of men in the company loved to sneak up close to spy on the women showering.

Liu Jie looked at the clock on the wall. It was just a little past six—still two hours until the rest of the workers arrived. He had time to get a good look.

As he approached, Liu Jie saw lights on inside but no sexy girls' silhouettes. Then he felt water at his feet.

"Huh? Water from the bathroom flooded out?" Big Bao asked anxiously.

Captain Nie nodded. "Yes."

"Was the door closed all the way?" I asked. "Did the victims die in the bathroom?"

"It was closed all the way. The old-fashioned locks needed a key to be opened from the outside, but they could be opened from inside without one," Captain Nie said. "But that lock was already broken, probably kicked in. The security guard said the door was closed and he didn't touch it, so he didn't know it wasn't locked."

"Makes me think it was someone from the company," Big Bao said. "Peeping that led to a rape-murder."

"The compound doesn't have a gate?" I asked.

Captain Nie shook his head. "The compound's never closed because there's a security system in the main building and nothing outside of value."

"Hold on, hold on," Lin Tao said. "Isn't anyone else wondering how the security guard knew without opening the door that the girls were dead?"

"The security guard said he looked down at his wet feet and saw the white socks in his sandals turning red. He realized it wasn't water and called the police."

17

"Can we do an experiment to see how long the shower has to run for the water to spill out?" Big Bao asked.

As I opened the door, the smell of blood rushed into my nostrils. To prevent water from further damaging the scene, police had shut off the water to the whole compound. But the weather was hot, and the bathroom had been airtight for days with a steady stream of warm water flowing, so even though the tap was off, it was still several degrees warmer inside. The warm, humid environment sped up the bodies' decomposition, so when we opened the door, the smell of blood and rotting flesh was heavy.

"In this environment, determining the time of death based on decomposition is impossible, right?" Lin Tao asked.

Several drains in the floor were sucking water out, but there was still some on the ground. We carefully set up a platform over the water and walked along it toward the bodies.

The two naked bodies were far apart. A blond girl was prone, six feet from the bathroom door, while a black-haired girl was huddled in the corner, lying on her side. Their faces and hair were bloated and stained with blood, so it was hard to make out their appearance.

"Yeah, the relationship between the level of decay and the environment is too great to get a precise time of death." I opened one of the victim's eyelids and pressed the skin on her back and sighed. "The lower abdomen is already turning green, and it's spreading toward the upper abdomen, which shows the initial stages of intestinal decay. This time of year, that would normally take at least three days. But the corneas are cloudy, semitranslucent, and you can see the pupil, which would indicate death occurred within the last forty-eight hours."

"So what do we do?" Lin Tao said.

"In this environment, corneal opacity and livor mortis will get us closer to the real time of death. It's normal for organs to decay faster in a warm, humid environment," I said.

Lin Tao looked up at the flickering lights. "Lights were on . . . If they died more than twenty-four hours ago but less than forty-eight, that would be the night before last."

"Good catch."

"If only bodies could talk," Big Bao said, "we wouldn't have to waste water testing how long it takes to flood the bathroom."

"When we came in, those two taps were submerged," a detective said with a tight frown, pointing at two faucets. He looked like he was going to pass out from the stench. "The water was so high, it covered about two-thirds of the bodies."

"Damn. If it's a rape case, our chances of getting bio samples decrease."

"Why?" Lin Tao asked.

"Semen is water soluble."

"Does that mean we can't tell if it's a rape case?" the detective asked. I shook my head. "Bodies *can* talk."

Blood had spread to every part of the floor, which made it impossible to reconstruct the crime scene using blood traces. Even the clothes on the bench by the door were wet. With this kind of scene, a forensic scientist has to start with some autopsy work and then coordinate with trace inspection to find clues.

I sent Big Bao to check out the body in the corner while I examined the one by the door.

"Who moved the body?" I shouted.

"No one," the officer responsible for site protection objected. "She was lying on her stomach like that when we got here. And look, the wounds on her head are in line with being knocked down from behind."

The back of the girl's head did have several jagged wounds that seemed to be caused by blows from a blunt instrument. The skull was exposed through the broken skin, and the black-and-yellow tissue on the edges of the wound was a horrible sight. No blood surrounded it.

"They just said the water only covered two-thirds of the bodies. If she was lying facedown, how did the blood get washed off the back of her head? There isn't even blood on the hair around it," I said. "And there's livor mortis on the back of the body, which could only happen if the victim had been on her back for more than twenty-four hours."

"Yeah, it looks like this one was lying on her back for twenty-four hours, then flipped," Big Bao responded, his voice echoing from the far corner.

"But . . . but really, no one could have gotten in," the officer insisted. "I've been on guard outside the whole time, didn't even go to the bathroom."

"Don't worry, buddy, I'm not accusing you of negligence. The victims died on the night of the twenty-seventh. Between the night of the twenty-eighth and when you all arrived, someone must have moved the bodies."

The officer blinked at me a few times.

Big Bao's voice came from the corner again. "Whoa, do you think maybe Liu Jie came two nights ago and killed them, then came back in the morning and moved the bodies for some reason before reporting the crime?"

"Could be, could be. People call in their own crimes a lot," the officer said quickly.

"But why move them?" I asked. "He'd expose himself."

"Don't worry about it," said Lin Tao, who had been brushing the door for prints. "Big Bao may really be right."

"Oh?" I stood up and walked over to him. The sudden movement caused me to feel somewhat dizzy, and I struggled to keep my balance on the platform.

"It's like this." Lin Tao saw my goofy posture and laughed. "There's a lock outside, but it's all rusted, hard to get fingerprints."

"If the murderer unlatched the door from the outside," I said, "he would have touched the side of the door, because there's no handle."

"Yup," Lin Tao said with a nod. "But this door's so crappy, I couldn't get anything of value. I did, however, find an incomplete fingerprint on the latch."

I squinted at it.

Lin Tao said to the technician behind him, "Did we get Liu Jie's prints yet?"

The tech nodded and took out a portable fingerprint card from his bag. Homicide police have the deep-rooted habit of collecting people's fingerprints as soon as they meet them.

Lin Tao compared it to the print he'd found.

"Fingerprints are so great," I said with admiration. "They don't take hours like DNA, just a matter of minutes."

"It's him." Lin Tao's confidence lit up the room.

"Fucker," the lead detective said. "I could tell that guy was bad news. Tried to fool us. He swore he didn't touch the bathroom door. How'd he leave a fingerprint, then?"

"Irrefutable evidence," I agreed. "Go interrogate him. Figure out why he killed the girls and why he moved the bodies this morning."

The lead detective nodded and set out.

"Well done, Lin Tao. Breaking a murder case with a simple fingerprint. Now that we're done, maybe we should go to Big Bao's grandma's funeral with him?"

"That's okay," Big Bao said. "Even if the case is solved, we still have to do autopsies."

"Thanks for the lesson," I said with a laugh. "But the bodies are going to the morgue to dry off. We can't start the autopsies while they're wet."

"Yup, yup," Lin Tao said. "We'd better wait. We need more evidence."

"No worries, your work is done. The rest is on us," I said, patting Lin Tao's shoulder.

"Hey, hey!" Lin Tao said, pulling away. "This is an expensive shirt."

Big Bao and I carefully packed the wet bodies into bags to be transported to the morgue. Then the three of us rushed to the funeral home for Big Bao's grandmother's funeral.

Northerners really do have a lot of different customs. Big Bao was berated by his parents for arriving late. With an indignant look, he wrapped a white linen cloth around his waist.

The ceremony included firecrackers, wailing, worship, and offerings, which took more than an hour. Then the host threw the fruit offering into the crowd, and everyone swarmed to eat it.

"Legend has it that eating the fruit offering to an old person can give longevity," Big Bao whispered to me.

I shook my head. "That's not right. How can you take the fruit given to the deceased's spirit and eat it yourself?"

"That's just the custom here," Big Bao said. "In a minute, they'll brush the urn with a willow branch; then it'll be ready for burial."

Another hour or more passed.

After the funeral, we drove back to the task force to await the results of the interrogation.

"You guys look tired," Big Bao said apologetically. "Qingxiang borders four provinces, so it's influenced by a lot of different cultures. Every village used to have its own customs, but over time, in order not to piss off the gods, we combined them."

"Be careful how you talk about the gods," Lin Tao warned. "You really don't want to make them mad."

"Actually, I'm really interested in hearing more about local customs, Bao," I said.

"Oh, there's all kinds of amazing stuff. For example, in the county north of here, if a child dies, they put the body at a fork in the road for three days. In the county south of here, they don't let the dead see the sun, so they wrap white cloth around the corpse's head. Other places put a coin in the deceased's mouth. Oh, and another smears mud on the body's face. Around here, the dead are wrapped in several layers of shrouds, and the types of cloth used are very important."

"Those aren't customs. They're superstitions, dances to the gods," I said.

"Careful, careful," Lin Tao fretted.

As we spoke, the car pulled up to Qingxiang's municipal public security bureau.

As soon as we entered the meeting room, we could sense the solemnity. All the officers were frowning, smoking, drinking tea, and staring at documents in a daze. But Captain Nie broke the silence, saying, "Liu Jie confessed."

"Yeah!" Big Bao said, and high-fived me.

"Don't celebrate just yet," Captain Nie said. "He confessed to molesting the corpses, but not to killing anyone."

"And the polygraph results backed him up," Director Zhang said.

"But he can't explain entering the scene and flipping the bodies, can he?" My head was spinning.

"He did explain that," Captain Nie said. "This morning, he heard the sound of the showers running, so he went to the bathroom to steal a look, but he noticed the door was unlatched. He went inside and his shock was soon replaced by lust. He molested the corpses, and then turned their front sides into the water to hide his prints."

"He molested some kids' rotting bodies? Smelling like that?" Big Bao said with disgust.

"Well, he was a bachelor," a detective joked. Captain Nie glared at him, and he swallowed hard.

"But was Liu Jie telling the truth?" Lin Tao said. "A polygraph can only be used as a reference, not to confirm or deny anything."

"You all determined the murders took place the night of June twenty-seventh," Captain Nie said. "After arresting Liu Jie, we tracked down surveillance video corroborating Liu Jie's story that he spent that whole night at an Internet café called Sky. Then, starting at noon on the twenty-eighth, Liu Jie was home sleeping. His neighbors and family are willing to testify. He didn't have time to commit the crime."

"I'm just saying, there's something off here," Lin Tao said calmly.

"He did more than defile the corpses! He undermined the crime scene! Obstruction of justice!" I sputtered, my face flushed with anger.

"Okay, okay," Lin Tao said. "It won't be nighttime for a few hours. Why don't we go to the morgue? You guys wait a minute while I get some work clothes. Gotta change this shirt."

18

"Careless." In the car headed to the morgue, I scolded myself for thinking the evidence against Liu Jie was conclusive. But evidence isn't just a fingerprint or a DNA profile; it's the thought and interpretation we apply. The victims' wounds would reveal more.

In the autopsy room, the two corpses lay peacefully on gurneys, the blood on them dry. We began with the black-haired girl who had been lying in the corner. Investigators said her name was Huang Rong.

"Guo Jing would be very sad," Lin Tao quipped, referring to the famous book character whose wife was also named Huang Rong. He solemnly took the camera and started snapping photos.

Shaving razor in hand, Big Bao squatted at the end of the table, singing "The Lion Gets a Haircut."

"Can you two please be serious?" I started examining the body's head, neck, chest, abdomen, and limbs according to standard procedure. It's especially important to look closely at the head and face: eyelids, lips, mucus membranes.

"There are a lot of wounds on the head," Big Bao said. "Hard to shave."

Forensic scientists have to be good barbers too, but we only know one style. Some do it with a straight razor; others buy professional trimmers. People think it's disrespectful to the dead, but in order to keep the hair from covering up injuries, we have no choice but to shave it all off.

If there are multiple wounds on the scalp, extra care has to be taken. It requires real skill to shave the skin around the wound.

"Conjuctivas are pale, mouth and nose uninjured." I continued my routine check.

Lin Tao stood to the side, flipping through the photos he'd just taken. "Why does this girl's nose look so black?"

I grabbed the hemostat and used it to stretch open the deceased's nostrils. "Whoa, way darker than usual." A white swab went in and came out black.

A test on the other victim, Xie Linmiao, had the same result.

"What's the deal?" Lin Tao asked. Big Bao leaned over.

"Doesn't make sense," I said. "The bathroom was reasonably clean, so how did the nasal cavities get so stained?"

"Maybe they got dirty in the mine?" Big Bao said. "Water washed away the stains on their faces, but not in the noses?"

"A sixteen-year-old PR girl," I said, "going into the mines over vacation? Seriously?"

"Maybe if they were bored," Big Bao said, lost in thought.

"I really doubt it, especially for girls who were hired for their looks," Lin Tao said.

I lifted the victim's hands. "There aren't black stains anywhere else on the body. Even the fingernails are clean."

"But what caused the stains?" Lin Tao said.

I nodded. "We'll send a sample over to the city bureau right now. It's getting late; we'd better keep going."

I cut off two fingernails for analysis and prepared a cotton swab for the mouth, genitals, and anus. Extracting those samples from a female victim was routine, especially for suspected rape cases.

"Even if they were soaking in water for a long time, we still have to try to get biological samples—"

"What's up?" Big Bao asked. He stood to stretch his legs.

"What's this?" I held a magnifying glass in one hand and squeezed Huang Rong's cheek with the other.

Huang Rong's rigor mortis had eased. The temporomandibular joint was loose, so when I squeezed her cheek, the inside of her mouth came into view.

I looked through the magnifying glass at her lower dental arch. There was a hair there.

"Why's that so strange?" Big Bao said. "She had a lot of blunt head trauma, remember? So some hair broke off, fell over her face, and when the body got moved, a few strands came off in her mouth. It's totally normal."

I touched the victim's mouth. "But this is pubic hair."

Hair from various parts of the body has clear morphological differences. Pubic hair is dark, curly, and appears flat in cross section; head hair is soft in texture, less curly, and cylindrical; armpit hair is lighter, soft, crimped, and semicylindrical. Quickly identifying the different types is an important part of forensic anthropology and critical to efficient on-site evidence extraction.

"Pubic hair's normal too," Big Bao said with a grin. "There's plenty on the floor in my bathroom at home. So when the water level rose, it got in her mouth. No big deal!"

I used a hemostat to grab the hair and tugged a bit. "No way. It's caught in her teeth!"

The room fell silent as everyone imagined the evil that must have taken place.

"Good thing there aren't many female forensic scientists. Otherwise this would be really awkward," Lin Tao said.

"Oh! That'd be so weird!" Big Bao exclaimed.

I ignored them, just clamped the hair and observed it carefully in the blinding autopsy room light. "Looks like there's a follicle. Yes. An intact follicle!"

This was crucial: a follicle meant we could get the owner's DNA.

The officer who'd just run the nasal swab over to the trace evidence lab came back panting. Seeing us all gathered around the hair, he shook his head and said, "Looks like I have to go right back, huh?"

"If we solve the case, your hard work won't have been for nothing," I said with a smile.

The two victims had strikingly similar wounds caused by dozens of blunt blows to the back of the head. Huang Rong's knees showed some subcutaneous bleeding, but other than that, there were no signs of damage. Not from constraints, not from resistance.

"Judging from the way the hymen and perineum are intact," I said, "the victim probably had not engaged in sexual activity while alive."

"That hair shows sexual activity too," Big Bao said.

"Do you think maybe they had a homosexual relationship," Lin Tao asked, "and then got into a fight and killed each other?"

I shook my head and said, "Impossible. The damage to the back of their heads is severe—they couldn't have done it themselves. Anyway, DNA analysis will tell us if that pubic hair belonged to someone with male or female chromosomes."

Opening Huang Rong's scalp revealed the dense white skull. One could make out two areas with major bleeding. The first was under the scalp around the dozens of occipital lacerations. The other was marked by blood adhesion to the top of the head, caused by a subgaleal hemorrhage.

"How can there be subgaleal bleeding?" I said to Big Bao, who was examining Xie Linmiao's body.

Big Bao nodded. "This one too."

Under the human scalp, there is a space between the skull periosteum and the scalp galea aponeurosis. This area ensures mobility between the scalp and skull. Sugaleal bleeding is generally caused by tearing of the hair. Hard to cause with an external blow.

"Wow, maybe Lin Tao was right," Big Bao said. "Women usually pull one another's hair when they fight!"

I didn't reply. After taking a good photo of Huang Rong's scalp wound and fracture morphology, I started sawing open the crown.

The electric saw ran fast and at a high temperature. The bone chips gave off a horrific cooked smell as they flew in all directions. I paused to rub my nose on my sleeve.

By the time I had Huang Rong's head open, Big Bao had done the same with Xie Linmiao's even though he started after me. He was dense sometimes, but the guy really knew his anatomy.

Next, we each put our hands near the incisions and observed for a moment. Then we lifted up the scalp on the front of the head to have a look, set it down, and paused to think over what we'd seen.

Both victims had contusions on the back of their heads along with massive bleeding. But they also had cerebral hemorrhages in the frontal lobe.

Brain trauma like that should have corresponding damage on the scalp, but these didn't. And there was only one explanation for that.

Big Bao and I said it at the same time: "Contrecoup injury!"

Lin Tao froze. "What's gotten into you two? Possessed? You gonna keep it up?"

Contrecoup injuries are a special kind of brain injury. One part of the scalp is damaged along with the brain tissue underneath. The force causes damage to the opposite side of the brain too, but from the inside, so there are no marks on the scalp. Contrecoup injuries usually happen during a fall or collision.

"How could there be a contrecoup injury?" My mind was racing.

"I got it!" Big Bao said. "The shower floor was so slippery that they both slipped and hit their heads!"

"What are you talking about?" Lin Tao scoffed. "I'm not a forensic scientist, and even I know the scalp wounds were formed by repeated external force. They wrestled with someone for a long time before they fell and died."

"Oh right," Big Bao said, scratching his head.

"They did fall," I said, "but they didn't slip. Someone knocked them over."

I pointed at the subgaleal bleeding on one of the girls. "Someone grabbed her hair and repeatedly banged her head against the ground or wall. Probably the ground, because the water in the shower only reached four or five inches high, and we didn't find blood marks on the wall. Don't forget, all a contrecoup injury needs is deceleration, and impact counts."

The autopsy continued. We inspected the abdominal cavity but found nothing abnormal. Xie Linmiao's chest and pelvis showed only mild postmortem damage—the results of Liu Jie's molestation.

"Looks like Liu Jie wasn't lying," Lin Tao said. "What a sicko."

Both victims died of their severe brain injuries. Judging by the contents of their stomachs, the murders took place four hours after their last meal. And the curly noodlelike substance in their stomachs told me their last meal was instant noodles.

When our work was finally done, I took off my jumpsuit and looked at the clock. I couldn't believe how late it was.

"Let's go back and get some sleep," I said. "Tomorrow morning we'll have the results of the physical evidence tests."

"What do you think so far?" Big Bao asked.

"Seems pretty simple actually. We can reconstruct the scene now."

"Oh?" Lin Tao said. "Do tell."

"Based on the subcutaneous bleeding on Huang Rong's knees and the hair in her mouth, the killer forced her to give him oral sex," I said.

"Then he killed both of them by grabbing their hair and smashing their heads into the ground. The whole time, he didn't turn off the shower, and after he killed them, he left. The water ran for one day and two nights until this morning when Liu Jie entered the scene, molesting and moving the bodies. The dirt in the nostrils is infuriating, but it could provide more clues. Liu Jie's flipping their faces into the water may have destroyed that evidence."

"Not completely destroyed," Lin Tao said. "We have to trust the city's trace evidence department. Maybe they can still detect the components even with such a small sample."

"You're saying the killer sexually assaulted Huang Rong, but what about Xie Linmiao?" Big Bao asked.

"There's no evidence of that," I said, "but the killer's murder method seems a little strange."

"Strange how?" Big Bao asked.

"Hard to say." I closed my eyes. "Let me think about it."

I spent all night plagued by nightmares about teenaged girls being raped and murdered in bathrooms. It reminded me of the serial murder case that tested my skills in Yuntai. After we started dating, Ling Dang had cried as she told me how her cousin Xiaoxiao was killed seven years earlier in her high school bathroom. There was evidence of rape, but the case went unsolved for years.

I looked through the archives and found that, in the intervening years, there'd been several similar cases, also unsolved due to lack of evidence. The bound victims were killed, raped, and dumped in bathrooms. There was a break in the killings, but they started again, and this time there was sperm. This led the forensic team to think the killer was someone with retrograde ejaculation syndrome, which causes sperm to go into the bladder instead of out through the urethra. We suspected the killer had suffered from the disorder and then been treated. We checked medical records of local hospitals, which led us to the killer, Shui Liang, a bank security guard. In my dreams, there he was again. I couldn't escape his eerily innocuous eyes or the look of disbelief and rage on the face of his young, beautiful wife.

I'd never forgotten the way he shouted her name when he was captured. "Pond! Pond!" It was a moment of great professional triumph, but that voice, that name . . . Something about it made my blood run cold.

I remembered walking into Shui Liang's apartment the night after we made the arrest. In the dim light, I saw a long-haired humanoid shadow. The sight, coupled with the windy weather outside, nearly made me faint.

As my eyes adjusted, I realized the monstrous form was just Shui Liang's wife brushing her hair.

"Miss, we're going to need you to cooperate with our investigation," I said brusquely to cover my fear.

The young woman put on lipstick as she slowly turned her head. There was no longer any sign of tears on her pale face, and she looked like a completely different person than she had earlier in the day when we'd arrested her husband. For some reason, that bloodless face made my spine go cold. There was an incredible toughness there, and something I didn't understand.

"Examiner Qin, of course I will cooperate with your investigation," she said, leisurely walking over. Her mouth was nearly on my ear when she added, "I'll definitely cooperate with your investigation."

She walked toward the door and disappeared into the darkness of the corridor.

As I slowly regained my senses, I wondered how she knew who I was. And what in the world was all that about?

The next morning, I was exhausted as I pushed open the door to the conference room.

"There's good news and bad news." Captain Nie's eyes were swollen, but he somehow managed to look suave as always. "Which do you want to hear first?"

"The good news," I said. "I had a shit night."

"We were able to get a clear genotype from the hair in Huang Rong's mouth. It's from a man," Captain Nie said. "So this case now has a starting point for screening suspects."

"As expected," I said. "What about the bad news?"

"We spent all night trying to figure out the victims' last movements, but it hasn't led us anywhere really useful. And DNA testing ruled out all the men from the property management company. So how are we supposed to find the hair's owner?"

I thought for a moment. "There isn't a large migrant population around here, is there?"

"There's a market town a mile away. It's fairly well-off, but there are a lot of migrants. But the property management company is in a pretty remote spot, so it's unlikely that a lot of people know about it, and no one would go there without some reason. I can't imagine how an outsider would know that two young girls were there alone."

"Then do you think the killer had an accomplice on the inside?" Lin Tao asked.

"We're working on that right now, pinning down all the workers' whereabouts and relationships," Captain Nie said, "but it's like a needle in a haystack."

I rested my head on my fist, thinking. Everyone in the room wore a desperate expression.

"Oh," I said, "what about the results from the nose swab?"

"It seems to be some kind of carbon ink," the trace evidence lab director said.

"Carbon ink?" I said. "Why would there be carbon ink in the shower room?"

"The girls got ink on their faces, so they went to shower?" Captain Nie theorized.

I shook my head. "The Internet-addicted generation has long forgotten about ink. Is it ink from a disposable pen?"

"No. Our chemical analysis pointed toward bottled ink that's barely on the market anymore."

"Uh . . . Captain Nie, you said you pinned down the victims' last movements. What'd you find?" Big Bao asked.

"Right. According to the street surveillance video, at six p.m. on the twenty-seventh, the two girls rode a moped into town," Captain Nie said. "They went to buy instant noodles. I know what you're thinking: Could someone have trailed them back to the compound from town? Our people scoured the videos for evidence of someone following on foot or in a vehicle and determined we could rule that out. So we're still focusing on the people who had specific information about the company or knew people on the inside."

"So the victims died after ten p.m.," I concluded. "Their stomach contents were consistent with instant noodles, and they died four hours after their last meal."

"Got it. Having a better estimate of the time will help us rule things out." Nie picked up his pen and wrote in his notebook.

I randomly clicked on the photos of the victims on my laptop, zoomed in, zoomed out.

"I just thought of something we could try," I said, breaking the silence.

19

"First, there's the carbon ink." I shifted uncomfortably under everyone's eager gaze.

"Come on, Qin, out with it," Captain Nie urged.

"After we first surveyed the scene, we thought Liu Jie had committed the murder, so around midday, we all went to Big Bao's grandmother's funeral." I swallowed. "It was a very long funeral, about three hours, because of all the local customs."

Big Bao sat next to me, nodding avidly.

I continued. "Big Bao told me that since Qingxiang is at the junction of several provinces, it's influenced by the customs of multiple regions. He said if a child dies, the body's placed at a fork in the road for three days; and some people don't let the deceased see light, so they wrap a white cloth around the head or cover the face in mud—or ink?"

Captain Nie slapped the table, startling me. "Right! Why didn't I think of that? But didn't that material come from inside the nose? The custom is to cover the face, not block the nose."

"When we got to the scene, both victims' faces were submerged in water. The water could have washed their faces clean or pushed something into their nostrils."

"Do you mean if Liu Jie hadn't flipped the bodies, we could tell whether Xie Linmiao's face was covered?" the lead detective said. "Fucker didn't mention that."

"The security guard was disturbed, and the bathroom lights were dim. He may not have noticed," Captain Nie suggested.

"Either way, that piece of trash needs to be held responsible for defiling corpses and destroying evidence," I said through gritted teeth.

"Well, if whoever killed them covered their faces, what's that tell us?" Captain Nie asked.

I took a deep breath and answered. "First, it's something older people care about. A young murderer wouldn't worry about burial customs. So I think the killer is older, but not too old for sex drive and physical violence—maybe between forty and sixty. And probably single."

"Makes sense." Captain Nie made a quick note.

"Next comes a more important question." I took a sip of tea. "Where did the ink come from? Surely the killer didn't commit the crime and only then go get the ink? If he just wanted to cover their faces, he could have used the slurry from the warehouse."

"So he must have had it on him," Big Bao said.

"And how do you carry ink on you?" I asked.

"In a fountain pen," Big Bao said.

"Exactly. That's critical. Not a lot of people use fountain pens anymore, which also supports the theory that the killer is an older person. Plus, blue-collar workers aren't usually big on fountain pens, so the killer is probably someone who works with language, like a teacher, clerk, writer."

"Older, single, works with words," Captain Nie said. "What a brilliant characterization. This definitely narrows things down."

"Thank you." The compliment helped my rhythm. "And I have another idea."

Everyone looked even more expectant than before.

"During the autopsy yesterday, I kept thinking there was something strange about the victims' skull damage," I said. "They both have severe blunt injuries consistent with being struck over thirty times. That means the murderer smashed their heads into the ground over thirty times. With that level of force, three to five times would be lethal, so why did he keep going?"

"Hatred?" Captain Nie shook his head. "No, can't be. We haven't found any evidence that the girls had enemies, so it's fundamentally a sexual assault case."

"Hatred is one explanation," I said, "but I'm thinking more along the lines of drunkenness."

"Drunkenness?"

I nodded. "A key characteristic of drunken crimes is recklessness. The excessive injuries could reflect the mad state of the killer's mind."

"Then why not say it was a madman who did it?" Lin Tao jumped in.

"The drunk and insane both do crazy things, but the insane are less likely to weigh future outcomes. An insane person probably wouldn't have bothered to cover the faces in ink."

"This analysis is excellent," Captain Nie said. "Based on what you've deduced, I don't think the killer could be too far from the scene. We'll look for older single men who like fountain pens."

"One more key point," I added. "Look at local restaurants and bars to see if someone fitting that description visited on the night of the twenty-seventh, got drunk, and left alone."

"Perfect," Captain Nie said. "We'll have a suspect in the next eight hours."

Restless as I was, I couldn't just accept that the forensic work was over and wait for results from the detectives, so I went along with them into town.

It hadn't been long since my stint with the North Central District Squadron, but I'd already forgotten how exhausting regular detective work was. We dragged ourselves out under the scorching sun to yet another little restaurant, the twelfth we'd tried.

"Night of the twenty-seventh?" the owner said. "We do good business here. How am I supposed to remember every customer?"

"Please try to think."

"Okay, let me look at our receipts from that night. See if I can remember anything."

I lit a cigarette while the restaurant owner shuffled to the back; I wasn't expecting much.

"Oh yeah," he called just moments later. "That old secretary in the local government, what's his name? Old Luo. He had a bit too much that night, was talking nonsense."

"Wait, wait, wait, wait, wait." A detective hurried to turn on a voice recorder.

Another flipped open a notebook. "Old Luo, former town government secretary. Who was he drinking with?"

"Himself." The owner laughed. "He ordered kung pao chicken and crayfish."

I put out the cigarette and listened intently.

"When did he arrive and when did he leave?"

"Aw, guys, come on. How would I know that?" the owner said. "Pretty late, I guess. We're open till ten. Oh, I remember something else. He fell on his way out the door; I had to help him up."

The detective nodded at me to say that the times matched up.

"Do you know Old Luo well?"

"Eh, he comes in sometimes," the owner said. "Old guy is lonely—likes to drink alone. But you don't think he's a murderer, do you? That coal thing with the teenagers? No way, he's a nice guy."

"No need to speculate, sir, and please keep today's questions to yourself." Saying this, the detective pulled me out of the bar.

"Age, characteristics, timing, drunkenness, everything fits," I said. "It's too much to be a coincidence. Are you going to go make the arrest?"

He nodded. "I'll report to the captain. You can head to your hotel and wait for good news."

20

Old Luo's name was Luo Feng. He was forty-five years old, and had spent his whole life as a government clerk, but he was in no way a politician. He was introverted and didn't make much. The women in town he liked didn't like him. The women who liked him, he didn't like. Really, he didn't think much of women in general. He fancied himself a man of letters. He was also single and addicted to pornographic DVDs.

On June 27, he went out for a blind date with a divorced woman the mayor had set him up with—but maybe she was warned off, because she stood him up. Depressed, Luo Feng went to his usual drinking spot and got wasted. He tried to follow a young woman home but got lost, disoriented by alcohol.

Luo Feng walked aimlessly to the property management compound. In that quiet, empty place, he heard the sound of the showers. He was familiar with the company's coal scam and PR methods. He knew they had some beautiful girls working for them. Could they be showering right now?

Desire burned in his chest as he kicked open the bathroom door. The girls' screaming just added fuel to the fire.

Luo Feng recognized the two "bitches" who had flirted with the mayor on the company's behalf. He made Huang Rong kneel down like the women in his porn movies.

They were just sixteen, and unless they were doing what they had to for work, they were terrified to be naked in front of men, to the point of losing their will to fight. So they didn't fight, but they did resist. Huang Rong knelt as she was told and started crying hard, refusing to open her mouth. Meanwhile, Xie Linmiao seized the opportunity to escape.

When Luo Feng saw Xie Linmiao begin to run, he rushed over and repeatedly slammed her head into the floor. With the room soaked in blood, Huang Rong gave in to his demands with the hope that she'd be spared. Of course, she wasn't.

The sexual release and physical exertion left Luo Feng collapsed on the ground and limp for several minutes. Then the onset of tremendous fear made him painfully alert. He'd heard that wiping a body's face with mud would trap its ghost inside, so he took out his fountain pen, spread ink on their faces, and fled the scene.

Feeling haunted by the ghosts he'd tried to trap, Luo Feng thought about turning himself in, but feared he'd get the death penalty. The police didn't have concrete evidence against him, but the interrogators insinuated they did. At first, Luo Feng tried to feed them some bullshit alibis, but when they suggested he might not face the firing squad if he cooperated, the disgusting man rushed to confess.

My relief was enormous. Creeps like Shui Liang from Yuntai and Luo Feng, the company security guard who'd abused the corpses, deserved the harshest punishments society could offer, and I used every tool in my investigative arsenal to make sure they got them.

21

"My dog is normally very well behaved—never eats junk outside and doesn't run away. As soon as I call him, he comes right to me." The woman shot a resentful look at the creature.

I'd seen that look before, from my mother when I didn't do well on a test.

The chow chow suddenly stood up, shook his fluffy hair, stuck out his dripping purple tongue, and barked, scaring Lin Tao half to death.

"You're afraid of dogs?" I asked Lin Tao, who was hiding behind me.

"No! I'm afraid of that slobber getting on my shoes. I just bought them and they're—"

"Expensive," I said. I knew him too well.

"That dog's not so little. Chubbier than normal for a chow," the detective said.

"Is not," the woman retorted with a huff, bending down to smooth the dog's fur. "He's just a little fluffy."

It was July 4, and the Eleventh Finger case was still on the minds of all the cops in Dragon City. The search for the body belonging to the eleventh finger was ongoing, so as soon as anyone spotted bones at a crime scene, forensic scientists were called in. When Chief Hu got the 110 call, he took Forensic Scientist Han to a northwest suburb. A man had called the police, saying his neighbor's dog had found a bone. The man used to be a butcher and didn't think the big bone belonged to a pig, so he called the city police, who'd called us.

The chow chow was highly displeased to have his treat taken away.

"The shape of this bone clearly tells me it's a human leg bone," Hu said. "Humeral head, nodule, trochlea, coronoid fossa, deltoid tuberosity."

"It could be from the Eleventh Finger body," Big Bao gushed. "Where was the bone found?"

Everyone was quiet.

"Bao, who are you talking to?" I said.

"Oh right," Big Bao said, blinking. "A dog found it."

"Uh, ma'am? Any idea where your dog might have wandered off to?" a detective asked, suppressing a giggle.

"Never goes far."

"The killer wanted us to find Zuo Fangjiang's body," I said. "So if this case is related, the body parts must be right around here."

"I doubt that," Hu said. "The eleventh finger's owner was killed before Zuo Fangjiang, remember? So it's been two weeks at least. In this hot weather, the smell would definitely be noticeable. Someone would have found it."

"Then they're not related." I pouted.

"Don't give up. Let's focus on this body, then go from there. There could still be a connection." Hu had been my teacher. He patted me on the shoulder and said encouragingly, "We've got thirty-some officers searching, mostly in the farmland and abandoned factories nearby. Why don't we go help them?"

Under the scorching sun, the search teams dripped with sweat. Even the police dogs seemed off their game—maybe the heat was wearing them out too. It wasn't until evening that an excited voice came over our walkie-talkies.

"We've got a body. A mile and a quarter northwest of the neighborhood, right by the side of the road." The walkie-talkie crackled. "Squads three and five are at the scene, setting up a protected area right now. Send forensic support."

The gravel road was barely wide enough for our van. I sat inside, thinking that if the body was missing a finger, we'd have a lot more clues and a better chance of solving the case. At the very least, it'd ease a month's worth of anxiety.

The crime scene was in the tall grass by the side of the gravel road. Investigators were already marking it with tape. A dozen or so local villagers came out to watch.

"This road leads to a cemetery," the station director told us. "It's pretty small. Some years ago, the city wanted to relocate it, but a villager nearly lit himself on fire in protest, so they abandoned the idea. Other than Tomb-Sweeping Day and people paying their respects during Dongzhi Festival, no one comes out here."

An officer pointed to the grass and said, "The body's almost completely rotted away. Digu found it."

Digu, a police dog, sat next to his officer, tongue waggling triumphantly.

The weeds on the side of the road were waist high. If not for the dog, no one would have found the rotting flesh. It had almost all worn away. Around the pile of bones were maggot shells and dead flies.

"Seems that the flies and their offspring tried to have a picnic, but their feast was toxic." I looked at Lin Tao.

"It's probably been here over a month, almost a skeleton," he said.

"Dismembered!" I poked with a branch and found several of the long bones had been cut in half. There were many complex, overlapping hack marks, just like in the Eleventh Finger case.

There was still some soft tissue on the bones. I asked Han Liang to turn on the searchlight on top of the van to transform the place into a temporary autopsy room. With four or five forensic scientists working together, the examination progressed quickly.

"The victim's pelvis and femur are connected, but the femur is split. The lumbar region was also hacked apart," Big Bao said. "It's totally like the Eleventh Finger dismemberment!"

"Whoa, you guys," Han called. "This body has exactly the same grooves cut into the pelvis and thigh as the Eleventh Finger body."

"The victim's torso and head haven't been separated. They're in the prone position, so the soft tissue on the neck against the ground didn't get eaten," Hu said. "I'm looking for blood vessels in the neck."

"There aren't any clothes around here," Lin Tao observed.

"About five feet from the body, the weeds are pressed down," said Forensic Scientist Wang, who had just arrived to provide support. "There's some matter there that's decayed as much as the body. It appears to be organs, and there are a lot of dead flies around."

I quickly put on rubber gloves and helped Wang pull out pieces of the muddy pile of maggot-ridden, rotten meat to have a look. Each time we touched it, more stench was released.

"The liver, spleen, lungs, kidneys, and intestines are all here," Wang said. "The trachea and tongue should be on top."

"No marks where the organs were cut apart," I said. "Again, just like the Eleventh Finger case. All the victim's organs were removed using forensic methods!"

"I think it's more than reasonable to connect these crimes," Hu said, raising his eyebrows. "They were almost certainly committed by the same person. This case is starting to make me nervous."

"The long bones of the limbs and the main torso bones all seem to be here," Big Bao said, gathering them up. "Twenty-two, twenty-three, twenty-four! Oh my God! The left hand is short three phalanges!"

The human hand has twenty-seven bones. Eight of them are carpal bones, fourteen are phalanges, and five are metacarpal. If Big Bao found three missing phalanges, the person's left hand was missing a finger.

"Ha-ha, even before DNA testing, we can be sure this is the owner of the eleventh finger!" Han crowed.

My skin began to crawl, and I suddenly had the sense that the perverted killer, disemboweler, and dismemberer was nearby, watching us. What could he want? Why pick a fight with the police? And why the forensic methods? I squinted at the crowd of rubberneckers, wondering if the killer really could be there and wondering if I could somehow recognize him.

"Slow down," Big Bao said. "Why was Zuo Fangjiang's body left in a trash can on a busy street while this body is out in the middle of nowhere?"

"Well," I said, grinding my teeth, "it may not be a busy area, but the body is right by the side of the road. Maybe the killer didn't know people don't usually walk here. It could just mean he wasn't familiar with the area."

Then I noticed Chief Hu was squatting down, silently looking at the skull.

"Find something?"

"Before, there were slight vital reactions around the wounds, so you all suspected the killer might've disemboweled the victim alive," Chief Hu said.

"No, I said a postmortem cell reaction probably caused that vital reaction," I said. "Big Bao's theory that Zuo Fangjiang was disemboweled alive is unfounded."

"Unfounded? Pale livor mortis, visceral shrinkage, bleeding to death—what are you talking about, unfounded?" Big Bao took off his gloves, fished out his cell phone, and showed me a photo.

"You put autopsy photos on your phone? What the hell?"

Big Bao blushed. "It's such a hard case, I thought looking at the pictures might help me notice something."

It seemed Eleventh Finger had gotten under Big Bao's skin too.

"Here's the thing," Hu said. "Zuo Fangjiang's body was decapitated, but this one has its head. So I looked closely at the neck. There's a large wound, the carotid artery is completely severed, and there's an obvious vital reaction. He bled to death."

"Drug, cut the throat, disembowel, dismember," Han said. "Probably in that order. The guy's throat was cut while the victim was alive. Maybe just as the dose of tetramine poisoning became lethal. I think Zuo Fangjiang may have died this way too, but with the head off, we can't tell if his throat has a similar wound."

I stood up, stretched, and found the crowd of onlookers had increased rather than decreased.

"What are they even looking at?" I said.

"Can't see anything with all this grass," Lin Tao agreed.

"Now we have to ID the corpse," Hu said, opening the corpse's pubic symphysis. "No need for the pressure cooker this time."

"Looks like another thirtysomething male," I said. "We'll get the height after we get back to the lab."

"Shouldn't be tough to ID the corpse with these remains," Han said.

Suddenly, the crowd began to stir. Some hightailed it back toward town while others just clamored noisily.

"What's going on over there?" I asked.

"It's haunted! There's a ghost!" someone shouted. More of the crowd started running off.

Our driver, Han Liang, had been a beat cop and knew a thing or two about riot control. He immediately shone the van's searchlight on the road back to the village to keep the people from stampeding.

"What the hell?" I said.

"Th-they said there was a . . . ghost." Lin Tao stepped closer to me. Without the searchlight, the grass around us was suddenly dark in the dim moonlight.

"A ghost?" I said with a laugh. "Can it fly? Come on, let's go look."

We couldn't work without the light, so we climbed under the tape to see what was going on. The villagers were basically all gone. There was only one left, an old man who needed help walking.

"What happened?" I asked.

"A lady ghost came out of the cemetery!"

22

With more than ten policemen around him, the villager mustered his courage. "I just came here to watch you work, that's all. I was gonna have a piss in the graveyard, but then I saw a ghost."

"What did the ghost look like? Where was she?" I asked, trying not to laugh.

"By the fork. Walk in a few steps and you can see her. Leaning against a tombstone, legs crossed, long hair blowing in the wind. Scared me to death."

Looking at the villager's expression, I could tell this was no joke.

"Let's go have a look," I said.

The man trembled as he slowly led us to the fork in the road. He pointed and said, "If you go in a little from here, you'll see her. Also, can you have someone escort me?"

Several officers shone their flashlights on the cemetery grass, illuminating the haphazard graves. And there she was.

In the distance was a rich family's tomb. A figure leaned against it, motionless, skin extremely pale. It seemed to be sitting with its upper body against the stone, head hanging, with its legs high in the air like someone doing exercises.

A normal person would have trouble holding that position, but the figure didn't move.

"Hey there, what are you doing?" the officer called.

Still the figure didn't move, but a sinister wind blew through its hair.

"Dear God!" Lin Tao said, trembling.

It reminded me of a story I'd heard when I was little. A man was walking through a field in the middle of the night when he saw an elegant woman in white with beautiful black hair blowing in the breeze. He whistled, and the woman turned around, but she had no face or head, just hair.

That story had stayed with me, and I'd always been a little skittish around long-haired women. The thought made me shiver.

The lady ghost kept her feet above the tombstone, still as could be. Her long hair swung in the wind, but no matter how it moved, we couldn't get a look at her face, even though we were only ten yards away.

"Who'll go with me to have a look?" I had to live up to my reputation for bravery.

A few of the officers and I put on shoe covers and started walking toward her.

It was a naked female body.

Leaning against the tombstone, its head bowed, long hair covering its face.

I'd been startled by people playing dead before, so I prodded it gently with a stick. Nothing. Gathering my courage, I used the stick to part the corpse's hair and uncover its face.

"Nope, no ghost here," I said. "Dead girl."

And unlike a ghost, a dead body is nothing to be afraid of.

One of the officers shifted his feet, and something whooshed down from a small tree nearby and fell on him. He jumped a foot, batting at his shoulders.

"It's okay; it's okay," I yelled. "It's just a rope."

The rope wrapped around the upper body and fastened it to the tombstone, deforming the breasts. Another rope kept the girl's hands behind her back. Two more tied each ankle to a nearby tree—or had, until the officer bumped into the little tree and knocked them down.

Though nothing was holding the corpse's feet anymore, they stayed where they were, high in the air and spread apart.

"Wh-what?" the officer said. "How did she do that?"

"Ever heard of a thing called rigor mortis?" I pushed on the knees, but they didn't move. The muscles were hypertonic, the joints stiff, which can be caused by rigor mortis or poisoning.

Seeing we weren't being attacked by a ghost, the other officers came closer, and the crowd of onlookers began to trickle back.

Lin Tao came over and saw it was just a corpse. No longer afraid, he raised his hand and said, "Stay back! I need to look for footprints! Out of the way!"

We undertook emergency site protection measures, cut the ropes, and put them in a body bag with the corpse. (Knots can sometimes reveal someone's skills or style, which could be an important clue.) The body went into the bag with its legs still stuck the way they'd been tied, which made for a strange sight from the outside.

There were several messy footprints that Lin Tao photographed one by one. "Some of these are fresh. Not a lot of people come here, so they're valuable. When we get back to the station, send me your footprints so I can eliminate them."

"This site has to be isolated," I said. "Cut off all the entrances. Once it gets light out tomorrow, we'll search the surroundings. I'd like to find the woman's clothing, but I doubt the van's searchlight will hold out that long."

Some of the young officers started to play rock-paper-scissors to decide who was going to do what job. No one relished the thought of staying overnight in the cemetery.

"No problem," Chief Hu told me. "I'll call for backup, and I'll tell them to bring flashlights. I'm worried it might rain, which would ruin the scene. So we'll search through the night."

"Looks like an interesting case," I said, momentarily forgetting the eleventh finger that had confounded me for weeks.

"You guys take care of this cemetery woman, okay?" Hu said. "The skeleton on the side of the road didn't reveal any good clues, so we just have to ID the corpse."

"Okay," I assured him. "Tying this poor girl to a tombstone took some imagination. I want to make sure we catch this one."

"With the rope tied like that in this kind of place and the victim in that posture, it looks like BDSM gone wrong," Big Bao said.

"Let's go to the morgue," I said. "Examine the body and then get some rest."

The body lay on the autopsy table in its awkward pose. Once Lin Tao finished taking photos, we began to break down the body's rigor mortis.

"Wow, the body's really stiff," I said. "And we know that rigor mortis is stiffest around fifteen to seventeen hours after death."

Having the legs spread like that did make it much easier for us to take the rectal temperature, though. "Wow, good call. According to the temperature, she died seventeen hours ago," Big Bao said.

It was 8:02 p.m. That meant the victim had died on that day, July 4, at three a.m.

"What would a woman be doing in a cemetery at three a.m.?" I said.

"I think it's a robbery case, you guys," Lin Tao said as he stamped the victim's fingerprints. "Look."

Her hands were pale, but there was an even lighter band on one finger of the right hand, where she'd apparently worn a ring.

"I agree," Big Bao said. "It's not a rape case. Hymen's intact."

"No signs of sexual abuse?" I was a little surprised. "Why was she naked, then? And in that position?"

Big Bao opened his hands and shrugged. "No idea. But there's no damage to the vulva."

"The perp must have intended to rape her," I said, "but couldn't for some reason. Or maybe the killer's a woman too?"

The victim's body didn't have any signs of constraint or resistance injuries, but there was mild peeling and bleeding where the ropes had chafed.

"Clearly tied up while alive," I said, "but she didn't resist, even afterward."

"Maybe she was drugged?" Lin Tao said. "We can get a blood sample and check."

"Or she was doing BDSM with a woman?" Big Bao said.

"I'm thinking," I said. "Tying a woman to a gravestone might be some kind of ritual. Making her into a sacrifice—or she wanted to be a sacrifice?"

Qingxiang City's six–twenty-nine case, the one with the ink on the girls' faces, had inspired me to start studying local customs. "Some ancient people practiced human sacrifice, but not tied to a tomb in a posture that suggested imminent rape."

"Makes sense," Big Bao said, pushing his glasses up on his nose with his arm. "Tomorrow we can find out who the tomb belongs to. Seems like a big family—maybe they wanted to sacrifice someone."

There was a deep rope groove in the victim's neck. Baking in the sun all day had turned the skin to leather. The inner surface of the victim's eyelids was bloodshot; blood in the heart incoagulable; fingernails black and blue.

"There are some subtle signs of resistance. There's slight peeling where the ropes rubbed against the limbs, and the rope tied from the feet to the tree was loose; it fell off as soon as that officer touched it,"

I said. "If this were BDSM, I don't think the strangulation would be so severe."

The case was murky. There was no basis to infer why the killer committed the crime. Our intuition was that it was some kind of sacrifice based on some old superstition, but then there were also the robbery angle and the aborted sexual assault. Or maybe those were a diversion to confuse the investigation.

Unable to get any more clues from the wounds, we extracted the victim's gastrointestinal organs to determine when and what she last ate.

Testing a victim's intestinal contents is a rather revolting process. The forensic scientist has to scoop them out one spoonful at a time and individually analyze each of the forms. This particular stomach was all but empty. All that was left was a pasty substance.

"Typically, it takes six hours for a person's stomach to empty out. If she died at three in the morning, at least nine hours after dinner, her stomach would have long been empty. Since there is something in her stomach, she probably ate around midnight—noodles, bread, something dry."

"Well, judging by the contents of the small intestine, she didn't eat dinner. But she probably ate lunch around one or two o'clock." Big Bao stood over the victim's small intestine, neatly dissected, on the autopsy table. "There's a large empty stretch in the middle of the small intestine, which means she didn't eat again until midnight, like you said."

"Most of the chyme has turned to paste," he went on, "but there're still some identifiable fibers, probably some meat and vegetables. Oh, tomato skin."

"Sounds like she was kidnapped after lunch yesterday," Lin Tao said.

With the autopsy complete, we were getting ready to extract the victim's pubis to estimate her age when the officer responsible for coordination came in and said, "Chief Hu wants you to hurry to the seventh-floor conference room."

I looked up at the clock and sighed. "Is there a development? It's already after eleven; we're exhausted."

"There is," the officer said with a nod. "We've ID'd the victim."

"That was fast!" I said. "Then we don't need to test the pubis—we can leave her intact. How'd you get it?"

"While you were doing the autopsy, our search team found the victim's clothing on a path near the cemetery. Another team took the fork up to the abandoned brick factory and found a bag of fresh cookies along with a purse. Inside were some business cards, cheap makeup, and a wallet. There were no bank cards or money, but there were discount cards and ID."

"Right, right. The victim ate something like a cookie around midnight," I said. "The bag probably did belong to her."

"The body's DNA is still being analyzed and compared with the woman's parents," the officer said. "But toxicology test results are back. The victim didn't take any depressants or sleeping pills."

"The victim didn't resist and wasn't drugged," I said softly. "But she stayed with the killer in a remote place for a long time and ate cookies, even went to the cemetery and undressed and didn't fight being tied up. How could that be?"

23

The victim's name was Qi Jingjing. Jing means "calm," and apparently her personality fit her name—quiet and introverted.

From the victim's relatives, friends, and colleagues, we learned that Jingjing's father had been laid off and couldn't find another steady job, so he'd been trying to get day-laborer gigs. Not long ago, her mother was diagnosed with cancer. The whole family's economic burden, including the cancer treatments, fell on the shoulders of Jingjing, and the young woman worked like a maniac to support everyone.

Jingjing worked in sales and marketing at an interior decorating company. The more she worked, the more she earned. Even though she was only twenty-one, she'd started in the industry after graduating from a technical junior high school and was already an old hand with lots of contacts in the building materials industry. In order to make extra money in her spare time, she worked as a broker. For example, if she introduced a raw materials supplier to a building materials factory, she would earn a fee.

"With a job like that," the lead detective said, "you're rarely in the office, so Jingjing's coworkers weren't surprised when she was out all day yesterday. They all said nothing unusual had been going on with her."

"Based on our examination, Jingjing had never had penetrative sex," Big Bao said. "Did the investigation turn up anything about her possibly being homosexual or asexual?"

The detective shook his head. "No one gave us any indication of that. In fact, and you'll be interested to hear this, on the day of the incident, she went on a blind date with a man."

"We checked the victim's phone," Chief Hu added. "She received a call around eleven a.m. on July third from her blind date, so that may be when she went. From twelve to two, there were a lot of calls. We investigated a little and found they were either clients or public phones, so no leads. Around three p.m., her phone was turned off."

"This blind date sounds highly suspicious," Big Bao said. "Who is he?"

"A businessman named Cao Zhe," the detective said. "A couple weeks ago, he came to Dragon City to open a shop, which is now under renovation."

"How tall is he?" Lin Tao took out an isometric shoe print photo.

After excluding the shoe prints of the villagers and police, Lin Tao identified several samples of the killer's shoe print.

"Cao Zhe's five six," the detective said. "Skinny."

"Really seems like it's gotta be him," Big Bao said. "But what girl just takes her clothes off? I bet the blind date was going well, then little bossman went looking for a secluded place to get romantic, but he turned out to be a pervert."

"The undressing wasn't necessarily voluntary," Hu said. "The clothes were all torn. That is, the killer cut them off with a knife."

"Using a knife wouldn't necessarily be about coercion," I said. "It could be because the body was already tied up and they couldn't be removed in the usual way."

"If that's the case, why did Qi Jingjing give in to being tied up?" Big Bao said.

I shook my head to say I didn't know.

"I doubt it was Cao Zhe," Lin Tao said. "Based on the footprints, the killer was probably about five eleven. There's a margin of error, but not that big."

"I don't think it was him either," I said. "How could a guy who came to Dragon City just a couple weeks ago know that area so well? Know the old cemetery, know the abandoned brick factory? I've been living in Dragon City for years, and I didn't know about them."

"Doesn't matter," Captain Nie said. "He may have been the last person to see Jingjing, so we arrested him, and he's currently being questioned."

I frowned and didn't say anything, annoyed at the captain's rashness.

"You all keep at it," Lin Tao said, apparently a little annoyed too. He looked at his watch. "Overall, this case looks like a robbery. I doubt it's the businessman, but I'll reserve judgment. It's late. We're going to call it a night."

When I got home late that night, my wife woke up bleary-eyed and made me a bowl of noodles. She sat down to keep me company as I stuffed my mouth.

"So what kind of case do you think it is?" Ling Dang asked.

"I think it could be some kind of ritual sacrifice," I said.

"Did you look at the inscriptions on the tomb?" she asked. "If it was a ritual, then it must have been done on some important day."

"Right!" I slapped the table. "Can't believe I didn't think of that earlier. Want to go with me and have a look now?"

"No way I'm going," Ling Dang said, her face full of fright. "And you shouldn't either. You need rest."

I laughed and gave her a kiss. "I was just kidding. The tomb isn't going anywhere—we can look tomorrow. But that really is a good idea, my better half."

"The whole thing sounds terrifying."

◆ ◆ ◆

Early the next morning, July 5, I got Lin Tao and Big Bao to drive with me to the scene. There were a dozen or so officers still searching for clues as I walked straight up to the tombstone where the body was found.

The inscription read: "Li Huaxai, Martyr and Anti-Japanese Hero."

So it was a martyr's box tomb built after the founding of the People's Republic. Rumor had it Li Huaxai's descendants had fought to keep the land as a cemetery, but the bodies were slated to be moved so developers could come in.

"Born September 8, 1910. Died July 4, 1941."

I felt a shudder of excitement. "The murder took place yesterday morning. Yesterday was the fourth day of the seventh lunar month!"

I watched Lin Tao and Big Bao shudder too.

Lin Tao smiled and said, "Looks like we're gonna solve this case."

Meanwhile, Cao Zhe's interrogation had led nowhere. Cao Zhe said he wasn't interested in Qi Jingjing and went home alone right after lunch.

"The video at the entrance of the place where he's staying confirms it," Captain Nie said with some frustration.

"See?" I was a little proud. "He didn't meet the criteria for the murderer. But did you get anything useful out of him?"

The lead detective shook his head.

"What time did they finish eating? Did Jingjing get any calls afterward?"

"There's a phone not far from the restaurant that takes prepaid cards. She got one call from that number after her lunch date."

"People still use those cards?" I mused.

"If you're trying to avoid being traced," Lin Tao said.

"Right." I looked to the chief and said, "The tomb the girl was tied to belongs to an anti-Japanese martyr, and she was killed on the anniversary of his death. I think you all should prioritize looking into that martyr's family members. There's a strong possibility that this was human sacrifice."

"I still don't understand why Qi Jingjing didn't resist," Chief Hu said.

I shook my head. "I don't know, but this is our only lead. Chief Hu, why don't we talk a bit about the Eleventh Finger case?"

"Good, good, good! Talk!" Nie said in a rush. It was clear that a month without a clue was weighing on the leadership.

"There have been some developments in the Eleventh Finger case," Hu announced. "We were able to ID the skeleton by the side of the road."

"That fast?" I was amazed at their efficiency.

"Been looking from the moment we realized it was missing a finger," Hu said. "Asked for assistance from the neighboring provinces and cities too. What's more, DNA testing confirmed the finger and the skeleton belonged to the same person."

Hu paused, then said, "The victim is Meng Xiangping, a urologist at Qingxiang City Hospital. This year, he was training in the provincial hospital. He would go back home every weekend, but on May sixteenth, he didn't show. His wife called the police on May eighteenth."

"The timing is consistent with our estimate," I said. "Xiangping died a little more than two weeks before Zuo Fangjiang. We only found Zuo Fangjiang first because his corpse was discarded downtown. So did we look into Xiangping's activity before he died?"

Hu nodded and said, "We did. May fourteenth, a Wednesday night, a coworker saw Xiangping in the hospital cafeteria. He was off the next day. Then, on Friday, the sixteenth, he was on call, but no one spoke to or saw him. Since he lived alone in a dorm, no one was keeping track of him until Saturday, the seventeenth, when his wife called his office."

"Is that all we got?"

"Yes. There's no way to track his movements after that point," Hu said with regret.

"What about his social relationships?" I pressed.

"Nothing yet."

Hu looked despondent. What was the link between the two men? Why were they killed one after the other, disemboweled, and dismembered? What was the point of all this?

"Let's focus on the cemetery case for now," Hu said. "We still don't have enough clues to track down the Eleventh Finger killer."

My human-sacrifice theory was soon discounted.

"I knew the date-on-the-tomb thing was a coincidence." Captain Nie laughed, a little bitter about having been wrong about Cao Zhe. "Human sacrifice? In this day and age?"

"How'd you rule it out?" I wasn't fully convinced.

"Li Huaxai's descendants haven't lived in Dragon City for over a year," Nie said. "He had only one son, who already died, a grandson who's fifty now, and a granddaughter who's forty-seven. The two of them take care of their eighty-year-old mother in Nanjiang. According to Nanjiang City's public security bureau, they haven't been back to Dragon City in the last year."

Captain Nie signaled for the lead detective to take over.

The detective opened his notebook and said, "All of Li Huaxai's family moved to Nanjiang last year. His great-grandson, eighteen-year-old Li Jianguo, is attending college away from home. He comes back to Dragon City occasionally and stays with his mother's sister. She's raised him since he was small, and they have a good relationship."

"And why isn't this Li Jianguo a suspect?" I asked. "Don't forget, the call to Jingjing was from a prepaid card. Only college kids would still mess around with that crap."

"Do you even know your great-grandfather's name?" Captain Nie asked me. "I'm talking name, not the day he died. A great-grandson, a college student, is he really gonna remember the day his great-grandfather died and murder a goddamn person for him as a sacrifice?"

I scratched my head. "Yeah, I guess you're right. Maybe this was just a robbery. What did Jingjing and Cao Zhe eat for lunch?"

"Tomato, fried egg, kung pao chicken, and some vegetables," the detective read from his pad.

"Looks like he was telling the truth," I said. "Consistent with what we found."

"Guess this investigation shows that examining stomach contents is useless," Captain Nie said haughtily.

"Right now, we don't even know if the victim and killer knew each other," Lin Tao said, trying to smooth things over. "Even if they were acquaintances, I don't think she would just let someone tie her up and cut off her clothes."

"But they also would have had to know that area really well," I said. "How many people know about the graveyard and the old brick factory?"

"A fair number. People who live around there all know," the detective said.

"Too bad you need a matching sample for footprints to be useful," Lin Tao said.

Suddenly, a detective rushed into the room. "Jingjing's debit card was just used to empty her account—twenty thousand yuan!"

Captain Nie jumped up. "Did we get the thief on video?"

The detective shook his head. "No, he was wearing a hat and glasses, so we can't see his face clearly."

Captain Nie sat back down. "So you busted in here for no reason."

"No," I said. "It's still useful. First, we know some of the suspect's physical characteristics. Second, we can be sure at least one of the motives was theft."

"Right, right." The detective nodded hard. "Five eleven, well-built, carrying a shoulder bag."

"That's consistent with our estimates from trace evidence," I said, looking at Lin Tao.

"But we still can't narrow the scope of the investigation," Big Bao said. "Dragon City has seven million people. How are we gonna find him?"

"Let's go back over the body and see if we find something new," I said.

"Without new developments in the Eleventh Finger case, we don't have much to do," Chief Hu whispered to me as we left the conference room. "Other than going back to the autopsy room, what else can be done on this case?"

I thought a second, then said, "The periphery search already gave us all the clues it could from Jingjing's belongings. So now we have to do the same for what the perp was carrying."

Hu lowered his head in thought.

"Those bags of cookies," I prompted.

"Yes, right," Hu said.

"So, check out the bags. See where they came from, where they're usually sold."

Hu nodded and said, "I'll tell the captain to have his men take a look. Maybe there are fingerprints or something."

"Our perp knows a lot about criminal investigation," I said. "He knew to wear a hat and glasses to withdraw the money. I doubt he'd leave fingerprints on the cookie bags. My recommendation is to start with the cookie manufacturer."

"Good idea," Hu said, turning to leave.

I looked at Big Bao. "Okay, let's get moving."

Lin Tao had gone ahead of us to the autopsy room. When we arrived, he said, "I just tested the victim's bag and wallet and didn't find anyone else's marks, not even glove smudges. There're only the victim's fingerprints. I think she may have given her money and bank card to the killer."

"That leaves two possibilities. One, they knew each other," I said, "or two, she was threatened."

"Like I've been saying, the victim didn't put up much resistance, maybe out of fear," Big Bao said. "We know Jingjing was a timid person."

I nodded silently.

After two hours of reexamining the corpse, we didn't have anything new. Though the previous examination was done late at night, we hadn't missed anything—or so I thought until I went to stitch the body closed again.

Sunlight brushed the victim's feet, illuminating a strange mark in the center of one of the toes.

I stopped my needlework and leaned over to look.

"What's up?" Big Bao asked.

"The other night, I didn't notice this shiny spot on the toe," I said.

"What is it?" Big Bao asked.

I shook my head and didn't say anything. I wiped the toe with a cotton swab, put it in an evidence bag, took off my lab coat, and hurried to the city DNA lab.

The DNA technician took my swab and began soaking and centrifugation. When it was ready, I peered into the microscope.

"Beautiful!" I shouted.

"Got it?" The tech pursed her lips into a smile.

"There's sperm! Hurry and do the DNA test!"

As I was waiting for the results, Chief Hu called with good news.

"We looked into the cookie bags. They're produced in Shaanxi Province and mainly sold there too. I don't think you could buy them in our province. And we were able to determine that the card was sold by Shaanxi Telecom. So the person who made the call was probably the killer."

"Shaanxi?" I said. "The killer came from Shaanxi? How could someone from Shaanxi know Dragon City so well? Crap, what do we do next? I just got some sperm from the victim's toe, but now it seems useless. I mean, Shaanxi's so big, even with DNA analysis, how are we gonna find him?"

"Heh, I've got more good news here," Hu said. "I'll be back at my office in a minute. Meet me there."

24

Chief Hu leaned against his desk, sipping tea. "If a timid killer went to a cemetery to commit a crime, what kind of area would he choose?"

"How do you know the killer's timid?" I asked.

"Hypothetically," Hu teased.

I thought about it, then shook my head.

Hu said, "If I were a killer, and very familiar with the area, I'd choose the spot I was most familiar with, like a relative's grave."

"Hold on," I interrupted, "why would the killer want to do it in the cemetery?"

"That's hard to say, but you didn't get my point yet?"

I nodded. "I got it. You're back to thinking about Li Huaxai's relatives. But the detective already said, other than his great-grandson, none come to Dragon City. Also, would a college student be stupid enough to sacrifice someone at his great-grandfather's grave? It has to be a coincidence."

"If you're saying the crime happening on the anniversary of his death is a coincidence," Hu said, "I agree. But my point is that if one of Li Huaxai's family committed the crime, he might choose a spot in that terrifying place that's relatively less terrifying for him. That'd be an unavoidable subconscious instinct."

"So let's track this kid."

"Not easy," Hu said. "Universities went on break two days ago."

"Then let's do a DNA comparison," I said. "I just found some sperm. But it's weird. Why would it be on the toe? Maybe a new trick from Japanese porn?"

"I don't know about that, but it's pretty safe to say he's our perp," Hu said.

"Oh?" I felt a rush of excitement. "On what basis?"

Hu gave a knowing smile. "Because Li Jianguo, Li Huaxai's great-grandson, goes to school in Xian; he's five eleven and well-built."

"Really?!"

"Yes. Where are you gonna find a coincidence like that? The cookies were from Shaanxi, the prepaid phone card was sold in Shaanxi, he goes to school in Shaanxi, just started break; the corpse was tied to his great-grandfather's tombstone; same physical characteristics . . ."

"Then let's get him," I exclaimed.

"We've already cast the net," Hu said. "And with the strength of our force, catching one evil little kid is nothing."

Once the lab checked the sperm against Jianguo's things from his aunt's house, the task force got the good news, and Li Jianguo was promptly arrested on a train from Nanjiang to Xian.

The task force confiscated all his shoes, but was unable to find any with a sole pattern matching those found at the scene.

"Looks like the kid must've ditched them," Lin Tao said in frustration after spending the afternoon studying two dozen pairs of smelly shoes.

"Good thing you found that DNA sample," Big Bao said proudly.

And Li Jianguo not only had a good sense of how to avoid detection; he kept impressively silent during questioning. Whatever he could deny, he denied. Whatever he couldn't, he was quiet about. After a variety of interrogation tactics failed, the task force finally used the DNA trump card. Faced with proof of his sperm on a dead girl's toe, Jianguo had nowhere to hide.

And just like that, the murderous teenage descendant of a revolutionary martyr cracked.

Jianguo grew up in Dragon City, where he paid his respects to his great-grandfather every year and learned to love the Communist Party. Until his grandfather died, his busy parents didn't bother to discipline him, and the kid ran wild. Though he had the smarts to attend a major university, he was only admitted to a third-tier school in Shaanxi.

In college, Jianguo got really into nightlife and met a party girl whom he soon moved in with. Under her tutelage, Jianguo went from a bratty freshman to a seasoned addict.

As with most people who get into drugs, Li Jianguo's life was pretty much ruined. Drugs were expensive, and a month's living stipend from his parents couldn't match what his girlfriend earned from a single night of prostitution. So if he wanted drugs, he had to put up with the girl he loved getting hot and heavy with other people every night. It was excruciating, but he decided that the physical pain of living without drugs was far worse than the mental anguish caused by his girlfriend's work.

After a while, though, he began to wonder about ways to get his own drug money. The only thing he could come up with? Robbery.

His goal was ambitious: to steal enough money to supply himself with drugs for all four years of college. Once he graduated, he'd go to rehab. The arrogant young man figured that if he ever did relapse, he'd just get a good job and buy the drugs himself.

At the end of freshman year, he barely passed his finals. During the train ride to Dragon City to visit his aunt, he thought about how to do the robbery. Who should he rob? A bank?

He stayed in Dragon City for two days and went to several banks to scope things out. It quickly became apparent that grabbing money from outside the bulletproof glass and getting past the heavily armed guards would be impossible. So he gave up on banks and started looking for single women. Three days later, he found his opportunity when he went to a restaurant for lunch and saw Cao Zhe and Qi Jingjing on their blind date.

The blush of her cheeks set him off on a fantasy. The guy with her was flashing a brand-name watch and a gold necklace. How could such a sweet girl go for a wealthy jerk like that? She didn't need him—she looked like an independent woman who had her own money.

Jianguo ate slowly at a table not far from them, thinking about whether to rob Jingjing. He saw her give Cao Zhe her business card and thought how good it would be to get one for himself.

After giving Cao Zhe the card, Jingjing went to the restroom. And Cao Zhe, looking impatient, turned and threw it in a trash can.

Dreams come true, Jianguo thought excitedly.

Cao Zhe and Jingjing's lunch was soon over.

Jianguo rushed to the trash and fished out the soiled card.

"Sea and Sky Decoration Co., Ltd., Marketing Manager, Qi Jingjing, 139XXXXXXXX."

That was easy, Jianguo thought with a smile as he left the restaurant. He went to the nearest prepaid phone machine and called Jingjing.

"Hello, is this Qi Jingjing? I'm calling from Shaanxi Real Estate Development Corporation," he said, using the accent he'd learned from his girlfriend. "We're looking to start a big project in West Dragon City, a deluxe housing development. After talking to various people, we think Sea and Sky is our best option for interior decoration. Would it be possible to meet and talk about working together?"

Jingjing was overjoyed. Sea and Sky had never had such a big project before.

Jianguo asked her to meet him at the entrance of his ancestral home, thinking he'd just take her inside to rob her, but no, that wouldn't work. Taking her to his family home would reveal his identity. He regretted suggesting it, but then remembered the abandoned brickyard nearby where no one ever went. That would work.

Drugs had aged Jianguo's body, so at only eighteen, he looked more like a thirty-year-old man. The man's handsome, world-weary looks took Jingjing by surprise, but also made her lower her guard.

Jianguo told her the residential area and cemetery would be bulldozed to make way for his company's luxury housing. As an addict and a denizen of the smarmy club scene, Jianguo had gotten good at winning people's trust.

As Jianguo led her down the path, Jingjing was thinking ecstatically about how much she would make from the project. This would cover her mom's cancer treatments and more.

It wasn't until a knife was pointed at her that she woke up from her dream.

Jianguo took Jingjing to the abandoned brickyard and forced her to take all the money from her wallet. There were only eight hundred yuan and a worthless ring. In order to make the elaborate robbery worth his while, he needed Jingjing's debit card—and her PIN number.

Knife casually in hand, Jianguo worked on Jingjing all afternoon and into the night in the abandoned brickyard, trying out harder and softer threats until he was sure the final password she gave him wasn't fake. When he found out there was so much in the account, he got very excited.

Flush with the monetary victory, he started to think about sex. But as soon as he got close to Jingjing, she resisted fiercely.

This pure woman won't play with me a bit? She gave me all her money, why not her body too?

She'd die before she gave that, Jingjing told him.

Jianguo looked at the starry sky out the factory window, took a bag of cookies from his backpack, and tossed it to Jingjing.

"You gave me the money, so I'll take you home," Jianguo said.

Thrilled to hear she'd made it out alive, Jingjing stood up, forgetting her handbag, and followed Jianguo. She hadn't imagined Jianguo would take her to that terrifying old cemetery. There were graves everywhere, the night sounds punctuated with strange birdcalls.

"Oh shit, I'm lost!" Jianguo said as he reached his great-grandfather's tomb, putting his acting skills to work.

"So what do we do now?" Jingjing said, holding her shoulders and trembling.

"You wait here. I'll find the way," Jianguo said.

"No, I'm afraid," Jingjing said. "Let's go back the way we came."

"I don't know the way back either," Jianguo lied shamelessly. "Why don't we just spend the night here and leave when it gets light."

Jingjing looked around at the overgrown weeds and gravestones. She closed her eyes and, with much regret, nodded.

"But what if I fall asleep and you go call the police?" Jianguo said. "I should tie you up to be safe. I promise I'll stay right here and not leave, okay? I swear on my honor."

Jingjing gulped and nodded. Her terror and exhaustion had overpowered her ability to think straight.

Which is how Jingjing found herself tied up on her back with her arms and legs splayed out. Jianguo flashed his knife and smiled sinisterly. "I promised not to leave, but I didn't promise anything else."

He cut off Jingjing's clothing piece by piece. Her smell and the way her body was positioned made his blood swell. He started taking his pants off.

The threat of rape and losing her virginity woke Jingjing from her paralysis. "Do you have a condom? I have AIDS."

Jianguo, pants half off, gaped at her in shock.

"Don't believe me? Wanna take the chance?" Jingjing spat, trying to sound convincing.

AIDS! Jianguo was very annoyed. He'd been on guard, but still got surprised by this trick! Either way, better safe than sorry.

He took out his junk and stared at Jingjing while he masturbated.

"Disgusting," Jingjing yelped as something sprayed her feet.

"Who's disgusting?" Jianguo snarled. He took another rope from his bag and wrapped it around her neck.

She knows what I look like. And there's that tattoo on my thigh. She'll call the cops. Witnesses must be silenced. Like in the movies.

Jianguo swore to the interrogators he didn't want to kill anyone, but at that moment, a voice in his heart whispered to him, "Murder Qi Jingjing." When she was no longer moving, he fled the scene, discarding her clothing across the field.

"I was afraid if she didn't die, she might get free of the ropes and chase me," Jianguo said.

"So you didn't sense her spirit chasing you the whole time?" I taunted.

Jianguo looked at me in terror. Lin Tao was apparently also frightened—he broke out in goose bumps.

"She didn't really have AIDS, right?" Big Bao said, a little worried.

Even though we wear gloves, a forensic scientist's biggest fear is working with bodies that carry infectious diseases. Contracting something lethal is a hell of a work-related injury.

"No," I said. "Already tested, safe. Relax. The poor girl was trying to preserve her virginity. She was smart, but that business card did her in."

"Not to mention her family," Lin Tao said. "Her mom has cancer; dad's doing odd jobs. What are they going to do?"

Big Bao looked pensive. "Good thing I don't have a business card."

25

"What's a latent disease?"

"Many people have latent diseases, but they lack pronounced symptoms. Once the conditions are right for the disease to emerge, they may suffer an acute or even fatal attack. The most common type is cardiovascular. For example, with a cerebrovascular aneurysm, you usually don't see clear signs of it, but if the head suffers a minor blow or the mood is suddenly excited, the aneurysm may rupture and result in death. Another common case is the cardiac conduction system. People often have latent problems that, when activated, can lead to the onset of disease or even cardiac arrest."

"So what latent disease did my dad have?"

"Your father's heart condition couldn't be considered latent. He had high blood pressure, heart disease, coronary stenosis, and lumen thrombosis."

"Then why didn't they catch it during his exam?"

Speechless, I looked at the health employee who'd examined the petitioner's father when he was still alive.

"He just did a blood test, no electrocardiogram, so it wasn't really an exam," Big Bao filled in.

"It was supposed to be an exam, but now you're saying it wasn't? I think it was! Stop bullshitting me. Are you going to execute this guy or not?"

"That's a question for the public security bureau. We're scientists." I tried hard to calm down. "But listen, the cause of death was disease. As a result, others can't be held criminally responsible. The most they could charge someone with is negligence."

"Why do you get to say what killed him? I think he was beaten to death!"

"Sir, we are forensic scientists. We examined your father's body and ruled out trauma, suffocation, and poisoning. We did find signs of potentially fatal disease. So our conclusions are in line with those of the city public security bureau."

"Bullshit. You bureaucrats all look out for one another. And you ruled out trauma, huh? What about the big spot on his leg? If that's not trauma, what is?"

I clenched my fist and forced myself to explain kindly, "The trauma I'm talking about is potentially fatal trauma, such as the rupture of large blood vessels or damage to vital organs. We didn't find any bleeding or even any minor injury, let alone something that would kill him. That bruise indicates he had a minor dispute, but it did not play a role in his death."

"You think you can take advantage of people like this? Murder cases have to be solved. Fucking bullshit."

"This is not a murder case. Because he died from disease."

"I don't buy it for a second. I'm going to Beijing tomorrow to petition."

"Don't, don't, don't. Aren't we explaining it to you now?" Captain Huang said, feigning a smile.

I never understood why the public security bureau would pay attention to those frivolous petitions, but it seemed like they spent the majority of their energy on them.

I have no problem talking to petitioners and giving them a forensic explanation that they can understand. But even rock-hard facts and patient explanations don't resolve many complaints.

This cursing jerk was making my blood boil, and Captain Huang's smile made me sick.

It wouldn't be unfair to call the guy a bastard. He was an outcast who'd been adopted by a single old man. After the old man gave him everything, the guy moved out. For more than ten years, he never gave the old man any money or so much as brought him tea. It wasn't until the old man had some dispute with his neighbor and died suddenly that the bastard went back to the village and started crying his eyes out.

Someone who causes trauma that kills another person bears some civil liability. The son could have gone through normal legal channels, but he knew he wouldn't be able to get much money that way.

"The squeaky wheel gets the grease," he told his adopted father's neighbors.

Those neighbors hated him and trusted the police, but that became fuel for the bastard's online hype machine. "They're all in it together, bullying my father," he wrote. "They obviously have a lot of influence! The public security bureaus have been bribed and don't even investigate murders anymore. Look at this picture of his leg, all black and blue. Yet these crooked cops still say he died from disease. Pay attention because, as a good son, I can't let my dad die in vain."

The page filled up with nasty comments about police officers.

My explanation was no use. As so often seemed to happen, traveling to another city to review a petition gave me no sense of accomplishment. Why was I even in Yuntai?

"Man, your groveling like that after he said he'd go to Beijing was really annoying," I told Huang.

"We should grovel for the people. We're servants, the people's servants," Huang said with a laugh. "I've been under a lot of pressure lately. These neighbor fights where one then dies from disease have been happening a lot, and all of them are petitioning. Families compete over who gets the most money."

"This isn't good. Society's not in harmony. There's going to be another murder case soon," I said, smiling.

Huang was the one who'd originally nicknamed me "Jinx," so I liked to use "jinxes" like that to mess with him.

"Hey, hey!" Huang shouted. "I've got more petitions than I can handle right now. If there's a murder case too, I'm gonna lose it. I'm seriously afraid of you, Jinx. Yuntai never has murder cases, and then you arrive here and start making prophecies."

As we walked into the Yuntai police station, everyone was bustling about.

"What's going on?" Huang asked Forensic Scientist Gao.

"Captain, you guys were busy in the meeting, but command says they found a body—could be a murder," Gao said. "We're getting ready to go to the scene now, sir. Forensic Scientist Chen will call you with a report."

"I really got myself a jinx," Huang said, his face full of frustration.

I felt a strange excitement. "I'll go to the scene too."

I found myself uncomfortably close to the same part of Yuntai where I'd broken the case with the serial rapist and killer. Being back made me shiver. Somehow, it felt like that case would always follow me.

As soon as we arrived, the villagers started talking hurriedly to one another. Some said the village was cursed and the girl's ghost was making trouble; others said the village's feng shui was off and would consume someone every year; others said they were going to move away.

The crime scene was a well in a field outside the village. A group of detectives surrounded the person who'd called in the case. His name was Jie Liwen, a skinny sixty-year-old man with strikingly black hair. He was squatting outside the police tape, silently smoking.

"Talk to us," a detective said. "This is a human life here. If you don't help us out, how are we going to catch the guy?"

Jie Liwen glared at the officer and said, "Really fucking unlucky lately, finding this thing. Who the fuck would kill someone and throw the body in my family's well? I hope they die with no children!"

As dawn was breaking, Jie Liwen had been getting ready to work in the fields as usual. He put a bucket into the well to get water, but no matter what he did, he couldn't get the bucket to fill up with water. That had never happened before, so in the faint light, he tried to see inside and made out an indistinct mass.

What the heck did some dumb kid throw in my well? he wondered.

There was nothing he could do, so he gave up fetching water and went to work. When the sun rose higher, he thought of the well problem again.

Squinting down again, he saw the well was full of straw.

"Fuck their ancestors," Jie Liwen cursed. He tried to puzzle out which mischievous village child would have put straw in the well.

It wasn't a very deep well, just five feet down to the water line. And it was narrow too—just barely the width of a man's shoulders. Scooping the junk out wouldn't be easy. He labored for hours with a shovel and bucket until the straw was just about all cleaned out.

Jie Liwen sat down heavily next to the well, panting and sucking on a cigarette, silently cursing the culprit's family for eighteen generations back. Then he wondered if he had offended anyone recently.

He stood up and grabbed the bucket, ready to finally get water, but when he looked down, he was shocked.

What the hell else is in there? he wondered. That doesn't look like straw.

He picked up a long branch and, hands trembling, lowered it into the well. There was something dark bobbing beneath the water's surface, and an oily substance bubbled up.

A dead dog? Jie Liwen thought to comfort himself. Deep down, he knew a dog wouldn't be that big.

He pushed down harder with the branch, and the thing sank and then floated back up and peeked out above the water.

It was the soles of two human feet.

"When was the last time you used the well?" a detective asked.

"I don't remember," Jie Liwen said. "Maybe two or three days ago."

"So you didn't use it yesterday or see anything abnormal then?"

"No, nothing."

The detective thought for a moment but couldn't come up with a follow-up question, so he turned and asked me, "Examiner Qin, should we secure the surrounding area?"

"Of course," I said, nodding.

"We looked all around," a technician said. "The footprints all appear to belong to Mr. Jie and the police. It doesn't seem like we'll be able to find any trace evidence."

I shook my head. "We still have to secure the area. There's still that area over there, especially that straw heap. Lin Tao will help you in a minute."

After getting my shoe covers on, I lay down by the well and looked inside. The corpse must have sunk to the bottom again, because there was no sign of it. Under the bright sun, I couldn't see anything down there.

"How'd Jie Liwen see anything in there?" I said. "I can't."

"Um . . . the body hasn't been pulled out yet?" Big Bao asked. "If we don't have the body, how do we know it's a murder case? Couldn't someone have jumped in there to kill themselves? Or gotten drunk and fallen in?"

"Come on," I said. "Would a suicide or an accident get covered in straw?"

"Oh." Big Bao hugged himself. "Um . . . maybe the victim fell, and then a kid just happened to put straw in?"

"Not impossible, but definitely not likely." I was still trying to see down into the well but couldn't make out anything.

"I'm trying to look on the bright side too, Big Bao," Captain Huang said, "but with Jinx here, it's gotta be murder."

I glared at Huang for a second, then picked up Jie Liwen's stick and stuck it in the well. I felt an object but still couldn't see anything.

"Fishing time." I threw down the branch and clapped my hands.

Huang had his men get to work.

"Wait, are they using an old-fashioned bamboo crane?"

"No matter what, we have to make sure not to damage this well," Huang said. All the petition cases really had gotten to him.

The officers started shouting, "Hey, hey, hey, left, left, left, careful, careful, okay, okay, okay, get it on, fasten it, fasten it."

After a frustrating half hour, they finally started to pull the rope up.

I got up from my spot on the grass to watch.

As the police officers called to one another, the rope came up little by little until a body emerged from the well. They laid it on a plastic sheet.

"It's not bloated or waxy, yay!" Big Bao said.

26

It was a man's body, tall and chubby. He wore pajama bottoms, and a long-sleeved shirt was tied around his neck with a rope. The abdomen had not yet turned green.

Because the groundwater here was cold, I couldn't use body temperature to determine time of death.

"Rigor mortis has eased, and livor mortis isn't fading when pressed. Today's the eighteenth, right? He probably died between twenty-four and forty-eight hours ago." I looked around and said, "Open ground. Transporting a body would be risky, so it probably happened at night. The victim was probably killed during the night of the sixteenth or early on the seventeenth and discarded in the well before sunup."

"Don't be so sure," Big Bao said, pushing up his glasses and carefully pulling back the shirt covering the body's chest. "How do you know for certain someone killed him? This shirt is suspicious, but it could be that he was insane and was just wearing it that way."

I shook my head. "Come on, Bao. You gotta pay closer attention. Look at his shoulders."

There were large, pale yellow wounds on the victim's shoulders and upper arms, exposing large areas of adipose tissue—likely the source of the oil on the water. With a little experience, it's not tough to discern whether a wound was inflicted before or after death. Injuries to a living body turn red from blood. Injuries that occur after the heart has stopped pumping appear yellow.

"They were probably inflicted when the killer dumped the body," I said.

Big Bao opened his mouth to speak, but he didn't.

I knew he was thinking the wounds could have been caused by us pulling the corpse out. But the abrasions had loose flaps of skin attached that indicated a direction of the force from shoulder to hand, which corresponded to the body's arms scraping the walls of the well as it went in headfirst. If they'd been caused by our pulling the body out, which was done feet first, then the force would have been in the direction of hand to shoulder, and the flaps would open in the opposite direction.

"When we get to the autopsy room, I'll teach you about the differences between actually drowning and being thrown in water after you're dead," I added.

The detective brought Jie Liwen to the body, pointed, and said, "Do you recognize him?"

Jie Liwen looked at the body, turned away to gag, then said, "I do. That's Old Jun."

The two of them were from the same village, same generation. But figuring out how they were related would require a degree in genealogy.

"Where did Old Jun live?" I asked, excited to have the corpse ID'd already.

"I can take you there."

The body was bagged and carted off to the autopsy room. I asked the officers to secure the scene and wait for the site survey staff to arrive before continuing their work.

We followed Jie Liwen along a path for ten or fifteen minutes before arriving at a dilapidated brick house.

"Well, here it is," Jie Liwen said.

Officers immediately spread out caution tape in front. We put on shoe covers, hoods, masks, and gloves before opening the unlatched door.

The inside was destitute, filthy. There wasn't one item of value. A wooden bed sat in the corner with some bedding and clothes piled on top.

The blanket was pulled back, and there was a pair of slippers at the foot of the bed. Cigarette butts lay strewn across the dirt floor. Opposite the bed was a square table with a chair on either side and a Chinese chessboard on top.

"Based on the positioning of the slippers and blanket, the victim was likely killed in his sleep," I said. "We'd better collect the cigarette butts for DNA testing."

Big Bao always knew a little bit about everything, especially anything having to do with leisure. "The people playing chess weren't any good. Red could easily finish black."

Given the dirt floor, there wasn't much chance of a good shoe trace, but I spotted broad streaks leading from the bed to the doorway.

"Someone dragged the corpse." I took out a tape measure and then pointed at the faint traces out farther on either side. "And those are from the victim's hands."

"Yes, I see," a detective said, taking pictures.

"Means one killer. Two could have lifted it."

Captain Huang grinned at me. "Already figured out how many suspects, great!"

The traces disappeared at the threshold.

I looked around a bit more, but nothing caught my eye, so I told the lead detective, "I'm going to go examine the body. Keep working and meet me at the task force in three hours."

The body weighed two hundred pounds. Big Bao, Forensic Scientist Gao, and I nearly broke our backs getting it onto the autopsy table.

"Whoa, he died from mechanical asphyxia," Big Bao said.

The victim's eyelids showed dense clusters of broken blood vessels; his fingernails and toenails were a dark gray-blue; the mucous membranes on the inside of the lips showed signs of damage. Big Bao was right—the victim was likely killed by suffocation resulting from pressure on the mouth and nose.

Even though we had a preliminary judgment, we had to continue with the rest of the autopsy. First, we had to look for further evidence of mechanical asphyxia; second, we had to rule out all the other possible causes of death. If we failed to rule out other possibilities, we would have to conclude there was a joint cause. For example, someone being hit on the head could die from a brain injury and simultaneously from massive blood loss. If two injuries were caused by two different people, both would bear responsibility for the crime.

In this particular case, we had to determine whether the victim had drowned, because drowning and suffocation present similar signs.

As Big Bao continued the exam, I focused my attention on the rope wrapped twice around the victim's neck. There was a knot on the front.

"Big Bao, what do you think the point of this rope is?" I asked.

"Rope? The rope was definitely tied to something," Big Bao said.

"Yes, ropes do tie things," I said. "I'm saying, what is this rope doing on this body?"

Big Bao thought it over. "Could it be an attempt at strangulation?"

I cut the rope away from the knot and removed it along with the shirt. "Look, the skin underneath the rope has a clear indentation, but the indentation doesn't show a vital reaction."

Big Bao nodded. "It was tied after death. So maybe the killer was trying to dress the body?"

"No. Dressing the victim at that time would be very easy. When old people die, their families hurry to change their clothes before rigor mortis sets in. So why in the world would the killer haphazardly cover the victim's chest like that—and tie it with a rope? What kind of outfit is that? Could it be a regional custom?" I asked, still obsessed with such customs after our recent experiences.

"Never heard of that one," Big Bao replied.

I put the rope and the shirt back the way they were. "The front of the shirt is hanging loose from the rope, but the back is tied up tight. That isn't normal. It's not a simple matter of tying the shirt around the victim's neck."

Big Bao looked them over for a second and said, "I've got it! The killer used the shirt as a blindfold. When Jie Liwen poked around in the water or maybe when we were hauling it up, one side of the shirt got loose."

"Very good, Bao, I think you might be right for once! But this rope wasn't only used to make the shirt into a blindfold."

I got a blank stare in response.

I used my steel tape measure to determine the length of the rope. "The circumference of the loop is about an inch longer than the neck circumference. If it were just for tying the shirt, it'd be a little long."

"That's normal," Big Bao insisted. "The victim's already dead, so the killer doesn't have to be so exact. And, since one side of the shirt fell out, it means it wasn't that tight."

"If it wasn't tight, why is there such a deep indentation on his neck?"

"Right. Um . . . ," Big Bao said, rolling up his eyes in thought.

"My analysis is that there were two reasons for the killer to tie a rope around the victim's neck. One, like you said, to blindfold the victim with his own shirt. And two, to tie a heavy object to one end to hold the body underwater. But the rope the killer used wasn't strong enough, so it broke."

I pointed to the broken end of the rope. "The break marks are rough, which means it was pulled instead of cut."

"Which means there's still something in the well," Big Bao said.

I nodded.

Big Bao laughed. "Okay, Jinx, can't wait to see Huang's face when he hears you want to dig up the poor guy's well after all."

The autopsy found internal bleeding, apical bleeding, and bleeding around the petrous portion of the temporal bone. But there was no liquid in the stomach as there would be with drowning, and the lungs didn't show changes from aqueous emphysema. This, along with the damage on his lips, allowed us to conclude that the victim did indeed die of mechanical asphyxia.

The victim's stomach was nearly empty. Along with the status of the rigor and livor mortis, we determined the victim died about six hours after dinner on July 16. The victim's back and shoulders had many crisscrossing scratches from being dragged after death. Some went from waist to neck, likely from when the murderer pulled him by his feet. Others went from neck to waist, likely from going into the well headfirst.

"Usually, when someone is smothered to death, there are more obvious constraint and resistance injuries," I said as I cut open the joints of the victim's limbs. "But this victim has neither."

Big Bao shook his head. "No, he does."

He cut the skin at the anterior superior iliac spine, revealing subcutaneous hemorrhages on either side of the pelvic bone.

"The killer probably straddled the victim while he pressed on his face. The victim was unable to move his limbs, which suggests the killer was stronger than the victim."

I looked at the tall, burly body and shook my head.

After finishing, we hurried over to the task force.

When we got there, the initial briefing was just starting. Captain Huang asked the forensic team to speak first.

I said, "The victim was likely sleeping when the killer straddled him and covered his nose and mouth, causing death by mechanical asphyxia. Time of death was likely six hours after dinner on July sixteenth. The killer then wrapped the victim's shirt around the victim's head and tied it there with a rope. This could be an indication of acquaintance crime. Sometimes people cover a victim's face after killing him—out of fear."

Huang nodded and addressed the room. "Mr. Jinx here just said with all these neighbor conflicts, we were due for a murder, and here we have it."

"Wait . . . It gets better," Big Bao said with a smile. "We think the rope around the victim's neck was tied to some kind of anchor, but the rope broke and the anchor sank. So we have to dig out the guy's well."

"That's no problem," Huang said with a surprising smile, motioning for the detectives to step in.

The lead detective opened his notebook and said, "The victim is Jie Lijun, sixty-one years old, living alone. He never married, but has an adopted daughter who met a man while working in the city; they're now married and live in Hubei Province. According to neighbors, she hasn't been home for a year. Also, the victim has an older brother named Jie Liguo who lives about three-quarters of a mile north. They didn't see each other much, but Jie Liguo's daughter-in-law was very good to Jie Lijun and brought him food every day."

"Huh? A niece? Could she be relevant?" Big Bao rudely interrupted.

"According to our investigation, the niece and nephew are very kind. Of course, the villagers are saying they might have an eye on the nephew's inheritance from his father."

"So much gossip," I said with a sigh. "Can't even be a truly good son these days."

"And there's a reason Captain Huang isn't worried about digging up the well," the detective said with a mysterious smile.

27

"Come on, out with it," I urged.

"It's like this," the detective said. "Jie Lijun's nephew, Maomao, and niece, Liu Cuihua, have always been good to him. Liu Cuihua brought Jie Lijun all his meals, and Maomao did all the work around his house. Jie Maomao takes care of his uncle's finances, using an account in his uncle's name at the Union Trust Fund to manage his small income and to pay his living expenses."

"Okay, so?"

"On the night of July sixteenth, Liu Cuihua brought food to Jie Lijun around six in the evening. When she came back for the dishes, she saw Jie Lijun was setting up the chessboard, saying he was going to play a few games, which lines up with our survey of the scene. We also learned that Jie Lijun had been studying chess for the last two years—he was completely addicted."

"Did he say who he was playing with?" I asked anxiously.

"Liu Cuihua knew there were a few old villagers who liked to play chess and often spent evenings at Jie Lijun's, so she didn't ask. On the morning of the sixteenth, Liu Cuihua went back with breakfast and found the bed unmade and the old man gone."

"Let me step in here," I said. "Jie Lijun doesn't lock the door at night?"

"The lock is broken. He was old and broke, so he didn't worry about attracting thieves."

I nodded, indicating for the detective to continue.

"Several days ago, Jie Lijun told his niece, Liu Cuihua, that he hadn't seen his daughter's new house since she'd been married, so he was planning on going to Hubei in the next few days. He was the kind of old guy who was always getting ideas in his head, so Liu Cuihua just told the old man he was a piece of work, and didn't think of it any further."

"You still haven't said who he was playing chess with," I exclaimed, getting dizzy from the suspense.

"I'm getting there!" The detective laughed. "Just now, the DNA lab came back with results from the cigarettes. They found a match for the man who called in the case: Jie Liwen."

"Oh!" I slapped the table. "Jie Liwen is now a prime suspect, so you're not worried about digging up his well!"

Huang smiled and nodded.

"Where were his cigarette butts?" Big Bao asked.

The detective took out the evidence list, opened photos from the survey on his laptop, and said, "By the outer stool."

"Black's side." Big Bao squinted to see the picture. "That makes sense! Red was about to beat black, which means Jie Lijun was going to win. Maybe Jie Liwen got angry and killed him."

"That's what I suspected at first," Forensic Scientist Gao said, "because Jie Liwen said he saw the feet sticking up after he removed the straw, but when we were getting the body out, I couldn't see anything."

I nodded. "I thought about that too, but maybe the light was different, or reflecting in there differently."

"Isn't this a case of toss far, bury close?" Big Bao said. "The killer threw the body into his own well. Afterward, he was afraid someone going by would see it, so he put straw on top. Then he was still afraid, so he called the police, thinking we wouldn't suspect him."

Huang nodded approvingly.

"But there's one thing that doesn't make sense," Big Bao said. "We figured the killer was stronger than the victim, but Jie Liwen is a little old man."

"Who said the killer was strong? I don't agree," Lin Tao said, having just returned from his site survey. "I inspected Jie Lijun's house and found a lot of tracks from a body being dragged. Are there drag marks on the corpse?"

I nodded. "A lot, very clear."

"When the body was dragged, the killer stopped every ten feet or so to rest."

Lin Tao pointed at an image of the marks on the ground. "These blank spaces are from dragging the body and then stopping. Which means the killer struggled to move it. So it probably isn't a very strong person."

"But when we examined the body, we found very little resistance," Big Bao said. "There was no damage to the limb joints."

I flipped through the slides and stopped at a photo of the victim's bed. "Hm. This can be explained. If the victim was sleeping, he probably had that blanket over him. Then suddenly, someone pressed down on his body and the blanket held him tight. With his arms trapped, there was no way he could resist. That kind of force spread out over such a large area wouldn't necessarily leave marks!"

Everyone nodded in agreement.

Huang said, "If no one objects, let's make the arrest. And dig up that well."

Digging up the well was a highly technical job. When we were standing there with no idea what to do, some smart officer called a well-digging company. They wore miner's lamps and brought a crane.

Thanks to the diggers' neat, efficient work, a large pit soon opened around the well. Next, the bricks supporting the well were dismantled. The wellhead opened up, and the claws of the crane began dredging up debris.

Our moods rose and fell with the roar of the diesel engine. Every time the crane went under, our hopes shot up, and every time it came up empty, they were dashed. And so we swung back and forth between hope and despair for over half an hour. The diggers just kept working silently.

Finally, amid a burst of cheers, the machine claw grabbed something.

I quickly put on gloves and ran over to examine it. With the lights of more than ten miner's lamps on my hands, I suddenly felt like a star in the spotlight.

It was a plastic bag, heavy and full, and tightly tied.

"Wouldn't a plastic bag that sank to the bottom be full of water?" Lin Tao said.

I checked it over. "Look, there are a lot of little holes poked in it."

Slowly opening the bag, I saw stones inside.

"You were right," Big Bao said. "It was made to weigh down the body. Where does all this work get us, though? What's the point of knowing there was something to weigh the body down?"

"Of course there's a point," Lin Tao shouted. "This type of cement gravel isn't found just anywhere. You usually see it around construction sites."

I nodded. "When the killer went looking for something to weigh the body down, he probably grabbed whatever was closest at hand. Is there construction anywhere near Jie Liwen's house?"

The detective shook his head, then paused and nodded. "Not right by Jie Liwen's, but a few hundred yards north, there's a house being built. We even saw a pile of gravel."

"I guess the disposal prep was done at the victim's home," Big Bao said.

I shook my head. "The well's south of the victim's home, and the gravel's to the north. It wouldn't make sense for him to go north and then south again."

"Let's not nitpick." Big Bao laughed. "I want to hear the results of the interrogation first."

But the interrogation didn't go as well as we'd hoped. Jie Liwen was agitated from the moment he was brought in.

"Shit, you got me in here; meanwhile the real criminal's out there living it up! I was unlucky enough to find a body in my well, and now I get dragged in here for questioning. You guys that clueless? Someone finds a body in their well, so they musta done it? Is that how you solve a case? Fucking unfair! Cops really are pigs!"

Back in the conference room, Captain Huang said solemnly, "We may have made a mistake, but we don't have a good reason to let him go. Jie Liwen admitted to playing chess with the victim that night, but said he went home at ten. And according to our external survey, Jie Liwen's behavior hasn't been strange recently."

"I don't think he's our guy," I said. "If the murder had been incited by the chess match, the response would have been spontaneous. But we determined the victim was already sleeping, so the killer snuck in from outside. We may have missed something important here. Why don't we let him go tonight, and when it gets light tomorrow morning, we'll keep working."

On his way out, Jie Liwen sprawled on the floor of the entryway, making a fuss. "I'm not leaving! You dragged me in here, and you won't get rid of me this easily! I want reparations! Emotional damage! Reputation damage! You don't pay, I don't leave!"

Depressed by the spectacle, I went back to the hotel, turned on my computer, and started looking over all the photos of the scene and autopsy from the very beginning.

My attention kept returning to that plastic bag. There was something familiar about it, but I couldn't think what it was. I lay down heavily in bed and quickly fell asleep.

That night, I dreamed of myself as a child, holding my grandfather's hand on the way to the market to buy groceries. My favorite dish was his mapo tofu, so I begged him to make it. At the tofu stall, the vendor took out a black plastic bag and used it to fish out a chunk of tofu from a basin of water. When the bag came up, all the water flowed out of little holes.

I woke up in surprise—it was almost eight already. I rolled out of bed and went to the bathroom to wash up.

"Hey!" Lin Tao yelled. "I'm showering in here!"

"No one's looking at your body, gorgeous. Don't be so uptight. I need to wash up so I can get to the task force and tell them what I figured out."

"I'm heading back to the scene myself. Last night I was thinking how there's so much straw in the well, but the straw heap is dozens of yards away. No one could have moved all that without some kind of vehicle."

As I brushed my teeth, I replied, "The corpse was miles away, so of course there was a vehicle."

"Ooh! Really? Well, I've got an ace up my sleeve too. Don't want to tell you now," Lin Tao said, playing coy. "First to the scene to get more evidence, then I'll tell you. But you should tell me what you figured out! How do you know the corpse was far away?"

"Okay. Why did that black bag have holes?"

"Don't know, maybe the killer thought stupidly that water would make it float?"

I shook my head. "The killer didn't make the holes. He was nervous throughout the whole process—dumping straw in the well shows his thinking was a bit off. Taking the time to poke a hundred perfect, tiny holes doesn't make sense."

"So then, what was it?"

"You go to the scene," I said, laughing. "I'll tell you at the station. You want to play hard to get; I will too. This breakthrough is something my grandpa told me in a dream."

28

"Our killer recently went to town to buy tofu," I announced. "That's a tofu bag. And, don't forget, Jie Lijun didn't cook his own food, so it wouldn't be from his place. That means the killer probably did prep work at his own home, gathering the bag, rope, vehicle, and picking up stones from the side of the road."

"The side of the road?" Captain Huang asked. "Are you saying the killer lives north of the gravel pile?"

"It's possible," I said. "The killer and the victim knew each other, so it's very possible there was some kind of grudge. Recently went to town to buy tofu, lives a little north of the victim, small, not very strong, could drive a vehicle, has a vehicle. It shouldn't be hard for you to find someone in the village who meets those criteria, right?"

"Sure," Huang said, "but we don't have any hard evidence. Even if we identify someone, we can't make the arrest, can't bring them in for interrogation without evidence. If that weren't enough, Jie Liwen is still sleeping in the vestibule, refusing to leave until we pay him for his troubles."

"Who says there's no evidence?" Lin Tao declared from the doorway, a photograph in his hand.

Everyone looked at Lin Tao expectantly. In cases without DNA evidence, trace evidence is a lifesaver.

"The straw we found in the well was thin and small, not bundled. That kind of straw isn't something someone could carry a lot of at once. The killer needed a vehicle to transport it. Last night, I realized a motorcycle or a scooter wouldn't do the job, so the killer probably used a pedicab or truck."

Lin Tao took a sip from his cup of tea and went on. "This morning, I went to look at the area between the well and the straw heap. The area's a mess, most of the traces are damaged, but pedicab tracks are distinct: three equidistant tire marks from the one in the front and two in the back."

Lin Tao showed the photo to everyone. "You guys find a suspect meeting Qin's criteria, and if he has a pedicab with treads that match these, I believe we can break the case today, right?"

"We have to!" Huang said, slapping the table. "Men, head out. I want you back with a suspect in three hours."

Before the three hours were up, the detectives were back—empty-handed.

"We found twenty-seven homes north of the victim's, with a total of thirty-two people fitting the body type."

"We checked all the tofu stands in town, and two of them use plastic bags similar to the one found at the scene. And the shopkeepers remember eleven of our thirty-two buying tofu from them recently."

"Of those eleven, seven do have pedicabs, but after comparing the tire treads, none matched."

"None?" I was a little surprised. "So you're saying we don't have a single suspect?"

The detective nodded.

"What about the other four? How did you confirm they don't have pedicabs?" I went on.

"There wasn't one when we looked."

"Then did you even ask them if they had one? They might have lent it to someone or something."

"We can't ask that. We'd reveal our investigative angle."

"Give me a break here," Captain Huang said. "You're going door to door looking at people's pedicab tires. Don't you think that might leak your investigative angle just a little bit?"

A detective sitting in the corner suddenly spoke up. "You guys? On the day the case was called in, I went to Jie Liguo's house to talk to the victim's family, and I think there was a pedicab in the yard."

I felt blood rush to my head. "Are you sure?"

The detective tapped a pen on his forehead. "I think so."

"But Jie Liguo is Jie Lijun's older brother," the lead detective said.

"And?" Huang said. "How many people have been killed by family members this year?"

"We didn't find any evidence of conflict between them. They just don't get together very much," the detective said.

"Well," Huang said, "Jie Liguo's son and daughter-in-law are awfully good to his little brother—maybe that's his problem. We just haven't had enough time to look into it."

"Does this Jie Liguo fit our criteria?" I asked.

"Yup," the detective said. "Skinny, bought tofu, he lives about five hundred yards north of the victim."

"Lin Tao, let's pay big brother a little visit," I said.

Jie Liguo was smoking in the doorway, a glimmer in his eyes. "What are you doing back here? My little brother died, so now you think I did it? Fuck off!"

I smiled, not responding.

Lin Tao walked back and forth in the yard, suddenly lay down on the ground, and then looked up at me. The slight crimp at the corner of his mouth told me he had it.

Lin Tao stood up, patted the dust off his knees, and walked over to Jie Liguo, bummed a cigarette, and said, "Dude, where'd you hide your pedicab?"

The casual question seemed to strike Jie Liguo square in the face. "What . . . what? What pedicab?"

"Your pedicab," Lin Tao said calmly, smiling at him.

"Pedicab?" Jie Liguo scoffed. "I don't . . . I don't have a pedicab."

Lin Tao didn't argue with him, just gave the detectives a look that said, Take him away.

His daughter-in-law, Liu Cuihua, came out of the kitchen. "What's going on?"

Lin Tao said, "Your dad's pedicab, where'd it go?"

Glancing at Lin Tao's uniform, Lie Cuihua seemed a little confused. She straightened her clothes and smoothed her hair as she lowered her head and said, "Last night he rode it off toward the fields."

We left an officer to keep an eye on the old man and headed toward the fields. I glanced back and noticed Liu Cuihua staring at us—no, at Lin Tao—in a trance.

When we got to the edge of Jie Liguo's field, we noticed a freshly smoothed section of the mud. Lin Tao said excitedly, "Is there a shovel in the survey van?"

A technician took a small shovel from the van. Lin Tao gave it a dismayed look and said, "I guess it'll do. Let's dig."

After some time and sweat, a pedicab wheel began to emerge. We all cheered.

29

Twenty-some years ago, Jie Liguo and Jie Lijun were closer, but then they both fell in love with the same village girl at the same time.

Which of the two thirtysomething bachelors should get to marry? Both sons needed a wife, but their parents had enough money for only one wedding, and for her part, the girl didn't know whether she liked the dark and funny Jie Lijun or the short, sharp Jie Liguo. The parents decided to let the older son marry and make the younger wait. They would look for a wife for him later.

On the day of his older brother's wedding to the girl they both loved, Jie Lijun didn't show up. He was found drunk in a bar, declaring he would never marry.

Happily, Lijun overcame his jealousy, and the brothers soon patched things up. But then Liguo's young wife died giving birth to their son, Jie Maomao.

Jie Lijun was devastated, convinced his brother had saved the child at the expense of the woman. Jie Liguo, grief-stricken, was angry and suspicious about what he saw as his brother's excessive mourning. It's my wife who died, he thought, not yours!

That feeling took deeper root in Jie Liguo's heart when Jie Maomao grew to resemble the tall, burly Jie Lijun more than him. When Jie Maomao was in middle school, Jie Liguo got drunk and told him he was really his uncle's son. Jie Maomao was confused at first, but soon he too began to believe his uncle was his biological father. It became something everyone believed, but no one wanted to talk about.

On July 16, Liu Cuihua argued with her father-in-law, and she was feeling sad as she delivered food to Jie Lijun.

"Uncle, from now on I'll call you Dad, okay?"

"Don't be silly; you're my niece."

"But Maomao's cheerful and broad-minded and so obviously resembles you. He's not at all like the man he calls Dad—mean-spirited, narrow-minded, holding grudges forever."

"Don't talk that way about your father-in-law; he's not a bad person."

"Anyway, we're going to take care of you, not him, in your old age. Maomao says so too. He says you two have the same blood in your veins, binding you more closely than just an uncle to his nephew."

"No, child, that's not right. I have my own daughter. She can help me when I'm old."

"She's an adopted daughter, not blood like us. And she's married and far away. We want to take care of you till the end of your days; you're so good to us."

"Ha, you're very kind, but please."

Unfortunately, Jie Liguo was listening to all this from the car.

Anger burned inside him. The affair between his younger brother and late wife had been confirmed. His disrespectful son was definitely a bastard. And the awful affair was his younger brother's fault.

In the dark calm of midnight, Jie Liguo was sleepless. He walked to Jie Lijun's house, burst inside, and smothered the sleeping Jie Lijun before he could react.

The traitor dead, Jie Liguo calmed down. He quietly went home, grabbed a plastic bag and some rope, and drove the pedicab back to Jie Lijun's. Ready to tie the bag of stones to the body, he noticed Jie Lijun's eyes staring at him in the moonlight. Frightened, he kicked Jie Lijun to make sure he was really dead. His hand shook as he wrapped the shirt around his brother's head, tied the stones on, and dragged the body to the pedicab.

On that clear summer night, Jie Liguo threw his brother's body into the well and covered it with straw.

When the police began their investigation, Jie Liguo carefully checked over his pedicab and was surprised to find a large bloodstain. The victim had been scratched and bled as the pedicab bumped along the road. Since he couldn't get the stain out, he decided to take the vehicle apart and bury it.

The blood from that stain was a match, and in the face of such strong evidence, Jie Liguo broke down weeping with remorse for the loss of his brother—and loss of his son.

"Who's to blame here?" Qin said.

"Jie Liguo's meanness," Lin Tao said. "But it must be unbearable to find out the kid you worked so hard to raise might not be yours."

"Yeah! What do you say we do a DNA test? I want to know who Jie Maomao's father really is," Big Bao said.

Lin Tao patted him on the chest. "Don't be so nosy, okay?"

"Hey, guys!" Forensic Scientist Gao said, pulling on my sleeve. "My treat tonight, let's celebrate."

"What, beef with noodles again?" I said with disdain. "Captain Huang coming too?"

"Huang can't make it." Gao laughed. "He's figuring out how to rebuild Jie Liwen's well."

30

"Good evening, everyone. Let's review.

"Victim one: Meng Xiangping, a thirty-one-year-old urologist at Qingxiang City Hospital, went missing on May fourteenth. His body was discovered on the outskirts of Dragon City on July nineteenth.

"Victim two: Zuo Fangjiang, the thirty-year-old CEO of the Tongtong Internet company in Nanjiang, went missing June second. His body was found on June sixth in a trash can in downtown Dragon City. According to all three cities' investigations, everyone with prior relationships to the victims has been cleared of suspicion. The two victims were strangers and have never had any contact with each other. However, we continue to believe these murders are connected, because both men were drugged with tetramine, killed with a cut to the neck, then disemboweled and dismembered."

It had already been two whole months since we found the disemboweled body and the Eleventh Finger case began. Given the gruesome nature of the crimes, the second body that had come to light, and the way the killer seemed to be taunting the police, we were hardly going to let it go. Besides, the thing was haunting all of us. Regular meetings were convened in the Dragon City conference room, but no new clues had been uncovered. The team was exhausted and increasingly worried.

"The video team's done all it can," the video unit captain said. "We've carefully gone over every second of surveillance video we have, but a lot of businesses' surveillance cameras are just decoration. We were able to determine that at six p.m. on the night of May fourteenth, Meng Xiangping was alone at the intersection of Yangtze River Avenue and Fanhua Street. And at eight p.m. on June second, Zuo Fangjiang got into a northbound taxi near the entrance to the ICBC Garden Road Branch. Those are the final times and places the victims were seen."

"Can I ask if, uh, Zuo Fangjiang ever went back to the hotel?" Big Bao asked.

"According to his hotel, Zuo Fangjiang checked in at noon on June second and left at five that afternoon. He didn't show up again after that."

"What about the cab?" I asked, rubbing my stubble. "Did we find it?"

"Well, yes, but it didn't tell us much," the video analyst said regretfully. "Because of the poor video quality, it took a lot of work to make out the license plate."

The lead detective on Eleventh Finger stepped in. "Yeah, so by the time we contacted the driver, two weeks had passed, and he couldn't remember where he took that customer to."

"They're so far apart: Yangtze River Avenue up north, ICBC down south," I said. "What about the tetramine? Any progress there?"

"We've done a lot of work tracking the source of the drug, but no luck."

"Could it have been for money?" I asked.

"We certainly can't eliminate that possibility," the detective agreed. "If these were spontaneous murder-robberies, and the killer is a psychopath, he's really going to be hard to find."

"What do you plan to do next?" I asked.

"Next, we'll keep looking into the victims' social relationships while we also continue to track down any new surveillance footage for the video unit to examine. They'll look for suspicious vehicles entering and leaving the area near the scene, and then my team will investigate them one by one," the detective said, stifling a yawn.

I nodded. "Sounds like you are putting in some serious hours on this. I hope we catch the guy soon so you can get some rest."

"Not tonight, I'm afraid," Chief Hu said. "A luxury apartment complex caught fire, and we've got a body."

"We'll come have a look," Big Bao said, gathering up his things.

"No need," Hu said. "It's probably not murder."

"That's okay. Since there's no Eleventh Finger work for us, maybe we can be helpful."

The luxury apartment complex on the east side of Dragon City comprised eleven six-story duplexes.

The crime scene was on the second floor of one of the buildings. When we got there, firefighters were gathering their hoses outside. One of the windows had been broken by the high-pressure water, but there were no clear burn marks around it.

"Hey, man, looks like the fire wasn't too big, huh?" I asked.

The firefighter shook his head. "Nah, didn't even see flames. We had it out in two seconds."

"Did you enter the apartment?"

He shook his head again. "No, that door is strong. The fire was out before we could break it down."

I walked through the building door, noting the security system there, and checked out the entrance of apartment 101. The steel door frame looked a little warped. I headed back out to the firefighter. "How do you know there's a body inside?"

The firefighter stopped gathering up his hose and looked up at me. "Oh, I get it, you're a forensic scientist, right? I read a novel about you called *The Corpse Whisperer*! I really admire what you guys do."

I blushed, too embarrassed to tell him I was the author. "Thanks. How do you know there's a body in there?"

"Oh." The firefighter scratched his head. "A cop climbed across from the opposite balcony and looked in through the sliding glass doors."

Just then, a Dragon City police officer arrived. He lifted his flashlight and said, "Hello, Examiner Qin. Good thing you're here. I'm pretty sure there's a body in there."

I nodded, put on my gloves, and looked at the front door. "First time I've seen a lock like this. And the door is made out of a really strong material, top-notch. No wonder you couldn't open it."

"And there's a glove mark on the handle," Lin Tao said, walking up with a small box. "No one besides forensic scientists, nurses, and sanitation workers should be wearing gloves."

"I swear I didn't touch this lock," I said, raising my hands.

"No." Lin Tao laughed. "I found it while you were chatting with the firefighter. Looks like it was made recently by someone leaving the apartment."

"Are you saying this is a murder?" I rolled my eyes.

Lin Tao lifted up the box. "Let's get this lock open and find out. How else are we gonna get in? The windows have security bars, and given the shape you're in, I doubt you could squeeze through."

"Shut it," I said. "You can pick this lock?"

"Got to." Lin Tao switched on his headlamp and went to work.

I stood behind Lin Tao with my hands pressed together in interest. "If you can open this thing, you're the man."

"I don't think it looks like a murder," Chief Hu said as he and Forensic Scientist Wang walked over. "We just talked to the security guards."

"Oh?" I turned and, seeing curiosity in the eyes of some nearby firefighters, pulled Hu off to the side.

Whether it's a murder case or not, we still have to keep investigations strictly secret—even from the fire department. Lots of people think the police withhold information for the sake of pretense. But actually, once information gets out, it makes solving a case much harder. For example, if someone wanted to take the fall for the real criminal, they could use key facts about the case to try and fool investigators.

"It's like this," Hu said. "The guards say the whole complex lost power just after ten p.m."

I looked at my watch: 12:35. "How long till the fire was discovered?"

"When the security office lost power, the guards went out to see what was going on and realized all eleven buildings were dark. There are six households in each building, so a total of sixty-six households. Only about forty-four are actually living here, and they all have a good bit of money. So at that time, it would've normally been all lit up."

"Yeah," I said with a nod. "With heat like this, there's no way these rich people wouldn't be running their air-conditioning."

"The security guards contacted property management. And property management contacted the electric company," Hu continued. "The electric company arrived at the complex at ten thirty and looked at the breaker, found a trip, reset it, and the electricity came back on."

"Circuit breaker?" Big Bao said. "Didn't they check which building short-circuited?"

"If there was a short circuit, resetting it wouldn't prevent another trip," Hu said. "They probably figured it was a random short circuit, so they reset the breaker, saw all the lights come back on, and left."

"So where's the circuit breaker?" I asked.

"It's on the corner of the back of the security building. There's an iron box there, and the circuit breaker's inside," Hu said.

I nodded. "So, if there was a problem with a circuit at the scene and they reset it, it still could have sparked, and if there was combustible material nearby, well . . . If the person in the apartment with the short was fast asleep or drunk, the fire could have gotten to him before he could do anything about it."

Chief Hu nodded. "The fire and power outage happening at the same time is too much of a coincidence. It's summer, so people are using more high-power appliances. We've seen a lot of personal injury cases from circuit breakers causing fires."

"But," I said, "when was the fire discovered?"

"After the electricity came back on, one of the security guards was still nervous because he recently read a news story about people dying in a fire caused by a short circuit, so he got his flashlight and went to look around."

"What time was that?" I asked.

"Eleven thirty," Chief Hu said. "About an hour after the breaker'd been reset. When the guard got to this building, he noticed the curtains were on fire and saw smoke rushing out of the windows, so he called for help. Ten minutes later, firefighters started putting out the fire, and our officers climbed up to the opposite balcony and saw a body on the bed."

"The firefighter I talked to said the fire was really small—they didn't even see flames," I pointed out.

"It wasn't that big, but there were flames. The curtains were definitely burned," Hu said.

"But an hour passed between the time when the circuit was reset and the fire was discovered," I said. "Don't you think that seems too slow? A bad fire should burn up everything in the house in a half hour. But only about ten minutes passed between when the security guard spotted the burning curtains and when help arrived. If our guys could see into the room then, the curtains must've already been burned up. That doesn't sound like a slow fire."

"I hear you," Hu said, "but that doesn't mean the fire didn't start slow and gain strength by the time it reached the curtains."

"This complex has a lot of surveillance cameras," Big Bao said. "I'll go have a look, then go over the map. See how much better rich folks' security is."

"Go ahead," I said, smiling. "It's going to take Lin Tao a while to pick the lock anyway. And after that, the trace evidence team will need some time to clear a path through the crime scene."

"He's picking the lock?" Big Bao said. "Why not just get an ax?"

"Are you forgetting what Captain Huang's doing right now?"

"Captain Huang?" Chief Hu asked. "From Yuntai?"

Big Bao started cracking up. "Yeah, he's working round the clock to fix an angry old guy's well."

"What are you laughing at?" Lin Tao asked as he walked over. "Come on, Qin, buddy. Door's open!"

31

"I hope you keep your job; otherwise we'll have a very clever thief on our hands," I said, sticking my head in to have a look. The first floor was neat and clean. If not for the pungent burning smell, you'd never have guessed about the fire.

Lin Tao and I went outside to the survey van for supplies.

"We ID'd the victim," a detective said, taking out his notebook.

"Yeah? Lin Tao, clear a path for us. I'll be right in."

"The victim is Dong Qifeng, thirty-two years old, one of Dragon City's youngest construction managers, part of a wealthy bunch."

"Oh, what a shame. Bright future," I said.

"Yeah, quite a rising star," the detective said, pulling out a passport photo. "She has a man's name, but she's a gorgeous woman."

The woman was indeed beautiful, and there was something majestic about her expression.

"She'd been married only a year. We're still getting the info on the husband," the detective said. "Dong bought the house herself, spent about three million. God, can you imagine money like that?"

"Since we suspect it was a circuit fire, I'm wondering about any renovations."

"Good point. The original developer renovated the duplex pretty recently. So if the fire started because of electrical problems, I suppose the developer would be at fault."

I nodded and offered the detective a cigarette. "Let's take a little walk—shouldn't smoke near the scene."

A few minutes and two cigarettes later, Lin Tao ran up, his face drenched in sweat. "All right, the path to the body is clear."

"That fast?" It meant the trace team didn't find any evidence—not good if this was a murder case. But if there was no clear indication that it was a murder, and there weren't traces to complicate the story, that could be a good thing. Accidents are always easier than murders for families to accept.

"I don't feel great about it," Lin Tao said. "The type of flooring in the apartment doesn't hold traces well. Unless shoes were dirty, they wouldn't leave a mark. We found a male shoe print on the first floor, but it has no ID value."

Maybe not, but a shoe print was interesting nonetheless. This was obviously the type of place where guests were expected to take off their shoes.

I didn't inquire further, just put on my jumpsuit and followed the passage Lin Tao made into the scene. The first floor looked totally normal, peaceful, with two pairs of high-heeled shoes by the doorway. I climbed to the second floor.

At the top of the stairs was a small living room with an elegant coffee table and stools. A tea set sat on top along with a wedding photo of a handsome man and pretty woman. I picked up the teapot, which was dry. There was no dust on it, however, which meant it was used often. The youthful, refined living room fit the attractive couple well.

Three doors led off the small living room. The floors in two of the rooms were dusty, which meant they hadn't been used in some time and that Dong Qifeng didn't have a housekeeper.

The principal scene was the master bedroom on the second floor. Just inside was a bathroom, its door closed, lights off. The space seemed peaceful, inviting, but once inside, I faced a horrific sight.

The room wasn't small, with plenty of room for a bed, nightstand, dresser, and TV, but it was devastated and blackened. Almost all the furniture showed clear signs of fire damage, with paint and finish peeling off. But the bed was the worst, bedding in ashes, springs bursting out.

A dead body rested on top. Most of its skin had been carbonized. It was hairless, the face unrecognizable.

"How awful." I sighed, remembering the photo of the beautiful woman.

"Was she burned alive?" Lin Tao asked. "I think I heard the 'boxing stance' is a sign of being burned alive."

The boxing stance means the body's limbs are curled up at the joints, which makes the body look like a crouched fighter. There was a photo in my college textbook of a burned corpse that looked exactly like a boxer, and ever since, whenever I'd see a fight on TV, I'd think of two burned corpses.

"Doesn't work that way," I said, shaking my head. "The boxing stance results from the muscular degeneration and contracture. The muscles contract, but the bones don't shrink, so the joints curl up. That happens whether the person is alive or dead."

"Then why would someone burn up like this with no signs of struggle or attempts to escape?"

Lin Tao seemed to be getting more and more interested in forensics.

"Oh, lots of reasons," I said. "Like maybe the victim was drunk or asleep, and the fire burned slow. Large quantities of smoke and carbon monoxide in an enclosed space will make the victim lose consciousness before he realizes there's a fire."

"Oh," Lin Tao said. "That makes sense. I think I've heard you say that burn victims rarely die of traumatic shock. How smoke inhalation and carbon monoxide poisoning making someone choke to death are much more common."

"That wouldn't be called choking to death," I said, trying not to be embarrassed for him. "When hot smoke and charcoal dust enter the respiratory tract, they cause a series of reactions that lead to throat swelling and suffocation. It's called acute respiratory distress syndrome."

"Right, right. How do you even remember all that medical terminology?" Lin Tao said, raising his eyebrows.

"It's my job, man. And there's another main reason why someone burned like this might not struggle: someone setting the fire after the victim's dead."

"But do you think it could be that big of a coincidence with the electricity going off?"

I circled the bedroom. The floor was covered in cinders and some water left by the fire department. Most of the walls were black from smoke. We'd be lucky to find any trace evidence at a scene like this. I looked at the most burned area and saw a strip of charred wire near the nightstand.

"In an enclosed room, with the combustion supporter unclear, we usually think of the place with the worst burning as the ignition point," I said, pointing at the nightstand. "There are wires here. Let's see what's connected to that outlet."

Lin Tao and I moved the nightstand away from the wall, revealing an outlet. A blackened charger was stuck in it, apparently from an iPhone.

The lack of discovery is a discovery.

I stood up. "Either the charger wasn't connected to a phone, or the phone was taken away."

"I think the case is clear-cut," said Chief Hu, who'd walked in while we were investigating the outlet. "Lots of people are in the bad habit of leaving their chargers plugged in all the time. I think, when the power went out, the victim was already asleep, and when it came back on, the charger sparked and set the sheets on fire. By the time the victim realized, she was already too weak to struggle."

"You may be right," the detective said. "I just got a call. The victim went to a bar to drink alone at six."

"I'm here!" Big Bao's voice boomed as he ran up to the second floor.

"I scanned the complex's surveillance video," Big Bao said. "The victim was dropped off at the entrance in an Audi TT, then entered alone as the Audi drove off."

"What time?" I asked.

"Nine fifty-one," Big Bao said. "Then the victim staggered to her front door. The entrance control system here is fingerprint activated, but apartment one-oh-one here is in a surveillance blind spot."

"So she probably came in and passed out," I said. "Though how drunk she was is hard to determine."

"Do you think someone accosted her at the entrance?" Big Bao asked, clearly fixated on the blind spot.

I shook my head and picked up two pieces of charred leather. "She changed into slippers. Would someone accosted change into slippers?"

"Regardless, we should get to the autopsy room ASAP," Hu said. "If it gets any later, we'll be up till dawn."

"I'll hang back and keep looking for traces," Lin Tao said. "If you find anything there, give me a call."

"Mind if I stay and look at the circuitry and surveillance?" Big Bao had recently really gotten into electricity too.

I nodded, then headed down the stairs with Chief Hu.

"Why does the chest have a wound?" I asked as Hu watched me use gauze to wipe charred clothing fragments off the victim's chest.

"Burning can lead to contraction of the skin, which causes a wound after a certain level of tension," Hu explained. "But you know that, Qin."

Burned bodies often show many suspicious signs of trauma, which confuses victims' families. For example, the phenomenon Hu was talking about can make a family think someone stabbed the victim. Or when high temperatures cause a skull fracture and large epidural hematoma, people assume the victim was hit on the head. In fact, it's a common feature of burn deaths that we call a "hot hematoma."

"Of course, but if the wound was caused by tension, it would occur along striae. It doesn't seem like this wound does," I explained, pointing. "Too bad the skin is burned so bad, it's hard to make out the striae path. Plus, we can't tell if the wound shows signs of vital reaction. If the wound was caused by contraction, there definitely shouldn't be one."

"Well, all this talk isn't doing any good," Hu said with a laugh. "After the autopsy, whether the body was burned before or after death will be clear as day."

Early in the Three Kingdoms Era (AD 220–280), County Magistrate Zhang Ju of the State of Wu did experiments with pigs to distinguish between those burned before and after death. The story of the successful field trial known as "Zhang Ju's Roasted Pig" was passed down through the generations. Zhang Ju discovered that whether burning happened before or after death is revealed by signs of "hot" respiratory syndrome—that is, the presence of carbon soot breathed into the lungs. Modern technology does something similar by testing for carbon monoxide in the heart.

Testing a victim's respiratory tract is often done with the "tongue scoop" approach. The forensic scientist cuts open the body's chest and abdominal skin and removes the sternum, then cuts the muscle along the lower edge of the jaw. Next, the scientist grips the tongue from underneath the jaw and pulls hard while cutting the connective tissue. This approach not only removes the tongue, epiglottis, larynx, esophagus, and trachea intact, but continues down to the internal organs. It's the most convenient way to get organs out if testing is needed, but forensic scientists avoid it if possible due to the toll it takes on witnesses.

Burn victims' skin gets very hard and takes a lot of physical effort to cut. By the time we got the abdominal cavity open, the three of us were sweating.

I hurried to remove the sternum and pulled out the pericardium.

"The victim's pericardium has a small gash!" I shouted. "The skin could have broken from burning, but not the pericardium."

Chief Hu and Forensic Scientist Wang quickly moved closer to see.

"You're right," Hu said. "There is a small gash. Is it possible you nicked it with your scalpel?"

To answer the question, I cut a V-shaped opening. The pericardium was full of blood.

"Definitely wasn't my fault," I crowed, filling a syringe with not-yet-coagulated blood. "The heart is also ruptured. If it were a surgical accident, there wouldn't be this much pericardial bleeding. The heart being stabbed probably sent it into arrest. Let's take this vial of blood to the toxicology department and get them to check the carbon monoxide content."

"But there was no sharp instrument that could cause cardiac rupture found at the scene," Hu said, "so it really is a murder case, and the power going out was just a coincidence."

Going ahead with the tongue scoop, we found the victim's respiratory tract very clean, no congestion or traces of soot.

"The victim died from cardiac rupture," Hu said. "The body was burned after death. You stay here, Wang. Qin and I will go request a task force be formed."

32

"What? Murder?" was Lin Tao's first reaction.

Some female officers stifled laughter at Lin Tao's surprise.

"Yes," I said. "The victim was stabbed in the heart."

"Preliminary physicochemical testing showed no carbon monoxide in the blood from the victim's heart," the chemical lab director chimed in.

"That means the victim was already dead before the fire started," I added.

"But other than some questionable shoe prints, the trace team and I didn't find anything suspicious at the scene," Lin Tao said. "It doesn't seem like a murder."

"The crime scene was destroyed by fire, and the killer didn't do anything complicated," I said. "So it makes sense if there's not much trace evidence."

"Can't be," growled a weary Captain Nie from the head of the conference table, irritated at having been called in in the middle of the night. "There was no blood at the scene."

"The heart doesn't bleed like an artery," I said. "It's surrounded by the pericardial sack, and we believe that the victim went into cardiac arrest after being stabbed, so not much blood would come out at all.

You're right that there should be some. But given that the scene was set on fire and then hosed down by the fire brigade, it's understandable that we wouldn't find it."

"That complex's security is flawless. Why hasn't the video analysis team got anything yet?" Captain Nie said.

"They're hard at work, I promise," the chief detective told him. "In the meantime, what should we do next?"

I turned my wrist to look at my watch. Already four a.m. Sometimes it seemed like I'd never see my wife again.

"I think we'd better get a couple hours of sleep," I said. "Lin Tao and I will take another look at the scene in the daylight."

Captain Nie nodded. "You've been working hard. While you're resting, I want the investigation division to track Dong Qifeng's last movements, who she met with and who she talked to on the phone. I want all relevant physicochemical and DNA test results by morning too!"

When I heard his words, my exhausted body slumped, embracing the promise of imminent sleep.

Just then, Chief Hu jogged into the room. "Looks like we'll be here all night, men."

"What's up?" Lin Tao asked.

"A custodian at Dragon City University found a body in a remote corner of campus."

"Forgive me," I said. "I'll look at the body soon, but I gotta sleep a couple hours."

"Are you sure, Qin?" Hu said. "We think it's connected to the Eleventh Finger."

For two months, we had been desperate for a new development in the Eleventh Finger case, so the conference room buzzed with anticipation.

Captain Nie gave clear orders: "Everyone in this meeting room who has worked on the Eleventh Finger case is to head to Dragon City University right now. Wake up any task force members at home. Call in backup as needed to take over the Dong Qifeng case."

"So?" Chief Hu grinned at me.

Jolted awake by the words "Eleventh Finger case," I nodded hard and said, "I'm coming. I can sleep when I'm dead."

By the time we got to Dragon City University, dawn was almost breaking. With students on summer break, campus was quiet. A small grove the kids used for romantic trysts was already surrounded by caution tape and full of busy survey staff.

"When I got here, rigor mortis was beginning to set in," Sun Yong, the forensic scientist on duty, said. "We concluded the victim died about five hours ago."

"Right now, I'm most interested in why you think this case is related to the Eleventh Finger," I said, looking at the body in the distance.

"After the victim's throat was cut, he was disemboweled. The tongue scoop method was used to remove the majority of the organs," Sun Yong said. "Like in the other two Eleventh Finger murders."

"Yes, definitely similar, but this body wasn't dismembered, right? Transporting it all the way here intact would be pretty hard, correct?"

"We believe the victim was killed right here," Sun Yong said, pointing to the Audi parked outside the small grove. "That car belongs to the victim, Cheng Xiaoliang. License and registration are inside. The photo matches the victim."

"Cheng Xiaoliang?"

"Cheng Xiaoliang, male, twenty-five, the only son of Dragon City U's party secretary," Sun Yong said. "We looked in his car. Everything's normal. No signs of a fight, no blood. Campus surveillance video shows him driving himself through the gates at eleven last night."

"Was there anyone in the passenger seat?" I asked.

"No one."

"So the killer was lurking on campus?"

"Not necessarily," he said. "The TT is a two-door with four seats. If the killer hid in the backseat, the cameras wouldn't have caught him."

"Then would there be video of him fleeing the scene?" I asked.

"Nah, there are lots of ways to get off campus. Cars can only enter through the north, south, east, and west gates, but people can go through the smaller entrances where there are no cameras."

"Once again, the throat was cut after the victim was drugged," Lin Tao said, pointing to the ground near the body. "How much you wanna bet it's tetramine?"

There was a lot of blood on the grass from the complex wound on the victim's neck. It looked like the victim had been defenseless when the carotid artery was severed.

"This is definitely the primary murder scene. Let's get back to the autopsy room ASAP," Chief Hu said.

It felt strange to rush to the autopsy room twice in the same night. Everyone was excited about another Eleventh Finger murder, but grim at the prospect of it going unsolved and of the killer continuing to beat us. And with the burn victim on top of it, we were feeling a little overwhelmed.

"The other bodies were dismembered before they were discarded. Why aren't there any signs of dismemberment this time?" I asked.

Chief Hu said, "Maybe the dismemberments were just to make the corpses easier to discard. They were probably killed and dismembered indoors. That wasn't to attract our attention—the disembowelment was.

So, since this murder was done in a secluded area outside, there was no need to dismember. This is personal, Qin. The Eleventh Finger killer is talking directly to us."

"Why was Cheng Xiaoliang heading to campus in the middle of the night?" Sun Yong said. "There are no faculty residences on campus, and the students are supposed to be on break."

"Maybe some of them stuck around," I suggested.

He nodded. "You're right, that's totally possible. And maybe Cheng Xiaoliang had some beef with another student and they got in a fight. And it just happened to be the same person responsible for the Eleventh Finger crimes! Could the serial killer be an undergrad?"

"Whoa, what the hell is this?" Hu, who was examining the victim's organs, suddenly shouted.

When examining the scene and body, I'd caught a strong odor of formalin, a solution of water and formaldehyde that forensic scientists use to preserve human tissue. It's easy to prepare, but laypeople don't use it, so I'd assumed I was hallucinating from sleep deprivation. Then I saw the object in Hu's hand.

Hu was holding a formalin-soaked ear. We all looked at Cheng Xiaoliang's head. Both ears were intact. So whose ear was it? My mind churned as I thought about the bodies of Zuo Fangjiang and Meng Xiangping. Suddenly, I had an epiphany.

I took off my gloves and pulled out the autopsy files. "I was right! When we found Fangjiang's corpse, it was missing an ear!"

"Really?" Hu said. "I completely forgot."

"Really!" I showed the record to Hu and said, "This is Zuo Fangjiang's ear! Even though we found him later, don't forget that Meng Xiangping died first. He was missing a finger. And we found Zuo Fangjiang first, but he was killed second—had an extra finger on him, but was missing an ear. If this is the killer's calling card, then Cheng Xiaoliang with this extra ear should be missing something else."

All of us scrambled to check over the body.

"Not missing anything but his internal organs," Sun Yong said, a little disappointed.

I looked at one end of the victim's trachea. There were knife marks going upward from the hyoid bone. I pinched open the oral cavity—rigor mortis hadn't fully set in. The cavity was empty.

"I got it. He took Cheng Xiaoliang's tongue."

"My God! The killer really is trying to provoke us!" Hu said. He ground his teeth. "He did the tongue scoop to remove the organs and left part of another body to tell us it's part of a series. Plus, he thinks like a forensic scientist! Who could be this messed up? What did we do to him?"

"The killer really is highly skilled," I said. "There are no good clues on this body. We'll have to look into Cheng Xiaoliang's relationships. The more people this guy kills, the more we learn his style. I just wish we had an angle for breaking the case."

"Damn," Sun Yong said. "He knows a lot about forensics, but that doesn't necessarily mean he knows a lot about criminal investigations. Hopefully the detectives can find something this time. We can't let this bastard keep killing."

"For now, let's get some sleep. Tomorrow we'll have not one but two special task force meetings." Hu laughed. "Up to our ears in murders around here."

I nodded wearily. "Yeah, I need to sleep. Lin Tao and I will go back and recheck Dong Qifeng's apartment tomorrow at noon."

After sleeping a few hours, I felt a little better. Walking outside, I saw my downstairs neighbor. The college girl was striking up a conversation with Lin Tao by the police car. I smiled. Girls are so forward these days, and men are shyer than ever. The world's changed.

Lips sealed, I sat my butt down in the car and waited pointedly.

Lin Tao said to her, "Sorry, gotta go. Let's talk again soon," then climbed inside too.

"Where to, gentlemen?" Han Liang asked.

"Dong Qifeng's house," Lin Tao said, then turned to me. "What took you so long, old man? If you were any slower, that girl would have gotten my number."

"Is that so bad? College student, charming."

"Come on." Lin Tao sighed. "Is anyone as charming as Su Mei? Not to mention a brilliant, badass crime scene investigator. Now that's a woman."

Before we knew it, we were at the scene. Lin Tao and I suited up and headed in.

"Since it's a murder case, there must be entrance and exit points," I said. "The area around the apartment is so heavily guarded, though."

"The exit isn't hard," Lin Tao said. "The front door on the first floor. That explains the shoe print and the glove mark I found, plus Big Bao told us the unit entrance door is a surveillance blind spot. But the entrance point is harder. You already eliminated the possibility that the killer followed the victim inside. Most of the windows have security bars, so the only possible entrance point is right here."

Lin Tao pointed to the small window in the master bath. It didn't have security bars.

I looked at it in shock. "It's so small, though. My head couldn't even fit through!"

"Your head is pretty big, Qin. No, I know. Of course it couldn't go through. I tried myself yesterday, couldn't do it," Lin Tao said.

"Maybe if the person was really, really thin?"

"One way to find out! There's a security camera outside this window. If they came in here, it was definitely recorded," Lin Tao said.

"Excellent. We'll just have to wait to hear from Big Bao."

"Hey, look over here," a technician said, opening the cabinet door of the nightstand.

The inside edge of the door hadn't been damaged in the fire, and blood spatter was visible all along it.

"Great eye!" I clapped him on the shoulder. "That solves one problem."

"When the victim was stabbed, the cabinet was open!" Lin Tao exclaimed.

I smiled and nodded. "So, the killer closed the cabinet afterward. That means he left us a clue!"

"But this blood probably just belongs to the victim. What new information could it give us?" the technician asked.

Lin Tao and I spoke at the same time. "Motive!"

I looked at Lin Tao and smiled. "If it was some kind of personal crime—revenge, passion—why go through the nightstand? And the victim's iPhone is gone. What does that tell you?"

"Oh, you think it was a robbery?" the technician said.

"Right," I said. "And not 'think'—it's basically certain. This was a burglary that turned into robbery and murder when the victim either woke up or came home unexpectedly."

"Based on the entrance and exit points, the nightstand door, and the missing cell phone," Lin Tao said, "I agree that it's a case of an interrupted robbery, not a premeditated killing. We'd better hurry to the task force."

As soon as we entered the conference room, Chief Hu boomed, "What took you so long? We've got a clue!"

"What is it?" I asked, taking out my notebook.

"Well," the lead detective said, "we detected human sperm on the vaginal swabs you did on Dong Qifeng. And listen to this. It matches the other victim, Cheng Xiaoliang."

33

"What?" I was shocked. "How is a basic robbery-murder-arson case linked with the Eleventh Finger killer?"

"We couldn't make sense of it at first either, but then we uncovered some things related to Dong Qifeng's recent activities."

The detective flipped through his notebook, organized his thoughts, and said, "Dong Qifeng got married a year ago, but no kids. She and her husband made an appointment at the hospital to get their fertility checked, but her husband found it insulting, so he fought with her, then left."

I'd been married for a little over six months myself, and we were hoping for kids too. As the daughter of a prominent OB/GYN, Ling Dang never felt awkward dealing with body-related stuff. She'd even recently suggested we go to her mother's department at the hospital to see why nothing had happened yet. I wasn't opposed, but actually getting there kept getting delayed by work. Looked like I'd have to make time to go after I was finished with this case. I didn't think there was anything wrong with me, but no harm in checking things out.

The detective went on. "According to our investigation, Dong Qifeng's husband is the son of farmers. After graduating college, he applied for an entry-level position at a small company in Dragon City. Maybe because of the difference in income and status—the woman high and the man low—the marriage to Dong Qifeng made him insecure. A week ago, he took a temporary leave from his job and left home. He's been back home in Henan, helping his parents on the farm. He hasn't had any unusual contact with anyone, so we're not considering him a suspect. As for Dong Qifeng, our research shows that she's been in a bad way since he left. She texted him every night. It started as scolding, then turned to begging. The evening of August fourth, after getting off work, Dong Qifeng went downtown to a bar called 108 Degrees by herself. But according to the surveillance video, she left the bar with a man at eight o'clock."

"Cheng Xiaoliang, right?" I said.

"Yup. Regulars and staff say Cheng Xiaoliang likes to go to that bar to pick up girls. His usual method is to take the girl out to his car and drink wine, then, you know."

"You know what?" Big Bao asked.

Everyone stared at him a second.

"You mean the two of them had already had sexual contact before Cheng Xiaoliang dropped her at the gate of the complex?" I asked, remembering Big Bao's report of an Audi TT on the surveillance footage. There was also a TT at the scene where Cheng Xiaoliang's body was found.

The detective nodded.

"Interesting, but is any of this really useful?" I said. "First, we know from the video that Cheng Xiaoliang didn't kill Dong Qifeng. Second, the same person couldn't have killed Cheng Xiaoliang and Dong Qifeng because they were both killed around eleven, and they were far apart by then. Not to mention that Cheng Xiaoliang was disemboweled, which takes time."

"But couldn't someone have hired two people to kill Qifeng and Xiaoliang separately?" the detective said.

I shook my head. "At the scene just now, we found evidence that the killer went through Dong Qifeng's nightstand and stole her iPhone. Although we're sure Xiaoliang's death is part of the Eleventh Finger series of murders, the Eleventh Finger killer clearly isn't a petty thief."

"Do you really think the two of them having sex and then being killed could be a complete coincidence?" Big Bao said.

"Sure, why not? Of course, we have to keep looking into their social contacts, especially any unusual opposite-sex relationships. I propose we split the task force between the two cases and communicate in a timely fashion. Do we have any clues from the time after Cheng Xiaoliang dropped off Dong Qifeng?"

"No. From the surveillance video, it looks like he went straight to campus. His phone records don't show that he contacted anyone at all."

So the Eleventh Finger case had hit a dead end once again. For a few moments, the task force sat in silent frustration.

"Oh, Big Bao, I wanted to ask you," Lin Tao said. "We determined Dong Qifeng's killer must have gotten in through a window in the master bathroom. Did you see anything on the surveillance video?"

"Not a thing," Big Bao said, and spread out a blueprint. "But when the complex lost power, the cameras turned off."

"Oh right!" Lin Tao slapped the table. "So what do you think?"

"Uh, I think," Big Bao said, pushing up his glasses, "the circuitry is such that each apartment has its own breaker, all of which connect to the unit breaker. Those unit breakers are connected to building breakers, which are finally all connected to a master breaker behind the security office. Supposedly, the electric company worker reset the master breaker and the whole complex got electricity back, but there's a big problem there."

"What problem?"

"If it was some kind of short circuit, then the individual apartment breaker should have been reset first, then the unit breaker, the building breaker, and only then the master breaker. If the electric company just reset the master breaker, the people in the building with the short couldn't have gotten electricity back. So why did they?"

"You're saying someone intentionally turned the breaker off?"

Big Bao nodded. "Right. Adding in your nightstand discovery, I'm thinking the killer turned off the electricity to the whole complex and went in through the window. When he accidentally hit the nightstand and woke Dong Qifeng up, he stabbed her, then grabbed the valuables and lit the room on fire. Next, he left through the front door. The cameras were still out, so none of it was caught on tape."

"So did he know his way around the complex, or was it dumb luck?"

"Oh, he knew it really well! Otherwise, he would've gone right for the window without disabling the cameras first."

"Makes sense," I remarked. "Captain Nie, I think you'd better start looking into people familiar with the complex's surveillance system. It could be someone who works there, or a worker involved in recent renovations. Someone short and skinny who needs money."

"But there are probably lots of people like that," the lead detective complained.

"I don't care how many there are! Line them up for me," Captain Nie sneered. "This case is solvable, much more so than the Eleventh Finger quagmire. Let's catch the killer fast so we have something to show the higher-ups. City and provincial officials are already leaning on us about the Dragon City University case."

"Heh, of course, a little prince died," I said. "People like that contribute nothing to society, but they still get all the attention."

Another detective stepped in to review details gathered about Dong Qifeng's business contacts, which struck me as pretty irrelevant at this point, so I zoned out. A few minutes later, my phone began to ring, and Lin Tao's name appeared on the display. I looked around in confusion. I hadn't even noticed him leaving the meeting room. Stepping outside, I took the call.

"Where'd you get off to?"

"When I heard Big Bao say the killer turned off the electricity himself, I ran over to the complex to see if there're any traces on the master breaker."

"You do have a good sense for evidence—I'll give you that. Any results?"

"A fresh fingerprint, good quality!" Lin Tao said. "The killer put on gloves before going into the scene, but forgot about that little detail when turning off the electricity."

Heading back into the room, I interrupted the detective. "Forget the business contacts; Lin Tao's got a fingerprint. Don't worry, Nie. We'll solve this case for you."

34

When detectives asked Zhao Bifeng for his fingerprints, he turned and ran. He never imagined one of the detectives had been a high school track star. The guy didn't get ten yards before being tackled to the ground.

It turned out that Dong Qifeng wasn't just a resident of the luxury complex—she'd supervised the construction. And she'd hired Zhao Bifeng to install the security system.

Zhao Bifeng knew Dong Qifeng was well-off, so he figured her home would be full of cash. Also, she was so pretty that he wanted to have a taste. But before he made his move, she married an insecure man who followed her everywhere like a stooge.

On August 4, when he heard his colleagues say Qifeng's husband had left home, he knew his time had finally come. According to a plan he'd been developing for a year, he'd sneak into Qifeng's house while she was sleeping, find the valuables, then cover her head, rape her, and leave. He even had a condom ready. But when he was looking for valuables, Qifeng woke up and started to scream. He got scared and stabbed her.

When she collapsed, lifeless, Zhao Bifeng panicked. Murder wasn't the plan. He set the sheets on fire and fled the scene. We'd never have caught him if not for his fingerprints on the circuit breaker.

"Well done with that circuit-breaker situation, Big Bao. If you hadn't figured out the electrical system, Lin Tao wouldn't have found that fingerprint," I said. "Without that and that bloodstain the tech found, Zhao Bifeng would be running free and we wouldn't be able to focus on the Eleventh Finger case."

"I can't believe Eleventh Finger has stalled out again," Chief Hu said. "My guys have been looking into all of Cheng Xiaoliang's acquaintances. Serious social butterfly, this guy. There are so many people that we've got nothing."

"As soon as the case got linked with Eleventh Finger, I knew it'd get bogged down," I said. "Having too many people to check up on is one thing; detectives losing heart is another."

"It's not just losing heart," Chief Hu said. "Now that this is turning out to be a real serial-killer situation—and especially now that a politically connected kid is dead—there's a lot of pressure on us. The men are overwhelmed."

"The scene where Cheng Xiaoliang died is really clean too. Besides the blood, I don't think we'll find any other trace evidence," Lin Tao said. "Just like before, the killer did a brilliant job cleaning up, didn't leave any clues for us to find. What's the game here? Is he trying to commit a series of perfect crimes? It really seems like only a law enforcement professional could do that."

Big Bao furrowed his brow. "There's nothing more forensics can do at this point. We have to let the detectives take the lead for now."

"You guys have been working like crazy," I said. "I have too. I've barely gotten any time with my wife since we got married. She's starting to think we can't get pregnant, but I blame stress and the fact that I get called to a new murder scene every damn night. I'm gonna rest a couple days, then go to the hospital and get checked out. After that, I'm going to give the Eleventh Finger case some serious thought and figure out how to stop that demon from hurting anyone else."

35

Fertility testing was terrifying, but Ling Dang and I were perfectly healthy.

"Guess we just haven't been worthy of a visit from the fertility goddess," I said with a grin.

"You can't blame the fertility goddess for your being gone all the time," Ling Dang countered.

"I won't go anywhere today. Tonight will be all about making a baby!"

"No new cases?" Ling Dang asked.

"Shh . . . ," I said. "Don't jinx it."

Before my voice even faded, the phone rang.

"Look, look, look," I said, pointing to "Command Center" on my screen. "I don't know what's up recently! Every time things get quiet, bodies start turning up. It's creepy."

"Yanggong County has a murder case. Please come lend support," the command center officer told me. "We need all available forensic and trace personnel, so please inform Lin Tao."

"But," I said, gritting my teeth, "we're on Dragon City's Eleventh Finger case. I'm afraid I'll have to stay here."

"I'm following instructions from leadership," the officer said. "The Eleventh Finger investigation has no new leads. The detectives will call if they need your input, but for now, your assignment is the Yanggong crime scene."

Hanging up, I looked at Ling Dang. Her face was calm, resigned. Even though she didn't like my running around the province like this, she understood how important my work was. To cheer us both up, I improvised a silly song, opera style: "My darling wife, we can't make babies, and poor Lin Tao can't find a wife, all thanks to these dastardly evildoers! Once the intrepid young hero catches them, he will return to his beloved to start a family!"

Mama Zhao was over seventy years old, living in the east end of Yanggong in a small traditional courtyard house. She had several children working in other cities who came back to visit once a year. They gave her some money for living expenses, but Mama Zhao supplemented it by collecting bottles and cans, which kept her fit.

As dawn broke on the morning of August 11, Mama Zhao was going about her usual business, strolling through the little streets by her home. She passed by the "junk rooms"—empty lots surrounded with bricks that had once been used for depositing trash. Because cleaning out the junk rooms took so much effort, under the new system for garbage disposal, people now just put trash cans outside their homes for the garbage truck to pick up; the old junk rooms were no longer used.

It wasn't that Mama Zhao needed the scavenging money so badly, but she liked the thrill of finding treasures in the trash cans.

The weather that morning was dreary and damp, but there was no sign of rain. Mama Zhao was enjoying the solitude of the dawn hour when she suddenly glimpsed a bulging bag in one of the junk rooms, its top tied with a white scarf.

Ooh, such a big bag. What could it be? she wondered.

As Mama Zhao got closer, a heavy stench made her stagger.

Crayfish shells, she thought.

Crayfish was a local favorite in Yanggong. By the time night rolled around, the streets were lined with vendors and people drinking alcohol and singing. Several tons of crayfish were reportedly eaten in the city each day, which meant a lot of shells. Sometimes unscrupulous businesses tried to save money on garbage pickup by discarding bags of shells in residential areas.

Buoyed by her strong sense of social responsibility, Mama Zhao held a cloth over her face and dragged the bag a few dozen yards to an abandoned pig farm.

Won't bother anyone here, Mama Zhao said to herself, clapping her hands in satisfaction. She watched as the scarf came loose and blew away.

Two emaciated dogs ran up and dug into the bag.

Eat up, Mama Zhao thought. Less stink that way.

Just as she was about to turn to leave, the dogs pulled out one of those pink, flower-printed sheets everyone seemed to own in the seventies.

Who would use a sheet to wrap crayfish shells? Mama Zhao wondered, suddenly suspicious.

As the sheet fell open, Mama Zhao didn't see the pile of crayfish shells she expected, but a human foot. The sight scared her so much, she had to sit down. After recovering from the shock, she felt her sense of social responsibility rise up again. She kicked the stones by her feet and managed to scare off the dogs. Then she pressed one hand to her rapidly rising and falling chest while unsteadily dialing 110 with the other.

"Those clouds don't look so good," I said, leaning out the window. "I sure hope they've already done all the preliminary survey work, because it's about to rain."

"I think you're right," Lin Tao fretted. "The evidence has already been damaged by time. If the rain god gets involved, it could be really hard to find good traces."

Soon the sky above the desolate highway began to darken, and beads of rain began beating on the windshield. Han Liang had to turn on his headlights and slow way down.

"Shit," I said, cringing as we passed the waterlogged remains of what must have been a dead dog on the side of the road. "I hope it's not raining like this at our crime scene. Water changes the rate of decay."

"How'd the sky get so dark this fast?" Big Bao said, pushing up his glasses. "It's not a solar eclipse, right?"

"No, just heavy cloud cover," Han Liang said. "We won't be able to see a partial solar eclipse till 2020. And not a total solar eclipse till 2034."

Han Liang had grown up in a rich family. After retiring from the regular police force, he gave up the chance to manage tens of millions in assets to become a full-time police driver. Even though he wasn't highly educated, he had a lot of experience and often surprised us with his wide-ranging knowledge.

Big Bao started counting on his fingers, probably figuring out how old he'd be then.

I reluctantly shook my head at the science student who was outrageously bad at math, then turned to look out the window. "Please don't send us rain. I know you're upset. That's why I came, isn't it?"

Lin Tao grabbed the back of my seat and asked nervously, "Qin, who are you talking to? Did you see something? A ghost?"

But we were lucky that day. When we got off the highway, the sky was completely clear. Yanggong hadn't gotten any rain at all.

The classic novel *The Dream of the Red Chamber* has a character named Wang Xifeng who can hear others before she sees them. A forensic scientist with a good nose can smell a corpse before he sees it. Long before we saw the crowd of onlookers, Big Bao said, "Yup, almost there."

The scene was at the end of a long, winding alley. A bag sat on the edge of an abandoned pig farm surrounded by countless flies.

The distance between the junk room where Mama Zhao found the bag and the abandoned pig farm was about sixty-five yards. The police had already set up caution tape, but since it was a dense residential area, officers were also standing guard to keep the locals from trying to get a closer look.

"Examiner Qin," Yanggong's Forensic Scientist Jiang said, walking over to me as he took his gloves off and shook my hand. "So good of you to come."

Jiang was one of the few county-level forensic scientists in the province to obtain the title of Deputy Senior Chairman of Forensic Science. He was around forty years old, capable-looking, and humble.

"Still haven't looked at the body," he told me. "We just finished combing the area around the junk room, but too many residents had already passed through, so there aren't any worthwhile traces left. The only thing we found was this, in a crevice between stones."

Jiang held up an evidence bag containing a cheap smartphone with a cracked screen.

"The phone still works," Jiang said. "We got in touch with some of the contacts and learned that it belongs to an eleven-year-old boy, Bao Guangmin. The boy went missing five days ago, on August ninth. So our first thought was that he might be the victim."

Lin Tao put gloves on and took hold of the evidence bag. He took a multiband flashlight from his survey kit and shone it on the phone.

"No traces," Jiang said. "When we found the phone, it was soaking wet and turned off. The local trace evidence team checked for fingerprints."

"Soaking wet? And it still turned on?" I said. "What brand is that?"

"Knockoff phones are the bomb," said Big Bao.

"So, did someone find the white scarf the person who called the police mentioned?"

Objects used in the disposal of a body are incredibly important. Sometimes it's the key that allows us to break a case.

Jiang regretfully shook his head. "The Yang River flows past the pig farm. Once the scarf flew off, there was no getting it back."

"There really aren't any traces here," Lin Tao said, looking up. "What about call records?"

"We looked, nothing unusual."

"No scene, no predeath movements . . . Looks like we'll have to let the body do the talking." I rubbed my nose, put on gloves, and headed toward it.

A couple yards away, the stench hit my olfactory nerves and made my eyes water.

Before me was a very common, beat-up, patterned plastic bag. It was so worn down, the words and logo were all but invisible. The bag was soaking wet, which I knew was the result of the body's decomposition. The corner of a sheet stuck out of it. Once pink, the sheet was now turning green from body fluids.

Judging by the size and shape of the bag, it contained the entire corpse of a child. The opening was already covered with flies. I picked up an unworn jumpsuit to use as a fan and shooed them away, exposing a snow-white human foot.

Big Bao was scratching his head as he said, "How odd. The kid's been missing so many days, and with the state of the bag, it should be either all bones or badly bloated. How can that foot be so clean?"

36

Slowly, we opened the sopping wet bag. It felt slippery, almost soapy to the touch. The stench surging from inside made me dizzy. I unconsciously raised an arm and covered my nose.

"Why don't we go look at the body at the morgue?" I quickly closed the bag tight.

"Why?" Big Bao said. "Is there gold in there or something?"

I looked at the crowd and said, "The victim's family is probably here already, and they don't need an audience for this. The body's in bad shape; it'd be too awful."

Big Bao gave a nod. "Okay. Just looking at the foot, I didn't think it had decayed at all."

"If it hasn't decayed, why's it smell so bad?" Lin Tao complained.

I waved over the morgue staff waiting outside the caution tape. "Put the whole thing right in the body bag if you can. It's a child's body—we want to be sensitive."

When we took off our gloves and got ready to go, a husband and wife pushed their way through the crowd. The woman cried, "Is that my son? Is it? Please tell me."

The death of a child can destroy a person.

I shook my head. "I'm sorry, ma'am. We still need to do DNA testing to identify the victim."

"I don't need testing. I can tell just by looking. I can recognize him." Her gaze fixed on the morgue staff.

"Ma'am, don't panic," offered Big Bao. "Even if you go look, you won't be able to be sure. It's better to let us do our work."

"How could I not recognize my own son?" the woman shrieked, her face covered in tears. "He's my own flesh and blood. He's only eleven years old. Eleven. We never let him do what he wanted. Just pushed him to study. I regret it. I'll regret it till the day I die."

The words made the man next to her howl.

"I'll look," he sobbed. "He's only got one descended testicle; it'll be easy to tell."

"I can't let you do that, sir." I waved frantically to the morgue staff, signaling to hurry and take the body away.

"Lord! What horrible son of a bitch could hate me enough to hurt my child?" the man roared at the sky, and the workers carried away the body.

◆ ◆ ◆

"Whoa," Lin Tao said, frightened by the body as we pulled it out of the bag.

"How can it already be so far gone?" Forensic Scientist Jiang asked, wrinkling his brows.

The level of decay for just five days surpassed everyone's expectations. Because Bao Guangmin had a frail body, the rotting subcutaneous tissue was already partially gone, revealing the bones beneath. Half of the face bones were visible, and the right ribs were also exposed. Internal organs were visible through the gaps. The arms and legs were beginning to turn dark green, and the skin on the hands and the right foot was almost all gone.

But the writhing maggots were the worst part. From far away, the body seemed to be moving, or made up of stampeding horses viewed from the air.

"That's so strange," Big Bao said. "Why is only the left foot not decayed?"

Starting from about two inches above the left foot, there was a marked difference in the level of decay. Above that two-inch band, the decay was advanced, similar to the level of the rest of the body; below that two-inch band, the foot was fresh. The difference was separated by a clear boundary as if marked by an ankle sock.

"Could it be because there just isn't much tissue under the foot skin?" Jiang said, then changed his mind. "No, his right foot is really bad, so that can't be it."

"Maybe he was wearing a sock?" Big Bao said.

I shook my head. "Even if he was, it wouldn't make a big difference."

"Right," Lin Tao chimed in. "When different parts of the body decay at different rates, there is usually a gradual change, but this body is unusual because there's a clear dividing line. Why?"

I thought a moment, then said, "I think it has something to do with why there are so many maggots."

"Ugh," Big Bao said, "I've never seen a body left outside have so many maggots."

"It's not just a matter of inside or outside," I said. "The body was wrapped in a sheet, then in a plastic bag, which was tied with a scarf. With so much wrapping, how did the flies get in? If the flies couldn't easily get in, they couldn't lay a lot of eggs, so there shouldn't be so many maggots."

"Yeah," Big Bao said. "It's got to be a group hallucination."

I elbowed him. "Be serious, okay? This is a dead kid. Didn't you see how the parents were crying? We have to catch the killer."

"So what's the relationship between the different decay levels and the maggots?" Lin Tao asked.

"I haven't quite figured that out yet. I'll let you know when I do."

"Gentlemen," Jiang said with an awkward swallow, "could we maybe do this autopsy outside? My bosses don't hire people to clean the autopsy room, so when we're done, we have to clean it ourselves. And if we get maggots all over the table . . ."

"How would that work?" Big Bao said. "There's no water outside."

"Let's step out and talk about it," I said. "The ventilation in here is no good. We're all dizzy."

The four of us stood around outside for five mindless minutes without coming up with a way to get the maggots off the body so we could do a proper autopsy. In the end, Han Liang solved the problem by offering us a simple spoon and bowl.

"Where'd you get this?" I said. "Sometimes it seems you can find things anywhere, even in a morgue."

Han Liang smiled. "Bowls are used to pay tribute to family members who have recently died. How could a morgue not sell them?"

Not seeing a way around it, I started spooning maggots into the bowl. Every time the bowl was full, I emptied it into an incinerator.

I tried to project calm, but it took tremendous effort to keep from vomiting. I forced a smile. "I've never done so much killing before."

Big Bao, who watched me go back and forth from the incinerator, said faintly, "I swear, I'm never eating rice again."

Looking at the bowl of maggots in my hand was really sickening. "Me neither."

The maggots finally vanquished, we took a closer look at the body. The outer layer of skin was gone, and the tissue underneath was very slippery. Wearing rubber gloves made it nearly impossible to get a firm grasp of the corpse's limbs, which made our work a lot harder.

First we checked his genitals.

"Only had one ball drop," Big Bao said. "Guess it must be Bao Guangmin."

"Yeah," I said. "His phone was at the site, the body's the same age, and with that abnormality, we can be pretty sure of the ID. Lin Tao, call over to local headquarters and let them know, please."

"Seeing a naked kid's body makes it impossible not to worry about sexual abuse," Big Bao said, gagging.

"I agree, but there's no damage to the genitals."

"He's a boy!" Lin Tao objected.

I ignored Lin Tao and turned the skinny body over.

Big Bao and I took out hemostats and lifted the skin around the anus. This was the flies' favorite area, so there wasn't much tissue left. There was only a thin layer of skin forming the baggy shape of an anus.

I used the hemostat to open the fold around the anus. "Sodomy usually creates a funnel shape caused by relaxation of the anal sphincter, but that's already decayed on this body."

"Oh," Lin Tao said. "That's what you're talking about."

"Look!" Big Bao pointed his hemostat at two spots around the anus that seemed to show some signs of damage, and the color was somewhat deeper.

I asked Lin Tao to take a flashlight and shine it near that part of the skin. It was indeed a hemorrhage.

When soft tissue ruptures, blood enters. Even though the body was decayed and turning dark green, we could still use different angles of light to identify darker parts where external force was used.

This bleeding tissue told us the body had been violated, and violated while the child was alive.

"This is a molestation and murder case," I said.

The Chinese penal code still reserves the term "rape" for women, so we couldn't say he was raped, only molested.

"That's a really important discovery," Lin Tao said. "They're still looking into anyone the parents had problems with. Since it was molestation, it wasn't revenge. Should I call again and let them know?"

I shook my head. "No rush. The two aren't mutually exclusive."

Examining the body did not go smoothly. We kept finding unexpected wounds.

"The victim's calves have lots of slashes, and they don't show a vital reaction. Someone cut him after he was dead," Big Bao said. "The cuts go all the way through to the tibia, the strongest bone in the lower leg. Was the killer just letting out anger?"

It made me think of the three outstanding murders in the Eleventh Finger case. Those victims also had slash marks on their tibias. It wouldn't be about venting anger. You could slash the face to do that.

"I think it's probably about wanting to dismember the body, but not knowing how," I said. "Like Eleventh Finger."

"Yup," Forensic Scientist Jiang said. "Look at this."

A few of the ribs on the right side were exposed. We'd thought it was the result of decay, but Jiang pointed out that the skin around the exposed ribs showed noticeable signs of charring and crimping.

"Since we know that the killer tried to burn the body," Jiang said, "those slash marks must be the result of attempted dismemberment."

"But the killer's skills aren't up to snuff. Neither attempt worked," I added.

Now that we knew what to look for, we found additional traces of burning on the inner thighs.

"I've seen a lot of burned bodies, but usually they're doused with gasoline or some other combustible. In this case, it looks like the killer held a lighter or a candle directly against the victim's body. How could that work? Stupid."

"Stupid," Lin Tao said with a sly smile. "You've got the suspect profile nailed."

37

We'd already been at it for over three hours. The afternoon light shone down as the unrelenting smell washed over us in waves. Desperate to be done, we started to divide up tasks. I took charge of examining the victim's stomach contents and determining the time of death, while Big Bao and Jiang started to look for the cause.

The victim's internal organs were too decayed for us to determine whether there was internal bleeding or congestion.

"The brain tissue has already liquefied. Let's see what we find when I move it," Jiang said as he carefully pushed the thick slurry of brain tissue down into the skull cap. "Aha, hemorrhaging around the petrous bone, a sign of mechanical asphyxia."

"I think I found something too," Big Bao said. "On the half of the face that's got skin left, I found some dark areas around the mouth and nasal cavity, which are probably the result of their being covered and pressed on!"

"Don't sound so excited about it," Lin Tao said.

"I'll see if there are any 'rose teeth,'" Big Bao said, ignoring Lin Tao.

"Rose teeth" is a forensics euphemism for dental bleeding, a sign of suffocation. The textbooks say teeth will become rose colored at their base during suffocation, a phenomenon that becomes more marked after they're soaked in alcohol. The textbooks also say that this method is somewhat useful, but not a sure thing.

That's because you do see it a lot in suffocation victims, but sometimes in nonsuffocation victims too. Forensic experts have researched the topic and have come to the conclusion that rose teeth and suffocation, though very frequently correlated, do not have a direct causal link. Still, being in the trenches of a forensic examination requires making use of every possible indicator, even if it's not conclusive.

As Bao prepared the bone forceps, I stood on the other side of the body, slowly sorting out the gastrointestinal tract. I used a scalpel to cut along the grain of the stomach wall, and the contents slowly appeared.

"I've got time of death," I said.

There was the crisp sound of crashing metal, and Big Bao froze.

"What happened?" I said.

"Uh," Big Bao said, swallowing hard. "The . . . The forceps slipped. The . . . tooth flew away."

"Flew away?" I said. "Go find it."

Even though any of the victim's twenty-four teeth would work, we couldn't just lose a part of a victim. We had to do everything possible to show respect.

We soon spotted the tooth on the ground. In the reflected sunlight, the base did reveal a faint red tint.

"With this much evidence, I think we can conclude the victim was suffocated by pressure around the nose and mouth, which led to death by mechanical asphyxia," Jiang said proudly.

"The time of death is clear too," I said. "Assuming we can find out the timing of his last meal. The shape of the rice in the stomach is intact and the stomach is full. Mostly rice, mushrooms, eggs, and tomatoes— especially rice. The food had just entered the duodenum, so the victim died about two hours after his last meal."

"Guess I know what I won't be eating tonight," Lin Tao said.

"The victim is Bao Guangmin, male, eleven years old, a fifth grader at Yanggong First Elementary School," the lead detective announced at the task force briefing. "He was an only child. His parents sell crayfish at night markets and rent a house in the city. On August ninth, five days ago, at one p.m., while his parents were washing crayfish, he slipped out the back door of the rental house and headed in an undetermined direction."

"Slipped out?" I asked.

"Yes," the detective said with a nod. "It was Sunday, so the victim should have been home doing homework. The parents were very strict about his studies, so we believe the victim snuck away to play. When the parents finished their work at the crayfish stall and arrived home at one a.m., they realized the victim was not home, so they started to look all over the city but were unable to find him. They called the police the next morning. The dispatch officer searched the area around their home but found nothing."

"Did Bao Guangmin call anyone before he snuck out?" Lin Tao asked.

"No. We looked at all the call records and didn't find anything useful."

The meeting room went quiet. Everyone was looking to me to introduce the forensic findings. I cleared my throat and said, "The victim died of mechanical asphyxia, likely from pressure around the nose and mouth. He died about two hours after his last meal. The principal contents of his stomach were rice, mushrooms, eggs, and tomatoes."

The detective nodded. "That conforms to our findings. The victim had lunch at noon on the ninth—rice, mushrooms, and scrambled eggs with tomatoes."

"In that case, the victim died around two p.m. on the afternoon of August ninth," I said. "We believe at least one motive for the killing was molestation. There was clear damage to the victim's anus."

Everyone lowered their heads and whispered in agitation.

The head of the task force, Deputy Director Gao Biao, said, "Then is our line of investigation flawed? It's been centered on a suspect."

"There's a suspect?" Music to my ears. "As I said, it might only be a partial motivation. It doesn't eliminate the possibility of enmity between the killer and the victim's family. What's the situation with the suspect?"

"The suspect is named Li Li," the detective said. "Male, eighteen, principal income is from crayfish stalls. He's poached business from the Bao family and caught a beating for it by Bao Guangmin's father."

"Then we definitely can't rule him out," I said.

"Oh?" Gao said. "You have any insight? Say the word and we'll arrest him."

"There isn't enough evidence for an arrest," I said. "I just think his age fits."

"You mean the crime was committed by a young person?"

I nodded. "There're two key points here. One, the victim was likely killed indoors in a remote place. An eleven-year-old boy would have the basic awareness to keep from being easily abducted. Seeing as he was tricked into going somewhere with the killer, the person who tricked him was either someone he knew or someone around his age, like a teenager. Children are more likely to trust teenagers. With adults, they're more cautious."

"Makes sense," Gao said. "I think I remember something like that from my college psych class."

"Second, we found a lot of strange wounds on the victim's body. Some of them are slash marks on bones that can't be cut apart—we suspect from a botched dismemberment attempt. Others are burn marks from holding fire directly against the skin—probably also a botched attempt at disposal. These methods for destroying a corpse would seem ridiculous to an adult."

"Yeah, but I don't think a teenager would think of them at all," Gao said.

"They would if they searched 'corpse disposal' on the Internet," Big Bao chimed in. "I saw a popular online post the other day about treating a body with lime, smashing it with a hammer, and dumping it in the sewer. That's as silly as it gets."

"Whether or not these botched attempts reveal the killer's a specific age," I said, "they definitely reveal a lack of experience."

"Time to bring Li Li in for questioning," Gao declared.

While we waited for them to apprehend the suspect and question him, Big Bao, Lin Tao, and I drove into the city so we could take a walk around. We weren't there to play tourist or eat crayfish from the food stalls. We wanted to familiarize ourselves with the area between Bao Guangmin's home and where his corpse was discarded.

Sometimes the drawings of a scene really fail to convey the orientation and spacing of a place, especially for those among us who aren't so good at math.

Bao Guangmin's home was in a residential area in the northwest quadrant of the city, the area with the most food stalls and nightlife. Bao Guangmin's parents were wise to rent there. Their house was only a ten-minute walk to their stall. But dense neighborhoods like that with the houses right up against one another were mostly constructed illegally. If a fire should occur, the trucks would have no way of getting in. There were no security cameras either.

It took us fifteen minutes to walk from Bao Guangmin's house to the road. Then we got into Han Liang's car and headed to the place where the body was discarded. The route seemed to cut through the city on a diagonal. A half hour later, we finally arrived at the southeastern quadrant where the body was found. It was also a residential area, but the houses weren't cramped together, and at only nine p.m., all was quiet.

I dialed the lead detective and handed my phone to Han Liang. "Liang, have an officer give you directions to Li Li's place," I said. "I want to take a look around."

We often called Han Liang our human GPS, because he traveled a lot, liked studying maps, and had a great sense of direction. There was nowhere in the province he couldn't find. He quickly drove us to the suspect's home in the center of the city.

Li Li's three-wheeled motorcycle was parked downstairs. The flat-bed contained cookware, his livelihood. Even though he lived in the city center, he commuted to his stall in the northwest quadrant every day.

The lights in his place were on, and weaving flashlight beams told me officers had entered to conduct a search.

I stood by the side of the car, thinking, and suddenly slapped myself on the head. "Idiot, we got the wrong person."

"Why?" Big Bao asked. "Doesn't he fit the profile?"

"Personally, yes. Geographically, no," Lin Tao said, thinking along the same lines I was.

We drove back to the task force where, as expected, we found a room full of frowns.

"Seems it wasn't him," Deputy Director Gao reported. "Nothing unusual came up during questioning, and there was nothing suspicious in his home. We're working on verifying his alibi."

"Yeah, he probably didn't do it," I said. "We were focusing on the criminal's characteristics, but we overlooked the key fact: time of death. Bao Guangmin ate at noon on the ninth and didn't leave home until one thirty. So there was only a half hour between then and when he died. Li Li couldn't have gotten Bao Guangmin home and killed him, even on his bike."

"Could Bao Guangmin have taken a cab to Li Li's neighborhood?" Gao asked. "After all, their age difference isn't that great, and maybe Bao Guangmin didn't know about the problems between Li Li and his father."

"No," I said. "Walking to a major road from Bao Guangmin's house takes fifteen minutes."

"Then could Li Li have killed him in his own neighborhood?"

"Also no," I said. "Dense area, victim died in the middle of the day, people everywhere. Plus, there's the molestation and the various attempts at corpse disposal. The crime must have taken place inside."

Gao looked dejected.

I understood. A case getting stalled like this meant more trouble ahead. Since the scene was destroyed and the body was so decayed, we weren't likely to extract any more clues, and we didn't have any good suspects.

After a few long moments of silence, Gao got up and opened the conference room door. "You guys worked hard all day; go get some rest. We'll stay here and figure out the next steps."

I accepted his offer gratefully. A good night's sleep would help get the horror of that awful autopsy out of my system. In the morning, I'd be able to get a new perspective on the case.

"I think," Big Bao said on the ride to our hotel, "we should focus on that line on the victim's ankle. It could be our breakthrough."

"Bao," I said, "great minds think alike."

38

After showering, I flopped on the bed. Lin Tao knew that I had a tendency to snore loudly when I was extra tired or shaken up. And examining the maggot-ridden body of a violated child had definitely given me a fright.

He eyed me and said, "Yeah, I think I'm bunking with Big Bao tonight."

Fatigue rolled over me like an avalanche. I began to drift off before I could even think about that dividing line on the victim's ankle.

But just before I passed out cold, Han Liang, lying in another bed, suddenly spoke up. "Remember on the highway, when you saw that dead dog—what'd you say?"

His unexpected words startled me awake, and I was suddenly moved. Han Liang had had a hard day too. As a full-time driver, he didn't get any free time, but his mind was still on the case.

"I think I said that water speeds up decay." Hearing it again, I felt a flash of inspiration and leapt up happily.

Han Liang was startled by my reaction. "So if the rate of decay depends on whether there's water or not, could the line on the victim's ankle be explained by water?"

"Yes, yes!" I shouted. "I love you!"

I raced over to Lin Tao and Big Bao's room in my underwear and desperately banged on the door. Big Bao looked surprised as I rushed into the room and sat down in a chair.

Lin Tao was already in bed. He propped himself up and pulled the blanket over his chest. "What's going on?"

"Han Liang helped me figure out the cause of the decay dividing line," I said. "We all know bodies decay faster in water, right?"

Big Bao nodded. "Sure. The body was wet. That explains why it decayed quickly, but it doesn't explain the line."

I grinned. "We've never seen a line like this before, because decay is a gradual process. What could cause such a straight line?"

Big Bao and Lin Tao both shook their heads in confusion.

"Standing water. Water surfaces are flat. Think about it. If the body was immersed in water, but one of his feet was sticking out, then the water surface would form a line like that around the ankle."

"But even then, there wouldn't be such a huge difference in the level of decay, right?" Lin Tao said.

"If we're talking about clean water, then definitely not," I said. "But what if we're talking about dirty water? Really, really dirty water."

"You mean like a sludge pit or septic tank?" Big Bao asked. "Why would dirty water like that have such a powerful effect?"

"I must admit, I have pretty good intuition," I said proudly. "Like I said, the line and the maggots were linked. We were wondering why there were so many maggots, more than we'd ever seen. That's the reason."

I grabbed a cup of water from the coffee table and took a sip, not caring whose it was.

"Maggots are the reason why dirty water makes such a difference. If the victim was immersed in a septic tank, the fly eggs would stick. And even though the body was wrapped up later, the fly eggs that were stuck to it would still hatch and accelerate corruption. The part below the ankle wasn't in the dirty water, so no fly eggs adhered, and it decayed much more slowly."

I looked at Big Bao, who seemed dazed, and added, "The strongest evidence I have to support this argument is how straight the line is. Only a liquid surface could make a boundary that perfectly straight."

Big Bao's and Lin Tao's expressions turned joyful.

"I'm going to call now and have the team check for septic tanks or still ponds near the victim's home," I said. "The victim died only a half hour after he left, so he was definitely attacked near his house."

"Then for now, our task is still sleep," Lin Tao said, lying down again. Then he stuck his head back up and said, "Damn it. The AC's too cold in here."

The next morning, the conference room table was covered with a map of the area around the victim's home. It matched what we'd seen on the ground—crowded little houses and winding, narrow streets.

"Residents' living conditions are better these days," a detective said. "When we got your call, we did a walk-around, but we couldn't find a public toilet or open septic tank or dead pond. The residents all have modern flush toilets."

"Really?" My heart sank. Even if the killer hadn't been caught, I hoped we'd at least find some septic tanks to help us limit the possible area where the killer lived.

I let my thoughts settle as I ran my finger down a road on the map. It quickly landed on a blank spot in the corner of the residential district.

"What's this?" I asked.

"Before the city redeveloped, there was a pig farm there. We didn't go in, but we got confirmation that there are no public toilets or ponds."

"Does it have to be a toilet or a septic tank?" Han Liang asked tentatively from the corner.

"No," I said. "Any place with very dirty liquid would work, but besides septic tanks and ponds, I can't think of what that would be."

"I could be wrong," Han Liang ventured, "but I think places where they raise pigs generally have a digester, similar to a septic tank."

"Digester?" I was surprised. "First time I've heard of it! Let's go look."

On the road, Han Liang told us about the appearance and function of a digester.

When we arrived, the place was overgrown with weeds, but some indistinct marks caught Lin Tao's attention.

"Those tire marks are pretty fresh," he said, eagerly snapping pictures.

Forensic Scientist Jiang and I walked ahead, and, suddenly, a huge pool opened up before us. It was overgrown with weeds that hid the surface of the filthy water. I threw a stone into it, which made a plop sound and caused many flies to take off.

"Whoa! This could definitely be the place."

"Why don't you guys care about these tire marks?" Lin Tao complained. "Don't you realize if the killer committed the crime around here, he had to transport the body six miles to dump it in that junk room?"

"True." I really hadn't thought of that.

Big Bao said, "So they must have used a car! But could a teenage suspect drive one?"

"Not necessarily." I shook my head. "You guys, what if the killer and the person who got rid of the body are different people? Think about it. A teenager still needs his parents, right? If parents know their child killed someone, they might help get rid of the body. Don't forget, we believe the killer was male, because of the nature of the sexual assault. But the bag was tied with a white scarf, which seems like something a woman would wear."

On the way back, everyone in the van was silent, thinking. The range of suspects had been narrowed greatly. And Lin Tao's tire marks were a big breakthrough.

At the same time, though, how could we take the next step and identify a suspect from this dense residential area?

Something in the backseat vibrated, breaking the silence.

Big Bao pulled up an evidence bag with a cell phone inside. It was Bao Guangmin's phone that had been found at the scene.

"What's this phone still doing here?" he asked.

"Oh," Jiang said, not bothering to look. "We didn't find any traces on it, so it's still in the van—didn't get a chance to put it in storage."

"Um, that's odd. The phone doesn't have a network signal, but it just got a WeChat message." Big Bao sounded excited as he warmed up to one of his favorite subjects. "You need a connection for WeChat."

None of us reacted. The kids all have smartphones these days, mess around with Weibo, WeChat, all those messaging apps.

Big Bao suddenly shouted. "Make a U-turn! Quick! Go back! Go back!"

Confused, but given Big Bao's breathlessness, Han Liang turned around and headed back the way we'd come.

Suddenly, Big Bao bounced up from his seat, banging his head against the roof.

"Holy shit! It got on Wi-Fi right here!"

Big Bao put on gloves, took the phone out, and started pressing keys. "Ha-ha! This is a private network that needs a password!"

"So what's that mean?" Forensic Scientist Jiang was getting dizzy from all of Big Bao's tech talk.

"It means the victim used his phone to get on a password-protected Wi-Fi network nearby, so when we go by, it automatically connects,"

Big Bao said excitedly. "Simply put, the victim was inside someone's house right near here, and they gave him a password to get online."

A stagnant pond. A Wi-Fi password. More and more, this was shaping up to be the bloodstained scene of the crime.

Big Bao and I took the phone and walked along the side of the road until we got to the point where the signal was strongest. We were standing in front of a small two-story building. Downstairs was a Changhe-brand van.

"All this searching—whoo—wasn't a waste—whoo!" Lin Tao sang to himself as he matched the tire-mark images to the Changhe van.

39

And just like that, thanks to the Internet, the case was solved.

The killer turned out to be a sixteen-year-old boy named Gu Feng.

Gu Feng wasn't gay, but he was extremely curious about sex. He was painfully shy, always blushing at school when a girl so much as passed by.

His single mother ran a clothing shop, which left her with little time to take care of him. He got good grades, but home alone after school, he would obsessively watch his hidden stash of porn DVDs.

Eventually, masturbation wasn't enough. But picking up a woman was out of the question.

It wouldn't be so bad to practice on a boy if I could get one to come over, he thought.

On the afternoon of August 9, Gu Feng was on his balcony, watching women on the street, when he saw Bao Guangmin.

That skinny boy almost looks like a girl, Gu Feng thought, and he threw a clothes hanger off the balcony.

"Hey, bro, can you help me get that?" Gu Feng shouted. "My ankle's sprained, hard to get down."

Bao Guangmin's parents and teachers had always taught him to help others, so he picked up the hanger without hesitation and walked up the stairs on the side of the small building.

"Thanks, bro. Come inside and hang out a while. I'll buy you a new mobile game."

Seeing Gu Feng's kind face, Bao Guangmin cheerfully followed him to the living room, got on the Wi-Fi, and started downloading the game.

Meanwhile, Gu Feng started playing porn on the TV screen. "Little bro, ever wondered about this stuff? You want to try it?"

The eleven-year-old knew nothing about sex, but he was afraid to admit that to Gu Feng. When he felt the pain, he started to scream.

Afraid the neighbors would hear and find out, Gu Feng covered Bao Guangmin's mouth and pressed him hard into the couch until he stopped fighting.

Realizing the boy was dead, Gu Feng panicked. He went online and searched for ways to dispose of a body, but nothing worked. So he waited till it got dark and threw the body into the digester on the old pig farm down the street.

The next morning, Gu Feng's mother saw police in the neighborhood looking for a missing boy nearby. When she saw her trembling son, she knew something was terribly wrong.

After getting the story out of him, she decided that leaving the body uncovered so close to their home was just asking to be caught. Being a protective mother, she went out in the middle of the night to pull the stinking corpse out of the digester, wrapped it up, and used her van to transport it far away from home. She was about as good at cleanup as her son was at corpse disposal, though. Lin Tao found DNA matching Bao Guangmin's in both the apartment and the van.

Gu Feng was charged with molestation and homicide, but since he wasn't eighteen, they wouldn't seek the death penalty. His mother was charged as an accessory.

"It's amazing how sex can be such a positive and negative thing," I said. "We all came from it. But it can also ruin your life."

"Yeah, just look at Lin Tao," Big Bao teased.

"Like you would know," Lin Tao shot back.

40

It had really been a wild year. Tough cases kept popping up. The forensic team got called in to help other cities so much, our department always looked closed and our families were forgetting what we looked like. People even complained to the Discipline Commission that our injury assessment work, which was used in nonviolent crime trials, was taking too long.

So it was no surprise when Binyuan City called. They'd found a body in the middle of nowhere, cause of death unknown, motive unknown, victim's identity unknown, investigative angle unknown.

Over the hot summer, we'd had a string of badly decayed bodies. Forensic scientists aren't afraid of disgusting things, but they are afraid of losing valuable clues and evidence to rot. Luckily, it was September now. Temperatures usually dropped.

Whenever a new case came in, adrenaline levels spiked. In ten minutes, we'd gotten leadership approval, called a car, readied our survey kits, packed our toiletries and clothes for several days of work, and were waiting by the front door for Han Liang to pick us up.

"There's an announcement," Big Bao said, squinting.

A poster on the bulletin board at the main entrance usually meant something important.

"Yeah? What's up?" I asked, setting up an out-of-office message on my email.

"Some kind of raise," he added calmly.

"What? A raise?" I shouted, putting my phone away. During all my years on the force, I'd gotten used to the pathetically constant salary.

The notice read:

Renewed Enforcement of Official Dress Code. Without exception, all personnel are required to wear their role-specific uniforms whenever on official business. Furthermore, all uniforms must be in new or like-new condition. Each officer will receive a few hundred yuan for new clothing items as needed.

"A raise? More like a straitjacket! They haven't been strict about dress code in years!" During college, I'd dreamed of wearing the forensics uniform, but after a while, the novelty had worn off.

"Clothes cost a lot. If you don't have to pay your own money for work clothes, that's basically a raise," Big Bao said, pleased. Big Bao actually liked to wear the uniform, because he was terrified of malls and learning to dress himself.

Hopes dashed after a moment of euphoria, I bitterly got into the car driven by Han Liang, who was already wearing his uniform.

Binyuan City was located in the north of my province, an area with flat plains and abundant resources. Despite its large population, it was a safe, stable place—murders and difficult cases were few and far between.

I think being a forensic scientist in a city like that has its advantages and disadvantages. The advantage is you don't work yourself half to death like some of us. The disadvantage is, with less experience, your professional competence advances at a snail's pace. That's why, when they came upon a difficult case, they called us in to be safe.

The crime scene was located in a small village near the western end of Binyuan, on a broad plain.

When we were still a couple miles out, I saw a reed marsh in the distance swaying with the wind. Blue caution tape was wrapped around the reeds. Since it was an undeveloped area, there weren't many onlookers.

Getting out of the car on the side of the road, we were met by officers.

"They put up caution tape this far from the scene?" Big Bao said, squinting at the police lights in the distance.

"Don't whine. If the tape's this far out, there's a reason," I said, putting on my shoe covers and equipment. Our team hiked in the direction of the police cars. We pushed reeds aside with our hands as we walked through deep mud until we finally arrived at the small pond.

The pond was in the center of a graveyard, though not so much an active one as an abandoned wasteland. An officer told us that rumor had it the pond water was running, fed by a brook that ran through the city. Reeds grew around the edges, as tall as a person. They went on in all directions over some miles of uninhabited land. Due to the graveyard's location, few people ever came by. Some local residents buried their relatives there according to custom, but it wasn't organized or crowded. On the long walk from the car, we'd see a burial mound every few hundred yards, some with stones, some without.

The scene was on the edge of the pond.

Binyuan City's Forensic Scientist Tao shook my hand, then started to bring me up to speed.

The case had been called in by a pair of high school kids. The night before, they'd gone to a karaoke bar in the city. When they were done at two in the morning, their school dorms were already locked, so they decided to spend the rest of the night walking around together.

While they were doing karaoke, it rained in Binyuan City. Even though the weather cleared up after midnight, the marsh ground was muddy. The girl was afraid her new sneakers would get dirty, so she proposed sitting on high ground near the road.

As they sat there talking and kissing, the couple heard a rustling sound in the reeds and saw the outline of a person in the moonlight. According to the kids, the silhouette was very, very tall and headless. It walked slowly toward them, but suddenly stopped, about a quarter mile away. Both parties froze and, before long, the figure, which they took for a ghost, retreated into the reeds. Frightened, they ran all the way to a small hotel where they talked for a while before calling 110 at five a.m.

When they got the call, two dispatch officers hurried to the scene. Seeing the size of the marsh, they called in a backup squad and technical team for support. The technicians soon found footprints, which led to a man on his back in the pond.

The man's head was lying on the shore, face stained with blood, chest submerged in the cold water. The technicians were preparing to remove the body when one felt warmth through his gloves. When he pressed the man's carotid artery, there was a weak heartbeat.

"Did the guy die?" Big Bao asked. "If not, why are we here?"

That made Forensic Scientist Tao laugh. "Lemme finish, will you? Our officers called for an ambulance and started driving in the direction of the hospital. The paramedics met them halfway, resuscitated him, and transferred him to the ambulance.

"Once they got him to the hospital, they found a wound on his forehead and immediately did a CT scan. They determined that an injury had knocked him unconscious. His skull was crushed by a depressed fracture, which caused a corresponding brain contusion and intracranial hemorrhage."

"Did someone hit him?" I asked.

Tao shook his head. "No. There was a frontal fracture and a contralateral-occipital-lobe brain contusion and bleeding."

"Ah," Big Bao said. "No need to overthink here. Such a clear contrecoup injury must have been caused by a fall. Doesn't that solve it? Someone went to the marsh to fool around, got startled by the two kids, ran, and fell into the water. Scene reconstruction finished! Why'd you even call us?"

I stared at Big Bao a second, then said to Tao, "Is he dead now?"

Tao nodded. "The hospital was preparing to perform a craniotomy, but before they could start, his breathing stopped."

"So what issues are you having now?" I asked.

"First, we're still not sure of the victim's identity," Forensic Scientist Tao said. "Second, we looked over the corpse in the hospital. There's a star-shaped wound on his head we can't figure out. The leadership currently believes the cause of death is accident or suicide, but from a forensic perspective, the wound on the forehead is hard to understand."

"Why?"

"The skin underneath the wound has a cystoid," Tao said. "Like you see when the forehead hits a hard surface that causes angular displacement, which is to say, there's a certain amount of shift the instant the forehead hits the ground. The shift causes the skin and bones to become staggered, tears the skin from the subcutaneous bone tissue, and forms a cyst."

"Cysts are really common in falls," I said.

"But that kind of rubbing displacement would have left mud on the face or at least in the wound, right?" Tao said. "And I think the star-shaped wound would have been unlikely to form on the muddy ground."

"There might not be mud because the doctors washed his face," Big Bao said. "And the shape could be explained by his hitting a hard object near the pond, like a rock."

"The doctors did wash the face, but they didn't do debridement and suture, so there should still be mud in the wound," Tao said. "And there are rocks near the pond, but we didn't find any blood on them."

"Either there really wasn't any or you just haven't found it yet," I said.

"Right," Tao said, "but we're afraid there could be a lot of controversy once this case develops, so we decided to ask you to come right away. I'm eager to learn from you and to get new insights into the case."

I smiled, clapped Tao on the shoulder, and said, "Thanks for the vote of confidence, brother. We'll do our best!"

Big Bao, Lin Tao, and I followed Tao through the marsh. The ground was soft mud. There were evidence markers all along our path, little signs with numbers on them.

"We found a few hundred footprints," Tao explained. "They've all been recorded. Some of them were ruined by the first officers on the scene; others are pretty clear. Right now we're expanding the scope of the search to find more intact prints."

"Have you done any comparisons?" Lin Tao said.

Tao shook his head. "We only have a few people in trace detection, so we just find them, record them, and go back and study them together."

"The victim was lying here," Tao said, pointing to a head-shaped depression in the mud by the pond. "According to the dispatch officers, there was quite a bit of blood on the victim's face, but by the time we saw it, as I mentioned, the doctors had washed it off. Still, we did a preliminary test of the recess around the victim's head and found no blood present."

I looked around. The marks in the mud were a mess, as if the police had been in a panic. On the other hand, the area around the pond had a lot of stones, a number of which could have made a star-shaped wound. And some were relatively clean and smooth, which might explain the lack of mud inside the wound. However, there were no blood marks on any of them.

"Maybe, when the police came to the rescue, they kicked the stone into the pond?" I said on a whim.

Tao frowned. "We really can't rule out that possibility!"

"Regardless, this doesn't seem like a murder case," Lin Tao said. "After all, he wasn't even dead when he was found."

41

The scene was simple, so Big Bao, Forensic Scientist Tao, and I decided to leave Lin Tao to finish up while we drove to the morgue.

When we arrived, morgue workers were just bringing it in. Tao approached with an enthusiastic hello and offered them cigarettes.

Given how much they see each other, forensic scientists and morgue workers are often friendly. The morgue workers envy the excitement of forensic work, while forensic scientists envy morgue workers' high salaries.

The body belonged to a small middle-aged man, who now lay peacefully on the autopsy table. Tao said the hospital doctors had washed his face, but there still was some dried blood there. The body's chest had tape from ECG monitor electrodes, as well as damage caused after death by a pacemaker and several small needle holes on the wrist.

"I've been wondering, since this body is neither tall nor headless, why did the students describe it that way?" Big Bao said.

"Not surprising," Tao said. "It's normal to see things wrong in the dark like that."

"Did your guys interview the doctors about how many needle holes they made? And if they put in a pacemaker?" I said.

Needle marks are critical for a forensic scientist. Injections are a very sneaky method of killing and favored by the smartest criminals. It's really not difficult to find needle marks, especially those made ante mortem. But if a victim is treated at a hospital, it complicates things. We can't differentiate between needle wounds made by criminals and ones made by medical staff unless we do complicated research like comparing the sizes of the needles.

"Five needle holes. They did try to put in a pacemaker," Tao said. "Our officers know how to preserve evidence; they've got that down."

"One, two, three, four, five needle marks here. Any way you look at it, it doesn't seem like a murder case," Big Bao said. He lifted the skin around the forehead wound with a hemostat.

"The wound could have been caused by a blunt or star-shaped object."

Saying this, I shone my flashlight on the inside of the wound and saw the tissue bridging from one side to the other. Because forehead skin is very thin, I caught a glimpse of the skull. It appeared intact with no protrusions that could have caused a rupture.

"This was probably caused by a blunt object," I said. "A stone would work."

Tao nodded. "I agree with that assessment, but don't you think an officer kicking the stone into the water is too big a coincidence?"

I didn't say anything, took off a layer of gloves, and picked up the victim's CT scan from the counter. Ever since handling the melted body that made my hands stink for days, I wore two pairs of gloves during autopsies. They kept the stink out, and once I got used to them, I found the extra layer didn't interfere with my work.

On all the bone-layer pictures on the CT scan, not one was normal. Looking through them, I determined that the victim's forehead had suffered a comminuted fracture. Since the periosteum hadn't broken, and it was just a common fracture, the likelihood that it was caused by a blunt object increased.

Meanwhile, the CT scan also showed me that the victim's head injuries were formed by deceleration. That means his head was moving quickly before coming into contact with a blunt object and stopping, resulting in the skull fracture and contrecoup brain injury. With that degree of brain injury, immediate treatment can usually prevent loss of life, but because the victim was out in the pond alone, the brain continued to hemorrhage. By the time he reached the hospital, there was no saving him.

"So he really did die from a fall," Big Bao said, looking at the scans in the light coming through the window.

I put my gloves back on and examined the victim's arm. "There are fingernail marks on both of the victim's arms. This wouldn't be easy for him to do himself, would it?"

I touched my own arms to experiment.

"It would be awkward," Tao said, "but it's hard to connect the marks to his death. Maybe he had a fight with someone, walked to the marsh, and fell down."

"Possible," I said. "An ID would sure help."

"I think we'll get it," Tao said. "Come on, gimme a hand."

Though a tough job, turning a body over without knocking off blood or dirt is elementary forensics. Tao and I carefully moved the body to one side of the autopsy table, then shifted it into a prone position. The body was stiff from rigor mortis, which made the process much easier.

"This looks symbolic," Tao said, pointing at a tattoo on the lower back. It was a crab with a centipede in its claws.

"I've seen centipede tattoos, but not crabs," Big Bao said, confused.

"His surname is probably Xia." Tao chuckled, playing on *xie*, the word for crab.

"Excellent! A tattoo like this definitely gets people's attention, so it should be easy to ID the body," I said confidently.

I picked up a surgical knife handle and got a blade from the disposable-supplies tray.

"Qin, what are you doing?" Tao asked.

"Doing? An autopsy." I couldn't make sense of his question.

"We can't do an autopsy," he said.

"What? Why not?"

"We don't have the ID yet. The bosses want us to get that first, then let the family decide whether we should do an autopsy."

"Huh? The Code of Criminal Procedure is clear, right? If cause of death is unknown, law enforcement has the right to perform an autopsy. What if a victim's family doesn't consent, so we don't do it, but the killer is a family member?"

"But the Code of Criminal Procedure also says we have to notify the victim's family so they have the option to be present," Tao argued.

"If we aren't able to notify the family or they refuse to come, we can just say so in the transcript!"

Tao thought this over a second. "That only applies to criminal cases, but we haven't found evidence of a crime here."

"But, Tao, we need to know the cause of death to determine whether it's a criminal case," I said, exasperated.

"Neither the preliminary examination nor the scene survey turned up anything suspicious," Tao said. "So, in order to protect themselves, the bosses want us to wait, or at least not rush. We don't know what might come up at the task force meeting tonight. Once we get a better grasp of the situation, we can make a final decision, what do you say?"

It was true that there were sometimes complaints about autopsies. Families accused police of stealing their loved one's body, damaging it, not respecting human rights. That the local authorities wanted to delay the autopsy to avoid trouble was understandable. Also, after some time in the morgue freezers, hard-to-detect damage on the skin would be more visible, so delaying the autopsy now wasn't the worst decision anyway.

At seven o'clock that evening, my team arrived at the Binyuan task force meeting room. The investigative and trace team, led by Lin Tao, was there as well.

Everyone seemed relaxed. Their work must have gone smoothly.

The lead detective was eager to start. Speaking in the local dialect, he said, "Secretary Zhao, fellow colleagues, let me begin."

The man in charge, Zhao Guanqiang, nodded.

The detective said, "At one o'clock in the afternoon, we determined the victim's identity and went to his home to take DNA samples. The DNA department just got the results back, confirming that the victim is indeed local resident Xie Qingong."

"Xie Qingong," Tao said with a laugh. "The crab that captured a centipede—fits with his tattoo."

The detective nodded and went on. "The victim, Xie Qingong, fifty-three years old, ran a small brick kiln and made decent profits— one hundred thousand a year, no problem. But he never married and had no kids. The locals think no one wanted to marry him because of his intermittent psychosis or mania."

"He was mentally ill?" I said. "Is that confirmed?"

"Yes. Although he didn't show up on any mental hospital records, we did find his medication records for mania treatment.

"According to surveillance video, the victim went downtown yesterday afternoon to a pharmacy before going to his son's home to eat."

"Son?" I broke in. "Didn't you say he was single, no children?"

"Oh, I forgot to say he adopted a boy named Xie Hao whom he called his godson. Everyone says he raised him all by himself like a real son. He manages the brick kilns now."

"What was the godson's reaction to the news?" I asked.

"Devastated," the detective said. "Xie Hao said that, last night after dinner, Xie Qingong seemed a little confused. But since he said he was going back to his own house, Xie Hao didn't worry much about it. Xie Qingong sometimes stayed over at his godson's house and sometimes went home."

"He usually went home," another detective corrected him, opening a map. "Xie Hao's home is in an isolated spot not far from where the incident took place. Xie Qingong's home is about a mile and a quarter north of Xie Hao's, also isolated. There's no surveillance in between them, so we have no way of knowing why Xie Qingong walked to the reed marsh west of his home."

"If he was manic, he certainly could have lost his sense of direction," Lin Tao said. "Our findings support the theory that the victim was lost when he entered the reed marsh and, once inside, could not find his way out. Then, because of his mania, he hit himself with a stone or else just slipped and fell in the rain."

"If I'm hearing you right, whether it was an accident or suicide, we have sufficient evidence to be sure the victim was responsible for the injury that led to his death?" I asked.

Lin Tao nodded. "Pretty sure. The victim didn't die at the scene, which doesn't fit the criteria of a murder, and based on our trace analysis, we were able to determine the victim's prior movements. Right now, we have sufficient evidence to prove the victim caused his own head injury."

"We do?" I gasped.

Lin Tao chuckled at my surprise. Then he cleared his throat and began to explain.

42

At first, the trace evidence team had taken a whole afternoon to sweep the reed marsh again. Since the reed marsh was very much untraveled, little could be extracted, but that wasn't necessarily a bad thing, because it meant each finding was important.

Excluding the area around where the victim was found, where traces had been destroyed by the rescue team, there were many fresh shoe prints elsewhere in the marsh. Since it had just rained at the time of the incident, the ground was very soft and the footprints had strong ID value.

After doing an on-site comparison, Lin Tao came to the firm conclusion that all the footprints came from the same pair of shoes. That is to say, only one person had walked around the reed marsh. And they didn't make one or two circles, but many. The prints went around the outer and inner rings of the marsh at least four times before disappearing where the victim died.

At that spot by the edge of the pond, the prints were mixed up with many others. Still, after eliminating the prints of rescue workers and police, we determined that the remaining prints belonged to that same person who'd walked in circles. There was no evidence of a second set of shoe prints.

I thought a moment. "But when we examined the body, it wasn't wearing shoes."

"The problem is this," Lin Tao said. "The victim was barefoot when the rescue team found him, but there were no barefoot prints at the scene, so we searched the mud near the pond. Sure enough, we found shoes with the same sole pattern and degree of wear as the ones that made the footprints nearby."

"I get it," Big Bao said. "You're saying when the victim fell, his shoes came off in the mud. And no one found them at first."

Lin Tao said, "So we can be sure only one pair of shoes walked through the reeds, and we have no evidence of another individual walking there. The victim went into the marsh alone. There's nothing that indicates this isn't a case of self-inflicted injury and death."

"Makes sense," Secretary Zhao said, "and the investigative team hasn't found any conflicting information."

"What's his godson say?" I asked.

The detective said, "Xie Hao is very sad and keeps asking when we can cremate the body."

Even though the trace evidence team had such clear findings, I still felt something wasn't quite right. I took the detective's laptop and opened the folder of photos and videos related to the case.

As I looked through them, I said, "Everyone's been overlooking something. The last surveillance video we have of Xie Qingong shows him buying medication from a pharmacy. That means he definitely took his meds that night. So why would he still have a psychotic episode? It doesn't make sense."

"Buying meds doesn't mean he took them," the detective said. "We asked Xie Hao, and he said he didn't see his godfather take anything. He may have forgotten or waited to take the medication before bedtime as directed."

The explanation made sense. I paused, and my gaze fell on a record of inquiry.

"According to this, the victim didn't usually have psychotic episodes, because his medication prevented them, but when he did, they lasted less than thirty minutes. We could say the victim entered the reed marsh in that amount of time, but walking around in so many circles would have taken at least an hour or more, no? If he'd already regained his senses, he wouldn't have gotten lost in the reeds. The reed marsh isn't that big; getting out wouldn't have been hard."

The conference room fell silent.

Big Bao said, "We can't rule out phantom disorientation."

Everyone started laughing.

"Phantom disorientation?" The detective said, "What, like someone being out in the middle of nowhere and getting possessed by a ghost? Who ever heard of a superstitious forensic scientist?"

The laughter annoyed Han Liang, who'd been quietly sitting off to the side. The elderly driver wasn't supposed to participate in case discussions, but he couldn't keep quiet. "Hey! You guys don't get it. Let me explain for Big Bao."

Phantom disorientation, Han Liang patiently told the room while I continued to look through the files, is a state of confusion. It happens when someone is out alone at night or in the wilderness and suddenly loses all sense of direction. They don't know where to go, so they keep walking in circles.

Phantom disorientation can happen to anyone. An organism's limbs have subtle differences—for example, each of a bird's wings has a slightly different span and level of strength. Likewise, a person's legs can vary in length and strength. If the stride length of a person's left leg is shorter than the right and he gets confused, he'll eventually walk in a big circle.

When people are alert, they use visual cues to adjust for physical differences. Those cues are lost when someone is confused, especially in a place with many similar markers like the woods or a cemetery, which exacerbates the confused mental state and results in phantom disorientation.

"Is this stuff reliable?" the detective said, no longer laughing.

"Of course," Han Liang said confidently. "I did an experiment once where I blindfolded my dog. She definitely ran in a big circle."

Everyone fell silent again.

"If you don't believe me, you can do an experiment yourself. Of course, phantom disorientation doesn't occur very often and it hasn't been proven yet, but that's just because scientists don't always study these things."

A detective was looking it up on his phone. "Whoa. It actually says the same thing online."

"Thanks, Han Liang," I said, acknowledging his lengthy but helpful explanation. "This is very interesting. Sounds like that could be what happened, but it's still a bit of a stretch, right? Tomorrow I'm going ahead with the autopsy."

"I'm afraid we can't," Secretary Zhao said. "The son wants cremation right away."

"What if I had solid evidence this might be a murder case? Then we could insist."

Secretary Zhao's gaze was firm. "Only if you can convince me."

"I think I can. First, the victim had fingernail marks on his forearms. They were fresh and occurred while he was alive. I tried different ways and found they're hard to make on yourself."

Secretary Zhao took notes rapidly.

"Second, if the victim hit his head and wounded himself at the scene, then there should be blood traces. The probability that the bloody object fell into the pond is very small."

Everyone looked at one another.

A detective said, "But what about the contrecoup injury? Qin, don't forget—the victim wasn't even dead when we found him!"

"I hear you. And without an autopsy, I don't have a good explanation," I said. "So I'll get to my third point. Looking at the original pictures of the scene, when the officers found the victim, the front of his shirt didn't have mud on it. If the victim fell forward into the mud and hit his forehead, that doesn't make any sense. Since the upper half of the body wasn't in the pond, there's no way the water would have washed it off. So where's the mud?"

The officers all looked at one another meaningfully. Now I had 'em.

But that wasn't all I'd deduced. "Fourth, I just watched the video from the officers' body cameras."

I hit "Play" on the computer, projecting the video onto the big screen. The scene discovery was pure chaos. Officers rushed to drag the victim out of the water. One pressed the carotid artery. He looked up and shouted, "Call one-two-oh—he still has a pulse!"

Chaos again, everyone rushing around. Some officers put the victim on a stretcher. As the officer with the body camera approached, there was a close-up of the victim.

I clicked "Pause."

"This image—what do you see?"

Everyone stared at the screen in silence.

"Please note the blood around the forehead wound."

"There's lots of blood on the face and the forehead too," Big Bao said. "Oh, I see now!"

I gestured for him to go on.

"The blood on the forehead definitely flowed from the wound to the hairline. Looks like it's already dry."

"Exactly! Gentlemen, notice the direction of the blood flow. If the victim fell forward, the blood should have flowed toward the ground. If he fell and then stood or sat up, it would flow toward the nose. If he fell and stood up and then lay down on his back, blood would flow to either side."

"Yes, but the blood flowed to the hairline. So after he fell, he must have stayed inverted for some time," Big Bao said.

Everyone gaped at us.

"Put us out of our misery, Examiner Qin," Secretary Zhao said. "Why did the bloodstain form like that?"

I shook my head. "I just saw the video a couple minutes ago, so I haven't had enough time to think it through."

"But," Lin Tao said, "why was there only one set of footprints at the scene?"

"True," I said. "Why was there only one set of footprints? Why is there a contrecoup injury? Why did someone dispose of a body before it was dead? I can't explain any of it. But it's suspicious as hell. And if there's reasonable suspicion, law enforcement has the right to decide to do an autopsy on the body."

"But his godson is really stubborn and totally against an autopsy," a detective said, looking daunted.

"Enough," Secretary Zhao said firmly. "I've decided. Tomorrow morning, we will autopsy Xie Qingong. Tell Xie Hao to attend. If he doesn't, make a note of it."

43

As I put on gloves and replaced the scalpel blade, I felt both calm and under pressure. Secretary Zhao's giving me the green light was an important show of confidence in my abilities and my intuition. Even though I had evidence this was a murder case, Lin Tao had evidence it wasn't. If we did the autopsy and didn't find rock-solid evidence of murder, the angry godson would make trouble for the local police, and it would be my fault.

Now that it had been frozen awhile, the body showed clearer signs of damage. The nail marks on the forearms had started to turn blue. Encouraging.

I dissected the forearms and found indisputable subcutaneous hemorrhaging—the victim had been restrained while alive.

"The victim has constraint injuries," I announced.

"Craniotomy next?" Big Bao inquired.

I nodded and used a scalpel to slice through the skin on the scalp. Dark blood immediately poured out. I grabbed a basin to catch it.

"How is there blood coming from under the skin?" Big Bao asked.

I shook my head. "It's not coming from under the skin—it's subgaleal bleeding. The scalp is dense; even if it bled, it would be very limited. This is coming from the subgaleal layer—the loose part that allows our scalps to slide around on our skull. Once it starts bleeding, it bleeds a lot."

Because the victim's subgaleal bleeding was mostly toward the top of the head, which didn't appear on the CT scan, and we'd been focused on the intracranial hemorrhage and skull fracture, we hadn't known about it until now.

"How can there be a subgaleal hemorrhage? Isn't that usually caused by hair pulling?" Big Bao asked.

I didn't answer as I separated the subgaleal layer from the scalp until the scalp was flipped down over the forehead wound. The skull fracture had cracks coming off it like spokes.

I used a magnifying glass to examine them. "I'm more and more convinced this is a murder case."

Lin Tao peered over my shoulder. "Why?"

"Look, the victim's forehead fracture has several central points, and the spokes are interrupted by other primary fractures."

"The fracture lines being interrupted," Big Bao explained, "means the victim's skull was struck repeatedly. You can't fall and hit your head in the same spot more than once."

"Even if it wasn't an accident, it could still be suicide," Lin Tao said. "Like if he repeatedly hit himself with something."

I shook my head. "We have to consider the injuries all together. Like Big Bao said, a subgaleal hematoma is usually only caused by the hair being pulled."

"So," Big Bao added, "looking at the two wounds together, someone probably pulled the victim's hair and threw him to the ground. That would result in deceleration of the head that could cause a contrecoup injury."

Lin Tao nodded, then shook his head. "But why would the killer not finish him off? Disposing of a living body doesn't make sense, does it? Also, why was there only one pair of shoe prints?"

I waved off Lin Tao's questions. "Don't worry. I've been thinking about this all day, and I've basically figured it out. Now that my suspicions have been confirmed by the autopsy, I'll explain it to the whole task force."

"Playing hard to get again." Lin Tao pouted, puffing out his lip.

I smiled. "Don't touch that dial."

I stood behind the podium in the task force room, shining a laser pointer at autopsy photos on the screen. Big Bao sat nearby, controlling the slide show.

"Based on the autopsy," I said, "we have concluded that someone wrestled the victim to the ground, grabbed his hair with both hands, and slammed his head repeatedly into the ground, causing serious injury."

"You still haven't answered my questions," Lin Tao whined.

"You're right. Well, injuries like this would have made the victim lose consciousness, which the killer probably mistook for death. That shows the killer was very flustered."

"That's not the key issue," Lin Tao said impatiently. "Why are there footprints from only the victim, not the killer?"

"Are you certain they're the victim's?"

"Of course! There was only one pair of footprints at the scene. If they weren't the victim's, how did he get there? Flew? Carried by a ghost?"

"Probably not a ghost, but couldn't a person have carried the victim?" I said.

Lin Tao was perplexed for a second, then said to himself, "Oh right."

"According to my analysis, after the killer thought the victim was dead, he threw the victim over his shoulder like a sack and carried him to a remote location."

I mimed picking up Big Bao, even though I definitely couldn't.

"Since he was in a coma, his head and feet were dangling. As a result, the blood from the victim's forehead wound flowed toward his hairline. Since the crime was committed indoors, not in the marsh, the front of the victim's shirt didn't get muddy. And this explains what the two people who called in the crime saw! The victim's body would have blocked the killer's head, so in the moonlight, the two looked like one huge, headless figure."

"How do you know the attack took place indoors?" a detective asked.

"Because of the shirt," I said. "And also, there was only one set of shoe prints. If the victim was killed indoors, he wouldn't have been wearing shoes, and the killer would have walked away from the pond without shoes."

"If the victim was carried like that, wouldn't his blood drip on the ground?" Lin Tao asked.

"Forehead wounds bleed relatively little, so if some blood fell into wet mud, it wouldn't be visible," I said.

"Then why did the prints make it look like the person was lost in phantom disorientation or whatever?" the detective asked. "Did the killer have that, maybe?"

"I don't think so," I said. "If the killer really was disoriented, he wouldn't have thought to keep carrying the body, just dropped it. My guess is the killer was searching for a safe place to discard the body, but panic made him indecisive. Then, when the high school kids shouted, he got scared and dumped the body near the pond he'd passed earlier. Since we didn't find wounds on the back, the victim was probably placed very softly on the ground, which would take some effort. That's when the killer's shoes got stuck in the mud."

"But if he left the scene without shoes, why didn't we see any barefoot prints on-site?" Lin Tao said.

"Because the killer was wearing socks. We know there's a little path from the main road to the center of the reed marsh. I think the killer probably left some faint sock prints on that path when he got away. And then the first responders barreled up the path and covered up those prints, which is why you didn't find them."

"That's perfectly possible," Lin Tao said, glowing. "It's a big area, sock prints are faint, and we were looking for characteristic marks like sole patterns, so we really could have missed them."

"Does this clear up everyone's doubts about it being a murder?" I asked.

Everyone nodded.

"Virtuosic, Qin. Everything they say about you is true, but now we've got a goddamn murder to solve!" Secretary Zhao laughed. "So, you wanna help us out with a profile of the criminal?"

"Of course. It's his godson, Xie Hao."

"Oh? Based on what?"

"First, the killer was flustered after the crime and rushed to get rid of the body. Especially if it was done indoors, the killer was likely close with the victim. Second, the killer placed the body gently on the shore even though it would be better hidden in the water, which indicates emotional attachment. Third, Xie Hao was strangely eager to cremate the body and tried to refuse an autopsy. Fourth, the victim didn't have other family, and our investigation hasn't turned up any problematic social or business relationships at all. Someone with a simple life like that—the killer can't be far."

Secretary Zhao nodded in approval. "Let's nail that asshole. Thinks he can murder his father in my district! So the scene of the crime is Xia Hao's home?"

"Seems likely," I said. "I think we have to do two things next: first, conduct a secret search of Xie Hao's home, and second, ask Xie Hao's friends to confirm whether or not the shoes found on-site belong to him."

◆ ◆ ◆

While officers detained the stocky Xie Hao at the brick kiln, we employed Lin Tao's lock-picking skills to enter Xie Hao's home.

It was a single-family cottage. Xie Qingong knew Xie Hao liked peace and quiet, so he'd spent a lot of money to buy him this house outside of town.

There were granite tile floors, solid wood furniture, and chic decor.

"Where should we start?" Big Bao asked.

"If your father was visiting, he'd probably be in the living room. Let's start there."

The seams between the granite tiles were all chalk white, but I found some marked with black.

"Bao, check this out. I bet you a bowl of beef noodles this is human blood," I said.

"Bet or not, I say it isn't," Big Bao said.

A quick tetramethylbenzidine test came up positive.

"All right, dinner's on you again!"

Big Bao was excited too. "Hey, case closed! I'll buy you all the noodles you want."

44

In addition to traces of the victim's blood, we found evidence of cleaning. And employees at the brick kiln identified the shoes we'd found at the scene as Xie Hao's, not Xie Qingong's.

Xie Hao tried to hold out, but after a few hours locked in an interrogation room with the bulldog-like Secretary Zhao, he was reduced to a sniveling mess.

"I loved my father, I know he didn't have an easy time raising me, and he gave me a better life."

"Then why'd you kill him?" Zhao asked.

"He was so stingy and indecisive. That's why we could never grow the brick business. I told him so many times: Put some more money into it; no matter how much we produce, it'll all get sold. But he always refused, refused, refused. He was the legal owner, so I couldn't do anything. I just wanted to get more business; that's it."

"So you killed him?"

"Two nights ago, he came to eat at my house, and I told him, 'Dad, you're sick, and medicine is expensive. With our current production capacity, we barely make enough to cover it. We have to expand production.' But for some reason—maybe he forgot to take his medicine—he started to hit me. So I reacted. It was self-defense!"

"Listen, you disgusting little ingrate," Zhao snarled. "I know you're feeling very, very guilty right now. But don't you dare bullshit me. Self-defense, my ass."

Xie Hao put his head down and started to cry. "Okay, fine. He really did start to hit me, but he wasn't that strong. I grabbed his hands fast and wrestled him down. Then he cursed at me, calling me a son of a bitch and saying I wasn't really his kid. I got mad and grabbed his hair and hit his head on the floor. I really didn't think he'd die or anything. I really didn't."

"How did you know he was dead?"

"I checked whether he was breathing—he wasn't."

"Idiot. If breathing is really weak, you can't feel it with your fingers. Another mind ruined by television," Big Bao said with a sigh from the other side of the two-way mirror as we watched the interrogation.

Under the interrogation room lights, Xie Hao went on. "I was so scared, didn't know what to do. I grabbed him and took off. I thought walking around the reed marsh would calm me down."

I tapped Lin Tao and Big Bao on the shoulder. "Let's go home. Zhao's got this covered."

"Missing that little wife of yours?" Lin Tao said.

"You know it," I said happily.

45

In recent years, most county police forces around the country had built their own autopsy rooms, which greatly improved our working conditions.

Once autopsy rooms became common, open-air autopsies became rare, and doing an autopsy at a hospital morgue even rarer. And thank goodness, because those were worse. The cold and roaring AC unit made the room like an icy coffin. Even grimmer, you were surrounded by bodies covered in sheets, and if you didn't pay attention, you might bump into one and reveal a pair of eyes or a pale hand.

Whenever I did an autopsy at the morgue, I felt watched.

I imagined the bodies saying, So that's how y'all do autopsies. Shame you have to do one on me. Will it hurt?

I'm sure it sounds strange, a forensic scientist being scared of a morgue.

Forensic scientists go through a strange progression. When you are just starting out in your career, it's normal to be a little scared. Then the fear turns into compassion for the victims. Later, hatred for the criminals. Finally, indifference. It's not emotional indifference but indifference toward life and death. You see past it all.

This seeing past it all is the result of accumulated experience and a shift in focus. When a forensic scientist is completely absorbed in finding clues and evidence, no fear, pity, or hatred matters. But for some reason, the morgue distracts me from the work at hand and turns me back into a sentimental, naïve version of myself.

Once the new autopsy rooms were constructed, I swore I would never go back to a morgue. Of course, that didn't last long.

In the middle of September, I got a call. The Eleventh Finger serial killer had added another victim to his list. And the place where the body was discarded? A hospital morgue.

It'd already been five months since June 6, when Zuo Fangjiang's dismembered body was found, then Meng Xiangping and Cheng Xiaoliang after that. Three months of countless officers working every angle and losing sleep. And still, we had no idea what demon was responsible.

The case was especially strange because the three known victims weren't connected in any way, and none of their money had been taken. So what was the killer's motivation?

Now, with a new Eleventh Finger murder, we didn't know how to feel. On the one hand, because we hadn't broken the case, another innocent victim was dead. But on the other hand, a new body could mean new clues.

It was a hospital on the brink of collapse. So many awful stories of medical malpractice had come out that no one was willing to go there. Over the last ten years, the facility had become horribly run-down, but no one wanted to spend money fixing it up. It got so bad, they couldn't even maintain a sanitary environment. Now all that remained was a relatively valuable piece of land.

"Patient A went to the hospital for a mastectomy. The cancer was clearly in the left breast, but the doctor removed the right." Big Bao sat in the car, rehashing the jokes that circulated about the hospital for the benefit of the new forensic interns. "Patient B went in for an appendectomy. Afterward, he was in horrible pain and went back to ask why. Wouldn't you know it, they forgot the anesthetic."

"Oh, and Patient C is a classic." Big Bao grinned. Then seeing the interns looking serious, he said, "Patient C went in for small-bowel hernia surgery, which should be a minor operation. They got the IV in, prepped his skin, shaved him, gave him local anesthesia, and right before they started cutting, he heard one of the doctors ask the other, 'Never done a hernia repair before. You?' 'First time for everything!'"

One of the interns let out a laugh.

"Hey now," Big Bao said sternly, "I'm not telling jokes. I'm teaching you medicine. A doctor shouldn't hurt people instead of saving them, and a forensic scientist who can't solve a case is a waste of space. So listen up!"

Over the years, I'd heard a lot of jokes about that hospital and hadn't known how much stock to put in them. Now, arriving at the frightfully dilapidated building, I realized things might be even worse than that.

The morgue was in a flat-roofed cottage at the eastern corner of the hospital grounds.

I looked at the unstable building in dismay. This thing had better not come down on our heads.

I saw a lot of technicians putting up caution tape at the morgue entrance and bustling about. I walked hopefully into the security office and started chatting with the guard.

"Who found the body?"

"On his way in this morning, a doctor saw a white bag in the doorway, one of our body bags," the guard said. "The doctor thought it was strange. The hospital hasn't had much business lately and no one has died, so how could there be a body? Even if there was a body, it shouldn't be in the doorway. So he looked closer and saw the body bag wasn't zipped and there were intestines coming out. He called the police."

"Your surveillance video, did the police take it?" I asked.

"Surveillance video? Do you know how much it costs to maintain that kind of equipment?" The guard snorted. "I don't think I've seen a working camera the whole time I've been here."

"But if the killer dragged a body to the hospital last night, someone must've seen that, right?"

"Nah, buddy. They won't pay for night shift. You know, I sit here half the day, still have to drive a cab at night."

"So there's no one here in the evening or at night?" I asked.

"The entire security staff, you're looking at it," he said, puffing out his chest.

I suddenly felt dizzy. This killer knew exactly what he was doing. No one would see him dump the body, but it would quickly and easily be found.

"Then is there any surveillance nearby, at least? Or if a car came in, there'd be headlights—maybe a doctor on duty would notice?" I made a final effort.

"Not so far as I know," the guard said. "Our gate is unlocked twenty-four hours, and at night the place turns into a parking lot for locals. We're supposed to chase them away, but no one bothers. Wouldn't notice if someone came this way and dropped the body."

I opened my mouth but couldn't come up with any meaningful questions, so I thanked the man and walked bitterly toward the caution tape outside.

Chief Hu was already there, dressed in a hazmat suit and holding two gloves soaked in blood. "The simpler a case seems, the harder it turns out to be."

I looked at him doubtfully.

"This victim has his ID right on him, like the killer is taunting us. Liang Fengzhi, male, thirty-seven. Our guys just checked and found out he's a lawyer, worked for a lot of firms, some in Dragon City, some not. He was currently working at the Hengda law firm in Yuntai City. He'd been in Dragon City two weeks, gathering evidence for an economic dispute case. His hotel said he left yesterday after three p.m. and didn't come back."

"How can we be sure it's the same killer as Eleventh Finger?" I looked at the words above the morgue entrance, hesitated, then put on my gloves and ducked under the tape.

"Disembowelment, slit throat," Hu said. "This time they didn't cut off the head, but the organs were taken out with the tongue scoop method. Probably poisoned again too. I keep wondering how we haven't been able to track something as toxic and tightly regulated as tetramine. We should at least be able to figure out how it's getting in and out of Dragon City, but still no leads. It's like the killer has his own untraceable stash of the stuff, but how could that be?"

"Well, this definitely links them," said Big Bao, a dark object in his palm.

It was a man's tongue, black and stinking—not from decay, but formalin.

"It's probably Cheng Xiaoliang's from August," Big Bao said. "Wasn't he missing a tongue?"

"And so this body is missing what?"

"He's got no, uh, thingy."

I gritted my teeth. "What a sick bastard. And we can't catch him." Big Bao looked to the sky and screamed.

The autopsy took four hours, two hours longer than standard. We looked the body over with the utmost care but still didn't find any valuable clues. We already knew the murderer's methods by heart: trick the victim into taking poison, let him die, cut the throat, and do a forensic disembowelment with the tongue scoop method, then dismember the body, steal a body part, bundle the corpse up with ropes, and leave it somewhere easy to find.

We were dealing with an extremely disturbed person.

The investigative work, for its part, took two days. Other than an outline of Liang Fengzhi's last movements, detectives learned nothing. They looked into every last person connected to the unlucky man—relatives, friends, coworkers in Dragon City and the people he'd worked with on the lawsuit in Dragon City, even the doctor who found the body and the taxi-driving hospital guard—and each one was ruled out as a suspect. Another dead end.

At the task force meeting, detectives reported that they couldn't find a single connection between the last places the Eleventh Finger victims had been seen, or between the times they went missing.

In sum, four totally unrelated people had been cut down by a sick killer for no reason.

Morale was sinking lower and lower. Only one person was upbeat.

"This tire mark is from the parking spot nearest to the morgue," Lin Tao said. "Even though there were many overlapping traces, I worked out which was freshest, using different kinds of light. I've already ruled out the car that belongs to the doctor who called in the case, so this could be a very useful clue."

"But we're not going to be able to check the millions of cars in the city," I said. "Even if we told the traffic unit to look for this needle in a haystack, and they somehow found a similar tire tread, there'd still be thousands that match."

"If only we could find the right car, I could use the specific wear pattern to show it's a match," Lin Tao said. "We need to have hope! Lots of cases are solved with blind luck. This could be one of those. I'm going to tell the traffic unit to keep it in mind just in case."

Though the clue was of dubious value, we waited expectantly for two days for good news.

We didn't get any. We got another murder case.

46

On September 20, with Mid-Autumn Festival nearing, an urgent request for assistance came in from Cheng City. We didn't even discuss it, just jumped in the car and rushed to the scene. We urgently needed a success to wash off the funk of the Eleventh Finger mess.

Cheng City was a wealthy city with few murders. But this one, we learned, was quite extraordinary, and the man who'd called it in was scared out of his mind. It took tremendous effort for the officers to calm him down and get the basic info.

When we arrived, Cheng City's chief investigative instructor, Zhang Ping, who was also a senior forensic scientist, gave us the rundown.

That afternoon, maintenance man Zhang Chunhe had received a call. Tenants were complaining about a heavy stench in the lobby of a building at one of their residential complexes, a property called the Guilin.

Zhang Chunhe had been with Fenghua Property Management for two and a half years, but he never went to the Guilin. It was a high-end complex, so it had good facilities and fewer problems.

Before Zhang Chunhe headed out, he looked over the complex's architectural drawings just in case. As a senior maintenance man, if he got there and didn't know what to do, it would be very embarrassing.

According to the drawings, behind the first-floor lobby were two fireproof doors that led to a stairwell. Underneath the stairwell was the entrance to the sewage well. Every building had a well to carry sewage away. There were also some electrical lines running through the well. Of course, electrical lines wouldn't cause the well to stink. It was probably a blockage.

But clogs would happen over a long period of time. Why hadn't anyone noticed the stench and reported it earlier? Especially these days when relationships between property managers and tenants were so bad.

Then Zhang Chunhe figured it out. The Guilin units were all two-family, two-elevator units. The first floor was an unoccupied storage room, and even people living on the second floor took the elevator. If no one went into the lobby or took the stairs, noticing the smell would be unlikely—especially with the barrier formed by the fire doors.

Zhang Chunhe had worked as a plumber and done dredging before, but it wasn't water he would be dealing with now but sewage. Even someone like him didn't want his clothing to stink.

Arriving at the building, Zhang Chunhe pulled on a waterproof jumpsuit and strained to open the sewage-well covering under the stairs. The well was black as night, and a truly nasty smell blew out from it. He was an old hand at dredge work, which he'd done for many years, but he'd never smelled anything that bad.

"Did an animal die down there?" Zhang Chunhe said to the property management staffer who'd accompanied him. "It's awful. If I'm really going in there, you gotta pay me extra."

The property management staffer retched and pinched his nose. He wiped tears from his eyes and nodded. "An extra two hundred."

Zhang Chunhe was a very adaptable person. At the mention of more money, he quickly got over the stench, put on a mask, and slowly lowered himself down the ladder.

Only a little light came in through the wellhead as he worked his way down. Before his feet had touched the bottom, he felt something bump against his back.

"What the heck?" Zhang Chunhe grasped the ladder with one hand and turned on his helmet lamp with the other. He craned his neck to look.

The sight made every hair on his body stand up.

Right behind him, a person was dangling, the head drooping down. Long hair covered the face.

"A ghost!" Zhang Chunhe shouted, so scared he nearly fell in. Fortunately, his adrenaline kicked in, and he didn't let go of the ladder. He quickly scrambled out of the well, ran outside, and collapsed trembling on the grass before taking out his cell phone and calling 110. The confused property management staffer was left by the well entrance, at a loss.

"You seriously want to go in there?" Lin Tao said, looking pale as he grabbed my arm.

"Yup," I said, looking at the well.

The sewage well had a vertical access tube leading to a square chamber—like a lowercase *b*—which made it impossible to see all the way inside the shaft.

But the so-called ghost wasn't hidden in a corner of the chamber; it was right in the access tube. I saw the shadow looming by the ladder.

"Being a forensic scientist means not believing in ghosts." I shone my flashlight inside, but I couldn't see the body clearly. The smell told me it had been hidden there for some time.

"The guy who called the case in said the ghost was floating," the detective said with a shiver. "He swore it was floating in the air."

"Floating?" I said with a laugh. "Did it yell, 'Boo'?"

"I mean it," the detective said, sensing my derision. "Zhang Chunhe said he was still a ways from the bottom, so the ghost couldn't have been touching the ground. If it was a person, how could it float in the air?"

And in fact, there wasn't much sewage in the well, so how could it be halfway up? Or seem to float? It really was a little confusing. And because of that confusion, in the hour before I arrived, the officers hadn't gone in to check it out.

"I'm not afraid of death, but I am afraid of ghosts," the young deputy director known as "Bold Boy" Zhao confessed.

"Forensic scientists are specialists, not coolies. Do you think it's our job to go fishing bodies out of wells?" To be honest, I was feeling a little timid myself.

I turned and observed Big Bao's and Lin Tao's pale faces. And when I looked at the detectives again, they avoided my gaze.

Before we got there, waiting for the province-level forensic experts was a valid excuse. But now, there was no reason not to go into the well to see what the situation was. If word got around that forensic scientists were afraid of ghosts, we'd become a laughingstock. It goes without saying we work to serve the needs of the people. Now their need was for us to go see what this supposed ghost looked like, so that was what we had to do.

I worked up my courage, put on my headlamp, and started down the sewer-well ladder.

My experience was just like Zhang Chunhe's. A few rungs down, I felt something bump into my calf. I still had eight feet to go before the bottom of the well, so there really shouldn't have been anything there, but there it was.

My hair stood on end. If I screamed, the people above would be scared silly. I tried to fight back the fear. Looking down, I could see a person suspended halfway down the well. The hair over the face and the body swaying as if it were floating made me think of horror movies like *The Ring* and *A Wicked Ghost*.

An average person would, without a doubt, look at this and see a floating female ghost.

But reason told me it was a body, not a ghost. My years of forensic work gave me strength, and I kept climbing down until I could see the whole corpse. I sighed with relief, then quickly went back to holding my breath; the stink of decay assaulted my nostrils.

It appeared to be a middle-aged woman, messy hair obscuring her face. She was hanging by her armpits from the sewage well's intricate wires. The wires were hard to make out in the darkness, which was why the body seemed to be floating.

Laughing in embarrassment, I turned to shine the headlamp on the ladder and saw a bloody impact mark on one of the rungs.

I climbed out of the well.

"The killer probably threw the body in from up above," I said, trying to comfort Lin Tao. "The body ricocheted off the ladder and then got stuck on all the wires in the middle of the well."

"So the killer threw the body in, heard it hit the ladder, and thought it landed," Big Bao said.

"How could it just happen to get caught on the wires like that?" Lin Tao said. "It's gotta be a curse!"

We were helpless in the face of Lin Tao's superstitions.

47

The victim was a woman in her thirties. She was a little on the heavy side, which, coupled with decomposition, made her look bloated. Her clothing was pulled up over her chest, revealing a black bra with dried blood above it.

It was nearing the end of September, and the weather had been warm up until two days before when temperatures plunged, which made it a lot more difficult for us to determine time of death. The body was only moderately decomposed, but still far enough gone to emit a very strong odor.

The abdomen was turning a color we called "corpse-green." We could only roughly judge time of death: in that weather, with the corpse-green appearing, it had probably been four or five days.

Unless a victim dies in his own house or someone who knows him is present or he has ID on him, forensic scientists face a nameless corpse. And identifying a corpse quickly is a very important step in any murder case.

"I'll tell you a joke." Big Bao had been in a good mood lately, always telling jokes. We believed that when a young forensic scientist started joking around, it meant he'd done the mental work of getting comfortable with death.

"When I was working in Qingxiang, I had a coworker," Big Bao said, "who was always claiming to be best at forensic anthropology, so guys in our bureau made fun of him, saying only dogs were as happy as he was to find a body. So he finds a clothed skeleton at a scene, and the detectives are desperate for an ID. He makes a big show of taking the bones back to the autopsy room and studying them. He's at it the whole afternoon, and his conclusion is that the victim was male and fifty years old. As soon as he says it, a trace guy who's been there with him the whole time reaches into the victim's pants pocket and pulls out an ID card. Female, name and address all there. The boss got mad and transferred the scientist to work as a prison doctor."

As he laughed, Big Bao stuck a hand in the victim's pants pocket. "Holy crap, good thing I checked. Here's her ID!"

"Li Yilian," a young detective reported, "was thirty-four. She worked in the state tax bureau, lived on the eleventh floor of the Guilin. Husband runs a large building-materials operation in Yuntai City, hasn't been home for a long time."

"Did her husband come back home about a week ago, by chance?" Big Bao asked.

The detective shook his head. "They don't get along well. The husband comes through only every two or three months. Colleagues in Yuntai are tracking his movements over the last few days but haven't found anything suspicious."

"A search of the sewer well didn't turn up any of the victim's personal items," I said. "But her formal clothing suggests she was probably on her way to or from work, so she should have had personal belongings with her."

I lifted the victim's right hand. "And look, there's a depression at the base of her ring finger, caused by wearing a ring for a long time."

I gestured to the victim's ears. "Her ears are pierced, which means she may have worn earrings. But we haven't been able to find her ring or earrings, so this could be a robbery."

"Robbery?" the detective asked. "In a sewer well? Her clothes were messed up. Couldn't it be rape or something that led to the murder?"

"Well, she wasn't killed at home," Lin Tao said. "I just broke into her apartment and had a look. Nothing abnormal there at all."

I smoothed out the victim's clothing. The bloodstained part had dried and gotten stiff. I told the detective, "I'll start with cause of death. The victim died of bleeding from multiple stab wounds to the chest."

"Obviously," the detective said. "I don't need you to tell me that."

"When we smooth out the clothing, we can see a lot of cuts in it," I said. "Now we want to see if they match the chest wounds, right?"

I lined them up. "Okay, they match. All the holes in the clothing correspond to holes in the chest. So, when the victim was stabbed, her clothes weren't pushed up, but hanging over her body normally, right?"

The detective nodded to show agreement.

I continued. "Now for your question about the sewer. No, the crime probably wasn't committed there. The wellhead is too narrow, the chamber too low, and the victim's pant legs show no signs of sewage, which means she never touched the bottom. Of course, the victim didn't just end up there for no reason."

I paused to look at a wound on the victim's forehead that showed no vital reaction. "The killer threw the body into the well. Due to initial acceleration, the body fell diagonally and the head hit the ladder, which caused it to ricochet and get stuck on the wires. The wires pulled her clothes up, which made it look like sexual assault."

"Then where's the primary murder scene?" the detective said. "No one would kill someone outside a building, then hide them inside it, right?"

"No problem," Lin Tao told the kid. "I'll find it."

"And I'll examine the body," I said.

◆ ◆ ◆

The victim had died from massive blood loss.

Her chest had been stabbed seventeen times. Eleven had gone between ribs and into the chest cavity. They ruptured the victim's heart, aorta, and lungs, which caused rapid blood loss and death.

We carefully examined each wound on the body—shape, length, depth—which allowed us to determine that the injuries were caused by a blade about two inches wide and six inches long.

Many people think that figuring out what weapon was used is useless unless it turns out to be something unique. In this case, we had a detailed description of the weapon, although every home would likely have a similar knife—a fruit knife or a steak knife, for example—or other instrument that fits the description. But figuring out what object was used isn't primarily to limit the scope of the investigation. More important, it allows later stages of the investigation to obtain valuable evidence and clues. For example, if we later searched a suspect's home and found several such knives, we would know to test them and possibly solve the case much faster.

This was a simple stabbing murder case, so the autopsy probably wouldn't turn up too many clues. We could only hope for a clear cause of death, time of death, weapon, and attack style.

The victim's stomach still had the remnants of corn. The food had not yet reached the duodenum, which meant she'd died within two hours of her last meal.

Additionally, we followed the standard practice of testing and photographing the victim's clothing. The back side of the victim's jacket was dusty. And it was worth noting that the jacket and pants pockets had bloodstains inside.

"How do you think the bloodstains got in the pockets?" I asked Bao with a smile.

Big Bao was getting better and better at fielding my questions. "There are two possibilities: First, after the victim was injured, she reached into her own pockets with bloody hands. Second, after killing the victim, the killer used his bloody hands to search the victim's pockets. The first would occur only in one set of pockets, whereas the other would put blood in all the pockets. In this case, there's blood in three of the victim's jacket pockets and two in the pants, so I think it's the second scenario, the killer searching the pockets."

"Good!" I said with a nod. "Evidence of searching the pockets further supports the idea that the killer was after money, which fits with the missing ring and earrings. We say bodies can talk, but now clothing is talking too. It says this is a murder-robbery."

After the autopsy, we rushed to the task force meeting.

"The victim's husband can already be ruled out as a suspect. He didn't have time to do it," the detective began.

"Yeah," I said. "The victim's jewelry was all taken. And her pockets all have blood smeared inside, the result of the killer searching them. Seems pretty clear this was robbery."

The detective nodded. "Further, according to our investigation, Li Yilian was last seen five days ago, on Friday night. A group of coworkers went out for dinner, and she left around eight. Been missing ever since. She didn't show up at work on Monday or answer her phone. She only comes into the office a couple days a week anyway, so her coworkers just assumed she went to Yuntai to visit her husband."

"Went out to eat?" I said. "The victim's stomach contents definitely didn't suggest a dinner party. All we found were some corn kernels. Maybe she didn't die after dinner on Friday after all."

"Oh, according to her coworkers, Li Yilian was constantly dieting. All she ate Friday night was that corn."

"As for the murder scene, we still haven't pinned it down," Lin Tao said, opening a slide show. "Like I said, we ruled out the victim's apartment, so next we inspected the stairs that she'd take to get up there. The section of stairs between the second and third floors shows signs of having been mopped recently, but there's no blood spatter on the walls. We even used tetramethylbenzidine to test for invisible blood, but didn't come up with anything. If the victim's heart was punctured in the stairwell, there should have been blood spatter, right? So my current theory is that the victim was killed somewhere else, carried here, and dumped in the well."

I frowned. "I can't agree. The back side of the victim's jacket was covered in dust, so she was probably supine in a really dusty place for some time. And her home probably wouldn't be that dusty. I see from your survey photos that the first-floor staircase is tile and the rest are cement. The tenants rarely take the stairs, so there's a lot of dust there. I think that indicates the victim was killed in the stairwell and left there for a while."

"Couldn't the jacket have gotten dusty from rubbing against the stairs on the way down?" Lin Tao asked.

"No. Dust from rubbing would have a direction to it. This dust is distributed uniformly over a large area. Also, when we examined the body on-site, livor mortis was concentrated in the lower back, which means the victim was supine for at least thirty-six hours after death."

"But if the victim was killed in the stairwell, why didn't we find blood spatter there? Doesn't make sense, right?" Lin Tao asked.

"Not every ruptured artery spatters," I explained. "On this victim, the broken arteries were all in the chest. The victim was wearing work clothing—long sleeves, jacket—so even if there was bleeding, the clothes would absorb it. A chest-wound victim wearing thick clothing rarely leaves blood spatter."

"Who do you think did it?" the detective asked.

I brought my fist down on the table. "Whoever the killer is, he's a resident of the building."

48

"Just because the building has a security system?" the detective asked doubtfully. "One building, thirty floors, two apartments per floor . . . That's sixty households who don't know one another. Someone trailing the victim could have snuck in behind her, right? Like someone from that dinner, or if they met a stranger afterward, couldn't they get in too? We all think an acquaintance did it. A stranger wouldn't be able to trick the victim into going into the stairwell."

"Maybe not trick," Big Bao said, "but chase or force. An acquaintance probably would have taken the elevator up and killed her near her apartment. Why drag the body between floors? Then throw the body in a sewage well? You'd have to be stupid."

"I agree," I said. "I think the killer either ran into the victim between the second and third floors, or he was lying in wait."

"If he was waiting, then it wouldn't be an acquaintance either?" the detective wondered.

"Maybe they knew each other a little, but they definitely weren't friends. Like I said before, after the victim was killed, she was in the supine position for thirty-six hours or so—long enough for livor mortis to fixate in the back. If the body had been tossed in the well and snagged upright on the wires immediately after death, the blood would have pooled in the calves and feet, and we'd see livor mortis there instead."

I cleared my throat and continued. "That the killer was willing to leave the victim in the stairwell so long tells us two things. One, the killer is very familiar with this building—he knew residents never take the stairs. Two, he didn't know the victim well. If someone had found the body, the killer was confident he wouldn't soon be suspected. He moved the body later to delay discovery, probably because it started to smell. He didn't know how to get the body out of the building without being seen, but he did know about the sewer well. Which is more evidence the killer knows the building. Because he lives there."

"Yeah, I see what you're saying," the detective said. "Knows the building, doesn't really know the victim—definitely fits with a neighbor in the building."

"Right," I said. "Plus, after the body was moved, the stairwell was cleaned. The killer probably got a mop from his own apartment."

"But why would the victim take the stairs? And the killer too?"

"Well," I said with a laugh, "I don't know about the killer, but it's pretty easy to guess why Li Yilian took the stairs."

"Really?"

"Her colleagues said she was always trying to lose weight, right? Living on the eleventh floor, taking the stairs every day, sounds like a good strategy!"

"Oh, good call!" the detective said. "According to her coworkers, she didn't belong to a gym or anything. Now we know what exercise she was doing, stair climbing! But why was the killer there?"

"We'll have to go back to the scene to figure that out."

Lin Tao, Big Bao, and I spent all afternoon in the stairwell between the second and third floor, scouring it for any kind of clue. We had to take a break at seven for another task force meeting, but then we turned around and went right back. Coming close to breaking the case wouldn't cut it.

Down in the lobby, residents were still ogling the caution tape around the sewer well. Even though we had already ID'd the body, the fear of a female ghost lingered.

As we entered the stairwell on the first floor, sound-activated sensor lights suddenly switched on. But looking up, we could see that the stairs between the second and third floors were dark.

"I didn't expect such a big discovery this evening."

"Yeah," Lin Tao said knowingly. "Every floor probably has working lights besides that one. Can't be a coincidence."

"You think the killer picked a dark place to do it?" Big Bao asked.

"Not sure, but I can find out."

Lin Tao ran out to the survey van to fetch a stepladder. He climbed up and carefully, carefully used his flashlight to look at the bulb. His face sparkled in surprise. "Qin, the lightbulb has fingerprints on it! They look fresh!"

"Get the prints," I said, handing him the camera. "Then see if the bulb was unscrewed."

Lin Tao recorded the evidence, then gently twisted the bulb. It lit up.

"Ha!" I said. "This really is a breakthrough."

"How?" Big Bao said. "You sure the prints belong to the killer?"

I nodded. "That bulb didn't burn out; it was unscrewed. Who'd climb up there and loosen a bulb? Only someone who wants to do something in secret. Which means the killer prepared ahead of time to make this spot dark so he could hide himself."

"If it's someone living here and we've got prints, we should be able to get him, right?" Lin Tao said, proudly reviewing the images.

"But how did the killer know the victim would come by?" Big Bao asked.

I thought it over and said, "The killer must've been very familiar with these stairs—knew the victim used them and other people didn't. Which means the killer is someone who would regularly see the victim taking the stairs . . ."

Lin Tao considered this a second. "So, not people who live above her, right? But people living on the eleventh floor or below might notice that the victim used the stairs every day!"

"Makes sense," I said. "That leaves only twenty-one households. I think we can break this case tonight."

As it came time for Big Bao to test his math skills again, he stuck out his fingers and called after us. "Hey, wait! How'd you get twenty-one?"

"Eleven times two, minus one," Lin Tao said, turning around.

In the task force meeting room, there was a big map of the Guilin building and a list of condo owners provided by management. Detectives were going through the list door by door.

"Three-oh-one's owner hasn't been home for a long time, four-oh-one has two elderly women living there—neither fits," a detective said. "This is a fancy complex. How could something like this happen?"

I pursed my lips and said, "What about six-oh-one, a rich kid living alone?"

Apartment 601 had been bought by a high-powered businessman named Han Shi for his son, Han Feng. The photo of a young kid with dyed red hair, a thick gold chain, and crooked eyebrows quickly caught the task force's attention.

A couple hours of investigation turned up traffic violations, assault, and drug use—all manner of delinquent behavior. Instead of questioning him directly, the task force decided to see if we could arrest him on drug charges and compare his fingerprints to the ones from the lightbulb.

Han Feng was quickly located in a private room of a nightclub, high out of his mind and in the arms of a cute girl.

Lin Tao grabbed the kid's limp hand, pressed a finger onto the paper, then after a three-minute examination under bright light, said, "We got him!"

49

Han Feng never worked, just hung out with his friends in bars, karaoke clubs, and skating rinks, chasing girls and drugs.

Sick of all the trouble caused and money wasted, his exasperated father finally decided to cancel Han Feng's credit cards, hoping the prodigal son would be forced to reevaluate his life.

But the punishment failed. Han Shi didn't know his son had become addicted to heroin. Han Feng sold his jewelry, cell phones, designer clothes—everything he had to feed his habit. When all that ran out, he had to find a new source of cash.

He remembered seeing a strange woman wearing jewelry in the stairwell. He couldn't remember what she looked like, but he remembered the jewelry. It looked expensive.

So Han Feng started lurking and watching. He spotted a woman who took the stairs every day before and after work. Hers was the only shadow that passed all day.

He lay in bed for two days, not just sleeping but designing the whole murder-robbery.

That night, to make his chosen spot darker, he loosened the light-bulb, then crouched in the corner. But the woman didn't come home after work at her usual time, so Han Feng waited and waited, worried he'd have to give up. Around nine, though, she finally arrived. He leapt out of the shadows, wrestled a shocked Li Yilian to the ground, covered her mouth, and desperately stabbed her chest with a fruit knife till she stopped struggling.

It was the first time Han Feng had killed someone, but he wasn't afraid. His head was filled only with thoughts of his next hit.

He yanked off Li Yilian's jewelry and riffled through her pockets, thrilled to find a significant wad of cash.

Han Feng rushed out to score the heroin he craved, shot up at home, and then passed out. When he woke up a day and a half later, he realized the body was still there.

There's that weird well downstairs, he thought. I'll just throw her in, mop up the stairs, and no one will ever know.

When detectives charged him with murder, Han Feng was surprised, but he was entirely without remorse. "I thought I was in the clear this morning. How'd you even find me?"

50

Captain Huang of Yuntai may have liked to call me "Jinx," but Big Bao was the real jinx, always tempting fate. As we were leaving Cheng City, Lin Tao let out a big sigh.

"All these murders! I wish they'd all just lay off for a minute and let us focus on the Eleventh Finger case!"

"Oh no," Big Bao moaned. "Just hearing the words 'Eleventh Finger' makes my head hurt. Let's forget about dead bodies for a minute, hurry home, hug our families, and have a nice Mid-Autumn Festival."

As soon as the words left his mouth, I felt a faint foreboding.

Holiday weather was sunny and breezy, perfect for the full moon. But ever since the Eleventh Finger case had started in June, neither the full moon nor recreation could capture my interest. The case was like a splinter, a bug bite, a rash. I might forget about it for a minute, but then there it was again, driving me nuts.

A reporter from a local TV station had a crush on Lin Tao, so he got invited to watch the live taping of a musical variety show. To take the pressure off, Lin Tao invited me and Ling Dang as well as Big Bao and his wife to come along.

"Look, look, look," Big Bao said. "Tonight's moon is so full, how romantic."

"Perfect for seducing your lady, Lin Tao," I said, eyeing the dozens of people in front of us in line outside the studio. "This side door isn't even open yet. When are they gonna let us in?"

"Don't worry," Lin Tao said, lifting his badge. "Everyone over here's a VIP. There're way more people at the main entrance."

"My first time as a VIP," Big Bao said, admiring his own badge.

Just then, some people circumvented the line and went straight into the studio.

The crowd rippled with resentment.

I smiled and said to Lin Tao, "See that? Those people are real VIPs. We should have brought lawn chairs."

"Shut up," Lin Tao snapped.

Half an hour later, the side door finally opened, and the crowd slowly surged inside.

Dingling-dingling . . .

My phone rang, and I immediately thought of Big Bao's jinx.

I struggled to get my cell phone out of my pocket in the crowd, and when I did, I saw two words displayed: "Command Center."

"Hey, you guys, hold up a sec."

"This is Sun Tongsu from command," a low voice said. "I just received a report that a body was found in a quarry on the outskirts of Dragon City. They're saying it's murder."

"Mhh . . ." My tongue stuck to the roof of my mouth.

"Today's a holiday, Examiner Qin. Have you been drinking?" Sun Tongsu said.

"No, no." I turned and looked at Lin Tao and Big Bao. They were making their way back against the crowd.

"Okay, good. Director Chen wants you right away," Sun said. "Please head to West Dragon City, the far end of Dragon City Avenue. There's a quarry there."

"Got it." I put my phone away and gave Ling Dang a guilty look.

Her drooping eyelashes flickered. "No worries. Mrs. Bao and I will keep each other company. You guys go. Drive carefully."

Ling Dang's gentle sadness made me feel even worse. It had been a long time since I'd taken her out on a real date.

Mrs. Bao made a flirty face and took Ling Dang's arm. "Go on, go. Ling Dang, they don't appreciate music anyway. It'll be better with just the two of us."

Watching them disappear into the crowd, I called Chief Hu and handed the car keys to Lin Tao.

"Hello, Chief. Happy holiday. Sounds like a perp sent us another present. Any clues?"

"Not sure yet," Chief Hu said. "All we know is it's a murder and the body was dumped. The men started survey work and cleared a path to the scene, but I still haven't seen the corpse."

"I'm wondering if it's connected to Eleventh Finger."

"Not likely," Hu said. "The body appears to have been burned."

"Burned?" I said. "Could the Eleventh Finger killer be expanding his methods?"

"Please! Don't jinx it!" Hu cried.

"I'm not the jinx," I said, shooting Big Bao a nasty look. "But I know one who's making us travel to the edge of town on Mid-Autumn Festival."

Big Bao looked sheepish. "Do you get reimbursed for gas if you drive your own car?"

◆ ◆ ◆

Although it was the provincial capital, Dragon City was pretty safe and not too big, so murders were fairly rare. But once Eleventh Finger started, all our best detectives were assigned to the case. If another tough murder case fell in our laps, manpower would be spread thin. I hoped this would be a simple one.

The car rolled over bumpy village roads for over an hour before we stopped and met Chief Hu, who pointed to a mountain with the front half dug out and said, "Over there."

If I wasn't seeing it with my own eyes, I never would have believed a place like that was hidden just outside our bustling city. I closed my eyes and took a deep breath, letting the sense of calm sink in. I'd always dreamed of a quiet country life.

"Wow, what a great place to hide a body!" Big Bao said, completely spoiling my moment.

Walking into the abandoned quarry was like entering a space apart from the hustle and bustle of the city. Only a tower and some dilapidated brick buildings remained. Half the mountain had been hollowed out, its yellow core exposed. Because the digging went very deep, the center had become a pond. Locals had paved the ring-shaped dirt road around it with gravel.

Under the light of the mid-autumn moon, I could make out the silhouettes of a few people strolling along the water.

"It's normally not so quiet," Hu said with a smile. "But today's a holiday, and it's getting late. Usually there are more locals here exercising."

"Exercising?" I asked.

Hu nodded. "A lot of people come to walk or jog around the pond in the evening—probably because the air's good. But after eight or so, it's dead out here."

"Wait, they run in the dark?" I looked up. If not for the exceptionally bright moonlight, the area around the pond would be pitch-black.

"Well, it's not totally dark at six or seven in the summer," Hu said. "No one comes in the winter."

"How do you know all this, Hu?"

"My hometown's five miles from here," he said, pointing.

"When did you get the call?" I asked.

"Came in at six-oh-five," a detective nearby said. "It was probably the first people coming to exercise."

"They found the body?" I said as I put on my gloves and stretched, watching the silhouettes and flashlight beams by the pond in the distance.

"No," the detective said. "They saw smoke. There're only stone and water in the quarry, so what would catch fire? Some of them went closer and saw the flames, so they assumed someone was burning trash."

"Do people often burn trash here?" I asked.

The detective nodded and pointed at the ground. "If you look closely, this gravel road has lots of black stains, all from trash fires."

"But they realized it wasn't trash?"

"Yeah, the locals said the fire started to die down. One said the burning object had a human shape, thought it might be a valley spirit or something. Another laughed at that, so the two of them made a bet. They got a little closer to check it out and realized it was a person on fire."

"A body, you mean," Big Bao said, curling his lip as Lin Tao leaned on him in distress.

"Right, a body," the detective said, scratching his head.

Next to the pond was a heap of ash on soft mud. Because the villagers used wet clothes to fight the fire, ashes flew in all directions. In the middle of the ashes was a curled-up, human-shaped figure.

The surface of the body was completely carbonized, all black. The face and head were especially dire, with the skull showing through in some places.

"Ooh," Lin Tao said. "I remember what you taught me on that construction-manager case. The boxing stance doesn't mean the victim was burned alive, right? To figure out if a body was burned before or after death, we have to look at the respiratory tract and carboxyhemoglobin levels in the blood. So to figure that out, we have to wait for your autopsy."

"Not necessarily," I said, staring at the ash pile.

"Huh?" Lin Tao said, bending down to follow my gaze into the ashes.

"Heat will make muscles contract, but not to such an extreme degree. Look, the thigh is bent all the way up to the chest; that couldn't be caused by fire."

"You're saying the body was already curled up before being set on fire?" Lin Tao asked.

I nodded as I opened the body bag and lifted the figure into it with Big Bao's help. The body was very light, not because the victim was frail but because fire evaporates all the water from the body.

"So we can't be sure it's a murder case, then," Lin Tao said.

I didn't say a word, just took out an evidence bag and started collecting ashes.

"These ashes are precious," Big Bao said. "We can get a lot of physical evidence from—"

He stopped short as all three of us spotted something at the same time.

Two long, black, rectangular objects appeared where I'd swept away the ashes. After having a technician take a photo, I carefully picked up the objects. They were probably metal, lighter than alloy.

"What is it?" Big Bao asked, squinting. "Metal, eh, yeah, should be the murder weapon, right?"

"Yeah," Lin Tao said, leaning in for a closer look. "But how could it be so easy to find?"

51

I carefully looked the two metal objects up and down, then dropped them in an evidence bag. I smiled and said, "Too light, couldn't be the murder weapon. But I can say with some certainty that this is a murder."

"How do you know?" Big Bao asked.

"Two metal rods, the same size and length, lying perfectly parallel beneath the body. What are they likely to be?" I asked.

Lin Tao frowned and thought it over. "Oh, I know. They're suitcase handle rods!"

"Exactly, from a rolling bag. It must have been cloth, because everything burned away but the metal rods. Which tells us the body was transported here in a suitcase before being burned."

"This would explain why the body is so curled up!" Big Bao said ecstatically.

"Right," I said. "Someone stuffed it in the suitcase. Don't get too excited, though."

"Oh right." Big Bao toned down his mood. "It's a murder; should be serious."

"Well, no need to be too sad either." I laughed. "Even though the force is shorthanded because of Eleventh Finger, I think this evidence is such that we can narrow the scope of the investigation and break this case soon."

Chief Hu walked over. "What's the plan, men?"

"Chief," I said, "would you ask an officer to take some of the ash to the lab to see if they can test for an accelerant?"

"Of course, I'll send someone now," Hu said.

"Great. Then we'll go to the autopsy room. With the body burned this bad, it'll be hard to get an ID. Hopefully trace detection can find some shoe prints or tire marks or something."

"It's after ten—I wonder if the show is still going on," Big Bao said, leaning against the inside of the car window and looking out at the moonlight.

"It was you, ya jinx," Lin Tao said. "You had to shoot your mouth off about relaxing for the Mid-Autumn Festival."

Big Bao smiled in embarrassment.

The full moon shone into the autopsy room, reducing the usual gloom. As I was about to turn on the lights, I suddenly heard a rustling sound.

There couldn't be anything in there besides the body on the autopsy table, right? I thought. No way the person is still alive—not with those burns.

Fear made it hard for my fingers to find the light switch. I muttered to myself as I took out my phone and turned on the flashlight.

A shadow suddenly darted out from a corner, flashed onto the table, and disappeared out a window. I jumped and dropped my phone in fright.

Lin Tao grabbed me. "Shit! Ghost!"

His overreaction calmed me down. I shook my arm free. "Dude, grow a pair."

I picked up my phone and used its flashlight to find the light switch. The large room was instantly bright. The body bag was right where it should be on the table, the victim lying peacefully inside.

Pointing at dusty paw prints, I smiled and said, "Ha, some ghost. Come on, trace guy. Test these prints and see what we can learn about the cat that just jumped out the window."

Lin Tao was a little embarrassed. He scratched his head and said, "What's a stray cat doing here in the middle of the night? There's nothing to eat."

"Ugh, I think burned bodies are even grosser than bloated ones," Lin Tao said, taking out his camera and covering his nose.

"Really?" I said. "Bloated bodies stink so bad, they make this burned one seem fragrant."

Lin Tao put up a hand to get me to stop talking, then retched a little and said, "How am I ever going to eat barbecue again?"

The victim was male, but we couldn't gauge age because his face was gone. When the fire started, he was probably lying with his right side against the suitcase, so the skin there was not highly carbonized. But his left side, which must have been facing up, was severely charred. The only way to get the body straight was to make cuts on the skin and muscle around the joints.

"Doesn't cutting like that damage the evidence?" Lin Tao asked. "Are you keeping track of how many cuts you're making to release the joints?"

"Yes. And the victim's original wounds, whether they occurred before or after death, can be distinguished from the ones we make during the autopsy."

"Oh? How?"

"Well, as you know, antemortem wounds will bleed and turn red; postmortem, they turn yellow," I said. "Now, since the body has been burned, whether they happened before or after death, the wounds are all black. And the heat made the skin around the edges crimp and harden. The incisions we're making won't be crimped, and a yellow layer of fat will be exposed, so it's easy to tell the difference."

It was hard to get good information with so much damage, but we found chest wounds indicating the victim was stabbed while alive. Since livor mortis isn't visible in burn victims, we couldn't determine whether they died of blood loss, so Big Bao took a scalpel to the abdomen to see if there was damage to the internal organs.

"Wait!" I shouted, and opened the victim's arms. Two pieces of cloth fell out from under the armpits.

I picked them up and shook off the ashes. "Clothing under the armpits is protected, so it usually doesn't burn like the rest of the clothes. I almost forgot to check."

Lin Tao took out a magnifying glass.

"Looks like two layers melted together," I said, using tweezers to separate them. "The inside is black, nice, maybe silk. Outside is thick, white, looks cheap."

"It's been eighty-some degrees out," Lin Tao said. "Who'd wear two layers?"

I smiled. "A doctor in a lab coat!"

The clue boosted my mood, and suddenly the moonlight outside seemed even more beautiful.

I cut open the victim's trachea and, as expected, there were no signs of ash. With no indication of acute respiratory distress, we could be sure the victim was burned postmortem.

The victim's rib cage was crisp and easy to cut through. Inside, all the organs were intact.

"Bodies are amazing." I sighed. "See how well our skin protects our internal organs?"

Lin Tao touched his own chest with a pained look.

"The victim's aortic arch is ruptured," said Big Bao, poking it with a hemostat.

"Then shouldn't there be more blood in the chest?" Lin Tao asked.

"Yes," I said, "but the fire evaporated the blood. In any case, this confirms the victim died from a sharp object puncturing the aorta and resulting in loss of blood."

"Stomach is empty—looks like the victim didn't get to eat any mooncakes for the festival." Big Bao shook his head regretfully.

"Shoot," I said. "I was hoping we could get some clues from the stomach contents."

"What about the pubic symphysis?" Big Bao asked.

It had been boiling away in the pressure cooker and was just about ready for examination.

"Looks like the victim was in his early thirties," I said, studying the pubic symphysis's shape.

"How many thirtysomething doctors could live in that little village?" Lin Tao said. "We've got the age and the occupation—should be able to get the ID pretty soon."

I shook my head. "Who said the victim lives in the village by the quarry?"

"True," Lin Tao said with a nod. "The body was in a suitcase, so I guess it could've come from anywhere."

"Well, not just anywhere," I said, shaking my head. "Not a lot of people know about that place, or how to get in. Regardless of where the victim was from, the killer had to be familiar with the area."

"So how are we going to ID the body?" Lin Tao said.

I took off my jumpsuit and looked at the clock. It was already one in the morning. "By pulling an all-nighter and sifting through these ashes."

The three of us took all the bags with ashes in them and shook them through a sieve, looking for any larger objects that could be useful evidence. We found a few zippers and a card-shaped thing.

"The zipper has a brand on it," Big Bao said. "GTFP—how do you pronounce a name that's all consonants?"

"Consonants? Ha." Lin Tao was amused. "GTFP is a high-end luggage brand."

"Good thing we've got a shopaholic on the team," I teased, "otherwise we wouldn't know which brands are any good."

"What do you mean 'shopaholic'?" Lin Tao said defensively. "It's called being fashion-conscious, okay? Fashion-conscious!"

"A high-end brand, huh?" Big Bao asked. "Could it mean the killer's well-off?"

"Not necessarily," I said. "What if the killer committed the crime in the victim's home and then used the victim's suitcase?"

"No. This means that the victim and killer were both well-off," Lin Tao lectured. "Using such a fancy suitcase to burn a body is a terrible waste."

"The left side of this card didn't get burned!" Big Bao exclaimed. "Feng? P? What's that mean?"

Big Bao and I looked expectantly at Lin Tao. He smiled. "Don't worry, boys. The shopaholic's got you covered."

52

"Did you forget our conversation when we were waiting outside the TV station?"

"About seducing your reporter friend?"

Lin Tao fake punched me and said, "About being VIPs. I said we were VIPs; you said we weren't . . ."

"Oh, it's a VIP card!"

Lin Tao grinned. "If I'm not mistaken, it's a VIP card for Silverworld Towers in downtown Dragon City. That's the only place they sell GTFP."

"So they probably stuck the card in the suitcase after buying it and then just left it there. Would a store like that keep a registry of their VIPs?"

"Definitely."

"Awesome!" I said. "Now we have something to show at the task force meeting."

By the time we hurried over to the meeting, it was already three in the morning. The detectives had no leads, so they were just waiting for us, looking tired and cranky.

"The victim died of blood loss from a knife wound to the chest." I looked at Director Zhang, who was heading up the task force. He didn't seem too interested in the cause of death.

"And," I continued, "the victim was a physician, thirty-some years old."

"And . . . ," I said, trying to create a little suspense, "we have reason to believe he was a VIP member of Silverworld Towers!"

Lin Tao's eyes widened. "I thought we weren't sure if the suitcase belonged to the victim or the killer."

"I thought it over on the way here, and I think it's gotta be the victim's," I said. "First, the cloth in his armpits. When do doctors wear white coats? At work. Which means the victim was probably attacked at work."

"Or after the doctor was attacked, the killer took the body to his own home and put him in the suitcase there?" Big Bao asked.

I said, "No way. The killer couldn't have curled the body into the suitcase once rigor mortis set in. That means there wasn't much time between committing the murder and putting the body in the suitcase."

I paused and went on. "Plus, this doctor had some money, which explains the fancy luggage."

"Oh?"

"He probably worked at a private clinic. Killing someone in a busy hospital and moving the body would be very difficult," I said.

"Makes sense," Zhang said. "I'll send some officers to check Silverworld Towers' VIP list for a thirtysomething doctor."

"There can't be many," I said. "By tomorrow morning, I mean, later this morning, we'll have good news."

It was after nine a.m. when my phone woke me up and I knew the good news had arrived.

"We're pretty sure we got the ID. A young doctor from a private storefront clinic in East Dragon City's Chengwang Town," Chief Hu said. "Director Zhang already sent a team over. You should go right away."

"How far is it from the scene?" I asked.

"About six miles."

"I'll be right there."

When my team arrived, Hu brought us up to speed.

"The doctor's name is Li Kehua," he said, "and he probably does make quite a bit of money. The clinic was open yesterday morning. Then, around two in the afternoon, people came to do their IV treatments and realized the clinic was closed. It didn't open again. Since it was Mid-Autumn Festival, everyone assumed Dr. Li had gone home to celebrate. At six o'clock this morning, after we found Li's name on the VIP list, we broke down the door and found blood on the floor."

"Six miles from the quarry, though?"

"Tells us the killer had a vehicle," Hu said.

"But why would the killer take the body that far away?" I asked.

"Maybe to hide it?"

"Doesn't make sense. The killer knew the place well, so he knew people exercised there and would spot the fire."

"Maybe he thought it'd make it harder for us to ID."

"Just shutting the body in the clinic would have been smarter, don't you think? Moving the body and burning it calls much more attention. Do you think it could be an acquaintance of the victim who was afraid once we got the ID we'd find him?"

"Hard to say," Big Bao said.

"You guys go in and look," Lin Tao said, already in his site-survey gear.

Inside were a basic exam table and two chairs, plus a scale, eye test chart, etc. Behind the table was a curtain, which was pulled back, revealing a cot pushed up against a wood-paneled wall that partitioned off a smaller back room. The room was very messy, filled with all kinds of medicine.

The bloodstains were mainly on the table, the doctor's chair, and the floor nearby. So the victim was sitting down when he was suddenly attacked with a knife. The blood spatter was very messy, indicating a struggle.

Under the chair for patients there was a thick red floor mat. Based on the dust pattern on the ground, it was clear the mat had originally been under the doctor's chair. There was also a pair of leather shoes under the doctor's chair.

"The victim wasn't wearing shoes," I said. "It looks like he sweated heavily, so he placed a mat under his chair and took off his shoes. When he was stabbed, he kicked the mat toward the patient's chair."

"The mat's all dirty," Big Bao said. "There's a lot of black and yellow stuff on it."

"Could be from the killer's feet," I said. "He would have stepped on it as soon as he got up. Because the mat has so much friction, the killer probably left shoe prints. Let's be sure to take it back."

"Look, Old Qin guessed wrong." Lin Tao stood in the doorway of the small room, shining his flashlight inside. "There are medicine cabinets in here, and next to them is a big spot with no dust. Something square-shaped in here was moved."

Lin Tao went into the small room, pulled out a tape measure, and added, "Exactly the size of a rolling GFTP bag!"

"If the killer went in there to get the suitcase, maybe there are footprints," I speculated.

Lin Tao shook his head. "The floor's bad for that. Even if there were some, they wouldn't be useful."

Sadly, we didn't find any clear footprints or fingerprints in the main room. And anyway, since so many patients passed through the clinic, even if we did find something, it'd be hard to determine whether it belonged to the suspect.

"Hey, Bao. Let's take a look at the doctor's things and see if there's anything helpful."

The exam table was a mess of prescriptions, medical devices, medical records, and wastepaper. After studying each and every scrap until I knew the doctor's scrawl by heart, I started looking through the drawer. As soon as I opened it, I saw an exquisite red card. Inside, written in the victim's handwriting, was a poem or song titled "The Touch of Never."

> Longing
> May never meet again
> Love
> May not last forever
> Our wishes put us together
> Our words made us suffer
>
> Only through fate
> Will you come my way
> Only our bond
> Will keep us fond
> Your love waters my fields
> And truth beats sweet words
>
> I never touched your smiling face
> Never gave your eyes a kiss
> But your shadow's in my heart
> Tearing me apart
>
> The grass watches the moon
> The moon reflects the grass
>
> Your sweet lips
> My fingers' fingertips

Only together

The touch of never

"Lyrics from a pop song? Sounds catchy."

Lin Tao shook his head. "No, it's probably original."

"Whoa, a poet too," I said. "Can you get what it means?"

Lin Tao was the "cultured" one. He read it carefully a few times. "As far as I can tell, this is a poem of love gone wrong, probably about an affair."

"Li Kehua wasn't married," a detective informed us.

Big Bao laughed. "Come on, Lin Tao."

Lin Tao said, "Hey, why couldn't it be the woman who's married?"

"If there really was an affair, this sudden murder and moving the body would make a lot of sense," I said. "We got the ID, and now we have a story. I think we can break this soon!"

Then I noticed something next to the doctor's seat.

"Strange," I said. "This trash can's lid is open."

I shone my flashlight inside. "And there's a piece of gauze in here."

"This is even stranger," I said, pulling out the gauze with tweezers. "There's blood on here, but it's very fresh and only covering a small area. If the patient was injured a while ago and needed his dressing changed, the blood would be dark yellow. And if the patient was just injured, there should be a lot more blood."

"So you mean the killer pretended to need a fresh dressing in order to take the doctor by surprise?" Big Bao asked.

I nodded. "Which tells us this was probably a premeditated crime. Use a little injury to fool the doctor, then sneak an attack."

"In that case, it really could have been the cheating woman's husband," the detective said.

"Very possibly," I said. "Let's get DNA testing on the gauze. I suspect the doctor may have been attacked immediately after he threw it in the trash. Some medical waste can spread disease, so a doctor would probably be careful about keeping the lid closed."

"Lots of new possibilities!" Big Bao said. "What should we do next?"

I shrugged and walked toward the exit. "Nothing we can do but send our new info to the task force and wait for the DNA results. Plus, it's still a holiday today. After last night, I want to go home and catch up on sleep."

Chief Hu came in and said, "The physical and chemical test results are back. The fire had an accelerant: gasoline."

"Did they test for the origin?" Big Bao asked.

"There's some staff looking at surveillance video from gas stations nearby," Hu said. "Others are asking around to see if anyone suspicious bought gas."

"Don't forget, the killer had a vehicle," I said. "Couldn't he have just siphoned the fuel out of it?"

"Nowadays, cars have curved filler pipes," Han Liang said. "It's really not easy to get the gas out. You could get the fuel out of a truck, but they use diesel."

"What about a motorcycle or moped?" I asked.

Han Liang nodded. "Yeah, you can get fuel out of bikes."

53

After a nap, I went to the task force meeting in high spirits.

The atmosphere was animated as they discussed the progress of the case.

"Seems Li Kehua did have an affair with a married woman," a detective said. "The woman's name is Ruan Fang. You noticed that poem had the character 'Ruan' in it, right?"

"Her husband is a company president named Wu Lixue," another detective said. "Chasing boys instead of being content as a rich man's wife causes trouble for everyone."

"President?" I frowned and thought for a moment. "Did you arrest him?"

The detective nodded. "The squad leader is questioning him now. Doing a DNA test too."

"Does this Wu Lixue keep birds?" I asked.

The detective raised his eyebrows. "Sure don't think so."

"I think you arrested the wrong man. The DNA won't match."

"Why?" He looked as shocked as if I had thrown cold water in his face.

I took out a transparent evidence bag. "We sent the floor mat for chemical and physical testing, and the test results came back with this."

"What the heck is it?" the detective said, frowning and leaning closer.

"The yellow things are a small grain often used to feed pet birds. The black thing is a chip of charcoal from a coal stove. In other words, the killer lives near bird feed and a coal oven. This company president doesn't raise birds, so where'd the bird feed come from? People in the city don't cook over coal, so where'd the charcoal come from?"

Just then, a DNA lab assistant came in and announced, "The suspect isn't a match."

"Isn't it possible that the blood on the gauze and the material on the floor mat don't belong to the killer?" Director Zhang said. "Your reasoning makes sense, Qin, but we can't be certain. We shouldn't let him go yet, right?"

"That's up to you."

"But who would want to murder that doctor besides him?" the detective said. "It doesn't seem like a robbery, right?"

"There's another possibility," Lin Tao said. "The killer may have seen something inside the clinic that he had to have, that he had to kill for."

"Like what?" the detective said, looking uncomfortable.

Lin Tao hadn't gone home for a nap. He'd been at the clinic, surveying. Seeing how charged up he was told me he'd made a discovery.

Lin Tao sat casually down at the conference table. He took a sip of water and popped a USB drive in the computer, then opened a slide show of photos he'd just taken.

"This afternoon, we focused on surveying the little back room," Lin Tao said. "Though the flooring there isn't conducive to holding traces, the dust distribution inside the medicine cabinet appeared to indicate recent movement."

"Did you rule out that the doctor moved things himself?" I asked.

"Yes. This doctor was disciplined. He had a chart labeling the position where each medicine was kept. If he wanted something specific, he could go directly to the chart and find it. But the movement traces we found were very chaotic, and many drugs were out of place. So the killer probably moved them. That also explains why the clinic looked ransacked."

"Was there something missing?" I asked, my eyes lighting up.

Lin Tao smiled. "Methadone."

"A lot of heroin users use it as a replacement," I said. "And as we've seen all too recently, an addict committing murder to get a fix is certainly plausible."

"Send Wu Lixue home," Director Zhang ordered. "Time to look for evidence related to drug users."

"I think the main line of investigation should follow from the trace evidence we found," I said. "We really have a lot of criteria now. Think about it: a drug user familiar with the area who keeps birds and has a coal oven and a small injury. With all these criteria and DNA, how could we not break this today?"

Still, I kept wondering why a drug addict would go to so much trouble with the suitcase and quarry and burning the body, all for a couple bottles of methadone.

Investigators dispatched officers from two stations, who searched the surrounding five villages and quickly found our bird-keeping, coal-burning, drug-addicted man. By eight p.m., Wu Biao was under arrest.

"Before we began," the detective responsible for the arrest said, "we looked at methadone clinics in the area that had been robbed previously, then used a crime map to determine possible whereabouts of the suspect, then followed your criteria to find him. It only took two hours to figure out where he was. When we searched his home, we found methadone pills that matched the ones missing from the clinic and—get this—one hundred thousand yuan."

"Huh?" Big Bao said. "A hundred thousand bucks? Then why would he have to steal methadone? Just go buy some drugs and you're done. None of this stabbing and shoving bodies in suitcases."

"He admitted that he pretended to need a new bandage from Dr. Li, then took him by surprise and stabbed him, but then he got scared and wanted to hide the body. So he took a suitcase from the back room, drove the body on his motorcycle to the quarry, siphoned out gas, and burned the body."

"That does fit perfectly with our hypothesis," Big Bao said smugly.

"We asked him why he didn't just go buy drugs," the detective said. "He said because of the big crackdown recently, you need really good contacts to find them, even if you have money."

"But where did the money come from? Did he have a job?" I asked. "Usually addiction drains all their money away."

"He couldn't explain the cash no matter how hard he tried," the detective confessed.

"I smell a rat!" I said.

"What do you think, Qinny boy?" Big Bao said, playing Sherlock.

I looked down and thought a moment, then smiled. "What do I think? Ha. I think we were wrong again."

"Wrong how?" Big Bao asked.

I turned to the detective. "There aren't a lot of people around here with the surname Wu, are there? What's the relationship between Wu Biao and Wu Lixue?"

"Wu . . . Wu Lixue? Didn't we release him? Oh shit. I get it."

54

The detectives quickly learned that Wu Biao was unemployed, apart from doing some dirty work as a hired thug, principally for Wu Lixue, his cousin.

Wu Lixue had a good career; he was worth over ten million before he turned forty. As you'd expect, his relatives and friends from the villages always came to him for jobs. The most useful one was his tough, reckless cousin.

Wu Biao was a junkie, so he needed a constant stream of money, which became the chain that bound him to Wu Lixue.

Wu Lixue doted on his wife, Ruan Fang, who was fifteen years younger than he and repulsed by the man she'd married. Her only job was shopping, but all that spending didn't fill the emptiness she felt inside.

Ruan Fang frequented bars, nightclubs, and gyms, hoping to find "true love." She soon met a handsome man at the gym who made her heart beat fast—Li Kehua.

Li Kehua wasn't tall, but he had a wonderful face and chest. He had retired from the provincial hospital at twenty-seven and started a private clinic in a busy town. That kind of courage made Ruan Fang melt. Similarly, Ruan Fang's beauty and charm drove Li Kehua wild. They'd been seeing each other for about a month when Wu Lixue caught on, but he decided to keep quiet.

On Mid-Autumn Festival, when Ruan Fang left to rendezvous with Li Kehua, Wu Lixue called Wu Biao and laid out the murder plan. Wu Biao had taped the call to protect himself, and the detectives were excited to submit the recording as evidence in court.

"One hundred thousand yuan to take a life," I said, shaking my head. "These rich people have no morals."

"That poem must have been a present Li Kehua was going to give to Ruan Fang the night of Mid-Autumn Festival," Big Bao said. "Seems like she was all about material things, but I guess something from the heart could still reach her."

"Right," I said. "And that young doctor really had some literary talent."

"Now moving and burning the body makes sense too," Chief Hu said to us.

"Yeah? I still haven't untied that knot."

"Wu Lixue hated Li Kehua so much for stealing his wife," Hu said, "that he told Wu Biao to stab the doctor more even after he was dead and then feed his body to dogs."

"Feeding it to dogs wasn't realistic, so he went and burned it," I said, following Hu's logic. "Wow. This Wu Biao is a pretty thorough hit man."

Lin Tao sighed. "If only people could just be honest with one another."

"Yeah, yeah," Big Bao said, "especially single hunks like you. Don't give in to temptation, man. Married women are to be avoided at all costs."

"Well, we cracked this one fast, so everyone can take a breath before we go back to investigating Eleventh Finger," I said. "This case should remind us that criminals don't always act alone. They can be hired. Our perspective was too narrow, and we nearly missed it; we have to do better next time."

55

The first thing I saw when I arrived at work in the morning was Big Bao telling a story to some young female colleagues from the DNA lab.

"Ten years ago, on a dark and stormy night, when I was still in college, a rustling sound suddenly came from the washroom. My roommates and I stiffened and went to look. One of our classmates was in there, scrubbing a uniquely shaped machete. When it was clean, he chopped up a cantaloupe for us."

Big Bao nodded to me before continuing. "While everyone was eating, he gave the machete an admiring look and said, 'Knife's not bad, huh?' We didn't care about his knife—we were stuffing our faces with the cantaloupe. But then he added, 'I stole it from the anatomy department! No worries, I washed off all the meat that was stuck on it.'"

"Eww . . . ," the girls chorused.

"That knife was used for autopsy training, to cut open those disinfected, preserved cadavers the school uses. We all knew no one ever cleaned those knives. People just stuck them back in the supply box with fat and muscle fibers all stuck on. Now you know why your mom told you never to accept food from strangers."

DNA technicians generally haven't studied medicine or anatomy, so Big Bao's vivid description made them squeamish. One of the girls said, "Forget about food from strangers. I'm never eating cantaloupe again."

"You sure?" Big Bao grinned. "I just saw a couple cantaloupes in your office. Should I take them?"

"What a jerk," I said. I knew Big Bao always had a motive for telling his stories. "Trying to trick these girls out of their snacks."

It was another slow week. Every day we just collected injury assessments, did bone age assessments, or wrote petition review reports. But with the still-open Eleventh Finger case constantly on our minds, we could never fully relax.

Feeling lazy, I turned on my computer and got ready to write a letter requesting two new survey kits, but as soon as the Word document opened, I got a call.

Big Bao was slurping down his ill-gotten cantaloupe, and his eyes widened. He gestured at the phone, asking me to answer it.

"Hello?" I said. "Hello, Chief Sun, how are you? What? Four?"

Big Bao stopped chewing.

I hung up the phone and said, "Qing District, four family members killed."

"Murder?" Big Bao slurred, his mouth full of cantaloupe.

"An explosion case, maybe an accident. But since so many people died, we have to go to the scene. I'll call Lin Tao and Han Liang."

Big Bao smiled as he slowly swallowed the cantaloupe. "All right! Finally a case! I've been growing hemorrhoids sitting around here."

Qing District was a subsidiary of Qingxiang City, relatively undeveloped. The scene was in one of its eastern suburbs. At least thirty police vehicles were blocking the road leading into the small village, so we had to get out and walk. Based on the level of police force presence, I knew it was a serious situation.

After we entered the village, there seemed to be an officer standing guard every few feet, nearly filling the narrow roads. The houses on either side of the road had all their glass windows blown out.

"Okay, then, this was not a small explosion," Big Bao said, looking around. "I've never surveyed a blast site before. I'm a little scared."

"Me too," Lin Tao said. "Do you think surveying a blast site like this puts our lives in danger?"

"'Seekers of fame and fortune, go your own way; those afraid of death, do not enter,'" I said. "That's a motto of the Republic of China Military Academy. The same applies to us."

"There was an accident twenty years ago," Han Liang said. "A forensic scientist was surveying a bomb site and absentmindedly stepped on an unexploded mine. He died bravely."

"Yeah, I remember that," I said. "We had the same teacher."

The whole way down the road, small groups of local villagers were being questioned by police.

"I'm tellin' you, you weren't there, I've never been so scared!" said a villager. "It was, like, four in the morning, we were sleeping. Then there was a bang. Didn't sound like firecrackers, more like a bomb dropped from an airplane. Then our house started to shake and buzz, and all the glass broke. I thought I'd gone deaf. I saw my wife's mouth moving but couldn't hear her. I thought it was an earthquake, so I grabbed my wife and started running. We ran downstairs and saw Old Fan's house was smoking and realized it had exploded, so I called the police."

"I'm so damn unlucky," grumbled a villager with gauze wrapped around his head. "When it happened, I was taking a piss and heard the bang, and a piece of glass hit my head. Now I need stitches? Every house got damaged. The government has to take care of us, right?"

"Old Fan's family always said their house had really good feng shui," another villager said, "but it's all the way on the edge of the village. And the windows didn't have any protection, so how is that good feng shui? Plus, it blew up, so where's your feng shui now?"

The man's full name was Fan Jincheng. Since Old Fan's house was easternmost in the village, all of its windows, apart from the front, looked out on the wilderness with unobstructed views. The view from inside really was pretty nice.

Qing District's police officers were using a neighbor's living room as a temporary task force room, its tiny coffee table surrounded by cops. When the three of us entered, some of the younger officers got up to let us sit.

"Gentlemen," Qing District Director Zhou Qiming said seriously, "thank you for coming. Things have been so quiet recently. I never thought we'd have such a big case—I mean incident—after Mid-Autumn Festival."

Officials liked to call criminal events "cases," but suicides and accidents they called "incidents."

"Do we know what happened?" I asked.

Zhou shook his head. "The site is sealed. Technical personnel are awaiting your arrival before they get started, so we don't know the specifics yet. I'm guessing it was an accident."

"Oh?" I said. "Fill us in."

Zhou cleared his throat. "The scene is Fan Jincheng's home. He and his wife lived there alone, but when the dispatch officer arrived, he confirmed there were four victims."

"Did they have hired help?" I asked.

Zhou shook his head. "No, it's family. We've already identified the four victims as Fan Jincheng; his wife, Ren Sufen; their grandson, fifteen-year-old Fan Cheng; and their granddaughter, seven-year-old Zhao Liqian."

"Two kids." I hated to see children die prematurely.

"Yes," Zhou said sadly. "According to neighbors, grandchildren often spend weekends at Fan's house. Today's Monday, and their parents were going to pick them up to take them to school. I can't imagine what they're feeling."

"Why do you think it was an accident?" I asked, trying to shake off the horror of losing children.

"First, our dispatch officer found the door locked and had to force it open. According to our investigation, the four of them got along wonderfully, so it couldn't have been suicide or anything. Second, the worst damage was in the kitchen area at the east end of the house. The village gets its energy from a gas pipeline, and the officer found that the segment connected to Fan's house was ruptured and still hissing gas, so he called to have the main valve shut off. That would indicate it was a gas leak that reached an explosive concentration in the air and was ignited by a flame or an electrical spark."

"Yes." I nodded. "Makes sense."

"Since four people died, including two children," Zhou said flatly, "the city and district are watching very closely, requesting that we find the source of the explosion quickly and handle it. First order of business is to definitively determine the cause of the explosion. The fire department was here earlier, but they didn't come to a firm conclusion. They extracted some samples for testing, but the results will take two days to come back."

I took a map of the village the detective had sketched and studied it carefully.

"What do you guys need to do?" Zhou asked.

"First we want to go in and see the scene," I said. "Then I'd appreciate it if you'd send morgue workers over to collect the bodies—I'd like to get them out of here. My team will collect residue and debris from the site and the surrounding area, then go from there."

"Sounds good," Zhou said. "You all go ahead and get started. I'll wait for your results. The investigative division will keep gathering information."

We left the meeting room and put on our survey gear.

Lin Tao said, "I'm a little confused. Why would four people, including two children, be near the kitchen at four in the morning? If they weren't in the kitchen, there would have been a wall blocking them and they wouldn't have died, right? They couldn't have been up that early to eat, I don't think. Kids don't usually start school till eight. Is there any reason to get up that early?"

"Shit, Lin Tao, you're right," I said, more alert now. "The timing really is a problem."

"This is a tough one. Four people dead, but we have no way to cross-check the facts with them. Who do we ask?" Big Bao said.

"Ask the scene; ask the bodies."

56

Through the main gate was a medium-sized courtyard and, behind it, the two-story main house. To the east were two one-story buildings with a kitchen and a bathroom. To the west was a row of one-story sheds filled with junk.

All of the glass in the windows was completely blown out. The kitchen roof was caved in, destroyed, which meant it was the blast's point of origin.

In the center of the courtyard lay two children's bodies. The girl's head was covered in blood, and there were bricks near it. The clothing on the boy's upper body was torn, and he had a large bloodstain on his chest that made it hard to locate the wound.

At the door to the kitchen lay the body of an old woman whose shirt was shredded and whose head, face, neck, chest, and abdomen were burned black.

After we did a brief examination of the three bodies and photographed them, we called in the morgue workers. As they carried the body bags out the gate, we heard the voices of the crowd outside rise.

Next we had to look at the primary scene, so we walked into the kitchen. The brick walls were cracked, windows blown out, the roof had collapsed, and rubble was covering a corpse from the chest down. The stove, water tank, sink, and cabinets had all collapsed, and fragments of pots and pans were scattered on the ground. The exposed end of the gas pipeline was wrapped up with a rag. Walking in, I was struck by a strong burning smell mixed with gunpowder.

The body buried in bricks was hard to even identify as human because its skin was charred. Ashes had stuck to it, so we couldn't distinguish its features either.

"I didn't see any burn marks in the courtyard," Lin Tao said. "All the damage is concentrated in the kitchen. It was clearly the site of the blast."

"It's not enough to just get the approximate location," I said. "We have to pinpoint the blast within one and a half feet."

As Big Bao watched Lin Tao take pictures, I walked out of the kitchen and into the main house. On the first floor were a bedroom and a living room. The floor inside was so clean, I assumed the first responders hadn't bothered going in. The bedroom was colorful and decorated with indecipherable "drawings" on the walls, so I figured it was a child's room. Two untucked quilts were strewn on top of the bed, and on the ground were two small red slippers that appeared to belong to a girl.

Running around barefoot? I thought with a frown. Maybe Lin Tao was right that there really was something strange going on here.

I went up to the second floor and found a hallway with three rooms coming off it. Two of them were piled high with junk. The third had a bed with two quilts, untucked.

Big Bao was waiting for me in the courtyard.

"How's it going?" I asked. "Did you dig the body out?"

Big Bao frowned and shook his head. "No need, just had to pull. Only half left."

"That serious?" I hurried over to the kitchen and saw the carnage.

The body had been severed around the navel, the stump's soft tissue charred, with black and green intestines softly hanging out. Some of the bowels had been blown off, leaving yellow feces scattered nearby.

The broken end of the dark red liver was exposed and emitted a powerful odor. Because of the enormous power of the explosion, the victim would have died quickly and without much bleeding. The little blood that did spill was burned away by the high temperatures.

Now that the body was exposed, the whole kitchen filled with the stench of human abdominal cavity, which masked the original burning smell.

I rubbed my nose and put on a second pair of gloves.

"Do we really have to sort through all this rubble?" Lin Tao asked.

I nodded. "We have to increase our chances of finding body parts. First, out of respect for the dead. Second, their distribution will help determine the direction of the blast."

"Then I'm afraid we'll have to check a lot more than just the rubble," Lin Tao said, looking at the collapsed roof and empty windows.

"Right," I said. "Based on the looks of the kitchen now, there aren't many more body parts here. They were probably thrown from the room by the force of the blast."

"It's not just body parts we're looking for," Lin Tao said. "How 'bout we divide the labor. You take the forensic team to look for the rest of this guy, and I'll have the technicians help me look for trace evidence of explosives."

I nodded in agreement as I set about rummaging through the rubble.

Big Bao came in, holding construction helmets. "Put these on. This place could come down on our heads."

The dozen or so pieces we found in the kitchen were really tiny, but I was eventually able to determine where they came from.

"Look, this soft tissue with skin, pores, and lots of rough black hair must be from the lower leg." I collected the tissue and spread it on a plastic sheet, sorted by category. "These bones are long but thin, which means they're from the tibia and fibula, also the lower leg. These are nail beds, and you can make out some foot bones, and this is soft tissue from the foot."

"This person's lower leg and feet were basically blown to smithereens," Big Bao said. "I can't believe how destroyed this all is."

Lin Tao said, "I was a little skeptical of those anti-Japanese TV shows where a bomb blows off a whole limb. But now I think I'm beginning to get the picture."

I nodded. "There are lots of different kinds of injuries at a bomb site. I'll tell you more during the autopsy if you want."

"We've gone through all this debris, so should we go look outside now?" Big Bao said as he picked up a basket.

I nodded. "Let's go together. Remember, every time we find a body part, we have to record about how far away it is from the kitchen."

There were a lot of body parts in the fields around the house. They were mostly larger pieces, and based on their morphology, probably from the thigh and calf.

"The most important thing is to find fragments of the pelvis, patella, and genitals," I said. "That'll help us determine the blast center."

Before we had walked far, we found a bone covered in bloody goo. It was semispherical, with a smooth front and back.

"Patella," I called. "About fifteen feet from the window."

As seven or eight forensic scientists combed the area, they found many soft tissue parts, along with a few fragments of the pelvis ten or so yards away.

"Are we done?" Big Bao said. "I'd rather not die of sunstroke. Mid-Autumn Festival's already passed; how is it this hot?"

I walked up to a scarecrow, took its hat, and said, "Your work is done, my friend. I'll keep looking. Oh wow, check it out!"

On the scarecrow's shoulder was a burned piece of human tissue. Based on the curly hair at its base, it was clearly a male reproductive organ.

"Are"—Big Bao looked at the straw hat in my hand—"you sure there's no soft tissue on that hat?"

Another hour of searching turned up a few more pieces of tissue. The farthest piece appeared to have come from the body's thigh and was thrown over a hundred yards away.

"That should be enough," I said. "Let's go do the autopsy."

"Start with the straightforward one," I said as the guys lifted the little girl onto the autopsy table.

The child was Zhao Liqian. Her forehead was completely caved in, her hair covered with blood. We could see the huge laceration on her forehead.

"What a cute kid," Big Bao said with a sigh. "I wish I didn't have to see this. Dead kids are the worst part of the job."

Based on the tissue bridging one end of the wound to the other and the contusion around the edge, a blunt object had caused her laceration and depressed skull fracture. We used a hemostat to pull out several yellow and red bits of brick.

"The victim's body position did not change after death," I said. "Combined with the debris extracted from the wound and the broken bricks around her at the scene, we can be sure the forehead wound was caused by bricks thrown by the explosion."

We found no other wounds on the small body. The frontal fracture pattern was not interrupted but was fully pressed inward, meaning the victim had died immediately after being struck in the head. That kind of wound would cause a large subdural hematoma and a subarachnoid hemorrhage, resulting in the formation of a small herniation and brain stem compression, which would lead to respiratory and circulatory failure and death.

The victim's stomach was empty, and we estimated the time of death was the same as the time of the explosion.

After examining the girl's body, we moved on to Fan Cheng.

Like his little sister, the boy showed no obvious signs of injury, only a small wound on the chest. When we moved the body, blood was still puttering out.

Fan Cheng's chest cavity was full of blood. We found a tear in his aortic arch and, in his thoracic cavity, the shard of glass that killed him.

"What crappy luck," Big Bao said, shaking his head. "If the glass hadn't hit him right there, he wouldn't have died."

"One is a large, blunt injury; one is a cut from fast-flying glass," I said. "These are both things people can't do. So the explosion caused their deaths."

"Are you saying you're sure it was an accident?" Lin Tao asked.

"No. The explosion was the cause of death, but it wasn't necessarily an accident."

"Don't you think it's a little funny? I think if the timing is suspicious, the case is suspicious."

"It's not just that." I told them about the shoes I found in the downstairs bedroom.

"A real shame," Big Bao said. "If only this boy had dodged that glass, he could tell us what happened himself."

"Dodge?" Lin Tao said. "Dodge how? Flying glass is no slower than a bullet. You think this is *The Matrix*?"

"Remember, even though these two injuries were caused by a blunt and sharp object respectively, the principle's the same," I said. "They're both caused by ejecta from the explosion."

"Right, you said there are a lot of different kinds of explosion injuries," Lin Tao said. "Let's hear it."

"Well," I said with a sly smile, "if we let the body tell you, you'll remember better."

57

The third body belonged to Ren Sufen, who was found near the entrance of the kitchen. Her wounds were mostly on her front. There didn't appear to be any surface damage besides burning on the chest and abdomen.

"The victim's skin shows second-degree burns. The rest appears to be undamaged," Big Bao said. "We'll have to open her up to find the cause of death."

"Hold on," I said. "Did you notice the white lines following the victim's skin pattern along the nose bridge, eyebrows, and corner of the eyes? That's from when light came out of the explosion and she reflexively closed her eyes. The wrinkled-up skin didn't burn, but the skin around it did, which made those lines. This tells us two things: First, she was alive when the explosion happened. Second, she was facing it."

Big Bao nodded.

The autopsy went very slowly because Ren Sufen's internal organs were so badly damaged. Her heart and lungs had significant contusions from hitting the chest wall. Her liver and spleen were ruptured but hadn't bled much because she'd died so quickly. In addition, her brain tissue showed signs of an extensive petechial hemorrhage.

"Tell me—I can understand all this damage to the internal organs, but how did the brain injury form?" Big Bao said. "Her skull was protecting it. You can't get a brain injury from a blast of air, can you?"

"Your forensic pathology needs some work," I teased. "It's all in the book. A shock to the chest wall causes a sudden increase in blood pressure in the chest. The superior vena cava's blood pressure soars, causing blood to flow back to the brain, which ruptures veins and capillaries, causing a petechial hemorrhage."

"Say more, wise master, say more." Lin Tao laughed.

"All three victims' stomachs were empty, which confirms they died at roughly the same time," I said, ignoring Lin Tao.

The fourth body was the most difficult, because it wasn't so much a body as half a body and ten miscellaneous pieces. The worst was that, whenever the half a body moved a little, more intestines would spill out. Their disgusting contents kept sticking to the autopsy table.

"This victim also died in the blast," I said, "but there are no white lines on his face."

"Meaning he wasn't facing the blast center," Big Bao said.

I nodded. "Right. His injuries are the most severe, so he was closest to the blast, but he was not facing it."

"That also means the blast came from inside the kitchen toward his back," Lin Tao said. "Really cool. Seems like you really can pinpoint the blast area to within a foot and a half."

Big Bao and I put the body parts on the autopsy table one by one, painstakingly cobbling together almost all of the victim's lower body.

"You forensic scientists must be pretty good at jigsaw puzzles," Lin Tao said. "It reminds me of the story of when you put that body together at North Central."

"The victim died from neurogenic shock caused by limb amputation," I said. "It could also have been blood loss. But whatever the specific reason, it was certainly from injuries caused by the explosion."

I looked at Lin Tao and the Qing District interns and said, "Now, explosion injuries are all about shock waves, high temperatures, and ejecta—explosive projectiles. The shock waves cause the most damage and can be divided into overpressure, negative pressure, and dynamic pressure. Overpressure blast injuries include the oppression effect (caused by pressing on the abdominal organs), the implosion effect (caused by the body's internal gasses compressing, expanding, and bursting), the fragmentation effect (a stretching force that rips the body into pieces), the inertia effect, and the differential pressure effect (intervascular pressure imbalance and thrombosis)."

"So complicated," Lin Tao said, scratching his head. "What do 'negative' and 'dynamic pressure' mean?"

"Negative pressure stretches the body, but dynamic pressure throws it, like when we see a grenade explode on TV and send Japanese soldiers flying.

"It all sounds really complicated, but at a real blast site, there are only five forms of damage." I pointed at the body on the autopsy table. "The two main forms of damage on this body are fragmentation wounds—because the shock wave created a stretching force, which led to the amputation of the lower body—and burns. There's no clothing left on the victim's back, whereas there is still some on the front, so that means there was more severe burning on the back, which supports our earlier conclusion that the blast center was behind the victim."

"What about Ren Sufen?" Lin Tao asked.

"Ren Sufen's injuries are minor on the outside and severe on the inside. Typical shock trauma caused by compression and impact injuries. These are three of the most common and serious injuries that occur at blast sites. The children's injuries are the fourth kind, ejecta injuries. Of course, there are other injuries that occur at blast sites, like carbon monoxide poisoning, falls, and crushing."

"Quite a lecture, Professor Qin," Lin Tao said, "but what good are all these mechanisms for solving the case?"

"Well," I said, "these body parts flew out through the window and landed really far, which means the blast was extremely powerful, and answers an important question."

I saw everyone watching me expectantly. "The weight of the victim's genitals and patella are about the same, but the genitals were launched farther, so the patella was thrown from a smaller angle and the genitals were thrown from a larger angle. The blast must have gone out radially from the center, which was parallel with Fan Jincheng's back."

"That would put the blast center under the sink," Big Bao said, looking at the ceiling as he pictured the kitchen.

I nodded. "The end of the gas pipeline was in front of Fan Jincheng, so it couldn't have been the center. If the room blew up after filling with gas, there must have been something under the sink that could produce fire or electricity."

"Wait, do you mean like a bomb?" Lin Tao said.

"In the early morning, the four family members rushed from their bedrooms toward the kitchen, and then the explosion occurred. It's very possible that this wasn't an accident."

On hearing our report, the task force members looked somber.

"So what do you think we should do next?" Director Zhou asked. "The investigation thus far hasn't found anyone with a conflicted relationship to the victims."

"We're going to keep sorting through the scene," I said, "to see if we can find any possible explosive residue, especially detonation device fragments."

"The fire department already did that," Zhou said. "They found some suspicious materials, but it was hard to be sure because a lot of kitchen appliances have metal parts that are hard to differentiate from detonation devices."

"Then we'll look too," I said, "and we'll also search the neighboring houses."

We spent that whole afternoon back in the dilapidated kitchen, paying special attention to the sink. Even though it had been blasted into nonrecognition, we still cleaned and examined every chunk of brick. But all we found was a black, rubbery substance.

"How can there be so much sticky rubber stuff here?" Big Bao said. "Were they hoarding tape under here or something?"

"No way. If it was a roll of tape, even blown up, the pieces wouldn't have scattered like this."

"So what could it be?" Big Bao said.

I shook my head to show I didn't know either. We headed back to the task force, ready to submit our findings to the investigative team.

We entered a cloudy room.

"These cops start smoking like chimneys as soon as there's a case," Big Bao said, wrinkling his nose.

"Don't look down on smokers," I said with a smile. "Maybe they're trying to quit."

I caught a glimpse of a sealed cardboard box in the corner with a clearly printed label: SPARE BATTERY.

"What's this?"

A detective said, "Found it in a pigpen by the entrance to one of the homes. Seems to be an electric car battery."

"A car battery in a pigpen?" I asked. "Who lives there?"

"No one at the moment. They're all working in the city," the detective said. "The pigpen's abandoned too."

"Why would there be a new battery in an abandoned pigpen?" My heart began to race.

I gingerly set the box on the conference table. Through gaps in the seal, you could see bare wires sticking out.

"Um, I don't believe car batteries have external wires."

But Big Bao already had his hand on the lid. "Enough talk. Let's open it."

58

Inside the box were six black, cylindrical objects. They looked like the rolls of coins people gave as gifts during the Republican Era. Red and green wires were connected to the top of each one.

"What the hell is this?"

"Dynamite," Han Liang said matter-of-factly.

"Dynamite?" I took a few steps back.

He nodded. "Wrapped like that, it's probably the ammonium nitrate used in mines."

All the hairs on my body stood up.

"Looking at the volume," he continued, "it's probably four and a half pounds per roll. Altogether, twenty-six pounds of ammonium nitrate explosives."

"That . . . That means . . ." Big Bao was in shock. "If it had a pull-wire, we'd all be dead?"

Han Liang smiled. "Calm down. If it hasn't blown up already, it won't. But yeah, if it did have a pull-wire, when you just opened the lid, not only would we have died, but the rest of the town would have gone up in smoke."

"See?" I slapped Big Bao on the back of the head. "You gotta think before you do things, man. My son hasn't been born yet. I don't want to get killed!"

"Ling Dang's expecting?" Han Liang said, bizarrely calm in the face of disaster.

"What? No, not yet, I just mean . . . ," I mumbled.

The truth was, I'd received a text the night before from Ling Dang saying she got a positive result on a home pregnancy test. I couldn't wait for this awful case to be over so I could go with her to the hospital to get it confirmed.

Shaking, I pointed to the box and shouted, "What do we do with this thing?"

"Well," Han Liang said, "pure ammonium nitrate is stable at room temperature. It's not sensitive to impact or friction. But at high temperatures, high pressure, and in the presence of objects that can be oxidized, it can explode."

I looked at the ashtrays full of cigarette butts. "Then we'd better get it out of here quick."

That a box of dynamite sat peacefully in a crowded room full of cigarettes for a whole afternoon was a stroke of luck. Once the physical and chemical crew had taken the box away, everyone calmed down a little and whispered to one other.

"Despite the close call," I announced, "we've made a huge discovery. The dynamite we just saw was wrapped in black rubber tape, which matches debris we found at the blast center. The explosion was caused by the ammonium nitrate dynamic."

"But this is a strictly controlled explosive," Director Zhou said. "And there isn't a mine nearby."

"According to our survey," a detective jumped in, "a lot of people work outside the village. There are definitely people with access to explosives."

"No one would do such a horrible thing for no reason," Zhou said. "Step up your investigation of the victims' family members, especially anyone who works in a mine and recently came back to the village."

"But how will we identify a suspect?" the detective said. "We don't have any evidence."

"Give us an hour," I said, "and we'll get you some."

I looked at Lin Tao. "We know the bomber went into that pigpen, and he definitely went into the victim's yard to set the bomb. When the officers arrived, the gate was locked, so the killer must've climbed over the wall. Think you could find some traces?"

"You know it," Lin Tao said with a slight smile. "Plus, there're bound to be prints on that box. I got this."

Zhou nodded appreciatively and then looked to me. "Qin, what are your thoughts on site reconstruction?"

"Simple!" I declared, brimming with confidence. "The killer went over the wall and hid in the victims' home, then planted the bomb. Actually, judging by the additional explosives, he may have been planning another. But while he was planting the first one, he made a noise and woke up the Fans, who turned on a light. Seeing it, the killer hurried back over the wall to escape. The old couple went downstairs and woke up Fan Cheng, who got out of bed and followed. When the three of them left the house, Zhao Liqian also woke up and, finding herself alone, ran outside without shoes."

I paused and took a deep breath. "At that moment, Fan Jincheng stepped on or came into contact with the detonation device and set off the explosion. The four of them died right then and there."

"So terrible." Zhou sighed. "If the timing were any different, the kids at least might have survived."

"Yes," I said sadly. "Fate is a slippery thing."

"No shortage of footprints around the pigpen," Lin Tao boasted when he returned to the task force, "including several prints belonging to the same person. We also found partials on the inside and outside of the wall near the kitchen. And guess what? They match those in the pigpen."

"Nicely done, my man!" I exclaimed, clapping him on the shoulder. "We've got the bomber's footprints!"

Lin Tao smiled. "But wait, there's more. The bomber was wearing canvas People's Liberation Army sneakers. Those shoes aren't so common these days, and the sole pattern is unmistakable. Plus, we found fingerprints on the cardboard box, very fresh. Other than Big Bao's, I mean."

"Excellent work," Director Zhou said. "A lot of fancy testing requires days, but you all used your naked eyes. High-tech tools are great, but the key to good detective work is still boots on the ground. Now it's time to find our man."

"The sooner the better," I agreed. "This piece of shit blew up some little kids. Who knows what he's capable of?"

Happily, we didn't have to wait long. Our officers headed out to resurvey the village, and one of them spotted a man carrying an old-fashioned bundle, ready to travel. On his feet were those old canvas PLA sneakers.

Suspicious, the detective approached the man for questioning. But when he saw the officer headed his way, the villager suddenly threw down his bundle and ran.

Did he really think he could get away? Before he ran three hundred yards, three of our men tackled him to the ground.

"Hey, let me go! Who do you think you are?" the villager squawked as he struggled.

"Police, and you know it. What's your name?"

"Fan Pao."

That made the officers chuckle because *pao* is the word for "run" in Chinese. "All right, Pao, you're coming with us."

The sole pattern and fingerprints confirmed that Fan Pao had blown up the house. Now we were all dying to know why.

59

Fan Pao's parents died young, so his uncle, Fan Jincheng, had raised him. Three years ago, Fan Jincheng had arranged for Fan Pao to marry a beautiful woman. The two of them were happy together and even welcomed a lovely son a year later.

Thanks to Fan Jincheng, the lonely orphan now had a good life. But Fan Pao knew he'd never make much money for his young family if he stayed in the village farming. So, two years earlier, he'd gone to work in a Shanxi coal mine. Although the work was dangerous and hard, the money wasn't bad.

During the Lunar New Year holiday that year, he took the ten thousand yuan he'd saved up and headed home to surprise his wife. He never expected to hear moaning coming from his own bedroom.

The man having an affair with his wife turned out to be his cousin, Fan Jincheng's eldest son, Fan Shengli.

"My dad took you in, gave you a nicer wife than you could ever get yourself, so what more could you want?" Fan Shengli laughed. "My having some fun with her just helps you out. Better to keep the fertilizer on the family fields than have her run off with some outside man, right?"

Fan Pao had been bullied by Fan Shengli his whole life. Nervous about his status within the family, he'd never dared to fight back. But even after twenty years of taking the abuse, he could never have imagined a betrayal like this.

Fan Shengli swaggered out of the house as Fan Pao's wife sobbed, and Fan Pao's mind spun.

Fan Pao was so used to Fan Shengli's bullying that he turned his pent-up anger on Fan Jincheng. The old man claimed he was giving me a wife, he thought, but it was a trick. He was really giving his own son a concubine.

The humiliation weighed heavily on Fan Pao as he went back to the mine in Shanxi. One night, he snuck into a storage shed and stole twelve sticks of dynamite, as well as blasting caps and detonators. Then he splurged on a gypsy cab to take him and his box back to Qing District.

Once home, Fan Pao set his awful plan in motion. He divided the dynamite in half, planning to blow both Fan Jincheng's and Fan Shengli's homes to smithereens.

That fateful morning, after planting the bomb in Fan Jincheng's dark kitchen, he knocked over a pan on the stove. The crash of metal gave him a terrible fright, so he hurried back over the wall. Just a few minutes later, he heard the deafening boom.

Fan Pao rejoiced. He hadn't imagined it would go so smoothly. Now he just had to wait for things to blow over before taking out Fan Shengli's house as well.

He never thought the police would figure out it was an intentional explosion—and certainly not so fast. Once they started poking around, though, he decided he'd better sneak off before they caught him. He was sad to abandon part two of the plan, but he consoled himself with the thought that, even though Fan Shengli didn't die, his father and Fan Shengli's son both died. Fan Pao felt avenged.

"You Dragon City guys really are as good as they say," Director Zhou told us. "If you hadn't cracked the case so fast, Fan Pao would have gotten away from us."

Lin Tao visibly swelled with pride.

Big Bao, on the other hand, was perplexed. "Hard to be happy when four innocent people died."

"Yeah," I said. "Poor Fan Jincheng and his wife gave Fan Pao everything, and this is how he thanked them, by killing Fan Shengli's children, even though they didn't do anything wrong. It's really unfair."

Still, getting to stretch our brains to solve a huge bombing case was exciting. On the drive back to Dragon City, Lin Tao, Big Bao, and I decided to get a drink to celebrate.

But Han Liang admonished us from the front seat. "Don't celebrate now, boys. Wait and get that drink after we break the Eleventh Finger case."

60

Forensic work isn't just about helping solve murders. A lot of the time, it's routine stuff like assessing injured people or doing toxicology for drug cases. Forensics is also essential for traffic accidents. We figure out whether the driver was under duress or some kind of coercion; we determine who was driving the car or sitting where to create a basis for liability. Since we were the provincial forensic department, helping municipal traffic departments was routine.

Major roads ran through Yanggong County, so they had a lot of accidents, and we often went there to survey accident scenes. This time, they had a difficult case on their hands.

As the story was relayed to us, a resident heard a loud bang outside at four o'clock in the morning. Going out to investigate, he found that a row of trees on the curb across from his house had been knocked down, and there was a tire in the road.

That road was a county highway in good condition and with little traffic. Young people often raced or went for joyrides there. One side of the road was a drainage ditch with about twenty feet of water. Since he didn't have a cell phone, the conscientious man ran half a mile before he found someone on the street and used their phone to call 110.

Officers rushed to the scene and undertook a rescue operation. After hours of work, they salvaged a Mercedes sedan and four bodies from the ditch.

Two of the victims were the president and vice president of a company in the county seat; the other two were escorts from an expensive karaoke bar. All of them had managed to climb out of the car after it hit the water, but because of injuries sustained in the crash, they weren't strong enough to keep from drowning. Blood tests showed that all four were intoxicated.

The cause of death and the cause of the accident were basically clear, but because drinking and driving was involved, the issue of compensation came up, and the four victims' families needed forensics to identify who had been behind the wheel.

Lin Tao, Big Bao, and I hadn't left town for a job in over a week and were getting a bit restless. When the call came in, we immediately jumped in a car.

But when it rains it pours. Just as we neared the crash site, I got a call from Chief Hu.

"Qin," Chief Hu said, "we need you back in Dragon City. Eleventh Finger has struck again."

"What?" My surprise woke Big Bao, who'd been dozing in the backseat. I put the chief on speakerphone and said, "It's been a month since the last murder, and five months since the first one. What the hell are we dealing with here? How is this monster still committing these crimes, and how do we still have nothing on him?"

"The killer's methods are simple," Hu said. "The simpler the methods, the easier to avoid leaving clues."

"This victim's also a thirtysomething male?" I said. "Same technique?"

Hu was silent for a second. "It's not quite the same this time. The victim is female, and her throat wasn't cut. Plus, she wasn't disemboweled."

"Huh?" I said. "Then how do you know it's related to Eleventh Finger?"

"Because Liang Fengzhi's genitals are in her pocket. And her breasts are missing."

I gasped. "The Eleventh Finger killer's signature! He doesn't need to bother cutting the throat or disemboweling his victims anymore, because he knows we're onto him and don't need any more provoking."

"Right, that's what we thought too," Hu said. "The killer is simplifying his process."

"So what do we do?" I said. "We're on our way to Yanggong to help with a traffic accident. Practically there."

"No rush," Hu said. "The boss is finally back from that special task force he's been assigned to all these months. The national police shot down the killer, wrapped up the case. Now that Chen's returned, he'll supervise this new murder himself. You just take care of that crash and head back as soon as you can."

"Terrific," I said. "We'll be back as soon as possible, and this time we're going to get the guy!"

I think my adaptive threshold is pretty broad. I can handle flavorful or bland food, hot weather or cold. At a crime scene, if the corpse is horribly rotten, as long as I get a chance to calm down, my mind can block out the stench after a few minutes.

Hu's call obviously sent my Eleventh Finger–obsessed mind racing, but once we arrived at the scene of the accident, I took a deep breath and focused on the task at hand. The people, the car, the road— Eleventh Finger was completely forgotten. Okay, mostly forgotten.

The car and bodies had already been removed and caution tape was up. I saw officers negotiating with repairmen. The accident had knocked down an electrical pole, and torn wires were scattered on the ground.

We could see streetlights and households nearby without power. The power company's phone must've been ringing off the hook.

Hoping to let them restore power as quickly as possible, we started our survey immediately.

The trees along the drainage ditch were bent down, but they hadn't snapped. Their bark was scraped off, and the fallen electrical pole lay near their tops.

"Looks like the car went into the water here," Big Bao said.

"The pole has flakes of silver paint stuck to it," I said, measuring, "which must be from the impact. The flakes are relatively high up, probably higher than the height of a compact car."

"What's your point?" Lin Tao asked.

"The vehicle tilted up after uprooting the trees. Although its frame may have been lifted by the trees, the weight of the vehicle and its passengers kept it from flying up. The fact that the impact marks are so high means the car may have flipped over."

I took off my gloves. "This scene couldn't have been staged. This was definitely an accident."

The totaled car had already been towed to a repair shop to be inspected, so we went to look it over. The vehicle was a silver-gray Mercedes, the front bumper fallen off, the hood surprisingly intact.

"This car's pretty messed up!" Big Bao said.

I circled the car slowly. "The trees at the scene are quite thin, and none broke. Because the soil on the curb is soft, the trees absorbed the impact while the vehicle was lifted up. There was no serious, direct impact. Look, the airbags didn't even inflate."

I stopped at the trunk. It was collapsed, completely distorted. I measured the depression on the top.

"This semicircular recess matches the diameter of the electrical pole, which means the car had already rolled. The whole topside of the trunk hit it."

"So the pole altered the vehicle's trajectory," Lin Tao said. "That's why it fell into the water. If it wasn't for that, the car would have eventually stopped. No one would have died."

Big Bao was focused on a Transformers bumper sticker. He laughed.

◆　◆　◆

"I'm sure the traffic department could have easily determined the path of the vehicle rolling over and going into the water," I said, "but the question of who the driver was needs forensics."

"Do you know?" Lin Tao said, bouncing a little in the moving car.

"Well, if the bodies don't have clear injuries, I've got nothing. Let's go see."

We were hurrying to the place I hated most, the local hospital morgue, the largest in the county.

The morgue was filled with refrigerated coffins with all kinds of bodies inside.

I rubbed my nose, pulled on my jumpsuit, and walked to the middle of the room where the four bodies lay on stretchers.

After several local forensic scientists hurried to remove the victims' clothing, I looked the bodies over and found no open wounds, not even any clear bleeding under the skin.

"Well, shit," Big Bao said. "No injuries, so how can we judge?"

I calmly examined each of the victims' limbs. "No, there are. They're just very light. I think we'll be able to make a determination."

"No serious injuries means there wasn't a direct collision," Lin Tao said. "That confirms our account of the accident."

I turned to a nearby traffic officer. "The family members agreed to an autopsy?"

"No."

"No? Didn't they want us to figure out who the driver was?"

"Yes, but they did not approve an autopsy."

After accidents, family members made all kinds of excuses, but they really just cared about compensation. But because of the influence of traditional Chinese thought, they often weren't willing to let their family members go under the knife.

I sighed. "Fine. Let's see what we can see without cutting."

Just doing an external examination greatly reduced our workload but also limited the information we could get. Fortunately, we had firm results in three hours.

I requested a meeting with the family members of the four victims.

"Did you get it?" the director of local traffic police asked. He was wary of my request to meet with the families, because even the slightest misstep could lead to complaints and petitions. What he didn't know was that my mind was already hundreds of miles away, focused on the fifth murder in the Eleventh Finger case. I was dying to get back as soon as possible.

"Sure did," I assured him. "Don't worry—I'll make this quick."

"After analyzing the scene and the vehicle, we have clearly determined the trajectory of the accident." I pointed at a photo slide.

"Cut the shit. We want to know who was driving," a guy jeered.

"Oh, my son, you died so horribly—" a woman howled, sending the room into a cacophony of quarreling and crying. The director himself poured everyone tea to calm them down.

Fortunately, I'd had Lin Tao remove photos of the corpses from the presentation; otherwise a riot would have broken out.

"Okay, let's talk about injuries, then." I coughed drily. "After examining the bodies, we determined that Male Number One was the driver."

"Bullshit!" that same man interrupted again. "The car was my son's, so you just assume he was the driver? Is that how you solve cases? What are you good for? Eating donuts?"

"So you're saying he couldn't have been driving his own car?" This time I was angry. "So tell me, who was? Or better yet, let me present the evidence."

The other victims' family members started to scold him and, cha-grinned, he sat back down.

"Male Number One had scratches from broken glass on his left arm and a contusion from a smooth, hard object on his right. Only the driver's side of the Mercedes has a window on the left and the gearshift and hand brake on the right. Male Number One also had a contusion on the right side of his waist, which lines up with the driver's seat belt buckle."

Male Number One's father hadn't jumped up to argue, so I went on. "Furthermore, Male Number One's body had bruising on the insides of both ankles, which means there was a hard object with a relatively coarse surface between his feet. The only thing in the car that matches this is the brake pedal. That wound is unlike all the other victims'. Also, the pants on his left knee had scratch marks. After inspecting the vehicle, we found the hood-release switch there with a sharp corner that could have scratched his clothing. None of the other positions in the car had objects hard enough to leave such a mark."

The driver's father seemed a little stumped, but he wasn't ready to let go just yet. "So . . . so tell me where the other people were sitting! If you can explain that clearly, maybe I'll believe you."

I smiled slightly, thinking we were lucky each victim's wounds were unique. "Female Victim One had bruises on each arm. The only posi-tion where both lower arms could come into contact with a flat object was the front passenger seat."

"So she couldn't have been driving?"

"No. Think about it for a second. If the driver hit the dashboard, the steering wheel would damage the chest. Female Victim One had no chest wounds. Also, of the four victims, only Female One's body showed no cuts from glass. And the only glass that didn't break was the front windshield and right front window. She was definitively sitting in the front passenger seat."

Hearing no objections, I went on. "Male Victim Two sat behind the passenger seat. His right side had scratches from glass, and his right temporal region had a large hematoma. As I wanted to explain earlier, the vehicle flipped over, so his head likely hit the door frame at that time."

Faint sobbing filled the room as I hurried to finish. "Last is Female Number Two. She sat behind the driver. Her right palm was cut up because, when the car was rolling to its right, she braced herself against the right window. If she'd been behind the passenger seat, she wouldn't have had enough distance to reach her arm out like that."

The conference room was silent.

"That's all. You have my condolences."

The driver's father opened his mouth to speak, but nothing came out. He slunk silently out of the room.

After the families had filed out, the director said excitedly, "Qin, in all my years in traffic policing, that was the most brilliant, persuasive analysis I've ever heard! Thank you!"

I was flattered by the praise but tried to show modesty. "Oh, it's nothing. The case's conditions were favorable, that's all. Glad we could help. Now we have to head back."

61

That traffic accident analysis made me feel pretty great, and I couldn't wait to tell the boss how his protégé was upholding his reputation in the field. Plus, it had been months—I missed the guy. Then it was time to head to the hospital with Ling Dang to see if our dreams had really come true.

But when we got to his office, Chen looked very gloomy.

"Boss, today I—"

"You're suspended," he barked.

"Suspended?" Lin Tao was the first to react.

My whole body felt numb. "Boss, who's suspended?"

He just stared at me, his eyes like torches.

I looked at dumbstruck Big Bao and astonished Lin Tao, then back at Chen. I gathered my courage and asked, "Wait, me? What'd I do?"

"Go home and wait to be summoned. Don't leave town."

"Summoned?" I racked my brain, thinking how I always played by the book, and about how many tough cases we'd solved while the boss was gone. Had I made some mistake? Something bad enough to need to be summoned?

The boss took a stack of photos out of his drawer and tossed it in front of me. "She look familiar?"

The woman in the photos wore a white knitted top, a black skirt, and lace stockings. She lay on the floor, pale as could be. She had clearly died of blood loss—the right side of her chest was soaked red.

I suddenly thought of the Eleventh Finger victim Chief Hu had mentioned—how the killer had cut off her breasts. This must be the same person. The last photo was taken while she was still alive. Her smile was lovely, but her face was definitely unfamiliar.

I shook my head. "I don't know her. Is she our fifth victim?"

"What were you doing during the National Day holiday?"

"That week? I was home with my wife, trying to figure out how to have kids."

"The victim's underwear had your DNA on it, Qin," the boss said sharply. "Ling Dang's trying to get pregnant, and you go do this?"

Everything went numb again. "What? I—I—I . . . How's that possible?"

Every forensic scientist's DNA is recorded in a database in order to guard against contamination during autopsies and sample-extraction processes. I hadn't attended the fifth victim's autopsy, so the only way my DNA could be on the victim was if we'd come into contact.

"Whoa, Director Chen, you can't possibly think the Eleventh Finger serial murderer is Qin here, right?" Lin Tao said.

I felt bewildered, wronged, angry, confused, and so much else that my heart felt clogged. The pressure was so great, I couldn't speak. I just looked directly at the boss, who stared back at me with a mixture of fury and concern.

After a brief stalemate, he said, "The victim, Liu Cuicui, was poisoned, strangled, and disemboweled using the tongue scoop method. From what I hear, the task force has always suspected Eleventh Finger could be someone on the inside, but they never expected to find your DNA."

"What was it?" Lin Tao said. "Hair?"

Chen was silent for a moment, then said, "Semen."

I had just gotten myself under control and was preparing to speak, but the revelation shocked me into incoherence all over again.

"I—I—I . . . Sh-sh-she," I stammered.

"Very little was found, but the DNA is definitely yours."

"No." Big Bao's face was unusually mature and authoritative. "Absolutely not. Qin would never. And anyway, we've been busy solving murder cases together almost nonstop ever since that handyman home invasion."

"Yes, I've been catching up on the reports," the boss said, "and it's because of all that excellent work that you aren't under arrest right now. You've never lied to me, Qin. Tell me, are you connected in any way to this or the other Eleventh Finger crimes?"

"No!" I shouted, finally finding my voice.

"Okay! I believe you, son. Otherwise, I wouldn't have told you so much. But this looks bad. The task force is willing to hold off charging you with anything, pending investigation, but you can't work for a while. Go study old cases in the archives so you don't waste your time."

How was I supposed to focus on closed-case files and a wall of whispering archives?

Me, a renowned forensic scientist, now a murder suspect. This was insane.

I picked up Liu Cuicui's photo, trying to figure out if I'd ever had anything at all to do with her. But after staring for a long time, I could honestly say I didn't know her at all.

It was getting late, but I still didn't go home. I didn't know how to tell Ling Dang what was happening, and we definitely couldn't go to the OB/GYN department right now. I texted her and lied, saying I was out on a case. In the deserted archives, I slowly paged through the files, trying to compartmentalize my spiraling thoughts.

Suddenly, the door swung open, and Lin Tao and Big Bao came in.

Big Bao said darkly, "We stole the materials from all five Eleventh Finger cases and made copies for you."

"He's not kidding about the stolen thing," Lin Tao said, looking behind him. "If the task force finds out, we're dead."

"Yeah," Big Bao said, nodding hard. "We don't want to get stuck in here looking at boring old archives like you."

I looked at my two brothers and felt moved. Other than the boss, they might be the only two people who really trusted me. "Thank you. I think I'm going to sleep here the next few nights. If you guys don't have anything to do, come help me look over these cases?"

Watching the two of them quietly leave, I wondered whether I would even be functional right now if not for their trust and support.

My strong adaptive powers came in handy again as the files slowly sucked me into a world without distractions. I even began to calculate the number of murders and unnatural deaths in each province and their ratios to one another.

I learned that, in a province with several million people, there were seven or eight thousand unnatural deaths each year. The largest number were traffic accidents; then came suicides and sudden deaths, followed by disasters and accidents. The suicide files were the most interesting. Forensic scientists had to be extra careful examining all suicide wounds to eliminate the possibility that they were actually caused by someone else.

For example, I found one case where the photos showed a victim with her throat slit, much like the Eleventh Finger victims, but the examiners had deemed it suicide. The reason was that the blood spatter around the body didn't show any gaps. If someone had been next to her, cutting her throat, as the blood flew through the air, some of it would have been blocked by the killer's body.

Province-level forensic scientists usually get called in on difficult cases, so they have less experience with unnatural death than lower-level forensic staff. I suddenly understood the boss's desire for me to use this time to fill in some gaps.

The archives also contained files on unresolved murder cases. Our murder-clearance rate was one of the best in the world, so there weren't that many. And a portion of the cases had clear suspects attached to them and just hadn't gone to trial yet. Still, there were several cases where investigators had eventually given up.

As I flipped through the cold cases, I realized it was almost two in the morning. Horror stories often paint two a.m. as a time when strange, terrible things happen. Sure enough, I looked down and broke out in goose bumps.

The file in front of me was an abandoned-baby case from earlier that year in Dragon City. To be more precise, it was a case in which the baby died and its corpse was discarded. In the photo was a trash can on the side of the road, and next to it was a woven wrap for carrying babies. Outside the wrap was a rope that had come loose from the smooth fabric.

I turned to the next page, a picture of the baby's body. There were no visible wounds. Its face mouth, nose, and neck were intact, but the face was bluish, so it had possibly died of disease. But what caught my attention were the marks on either side of the baby's thighs.

The night was dark, and so many terrible things had happened, but sitting there next to the filing cabinet, I felt not fear but incredible excitement.

Because I knew those marks were the key to solving the Eleventh Finger.

62

The sides of the baby's thighs had many postmortem strap marks. So after the baby died, whoever abandoned the body tied string around the legs to make it easier to move. But because the legs' soft tissue was thick and elastic, the string came right off, leaving those distinct marks.

Additionally, the baby's outer thighs showed cuts from a sharp object. The clean lines told me it was a knife, but the person only scratched the skin without injuring the muscle.

"Rope grooves!" I yelped, my voice echoing in the room.

After several attempts to tie up the legs, the killer must have resorted to that method to keep the strings in place. The technique was entirely consistent with the one used to tie up bodies in the Eleventh Finger cases.

Could it be the same person?

I eagerly scanned the rest of the file.

The forensic scientist on that case was Zou Shuwen. Two months later, he retired, so when we found the rope grooves on the bodies in the current cases, Old Zou wasn't around to tell us about the abandoned-baby case.

According to the file, Zou had performed a local dissection and examined the baby's heart. He found Ebstein's anomaly, a rare congenital heart defect in which the tricuspid valve leaks blood backward into the right atrium. As a result, the right atrium becomes enlarged, and if the leak is severe enough, congestive heart failure can result.

It was an abandoned-dead-baby case, not a murder. The unit handling it did some investigating and found no clues, so the case was closed.

Then I saw a note that made my head spin with excitement. Apparently, the baby wrap from the photo was still locked in the Dragon City bureau evidence room, never having undergone DNA testing.

I was about to call Lin Tao and Big Bao but then realized they would be sleeping. I could tell them the good news tomorrow.

I was elated not just because the injustice done to me would soon be righted, but because the terrible serial killer that had been toying with us all these months would finally be brought to justice.

Exhausted, I passed out on a row of chairs in the archives.

As soon as I woke up, I called Big Bao and Lin Tao and told them about my discovery. Lin Tao couldn't contain his excitement, while Big Bao blankly asked, "What's your point?"

Lin Tao and Big Bao hurried to the task force to report my findings and requested the baby wrap be immediately sent for testing. Then they came to the archives to go through the files with me.

"Even if we get the suspect's DNA off that baby thing, what do we do with it?" Big Bao said. "Ten million people live in Dragon City. We can't even use DNA to find a suspect in a little town of one thousand. How are we gonna do it in a provincial capital?"

"We can't use DNA to find the person," Lin Tao said, "just to confirm it's him once we have a suspect. I actually think the best thing right now is to make a criminal profile."

I nodded. "Okay, let's see, this person is psychologically disturbed. He's ruthless. And I bet he's already had problems with the police, which is why he's been trying to provoke us."

"Don't forget," Lin Tao said, "he must have a personal grudge against you, or he wouldn't be trying to set you up! What I want to know is how the hell he got your DNA."

I blushed. "I swear, my conscience is clear!"

"I was arguing with Forensic Scientist Han about whether the killer is male or female," Big Bao said, racking his brain. "Right now, I really think he was right that the killer's a woman."

"Oh? Why?"

"He made the point that the killer's cut marks didn't seem strong like a man's. And poisoning is much more common for female murderers."

"Yeah, but you didn't agree with Han before, so what changed?" I asked.

"I've thought about it a lot the last couple days. Like you told us before, with serial murders, you have to look at all the cases together," Big Bao said. "One key connection in these cases is that the first four victims were all men."

"But the fifth was a woman," Lin Tao said. "So how does that work?"

"Think about it. What kind of person is easily tricked into drinking poisoned alcohol or water? Either an acquaintance or someone who's trying to sleep with you. There was no connection between the first four victims, no common acquaintances. So the only thing left is sex."

I slapped the table. "For once, Big Bao, your reasoning makes perfect sense! But then why would the last victim be a woman?"

Big Bao pulled a report from his bag. "These are the results of the latest investigation. The last victim was gay!"

Lin Tao and I were both stunned. It was a perfect confirmation of Big Bao's theory.

"And get this," Bao said. "The men were all either single or away from their wives. There was the doctor who came to Dragon City to study, the lawyer and businessman who came for work, and a rich playboy. What they all have in common is susceptibility to having an affair.

The woman must be the same. I really think our hypothesis is correct. We're going to catch the killer!"

"But why would she switch to a woman this time?" I asked. "Did she want to keep us from making that connection?"

"We can't rule out that possibility," Lin Tao replied. "Of course, it could be that she's also attracted to women."

"So what should we do now?" Big Bao asked.

I rubbed my temples. "Do you guys know which bars lesbians go to? There can't be very many in Dragon City."

"What?" Lin Tao said. "You want to sit and wait for her to come to you?"

"Yeah, hold up," Big Bao said. "How are you going to pick a neighborhood? And even if you somehow get the right bar, how are you going to know who's the killer?"

"I'm not sure. But I somehow think if I can just run into her, I'll be able to tell. Don't forget, she wants to frame me. I should be able to notice something that's off."

"Hm," Lin Tao said. "That makes some sense. Since she tried to frame you, you definitely have some connection. I bet she's a jilted girl you dumped."

I turned red again. "Hey! Ling Dang was my first love!"

"Stop flirting, you two," Big Bao said. "You still didn't address my first question. How are you going to choose the location? Dragon City is big!"

I smiled and took out a drawing compass. "When we had some downtime between cases recently, I boned up on crime mapping. It's very popular abroad, but a lot of people here think it's superstition. Remember how Su Mei made that computer program to simulate currents and locate that grave in the sewers? It's kind of like that, but with crimes."

"Oh yeah," Big Bao said. "And the local guys used that to find the heroin addict in our doctor murder case, right?"

"Exactly, and it worked. Some experts think the early crimes in a serial case happen within a certain radius of the killer's principal activity zone, then expand outward."

"That does sound a little abstract," Lin Tao said.

"Got nothing to lose," I said.

"Are you going to use the places where the bodies were disposed of?" Big Bao asked.

I frowned. "We know the killer has a car. The bodies could be disposed of anywhere, so that won't work. I say we map the places the victims were last seen alive and see where the center is."

Big Bao grabbed a map of Dragon City and a red pen. "Meng Xiangping went missing at this hospital, here. Zuo Fangjiang went missing at this bank, here. Cheng Xiaoliang lived near the university and was killed there. Liang Fengzhi went missing here. Should Liu Cuicui go on the map too?"

I nodded and took the pen. "According to the reports you stole for me, Liu Ciuciu was murdered in her rental house in this trendy neighborhood."

I used my compass to connect the points. The result was a lopsided oval. In the middle, I drew a blue circle. "Look, what's this place?"

"It's the 3754 District!" Lin Tao shouted. "That neighborhood is all nightlife—bars, clubs, karaoke. You nailed it!"

I smiled. "Amazing. I don't know about you guys, but I'm a crime mapping convert! It looks like Bao was right. The killer very definitely used attraction to gain her victims' trust."

"I'm a little confused, though," Lin Tao said. "The initial investigations of the victims should have looked at bars and nightclubs. Wouldn't they already have checked the surveillance video? Why didn't they find anything?"

Big Bao raised his hand. "I can answer that, actually. I have a friend on the video team. He was complaining to me a few days ago, said they have an office full of hard drives. They're scouring video footage from all over the city—without a crime map, it's way too much. Plus, the victims weren't wearing very distinctive clothing, and bars are really dark. So they either haven't gotten to the video from the bars on that street, or they looked at it and didn't spot anything."

"Makes sense," I said. "So what are we waiting for? The killer took part of the last victim's body. She's definitely planning another murder."

"Let's go!" Lin Tao said. "That neighborhood is crawling with hot women. If nothing else, we can enjoy the view."

But Big Bao looked worried. "Qin, are you sure you can spot the killer? And isn't this dangerous? You're a great forensic scientist, but you're not Superman."

Big Bao's concern was like a needle bursting my balloon. He was right. Could I really just walk into a bar and find the killer? And what would happen if I did?

63

Just then, Big Bao's phone rang.

"Hello?" Big Bao saw it was a task force detective and answered on speakerphone.

"Results are back," the detective said. "The baby wrap had two people's DNA on it. One was the baby."

"And the other?" Big Bao asked anxiously.

"The baby's mother."

"Did you check the DNA registry?" Big Bao asked. "Any hits?"

"No."

"Guess we'll have to go find her ourselves," I said as I gave Big Bao a pat on the back. "But you're right about it being too dangerous for me to just sit in a bar. We may be forensics guys, but what we need is an old-fashioned detective stakeout."

The three of us sat in the car we'd borrowed from Han Liang, parked at one end of the main drag of the 3754 District. Fashionably dressed men and women bounced between bars and clubs.

"I feel old," Big Bao lamented. "Can't believe anywhere in Dragon City is so busy this late."

Less than an hour later, he was snoring.

I gave Lin Tao a cigarette, and we rolled down the window and lit them, not speaking. Only the glare of the neon kept us awake.

Suddenly, Big Bao blurted out, "Four fours! Raise eight, right?"

"What?" I said, laughing.

"He started learning a new card game called Broken Egg," Lin Tao explained. "He's already addicted."

"You mean he's talking in his sleep?" I said.

"You didn't know he talks in his sleep?" Lin Tao grinned.

"Does he still sleepwalk too? One time he walked into the autopsy room and scared the crap out of me."

As we laughed, the street began to fill with men and women walking unsteadily in twos and threes.

"Closing time," I said, straightening up.

"People don't call it that anymore," Lin Tao said. "Do you think this is still the nineties?"

As the flow of people increased, I scrutinized each face, trying to find a needle in the haystack. It was almost two a.m. again, and the bad sleep I'd had from crashing in the archives was catching up to me. I began to feel drowsy.

The bar crowds slowly dispersed, but we hadn't seen anything of note.

"I don't think this is going to work," said Lin Tao, key already in the ignition. "We can't just keep waiting around with our fingers crossed hoping the Eleventh Finger killer will happen to walk by our car and you'll happen to recognize her."

"Wait," I said. "Did I just hear someone yell?"

"What?" Lin Tao strained his ear.

A sharp female voice came in through the window. "Pond! Pond!"

All the hairs on my body stood on end.

A woman wearing a gold skirt and black stockings entered our field of vision. A girl came over and said a few words to her. Then the woman started walking away alone.

Unlike everyone else, she seemed completely alert. She took out her phone, shook her shoulder-length hair, and seemed to sigh.

As the light of the phone hit her face, I saw she was gorgeous.

"Anyone else think 'Pond' sounds really familiar?"

Lin Tao frowned. "She looks familiar too. Oh God, oh God. I know who it is."

"Who?" I asked, staring out the car window.

"Shui Liang's wife," Lin Tao said as he shook Big Bao awake.

Shui Liang was the bank security guard serial killer in the Yuntai cold case I'd gone back and solved. He had been sentenced to death, and the sentence had been carried out. When we searched Shui Liang's house, we met his wife briefly, and she spoke one ghostly sentence to me. Pond sounded familiar because that's what Shui Liang screamed as they carried him away.

"Holy shit! It's her!" I said. "She said then she wanted to cooperate with me, but really she wanted to incite me by becoming a serial killer!"

"When she said she wanted to cooperate with you, I thought she meant she was gonna seduce you," Lin Tao said with a humorless laugh. "So how did she get your DNA? You didn't . . ."

"No way!"

"Female, perverted by suffering, hates you, hates the police," he said. "She fits the profile perfectly."

"C'mon! Let's get her!" Big Bao said, wiping the drool off his mouth and pulling out handcuffs.

"Where'd you get those?"

"I took a combat training course. Everyone got billed for equipment." Big Bao opened the car door.

I held him back. "Did I miss something? You're a forensic scientist! You examine bodies! You did a two-day combat course, and now you think you're the Terminator?"

"I got an A!" he insisted.

"Easy, big fella," I said. "If she's the Eleventh Finger killer, we definitely won't let her get away, believe me."

"Next we have to secretly get a sample of her DNA, right?" Lin Tao said.

I shook my head. "No. Let's follow her and see where she lives. That's more than enough for tonight. This woman is tricky. If we try to get her DNA now, first, it would go against protocol. Second, it could arouse suspicion, do more harm than good."

"But how will we know if the DNA on the wrap was hers?" Lin Tao said.

"I have an idea."

Pond lived in a small detached house near the strip. After we watched her go inside, we quietly left.

That night, I slept better than I had in ages.

The next morning, Big Bao and I went to the DNA testing lab to find the lab director. "Director Zheng, I'm sure you have a ton of work right now, but I really need you to do me a favor."

She stared at me wide-eyed. "Weren't you suspended?"

"It wasn't justified," I said as I led her into the lab. "And it's just a simple favor. Remember that old Yuntai case with the rapes and the security guard? After Shui Liang was captured, did we get a DNA sample from him?"

"Of course," Zheng said. "We take samples from everyone when they're brought in."

"And you guys processed an abandoned baby's wrap yesterday, right?" I said. "I need to know if a genetic relationship can be established between Shui Liang and the DNA from the wrap. And I need it right away."

"You think the abandoned baby was his?" Zheng said. "What an unfortunate family."

Before long, Zheng came out of the analysis room. "It's a match. Shui Liang, the abandoned baby, and the mother are related."

"Oh my God, Qin," Big Bao said. "That indirectly confirms the suspect in this case is Shui Liang's wife!"

"Bao," I said, "this is very serious. I need you to hurry and get this information to the task force. Have them put the suspect under immediate surveillance."

The task force was overjoyed to hear that there was finally a real break in this impossible case. They immediately dispatched an elite force to search the woman's house and the VW Beetle parked in front. When one of the female officers took a bucket out of the trunk, she couldn't help but scream. In the bottom was a plastic bag containing a human breast.

64

The DNA map printed slowly, so slowly. Lab Director Zheng tore it off and pointed with a ruler. "The stains in the victim's car and courtyard contained human blood matching from Meng Xiangping and Zuo Fangjiang. The soft tissue in the plastic bag is a match for Liu Ciuciu."

The room burst into cheers.

The mountain that had been slowly crushing all the task force officers was demolished at last.

That afternoon, Pond arrived home and found two heavily armed police officers standing in the yard. She turned to run, but several plainclothes officers had closed in behind her.

She straightened her clothes and hair, put her hands up, and smiled slightly. "If you fail, you must pay the price. I've long been prepared for this day."

"You failed, all right, but you can't pay the price," Lin Tao said, glaring at her. "Demons go to hell."

None of the officers were willing to interrogate her, all unable to believe that this beautiful woman was the perverted, brutal demon who'd killed five people and toyed with several dozen police personnel.

She said plainly, "I won't talk to anyone but Qin."

EPILOGUE

My name is Hai Run. I'm twenty-seven years old, from Yuntai.

The characters in my name all have the radical that means "water" as part of their characters, and I've loved water since I was little. That's why my close friends call me "Pond."

Since birth, I've always been the best. Once I started going to school, my supplies and bags were better than everyone else's, and all the boys liked me. Although my mom passed away when I was six, my father took care of me like a mother and father combined.

He was an entrepreneur, even though he wasn't born with any connections. He manufactured and sold tetramine to get his first chunk of money. By the time I was in middle school, he'd switched to real estate and become an important man. When I started high school, he was already chairman of the biggest company in Yuntai.

My father was very busy, but he never neglected me. And no one dared to bully me, because they were afraid of him. My teachers never yelled or hit me. Even if I skipped school or didn't do my homework, they would just laugh. My life was smooth sailing till I was twenty-five.

Even though I was obviously beautiful, I always liked roughhousing and playing soccer with the boys. Dad often tried to tell me that girls have to do girl things or no boy will want them. That clearly wasn't true—my desk drawer was full of love letters. But I didn't like any of those boys. They were all rule-followers and cowards.

I just wanted to have fun, so my grades weren't great. Based on my college entrance exam, I could have attended a university, but I chose nursing school instead. The reason was simple—I liked the outfits.

Dad was fiercely opposed. He said, "Why not study accounting? Better than waiting on people as a nurse." But I was very assertive, and eventually, he had to accept my wishes.

Nursing school was almost all women, and I kept having confusing feelings about some of them. Once, a female classmate got drunk and kissed me, and it felt really good.

When I told Dad about the strange feelings, he wanted me to drop out and get away from all those women. His plan was to send me abroad to learn about the world and how to manage my money. I was his only child, so he had to consider the problem of passing on his enormous assets. I'd never even left Yuntai City, so I wasn't willing to go live in a strange country. But I did agree to drop out, because after that first year, I knew there was no way I was willing to do the dirty, tiring, risky work of a nurse.

With Dad's help, I transferred to Yuntai University to study finance. But I could never pay attention in class. Accounting, Western economics, management studies, statistics—it was all boring nonsense. In one ear and out the other.

The only thing I could think about was whether I liked men or women, and how to get my dad to accept it.

That summer, I was walking into a bank when I felt someone reach into my pocket. Nobody robs me! I turned and grabbed the asshole, not expecting he would take out a knife and cut me.

I saw the bloodstained knife and thought I was going to die.

At that moment, a man in a uniform suddenly rushed out of the bank. He aimed his gun at the thief and yelled, "Down on the ground!"

The cut on my arm wasn't serious, so I decided not to bother pressing charges. I didn't have the mental energy to think about thieves. The tall, handsome guard who came to my rescue caught my eye, so I got his number. His name was Shui Liang, and since Shui means "water," I knew it was meant to be.

◆ ◆ ◆

My father used all his connections to pry into Shui Liang's past, but Shui Liang wasn't offended. He said he understood a daughter's happiness meant everything to her father.

Even though Shui Liang had been born poor and didn't have a very good job, my father said he had integrity, so he supported our relationship.

If I tried to list all the ways Shui Liang was good to me, it would take all night. He was incredibly loyal. I trusted him, trusted him completely. I loved him with all my heart. He said he would never leave me.

Our marriage was very happy, and my father gave us anything and everything. Last year, our love finally crystalized in an adorable baby boy.

My father treasured the baby and eagerly took care of him on weekends. That gave us some time alone. Everyone was so happy.

But our perfect family was broken that day.

Because of you, Qin.

The day you took my Shui Liang away, my father and I were sure you had the wrong person. How could such an honest, kind person be a murderer? We refused to believe it.

So my father reached out to his connections on the police force. They said you had conclusive evidence my Shui Liang had raped and killed a bunch of high school girls.

The shock gave my father a cerebral hemorrhage. He fell asleep and never woke up.

I still don't dare to think too much about that time. My two loved ones left me on the same day—my husband arrested for rape and murder, my father dead from shock and anger. That day, I cried all the water out of my name. I cried the whole night.

To think that my darling husband could actually do something like that, even after we met, even while I was pregnant. Are there no good and decent men in this world? I hated him, but deep down, I still loved him. That tension between love and hate ripped open my heart.

And my beloved father, for whom I was the most precious thing on earth, gave me everything I wanted, and I'd gone and chosen a man whose evil killed him. My guilt was like a knife in my broken heart.

But the one who truly tore my perfect family apart was you, Qin Ming. You thought you solved a big case, did a great job, huh? But your triumph is built on my anguish. The next day, I made up my mind to use all the money I'd inherited from my father to make sure you got a taste of the pain you'd caused.

But when I went to my father's company, I found out I had nothing. Some of the vice presidents had been maneuvering to steal the company from him, and his death just made it easier. Only a few days had passed, but they'd already managed to take over my whole stake in the company.

Luckily, my father still had several hundred thousand yuan in savings, and he'd bought a small house in my name in the provincial capital, so I wasn't homeless.

When I got to Dragon City, everything was unfamiliar. With my father's savings, my son and I were able to survive while I figured out what to do next.

Then fate struck again. One night, my son suddenly had difficulty breathing. By the time I got him to the hospital, he seemed fine. The doctor said it was nothing and that I shouldn't worry. Relieved, I took my baby back home. But when I woke up the next morning, he was dead.

If that horrible doctor had any regard for human life, my son would not have died.

Now the last thing I cared about in the world was gone. I had nothing, so why go on living? I didn't cry again, because I had already cried all the tears in my heart's pond.

The baby's legs were flabby, and my trembling hands couldn't get the wrap around him properly, so I tried string, but that didn't work either. I tried using a knife to cut grooves for the string, but I couldn't go through with it. Sometime later, his beautiful little body grew stiff, so I wrapped him up, ready to jump together out the window.

Crouching there on the ledge, I thought of you. I still hadn't gotten my revenge.

So I started researching forensics online. Tongue scoop, dismemberment—they may seem frightening, but I'd already lost my humanity. I wasn't afraid of the dark, wasn't afraid of blood, wasn't even afraid of death.

I started going to bars and found out how awful men are. They all deserved to die.

There was an old box at home with some tetramine inside. My father had said even a little bit of the drug could kill someone, so I was never allowed to touch it. He'd kept the box as a memento. After all, it was the bedrock of his fortune. I looked on the Internet and read about tetramine's stability, how even after many years it won't lose potency. And how as soon as the police find it, they trace it to the source. But mine was untraceable. This was my magic ancestral weapon.

My first bar adventure was with a doctor. I hate doctors, and married doctors who go out to pick up women I hate even more, so I killed him.

I used forensic methods to disembowel the body, then dismembered and discarded it. But after two weeks, the body still hadn't been discovered. I decided to put the next one somewhere you couldn't miss it. I would let you find it, let you solve the case. Aren't you good at solving cases? I wanted to see if you could guess your murderer was a woman.

I got the idea from a TV show to put one part of a victim with the next body so they could easily be connected, but you idiots still couldn't solve it. I made sure the killing was done very professionally, with forensic techniques, so suspicion would fall on you. But you cops never want to suspect your own people.

Then a golden opportunity arose.

Standing in the crowd outside the caution tape as you surveyed one of my perfect scenes, I heard you and a handsome guy talking about going to the fertility doctor. I followed you there, and perhaps heaven helped me, because the nurse who took your sample was an old classmate of mine. I was easily able to distract her with gossip while stealing a bit of that semen sample.

If I couldn't frame you, at least I could ruin your reputation. So I found a woman to plant your DNA on. Her death would help me get my revenge. Revenge for Shui Liang, whom I loved and hated, revenge for my father, my son, and myself.

Maybe I lost, but I'm at peace. I can go see the three most important men in my life. They're waiting for me.

ABOUT THE AUTHOR

Qin Ming, a lead medical examiner by trade, started his long career early and earned the nickname Old Qin. His perceptive analysis of countless bodies earned him another: the Corpse Whisperer. He uses his deft hands to right wrongs and his Buddhist heart to wish for world peace. His bestselling novels have sold hundreds of thousands of copies.

ABOUT THE TRANSLATOR

Photo © 2014 Bethany Ruth Christy

Alex Woodend is a writer and translator whose fascination with Spanish and Chinese began at Franklin & Marshall College. He continued his studies at Columbia University, where he wrote his master's thesis on early post-Mao literature.

The translator of the Captain Riley Adventures series and other titles, he currently lives in New York and is at work on more translations and original fiction.